DOCTORS' WIVES

DOCTORS'
WIVES

Frank G. Slaughter

Doubleday & Company, Inc.
Garden City, New York

AUTHOR'S NOTE

Quotations identified as "from a medical journal" in the text are from "Psychiatric Illness in the Physician's Wife," *American Journal of Psychiatry*, Vol. 122, pp. 159–163, August 1965, Copyright 1966, American Psychiatric Association. They are used with the kind permission of the editor of the *Journal* and the author of the article, Dr. James L. Evans.

I first learned of the "iron sludge" technique for treating intracranial aneurysms from an article in the September 26, 1966, issue of *Newsweek,* describing the work at the University of California at Los Angeles of Drs. John F. Alksne, Robert Rand and Aaron G. Fingerhut. The brain operation described in the latter part of this novel is a modification of their technique.

Frank G. Slaughter, M.D.
January 15, 1967

DOCTORS' WIVES

CHAPTER I

It was shortly after four, when Mabel, the blonde and buxom waitress on the afternoon shift in the Snack Bar across the street from the hospital, went out to sweep the parking space in front of the shop. She'd come on at three and the change from the late summer heat to the air-conditioned interior always made her arthritis painful, so she was glad of an excuse to get out in the warm September air for a few minutes before the five o'clock rush began. The shop, all glass, stainless steel, red-cushioned stools at the counter and booths against the wall, occupied one corner of the Faculty Apartments parking lot. Across the street, above the ambulance unloading ramp, blue neon lights spelled out EMERGENCY ENTRANCE.

Weston University Hospital occupied the entire opposite side of the long block across from the Snack Bar, a mass of buildings with connecting walkways, built of cinder blocks painted white and tall columns of steel-framed windows. On the lunchroom side of North Avenue one end of the block was taken up with the towering building that housed the Faculty Clinic, a privately operated medical group to which much of the medical school faculty belonged. Only about five years old, the clinic had already been enlarged several times and, during the daylight hours, a constant stream of people flowed through its marquee-covered portico at the far corner of the block.

The Faculty Apartments, owned by the university, occupied the entire end of the block, facing west on Weston Boulevard.

Diagonally across the street from it, in front of the main entrance to the hospital, stood the housing facilities for married residents, interns and students, consisting of four apartment complexes with an enclosed playground. The main classroom buildings for the medical school were on the opposite corner of Weston Boulevard and North Avenue from married student housing, convenient to the hospital and all parts of the group of buildings that made up Weston University Medical School.

"Where'd you go on your day off yesterday, Mabel?" Abe Fescue, the short-order cook, lounged in the open door of the empty lunchroom, smoking a cigarette that was forbidden inside. A small transistor radio atop the counter, also forbidden when customers were in the shop, filled the air with a rock-and-roll tune.

"On the Parkway," said Mabel. "I like to drive up there this time of the year."

Located in the foothills east of the Great Smoky Mountains, Weston was primarily a manufacturing city. It had become a major medical center when the medical school had opened some fifteen years earlier, quickly outstripping in importance and stature the small, older university of which it was a part. Rogue River curved around the city, with a dam some ten miles to the south forming a lake and a source of hydroelectric power that had made the town a natural location for a major textile operation.

"Fall's comin' early this year," Mabel added. "The leaves are already turnin' up towards the Knob."

"Won't bother me none," said Abe. "Come Thanksgiving, I'll be heading south for Miami."

"You short-order cooks are like birds, always flying north or south. I suppose you'll lose all your money at the tracks again this winter and come borrowin' from me next spring like always, so you can pay your rent the first month."

"This is going to be my best winter." Abe was a thin man of indeterminate age. His face was scarred by acne from childhood, and the inevitable tattoos, relic of Navy service, almost covered his upper arms. "Why d'you stay around here winters anyway, Mabel? You could make twice as much in tips working in South Florida and still get your old job back in the spring, when the weather turns warm again. Good waitresses are like short-order cooks; they can get a job anywhere."

"I like it here." Mabel looked with affection at the neon lights of the emergency entrance and the towering walls of the main hospital. "When I was a little girl, I had my heart set on bein' a nurse; then I married a louse and by the time I got rid of him, it was too late. I've got a lot of friends in the hospital, and workin' here, I keep track of most everything that's goin' on over there. Makes me feel like I'm part of it."

"You own some of it, too, from all those checks you've picked up for students that couldn't pay," said Abe. "Don't be a sucker all your life, Mabel."

The waitress took no offense. She didn't expect anyone to understand that the hospital and medical school staff were just like a family she'd never had. Coming and going through the years with their waffles, hamburgers, steaks, hashed browns, scrambled eggs, and coffee, she had heard all their troubles and their joys. Sometimes, when a student was broke and hungry, she paid for the food checks herself, and maybe she did lose a little that way—she'd never stopped to figure it up and wasn't going to. Helping them gave her the feeling of being a part of the exciting world of medicine, a sense of being needed she had never found until she'd come to the Snack Bar when it had opened nearly ten years before.

The sweeping finished, Mabel lit a cigarette of her own, tossing the match into the gutter. It was only the first of September and still warm, but there was a faint touch of fall in the air. Up on the Parkway, where she'd driven for a few miles the afternoon before, it had been a lot cooler, a tangible promise of what was soon to come.

In the haze of the late afternoon sunlight, the mountains were a bluish-tinted backdrop for the green-clad foothills to the east and the valleys between, with the fields of corn brown and sere as they waited for the harvesters. Later, when winter finally came, the mountains would take on a mantle of snow and the students would be driving up on weekends for skiing and fraternity house parties.

Down here in the valleys, though, it was still warm enough for water skiing—by the hardy. As Mabel smoked, she saw a girl skiier in a bright yellow bikini flash across the lower end of North Avenue, where it dead-ended into Riverfront Drive, a block below the intersection of Weston Boulevard.

"Looks mighty quiet over there." Abe nodded toward the hospital. "You can hardly believe all hell could break loose any minute in that emergency room."

"Won't be much goin' on today, a lot of the doctors take Wednesday off to play golf. Besides, only the first-year students are in school yet. The rest won't come in for another week."

"Maybe business will pick up then and we'll have a chance to get a bonus on weekends." Abe tossed his cigarette butt into the gutter with a flip of his thumb. "Guess I better get some tomatoes sliced for the five o'clock rush. You coming in?"

"Not yet. I want to enjoy the fresh air awhile longer. Hope Jeff Long and that little Monroe girl come by tonight when she goes off duty. She's had enough trouble—with that skunk of a husband leaving her as soon as he was able to support himself and now her little boy havin' trouble. Janet deserves somebody nice like Dr. Long."

"There you go with another of them soap operas you're always dreaming up."

"What's wrong with soap operas?" Mabel's Irish temper had been stirred at last. "Some of the best people listen to 'em. The last time I was through the clinic, I was talking to Mrs. Weston—"

"The D.A.'s wife?"

"Yeah. She listens all the time. I could name you a lot of other important people who do, too."

"Give me a ball game any day—or a horse race."

"Go on inside and slice your tomatoes. You got no feelin' for the real things of life."

"And me married four times?" Abe grinned. "I could write a book about what you call the real things of life—nagging, bitching, sleeping around, having abortions. Who wants 'em?"

The door closed behind him as he went inside and Mabel could see him moving toward the end of the counter, where a door gave access to the cooking area behind it. The charcoal grill was already hot, waiting for the procession of hamburgers, chopped sirloins and tenderloins that would pass across it during the next five or six hours. The round metal rings in which the hashed browns were cooked on the flat metal grill with the gas flames beneath were stacked neatly at one side, a package of eggs occupied the shelf above, and the drawer beneath was filled with loaves of bread and packages of rolls sprinkled with sesame seeds.

A brief lull would occur around ten, if they were lucky, giving them time to clean up before they were swamped again by a flood of nurses going off duty at eleven, meeting interns and residents there for a brief rendezvous before checking in at the Nurses' Home on the other side of the hospital block.

Halfway around the end of the counter, Mabel saw Abe stop suddenly and turn quickly to push open the outer door. "Hey Mabel!" he called. "Some doctor just shot his wife."

"Who was it?" The waitress covered the distance to the door at a trot.

"Didn't get the name. The announcer broke into the music and I knew you'd want to hear it."

"I hope it's nobody at the hospital. Quick! Turn the radio up!"

The cook grabbed the small radio and twisted the volume knob.

"Now see what you did!" Mabel cried, when it came off in his hand, ending the broadcast in a squawk. "How are we going to know who it was?"

"Watch the emergency entrance of the hospital while I try to get this damn thing going again," Abe said. "Of all the times for . . ."

ii

Amy Brennan was driving home from the District Six meeting of the state medical auxiliary, tooling along the new four-lane interstate highway through the foothills at seventy-five miles an hour. The air conditioner of her new Eldorado was purring and the FM radio was playing a Brahms concerto softly, soothing her thoughts, after the cat-scratch battle with the representative of the downstate faction who had invited herself to the meeting.

Everybody had known the visitor was there to curry support in favor of her own candidate for president-elect when the auxiliary met during the convention of the state medical association next month. But Amy had played it cool—she could say that much for herself. And it hadn't been easy, especially the way her temper had been on a hair trigger lately, since her campaign to become president-elect had taken her on a tour of the state, visiting each of the districts.

"Cool Amy," Pete had sometimes called her in the early days of their marriage, but lately they'd hardly seen each other enough for him to call her anything. Ostensibly, the purpose of the tour of the state auxiliaries had been to talk about the role of doctors' wives in preventing the further spread of Medicare, but its real purpose had been to line up votes for Amy. Since she was a little girl, she hadn't left anything to chance, if she could help it, and as a result, her carefully planned campaign was now rolling like a juggernaut. The representative of the downstate faction had soon seen the handwriting on the wall, as far as her own candidate was concerned, and when she'd been forced to fly home without an endorsement from the members of District Six, it had been the same as conceding Amy's election.

The campaign had been a tough and exciting one, for District Six was no pushover. A lot of doctors in the area had no love for the medical school at Weston and even less for the Faculty Clinic that had taken away some of their most prosperous patients. With so many four-lane highways crisscrossing the land-

14

scape it was easier for a patient to drive to Weston for one of the fast but complete diagnostic studies for which the clinic had become famous than to wait in the office of a hometown doctor for an examination that couldn't touch the clinic's for thoroughness. Doctors' wives usually echoed their husband's prejudices, however, and with Pete Brennan president of the Faculty Clinic Corporation, as well as the leading neurosurgeon in the state, Amy had been forced to work especially hard to get their approval.

She had enjoyed it all, though, particularly the political maneuvering and infighting that had brought her, at thirty-nine, to the top of the heap in the womens' side of state medical politics. And she couldn't help chuckling now at the thought of how she had maneuvered the downstate faction's representative into admitting her candidate's liberal sentiments, even to the point of apparently favoring Medicare—the next thing to labeling her a communist and the kiss of death among the conservative-minded wives of District Six.

Still, she decided as the sleek car flowed along the new highway, it would be just as well to play down the tactics she'd used against the other candidate when she talked to Pete. He was sometimes a bit sticky about her political maneuvers and they'd even quarreled about it once or twice. But her brother Roy would love to hear about them. As District Attorney for Weston County, Roy was moving into a wider sphere of political operations, and wanted Amy to take charge of women's activities in the race for state attorney general he was planning to make next year against the incumbent, Abner Townsend. But Amy was too busy right now with her own plans to think of anything beyond the convention next month, so she'd made no commitment.

Everybody had come through when she'd called on them, she remembered with satisfaction. Roy's wife, Alice, didn't go in for organizational activities as a rule, but she'd made an exception for her sister-in-law and helped Amy entertain visiting doctors and their wives. Lorrie Dellman, Maggie McCloskey, Della Rogan, Grace Hanscombe and Elaine McGill had been loyal, too:

but then they had all stuck together pretty closely since Amy had organized them into what Pete liked to call the "Dissection Society."

Pete claimed that all the women did at their monthly sewing-circle get-togethers was to dissect the characters of people they knew—mainly other women. What he didn't know was that Amy had been carrying out a plan in organizing the group from among the wives of the six men who had formed the nucleus of the faculty for the new Weston University Medical School which had been organized at the end of the Korean war. That plan had even then been concerned with promoting Pete's own future, both in the medical school and in state and national medical politics, for which she was already setting her sights.

Pete Brennan, Paul McGill, George Hanscombe, Joe McCloskey, Dave Rogan and Mort Dellman had all been together in Korea, where Roy Weston had been working in the Inspector General's office. Roy had persuaded the six of them to join the faculty of the new medical school when they got out of the Army after the armistice. And none of them, Amy was sure, had ever regretted the move. Relaxing now as the big car sped homeward, she turned her thoughts to the first time she'd met Pete.

It had been at the Weston Country Club, the Saturday night dance everybody who was anybody in the city attended. He'd been in a group around the piano where Lorrie Porter was playing while the orchestra was taking a break, improvising jazz with the lazy competence Lorrie brought to everything she did.

Tall and a bit florid, Pete was then—and now—a solidly built man with the map of Ireland written on his face and in his blue eyes. He had caught Amy's attention at once. Being tall for a woman, she was naturally attracted to big men. Two years out of Vassar and four years post-debutante, with reddish blonde hair that needed no rinse and a good figure, she could have had her choice of a half-dozen men in Weston and elsewhere, but she'd always been particular. Not for her was just an average husband; the man she married, she had long since decided, must be a leader and a professional man—which meant most likely a lawyer or a doctor.

Amy had come to the club that night with Roy and Alice. As her brother crossed the crowded ballroom with a drink for her, he'd seen the direction of her gaze and grinned. "You look like a bird dog at point, Sis. Want to meet him?"

"Who is he?"

"Major—Dr. Pete Brennan. Just out of the Army and signed up with a half-dozen others of my friends from Korea for the faculty of the new medical school."

"What's his specialty?"

Roy looked startled. "What difference does that make?"

"Surgeons and internists are the aristocrats of the medical profession. You ought to know that, Roy."

"Never thought about it, but Pete qualifies. He's a neurosurgeon and surgical chief of the 319th General Hospital in Korea."

"Is he married?"

"No."

"Attached?"

Roy grinned. "Would that make any difference?"

"No. But it's simpler if he isn't involved."

"Far as I know he's a rover, which ought to make him feel at home in Weston—before marriage or after. The seven of us spent a lot of time together in Seoul, playing poker, drinking a bit, the usual things. All of 'em are top-notch men and Pete's the pick, a fine surgeon and an excellent administrator. Women are attracted to him like flies to a sugar bowl, though. What makes you think you have a chance to nail him?"

"I'm the kind of wife an ambitious doctor needs, for one thing. And I'm not exactly hideous."

"Come to think of it, you aren't," Roy grinned. "But since he's my friend, maybe I should warn him against a conniving female—"

"You do and I'll kill you," said Amy. "If he does his part, I can make Dr. Peter Brennan the most popular surgeon in town and the richest—maybe even the biggest doctor in the state. What more could he ask for?"

17

"To be loved for himself."

"He'll have all that he needs, too."

"If Pete goes for you, Sis, it isn't going to be something you can just turn on and off," Roy warned. "The woman who marries him will know she's married to quite a man. And she'd better be a real woman, not just somebody who's scheming to get ahead."

"For that I ought to punch you in the nose." Amy's temper had always been quick. "Go to hell! I'll introduce myself to him."

"I just wanted to make sure you knew the score. Come on."

They had been married less than six months later in the biggest wedding Weston had ever seen. One by one the other members of Pete's group had been married, too: Mort Dellman—actually not an M.D. but a Ph.D. biochemist who was also a laboratory whiz—to Lorrie; Dave Rogan, the psychiatrist, to Della; Joe McCloskey, the urologist, to Maggie; and Paul McGill, whose specialty was dermatology, the skin, to Elaine. All had been snapped up by local girls or—as was always happening with doctors—by girls working at the hospital. George Hanscombe, the internist of the group, had been married since the end of World War II to an Englishwoman named Grace Barrett.

The five doctors' wives—plus Lorrie Dellman and Alice Weston—had been the nucleus around which Amy had begun to build her own clique long before she'd become interested in the medical auxiliary. With her instinctive flare for oganization, she'd known the group would be of help to her someday—and to Pete. Besides they were all congenial and Alice and Lorrie were distant cousins.

As a starter, she'd invited them to a luncheon at the old Weston place, with its tall columns, spacious grounds and faithful retainers. At a time when most of the others had been living in apartments while their husbands got started again after Korea, the possibility that they might one day enjoy the sort of luxury Amy accepted as a matter of course, had been a magnet—to all except Lorrie and Alice, of course. Daughter of old Jake Porter, Lorrie, too, was to the manner born—and didn't give a damn—

while Alice had grown up in Jake Porter's home as his ward. Being a Weston carried with it a lot of advantages, too—of which Amy was quite cognizant. Even though her father had not been a ranking member of the management of Weston Mills when he died, he'd still owned a considerable amount of stock. And thanks to the business acumen of Jake Porter in negotiating the deal by which Tropical Fabrics had taken over the mills, Amy had become financially independent.

Not that she and Pete had needed her money long. As Roy had said that first night at the club, Pete Brennan was a born leader of men, with enough Irish charm thrown in to talk any woman out of her inhibitions—as Elaine McGill had once reminded Amy somewhat maliciously. But then Elaine's husband, Paul, was a dermatologist and, while nearly everyone had skin trouble at one time or another, even if they escaped acne as teenagers, doctors in that specialty didn't draw down the big fees surgeons got. So she could hardly blame Elaine—who'd been a schoolteacher—for being envious.

Amy sometimes suspected Elaine and the others of secretly yearning to share some of Pete's vigor, too. And sometimes she would almost have been willing to divide it with them—until he'd begun to taper off after those frequent evening faculty conferences had started about a year ago.

Pete had risen fast in the medical world; Amy had to hand him that. He'd had more than one offer from larger and more important medical schools to join their faculties. But since the Faculty Clinic had become a veritable bonanza almost overnight, his salary as a Clinical Professor of Surgery at Weston University Medical School was now the least part of his income.

Pete was very popular with his fellow doctors, and with practically no effort had been elected second vice-president of the state medical association last year. At the next convention he was sure to be raised to first vice-president, the next year to president-elect, and the next to president. But thanks to a year of intense politicking Amy would be president of the auxiliary at least a year before Pete picked up the gavel of the state association.

The thought of reaching her immediate goal before Pete was able to achieve a similar status at the state level brought a warm feeling of satisfaction—succeeded almost instantly by a stab of fear. Until just then, she hadn't stopped to wonder how Pete would react to her reaching the top in women's medical politics before he attained a similar position in the state society. And at the thought that she might have let her ambition endanger her marriage, Amy's right hand moved from the wheel to touch the spot on her left temple where the familiar throbbing pain of migraine had just appeared.

"Damn!" she said aloud. A migraine attack now could mess up everything. With the all-important district meeting successfully concluded, she'd planned to be particularly nice to Pete tonight and had hurried home, although originally she hadn't expected to get back to Weston until tomorrow. As soon as she got home, she had planned to call him at the clinic and suggest that they meet at the club for dinner. First they'd have a few drinks at the bar where several of the Dissection Society girls were sure to be. Some of them spent as many evenings at the club as they did at home and in the ladies' lounge she could give them a quick account of her triumph.

When dinner was over, she and Pete would return to the big house with the white columns on the knoll overlooking the river. Like most of the other university children, Jenny and Michael were still away at summer camp. They wouldn't be back until after Labor Day, and she'd given Ethel, the live-in maid she'd inherited along with the house, the night off by telephone—just after buying the new nightgown before leaving for Weston. From there on, she knew she could trust Pete to pick up the cues.

Mentally adding the times Pete hadn't been home to those she'd been away for the vitally important district auxiliary meetings, Amy was startled to discover how little they had really been alone together in the past year. All of which made tonight particularly important—if she could just stop the damn migraine that was now like a spike being driven into her skull.

Glancing at her watch—an Omega with a diamond-studded

band given her by Pete after he'd collected a five-thousand-dollar fee for a disk operation on the wife of Sam Portola, who headed the syndicate that now owned Weston Mills—Amy saw that she could just make George Hanscombe's office before five for a hypo of ergotamine tartrate and Demerol to relieve the pain—if the lights were right coming off the interstate. It was just then that the soothing tone of the Brahms concerto was broken by the voice of the radio announcer: "We interrupt 'Music for Mid-afternoon' to give you a special news bulletin."

Amy reached for the radio switch, wanting no news of a new backset for the U.S. forces somewhere in the world, or another race riot, to heighten the steady throb of the migraine. With her hand halfway to the controls of the radio her muscles suddenly went rigid, however, and the Cadillac swerved dangerously as the fingers of her left hand tightened on the wheel.

"Tragedy struck this afternoon in Weston's fashionable Sherwood Ravine district," the radio announcer continued. "According to a report just phoned from an observer on the scene, a prominent Weston physician, Dr. Mortimer Dellman, shot to death a few moments ago his attractive wife Loretta. Details of the tragedy have not yet appeared on the news tickers but a man with Mrs. Dellman at the time, said to be a prominent physician, was also seriously wounded."

Amy leaned forward to hear the broadcast over the rush of wind around the car.

"Police have thrown a cordon around the home of Dr. Dellman but one ambulance was seen to leave for University Hospital and another has just arrived. Stay tuned for further developments in this fast-breaking marital tragedy of high society."

CHAPTER II

The clock on the dresser said four when Elaine McGill eased herself out of bed. Crossing the bedroom of the small lakefront cottage to the dresser for a cigarette, she lit it with the gold-plated lighter Paul had given her for their tenth anniversary. Two hours, she thought, should be ample time for the sperm deposited around her cervix to find their way into the uterus. In fact one of them should already have joined up with her own ovum, if she'd figured the time right and interpreted correctly the rise in temperature she had so carefully noted with an accurate thermometer record every day for the last six months. That rise, according to the textbook she'd studied at the hospital library, was supposed to indicate ovulation—and the best time to achieve pregnancy.

Elaine had spent a lot of time studying the reproductive function these past several years when she had been trying so desperately to become pregnant. The more she studied, the more she marveled that something so vitally important to the preservation of the human race had seemingly been left largely to chance. Everything about it, in fact, violated her innate sense of logic, of an orderly and divine planned motion of the spheres and the smaller units of the cosmos.

Before marrying Paul McGill, Elaine had been a mathematics teacher in Weston High School. She had been working on her doctorate when the handsome dermatologist had joined the faculty of the new medical school along with Pete Brennan and the others.

Not that Elaine had orbited anywhere near Amy Brennan's sphere before her marriage. She'd grown up in North Carolina, gone to N.C.C.W.—now the University of North Carolina at Greensboro—and taken her Master's degree in mathematics at Columbia before coming to Weston. But since Paul McGill had been one of the Five Horsemen of the Apocrypha—Dave Rogan had cooked up the absurd designation while they were in that Army hospital in Korea—she'd naturally joined Amy Brennan's Dissection Society.

Serious-minded as she was and something of an intellectual, the fact that Paul was ten years older than she had only intensified his attraction for Elaine. They had been married about four months after he joined the medical school faculty but for a while having children hadn't seemed financially advisable. With the opening of the Faculty Clinic, however, Paul's financial prospects had changed almost overnight and Elaine had immediately stopped all use of contraceptives—except for a few months' use of "the pill" when it had first come out and reports said women who used it were more likely to get pregnant after they stopped than before.

Elaine had been happy in Weston until her apparent sterility had begun to trouble her. Now, after nearly fifteen years of marriage, she sometimes found herself wondering resentfully why she had to be barren when a substantial part of the human endeavor, it seemed, was directed at bringing about the union of two cells, the sperm and the ovum, at just the right moment in the menstrual cycle of a woman.

Everything that went before was actually window dressing to that simple microscopic event, the ultimate *climax coitum,* so to speak, that kept a large part of the world's business running at a profit. The girl in the bikini on the billboard smoking KOOLS; the baseball player in the shower shampooing with PRELL, spraying himself with LIFEGUARD after toweling, and slicking his hair down with BRYLCREEM, if he was "man enough to try it"; the exotic perfume guaranteed to draw men like flies because its "secret" ingredient was really musk, the stink of animal sex lure; dinner by soft candlelight with gypsy violins playing; the view of Los Angeles from Mulholland Drive at midnight—all were designed to bring about, almost as an anticlimax, the gutsy business of thrust and parry, until the *coup de grâce* was delivered by the explosive force of mutual ecstasy and languor immediately seized spent bodies to bring on sleep, so the final microscopic stages of the union could be accomplished.

All of it—the whole elaborate mechanism that kept hundreds of industries humming to promote human sexual union while pharmaceutical houses were equally busy manufacturing "the pill" that prevented its full completion and accounted for a sizable slice of the G.N.P.—had one purpose, one driving force more powerful than the hydrogen bomb, or even a great earthquake. The force that united a male and a female during a few brief moments for the purpose of preserving the species.

That same force made the chromosomes and the far smaller genes of the human sex cell march together with relentless tread to become one. In this new being were joined all the characteristics of both parents: the gene for hemophilia that, carried only by the female, would one day destroy the offspring with uncontrollable hemorrhage; the genes for the male parent's blue eyes or the web toes handed down from great-grandfather Albert; the *arcus axillaris*, a tiny muscle that crossed the armpits of perhaps one individual in a million for generation after generation with no perceptible purpose, except that eons ago some primate ancestor had needed it; the short legs and long body from the father's side combined with the large buttocks from the mother's —all these and a million more characteristics distributed by chance, or by divine pattern from a heritage of incalculable years, came together in the chromosomes of two people who met, cohabited and, because they wanted to or because in the heat of passion someone forgot to take a pill beforehand or inject a household cleanser afterward, produced a new being.

Perhaps the final penetration through the cell membrane of the ovum by the head of the single spermatozoon that made impregnation possible was fully as ecstatic as the union of the bodies preceding it. Who could say, when not even Sigmund Freud had been able to dredge up a memory of that climactic moment from the formless plasma of the unconscious? Certainly there was no ecstasy for the tail of the gobbled-up male cell; once its function of moving the sperm through the female generative tract to penetrate the cell membrane of the ovum had been accomplished, it died unheralded and was absorbed, very much as the black widow spider eats its mate after the latter fulfills its single purpose, reproduction.

It was all too hit-or-miss for logic to play much of a part in it, Elaine McGill had long since decided, but she had made one final try anyway. That try had brought her this Wednesday afternoon in September to a lake cottage the Hiltons had lent her and Paul while they were in Europe on a sabbatical, brought her here with a man she hardly knew and whom, she told herself firmly, she had no desire to know after today.

One thing she didn't have to worry about—detection. Paul always played golf on Wednesday afternoon and stopped at the Nineteenth Hole of the Weston Country Club for a drink after his shower. He rarely got home before six and long before that she would be back in Sherwood Ravine, preparing dinner while the memory of what had happened here this afternoon rapidly faded—forever.

The sensible thing, she knew, would be to dress and leave now, while Mike Traynor was still asleep. She could call him from a service station on the way back to town and make sure he was awake; he'd said he had to take over for one of the interns in the emergency room of the hospital at five o'clock. But something held her back, something she wasn't quite ready to admit into conscious thought, but which nevertheless stirred her pulse to a swifter beat.

Pausing before the mirror on the bathroom door, Elaine admired her own naked image there, knowing she was even more lovely today at thirty-nine than she'd been fifteen years ago when Paul, newly appointed Assistant Professor of Dermatology in the medical school, had married her. Her body had filled out during those years; a woman who knew she was loved always gained weight. Her dark hair was wound about her head now in a coil of coppery braids; Paul liked it tumbled about her shoulders when they made love, so it had seemed somehow unfaithful to him to let it down this afternoon.

Her breasts were just full enough, she thought, though she had felt the demanding mouth of an infant upon them only once. She'd been especially despondent over her inability to conceive last year and Paul had sent her on a visit to her sister in Philadelphia, who had just had a baby. One afternoon when Sally had been out, Elaine had taken the bottle from the infant and given it her own breast instead.

Even now, she could remember with a shiver of pleasure the feel of the small mouth upon her breast, the rasp of the baby's tongue upon her nipple. But she'd been dry, of course, and the baby had soon set up a howl, so she'd hurried to put the rubber nipple back into his mouth—after which he promptly fell asleep.

Her waist, reflected in the mirror, was still sweetly curved, the hips just full enough to make men turn to look at her when she walked across a public room. The legs, she knew, were superb. She'd won a "perfect leg" contest at a summer resort at the end of her third year in college and had been besieged the rest of the summer every time she appeared on the beach by college boys on the make.

Both she and Paul had superb bodies and good minds, even though at fifty, he was a good eleven years older than she and seven or eight more than Pete Brennan and the others, who made up the ruling hierarchy of the medical school—except George Hanscombe who was the oldest one of the group. So why had the children they wanted so passionately been denied her and Paul, when someone like Lorrie Dellman, who really didn't give a damn, was like a brood sow—until Mort had put his foot down and had her tubes tied off after the last Caesarean.

It wasn't that she and Paul hadn't tried hard to start a family. God knows she'd run the poor man ragged the four or five nights of each month, when her carefully determined ovulation cycle had indicated she was able to become pregnant. Jack Hagen, the gynecologist at the Faculty Clinic, had tried every test known to man on her, too, and all the treatments. Hormone injections, tubal insufflation—pumping air up through the uterus and tubes until your belly felt like a balloon—she had undergone the whole gamut but with nothing to show for it.

Finally, she had persuaded Paul to have his sperm examined but they'd drawn a blank there, too. Mort Dellman in the medical school laboratory said he'd never seen wrigglier sperm than Paul's. But they still didn't seem able to propel themselves up the short distance of maybe five inches to her Fallopian tubes and penetrate the ovum she broke out of its follicle every month as regularly as clockwork—if the evidence of her thermometer was to be taken as valid, which Jack Hagen assured her it could.

At first, Elaine had thought the reason she didn't get pregnant might be because Paul was so hasty that he hardly ever managed to get inside her before he lost his seed. But when she'd finally gotten up the courage to ask Jack Hagen about that, he'd assured her it probably didn't make any difference. Only two things were really needed for pregnancy, he'd said: a viable ovum, which a healthy woman like her produced regularly about every twenty-eight days, and the presence of sperm—capable of fertilizing it—in the entrance to the generative tract within twenty-four hours or so of the monthly ovulation. Paul always got that far—though usually not much farther.

"Premature ejaculation," Jack Hagen had labeled Paul's trouble. He had further volunteered that a lot of men, even young ones, suffered from it—mostly because of nervousness or some defect in their psychological sexual development. Elaine had toyed for a while with the idea of suggesting that Paul see Dave Rogan, who was a close friend as well as a psychiatrist, but had given it up, knowing Paul didn't like to talk about his trouble.

In time, Elaine had learned to take care of the fact that Paul was rarely able to bring her to a climax, but way back in her mind there was always the nagging wonder whether she wasn't being denied something. Lorrie could have told her, she was sure. God knows Lorrie seemed to enjoy sex, judging by the number of times she'd put horns on Mort. Even a louse like him deserved better and once or twice, when she'd seen Mort undressing her with that feverish look he got in his eyes after a few drinks, Elaine had even considered encouraging him a little. Mort was certainly fertile; he—or somebody—had kept Lorrie pregnant most of the time, until her tubes had been tied.

Paul had put his foot down on any question of artificial insemination, when Jack Hagen had advocated it. In fact it was the only question on which he and Elaine had really quarreled since their marriage. What was to be gained—he wanted to know—by injecting another man's sperm into her cervix, when Mort Dellman had labeled his own O.K.? The trouble, he insisted, had to be connected with the acid-base balance of Elaine's own generative tract, a condition that must be destroying the sperm before they could reach the ovum. Besides, he said, the whole thing was immoral—Paul was very strait-laced about sex. And since no doctor would inseminate her without the written permission of her husband, she had been forced to resort to an older, if less honored, method this afternoon.

It ought to work, too, she thought, looking at the tousled dark head on the pillow. Mike Traynor was as perfect a specimen as she was—and she'd been careful to pick a lover, even if for only a single appearance, with Paul's coloring and general features. Working the whole thing out and finding the right donor—it assuaged her own moral scruples a little to label Mike thus— had taken a long time. Logic told her it would have been more scientific to use the computer, nerve center of the new data-processing system Mort Dellman had devised to speed up examination procedures in the Faculty Clinic. That of course had been impossible but, as a mathematician, Elaine was sure she had worked it all out logically anyway.

Once she'd found Mike Traynor, she'd been forced to play a role she had never played before, that of a strumpet. But it had all been justified by the need for a child, she reminded herself again—though hardly by the fact that she had found herself enjoying the role. Or that the sight of Mike Traynor's dark head on the pillow now should stir an answering warmth within her body.

In the end though, sex hadn't really been any different with Mike Traynor from what it was with Paul—only a little longer. Fearful of destroying the acid-base balance, or whatever it was Paul had been talking about, she had lain upon the bed afterward, tense and unfulfilled, waiting for the new seed which had just been implanted in her generative tract to reach her ovum; Mike Traynor, on the other hand, had gone to sleep.

The bell on a nearby church steeple tolling four reminded Elaine that Mike had said he had a class at five; he was a senior medical student at the university substituting as an intern on medicine for the summer. The cottage by the lake in the foothills of the Smokies where so many of the medical faculty had summer places was a good half hour from Weston, so she decided to wake him. Going to the closet, she put a wrapper about her naked body and tied the sash. Then, with the half-smoked cigarette between her lips, she went over to shake Mike awake.

He rolled over and looked up at her, his eyes foggy with sleep. Then he grinned and reached up to take the cigarette from her lips and put it between his own.

"Well, aren't you the eager one?" he said. "And you so shy before."

"Wh—what do you mean?"

"Did you think I didn't realize you never crossed the wire?"

"Wire?"

"This kind of a race should be a photo finish. But when I get going, I can't always slow down—at least not the first time. Now the second—"

"It's four o'clock—you said you had a class at five." She knew she didn't sound convincing.

"I can get to class in twenty minutes. Anybody liable to come here before five—like a husband?"

"Nobody knows I'm here. He's playing golf."

"Then what are we waiting for?" With a movement so casual that it was completely disarming, he sat up to loosen the sash

30

holding the wrapper around her waist and push it off her shoulders. Startled by the action, she made no move as the garment fell to the floor in a pool about her feet.

"Man! O man!" His admiration, she knew, wasn't feigned. "Imagine all this being wasted on Old Dermatographia."

"Who?" she asked—a little breathlessly. Things were moving very fast, but she was far from sure she wanted to slow them down.

"That's the name the students have for your husband. He's got this pet theory that a person's nervous make-up can be determined by the way the skin reacts to being marked with a fingernail. Dermatographia means writing on skin—you know—like writing on a blackboard."

"I remember hearing him speak of it."

"He's always stroking the patient's backs; if they've got a quick nervous reaction, the mark turns red. You'd be amazed how often he can spot people with psychosomatic ailments, just by writing on their skin."

"Does he do that to women patients?"

Mike grinned. "It's bad enough to put horns on a guy without revealing his secrets. I've got principles, baby." He touched her breast and whistled softly when the nipple became erect, straining at the touch until the dark skin of the areola took on a pigskin-like appearance. "Come here, beautiful."

The first time she had merely accepted him, shutting her mind and her emotions off from what was, for her, purely a mechanical act carried out to ensure creation of the child she hoped to bear. This time he took her and the difference was so great that just before the explosive moment of orgasm she was sure she would faint dead away. Then it was over and this time she knew—with some deep primeval instinct granted occasionally to women—that the sperm would reach the waiting ovum.

"Now that was a photo finish if there ever was one." Mike Traynor exhaled a sigh and reached for the cigarette he'd put into the ash tray by the bed. "And what a race!"

As he left the bed and started putting on his clothes, Elaine pulled up the sheet to cover her naked body. With the movement she shut him out of her life as casually as he had come into it, sternly repressing any thought of the explosive moment of pleasure she'd just experienced in his arms. Now that she was going to bear Paul a child, her mind had already erased even the thought that another man's seed had made it possible.

"See you later, baby." Mike Traynor waved good-bye from the door but Elaine didn't bother to acknowledge the farewell. She was lying with her knees drawn up as Jack Hagen had told her to do. Fifteen minutes, he'd said, should be long enough but she decided to take a little nap just to be sure. There'd be plenty of time to get home before Paul finished his golf game and his drink at the club.

She heard Mike Traynor's old car sputter into life but didn't hear the radio that came on when the switch was turned. Only the last words of the news broadcast reached Mike's ears, but they were enough to make him gun the car and head for the hospital.

"*Christ!*" he thought. "*If this was last Wednesday, the guy being taken to the emergency room from Dellman's house could be me!*"

ii

"Well, that's that." Police Lieutenant Eric Vosges watched the ambulance with its sheet-covered occupant move down the curving driveway into the street. "The cream of Weston society, and she winds up in the meat wagon with a bullet through her, as dead as any whore on Houston Street that held out on her pimp. What was she anyway—a nymphomaniac?"

"Unh-unh!" Sergeant Jim O'Brien pushed the battered hat back from his forehead and spoke without taking from his mouth the pipe that was always there when he was awake. "Nymphos sleep around hunting for a man who can satisfy them. Lorrie Porter— that was her maiden name—really liked it. I can remember the first time she got into trouble, couldn't have been more than sixteen when Amy Weston's brother knocked her up—"

"The D.A.?" Vosges' tone was only slightly shocked. Brought in from outside to put beef into Weston's police force after some students at the university had staged a panty raid on one of the girls' dormitories that had turned into a riot, he had quickly discovered that Weston wasn't much different from any other university city of a hundred-odd thousand people.

"Roy wasn't the first," said O'Brien. "Jake Porter—he was the real power in Weston Mills then—knew Lorrie had round heels even at that age, but he didn't do anything about it. Guess Jake figured it was in the blood. After all, he's still chasing girls at seventy-five—and able to do something about it, with a little help, when they let him catch them."

"But Mrs. Dellman had everything!"

"Everything except what she wanted, I guess." Sergeant O'Brien scratched his head. "Don't ask me what that was."

"You were speaking of the D.A."

"That's done and over with a long time ago. Roy wanted to marry Lorrie, but the old man would have none of it. He knew his daughter well enough by then to know she'd wreck Roy's future. The abortion was done by a madam down on Houston Street and everything was okay, until the girl started hemorrhaging and had to be brought to the hospital. It took some doing but we managed to cover it up."

"Was that wise?"

"It was if you wanted to stay a cop here in those days—and probably still is. The town was owned then by the Westons and Jake Porter. You played the game their way or you struck out."

"Do enough of the old ways remain to get him off?" Vosges nodded to where Mort Dellman was being ushered into the back seat of a police cruiser.

"Probably. What I can't figure out is why he did it. It's no secret that Dellman married Loretta Porter for her money. He isn't an M.D. like the others that started the Faculty Clinic; I think he's a chemist or something. But he's a born administrator;

runs that place like a machine. Nobody around here likes him much, though, and he wouldn't have gotten into the country club if he hadn't been married to the daughter of the man who built it."

"He's done all right for himself—until now." Vosges eyed the obviously expensive house with the large kidney-shaped swimming pool at the back under the pines.

"Marrying Lorrie helped," Sergeant O'Brien agreed. "But ever since he organized that medical production line they've got at the Faculty Clinic, Dellman's had a firm hold on part of a gold mine."

"Do the doctors there do good work?"

"You've got to go clear to the Mayo Clinic for anything better." Vosges shook his head. "And he wrecked it all today with one shot."

"That's what bugs me. Why would he do it?"

"The unwritten law still holds good in most parts of the country."

The grizzled policeman shook his head. "You can't tell me that in the twelve years or so he's been married to Loretta Porter, Dellman didn't know that practically every guy in town with hot pants was shacked up with his wife at one time or another. He must have had dozens of opportunities to shoot some of our most prominent citizens, if he'd wanted to. So why did he pick on this particular one?"

"Who knows?" The police lieutenant shrugged. "Think the guy he shot will make it? He looked pretty rocky to me when the ambulance took him away."

"Ten years ago a bullet in the middle of the chest would have been curtains, but they've got some pretty hot doctors at the University Hospital these days—especially that refugee fellow Dieter. Patched a hole in my nephew's heart a year ago, right after he first came here. The boy had been an invalid since he was a baby, now he's out for the swimming team at the university." O'Brien knocked out his pipe and started filling it again. "I still say there's something screwy about this setup."

34

"Maybe it was her he intended to kill."

"That don't fit either. Old Jake Porter is the richest man in these parts and Lorrie would have inherited a sizable chunk of his dough. I don't see anybody as smart as Dellman deliberately cutting himself off from that. Besides, he's done his share of tomcatting around town, so what right does he have to feel so virtuous?"

"What's the answer then?"

"That's what's bugging me. I can understand him plugging the guy—if it was somebody he didn't like. But he's known the poor devil for years. They were all in the army together in Korea, came here when the med school opened, and worked together every day. I tell you, Eric, there's something about this thing that doesn't gee."

"Don't strain," Eric Vosges advised. "If this town's like most, it will all come out in the wash."

CHAPTER III

It was a quarter past four when Della Rogan and Grace Hans-combe parked the golf cart they had been using in the space reserved for the vehicles beside the caddy house.

"Eighteen holes is too much at my age, Della," Grace said with a groan as she got out of the cart. She wore light beige Bermuda shorts, a yellow blouse and a yellow bandeau to hold her blonde hair away from her face while playing. At forty-eight, Grace was still well-preserved, with the fresh outdoor look many English-women seem to be able to retain through life.

"I'm glad I'm not a champion," she added. "The work of staying in shape would kill me."

"You're champion unofficially," said Della, as she lifted her clubs from the cart.

"Today was a fluke. I don't know what put you off your game, Della, but it must have been something earthshaking for me to beat you. Come to think of it, you haven't been yourself since you came back from that tournament in Augus—"

"Forget it, Grace!" Della's voice was sharp.

"Look here! I was only—" More angry than hurt, Grace stopped as Della shouldered the clubs and started toward the driving range. Then raising her voice she called: "If you decide to be friends again, stop by the house for a cup of coffee in the morning. I've been feeling so damned lousy the past few mornings, it'll be a relief to have even a grouch to talk to."

When Della didn't answer, Grace turned toward the clubhouse, leaving her clubs for one of the caddies to take to the locker room, where they would be put away by the maid. It was one of the prerogatives of being the wife of an officer in the club, as well as chairman of its most important women's committee—after golf, which Della Rogan headed. Being the wife of the city's leading internal medicine specialist did have some advantages—along with the disadvantages—she thought, as she headed for the bar and a tall drink, besides representing quite a jump from being a barmaid.

ii

Walking across the grounds toward the driving range, Della Rogan was surprised by the weight of her clubs. It was the first time in weeks she remembered carrying them herself. The caddies always did that, and there was always a golf cart to transport her from green to green so she could save all her energy for the vitally important strokes themselves.

Crossing the putting green adjoining the swimming pool, where a group of young people were squealing happily in the late afternoon sunlight, she approached the driving range, and putting her bag into the rack beside one of the driving slots, took out her favorite driver.

"Leroy," she called. "Bring me a bucket of balls, please."

A grizzled colored man looked out of the adjoining caddy house. "Yes'm, Mrs. Rogan," he said, and disappeared momentarily, before reappearing from another door carrying a bucket of golf balls. "Want me to tee 'em up for you?"

"No, thank you, I just want to practice my drive a little."

Della picked a wooden tee from one of the side pockets of her golf bag, an elaborate one of tooled leather—and very expensive. Dave had given it to her as an anniversary present just before she'd left for the Southeastern Women's Open Championship at Augusta. Remembering the tournament—and what happened afterward—she shoved the tee into the ground with suddenly shaking fingers, placed the ball upon it and took her stance, the driver gripped tight in her sun-browned hands.

Whack! She drove the ball hard, watching it soar far down the range, straight as an arrow, before dropping to the ground.

Could a guilty conscience have had anything to do with Dave giving her the bag? she wondered. It was very expensive, but she'd casually mentioned seeing it in the pro shop so he'd known she wanted it.

Whack! The second ball started true, then began to veer in a perceptible slice, striking the ground well to the left of the first one.

She'd been away an awful lot this year playing in tournaments. Dave hadn't accompanied her, of course; a psychiatrist couldn't just pick up and go traipsing off whenever his wife played golf. They'd quarreled bitterly over his not being able to attend the Southeastern Women's Open at Augusta, but he'd insisted that, with several patients at a crucial point in their therapy and testimony in a court case coming up, he just couldn't interrupt it. Besides, she knew, he didn't mind staying home and was fond of the kids—both away at camp now like most all faculty children. And there was always Mattie, the live-in maid, to take care of them when Della was away.

Not many wives of doctors on the medical school faculty had a live-in maid, but with Della gone so much of the time playing golf, it had seemed the thing to do. In fact, she remembered now, Dave himself had suggested it. At the time it had only seemed an act of consideration on his part, but maybe there had been another reason why he'd been willing for her to be away so much, a reason she might not even know of until it was too late. Just that had happened to others—even to some of her friends.

Teeing up again, Della stroked the ball almost viciously, but this one sliced even more than had the others and she put down the club quickly because her hands were trembling so much that she was afraid she would drop it. Unconsciously the cause of her sudden doubt of Dave was the knowledge of her own guilt, but

she refused to allow that thought access to consciousness, knowing its capacity to blast into bits her snug little world of club
life, golf tournaments and the row of trophies on her mantel. It
was simpler to suspect Dave and transfer the guilt to him; the
trouble was that her love for him and her knowledge of his love
for her made it practically impossible to convince herself.

If Dave wasn't so damned considerate of her, she thought
with a flash of anger, maybe nothing would have happened at
Augusta. He never objected to her playing in tournaments, even
when it meant leaving him and the children for several days, and
lately he hadn't even been making many sexual demands on her.
Which had seemed just as well at the time; after eighteen holes
of golf, plus an hour or so of practice shots, she was usually too
tired for that sort of thing. Come to think of it, they hadn't
made love in six weeks. With the Southeastern Championship at
Augusta and now getting ready for the club championship here
at Weston, she'd been away nearly half the nights and exhausted
the others, but Dave hadn't seemed to mind.

Or had he? she wondered, as she swung on the ball.

Whack! She stared at the spot where the ball should have been
with unseeing eyes.

Could he possibly have heard of what had happened at Augusta
—after she'd won the Women's Southeastern?

"You all right, Mrs. Rogan?" Leroy's soft-voiced question
startled her.

"Of course I'm all right. Don't be impertinent!"

She was breaking the club rule that frowned upon any tongue-
lashing of its employees, for caddies and attendants were harder
to find every year. Dave was vice-president of the club in charge
of personnel and she'd often heard him say that, with the government changing the wage-and-hour laws every session of Congress,
nobody knew where they'd be able to get help any more.

"Why did you ask, Leroy?" She forced herself to be conciliatory.

"You just topped your drive, Miz Rogan. Ain't seen you do that
in ten years."

Della looked down the driving range and, seeing nothing where the ball should have landed, let her eyes drop slowly. It seemed an eternity before they found the small white object, hardly a dozen feet from where she was standing.

"Take my clubs to the locker room please, Leroy," she said in choked tones. "I've got to have a drink."

iii

Alice Weston never looked at TV in the afternoon, once the last soap opera was finished. By that time, she was so emotionally spent that she had to lie down for a while before taking her bath and dressing for dinner. Having never known real unhappiness, Alice found the tribulations of the sad people inhabiting the dream world of the afternoon soap operas almost more than she could bear. She never listened to the news: real-life misery always left her depressed for a long time. But she bore the soap operas bravely, out of a sense of duty. After all, it didn't seem right for one person to have everything and not suffer a little for the troubled world—if only through the proxy of a TV screen.

A half-hour in bed in the afternoon with the blinds drawn was like a cathartic, however, flushing away the troubles of the soap opera world and leaving Alice ready for her bath in preparation for the ritual before-dinner martini she and Roy always shared— when he was home. Vanessa, the full-time cook-maid, prepared the dinner, did the cleaning and even the grocery shopping, so Alice had little responsibility as far as running the house was concerned. But Roy did like for her to prepare his martini with her own hands, the vermouth barely flavoring the gin, the olive bruised just enough for a hint of the bitter oil in its skin to seep into the drink itself.

They'd been married almost twenty years, since she was eighteen. Yet not once had Alice ever confessed to Roy that she always diluted her own drink with water while she was making it. The stimulation of alcohol whenever she allowed herself to drink

that much, which was almost never, always made her a little un-
sure. She knew people did awful things when they had too much
to drink. There was always a lot of that sort of thing in the soap
operas and she was afraid of what alcohol might do to her own
tidy little world.

Then she remembered that Roy had said he wouldn't be home
for dinner—some sort of a pretrial conference would make him
late. Maybe she'd call Corinne Marchant to come and stay awhile
with her, she thought, and the idea made her feel happy, driving
away the sadness left over from the afternoon TV serials.

Alice had just taken off her dress and was stretched out on
the bed in her slip in semidarkness with the window air conditioner purring softly—even with the mountains only fifty miles
away, Weston got pretty warm in early September—when the
phone at the bedside rang. Drowsily she lifted it from the cradle;
like the rest of the room and herself, the phone was pink and
white.

"Alice?" She recognized the high-pitched, somewhat querulous
voice of Jake Porter.

"What is it, Uncle Jacob?" The tough old man had taken Alice
and her widowed mother in after her father's death and practically raised her as his own daughter, so she always felt about him
like she felt about one of the Biblical patriarchs. For that reason,
she'd never been able to bring herself to call him Uncle Jake, as
Roy did—though everybody knew Jake Porter bore no resem-
blance to a Biblical character, except perhaps King David in his
Bathsheba days.

"Where's Roy?" the old man demanded.

"I don't know. At his office, I suppose."

"I've called there. They don't know where he is."

"He said he wouldn't be home until late. Do you want me to
have him call you when he gets here, Uncle Jacob?"

"I can't wait that long; I need him now. Roy's got to clamp the
lid on before this town erupts like a volcano."

"We couldn't be having a race riot in Weston." One of the

42

characters in "Edge of Day" was a beatnik who was always brag-
ging about how he had been in the march to Selma. Just seeing
him on the TV screen upset Alice so much that she almost had to
turn off the rest of the story, as soon as he appeared. Almost—but
not quite.

"Hell, no!" said Jake Porter. "You mean you don't know what's
happened?"

"Know what, Uncle Jacob?"

"The news. It's all over the TV."

"I never watch the news. It upsets me."

"Lorrie's been shot—killed by that son-of-a-bitch she married.
A man with her was shot, too."

"Oh!" As the room started revolving slowly, Alice clung desperately to the receiver, the only solid thing immediately at hand.
She knew she was going to faint. Mother always said her nervous
system was too delicate to stand shocks and had carefully
shielded her from them.

"Don't you faint, Alice!" The old man's squawk in the receiver
was like a cold douche, reviving her a little. "I've got to find Roy."

"Who?" From some deep reservoir of courage she'd never been
called upon before to tap, Alice found strength to ask the question. "Who was the man with Lorrie?"

"The radio broadcast didn't give his name. I think they said he
was a physician but I was so upset when I heard it that I can't
be sure. I called the hospital but they won't tell me a damn thing
either."

"Why the hospital?"

"Damn it, Alice! Haven't you heard what I've been saying?
Mort Dellman caught a man in bed with Lorrie this afternoon
and shot them both. Lorrie's dead and the man's seriously
wounded. He could be Roy."

The telephone dropped from Alice's fingers as the familiar
cramping pain just to the left of her navel doubled her up in
sudden agony.

"Alice!" The old man's voice came from the phone. "Alice!
Are you there?"

Clutching her abdomen with her left hand, she managed to pick up the phone again. "I've got to go, Uncle Jacob."

"Go?"

"To the bathroom. I'm having a colon attack."

The explosive cramping agony came again and she dropped the phone. Rolling over on her side, she slid from the bed and started to crawl toward the bathroom on hands and knees, gasping with agony when every move brought on the terrible cramping pain.

"Hell, Alice! Don't you have anything better to do at a time like this than—" Her own cry of pain blotted out the pungent word but from the door of the bathroom she heard, as if from a great distance, the final exasperated splutter of the old man over the phone hanging from the bedside table by its cord.

"If your mind was half as active as your gut, Alice, you'd be the smartest woman in the world."

iv

Maggie McCloskey was sitting in the small bar across from the ladies' lounge when Della Rogan came in and ordered a gin and tonic. The men still pre-empted the Nineteenth Hole, but the club had turned what was once storage space back of the main bar into a small, intimate room where the women could have a drink in shorts after the game.

Maggie was on her third or fourth, judging by the rather glazed look in her eyes, but Della didn't want to speak to her until she had swallowed the first drink and ordered another. She didn't want to be reminded that, of all the members of the Dissection Society, Maggie was the only one who had gone so far as to get a divorce—yet.

Born Margaret Smith, Maggie had been a secretary in the psychiatric department of the medical school before her marriage to Joe McCloskey, and Della an X-ray technician. They had both come from the same town in eastern Tennessee, but Della had lost track of Maggie until they'd met again at the new hospital

44

and medical school of Weston University some fifteen years earlier.

Back in Tennessee Maggie had grown up on the other side of the tracks from Della and, though Della never reminded her of it, or even thought about it, Maggie had seemed determined to run herself down, even after Joe McCloskey married her. Actually, as Della very well knew, Maggie had no reason to feel inferior to anyone. She had been an extremely capable secretary to Dave Rogan and had been instrumental in bringing Della and Dave together, when they had double-dated once with Maggie and Joe.

Just what was the trouble between Joe and Maggie, no one could ever be sure. Joe was a small, somewhat prematurely bald man, with courtly manners and a degree of kindness and tolerance somewhat unusual in a urologist, whose work brought him in contact with some of the seamiest aspects of human behavior. Della had always suspected that the main trouble was Maggie's feeling of inferiority, which again didn't make sense. For Maggie had been very pretty when she and Joe were married and was still a handsome woman, though the marks of dissipation had begun to mar her beauty, particularly since the divorce, when she had been drinking more heavily than before.

For whatever reason, liquor only seemed to exaggerate Maggie's increasingly frequent lapses into the customs and language of her early upbringing. In fact, Della sometimes thought she was deliberately flogging herself by making people disgusted with her and her behavior. And being naturally kind and genuinely fond of both Maggie and Joe, she felt sorry for Maggie and tried to help her, often at the expense of her own feelings, when Maggie lashed out blindly, striking at anything within reach.

Physically, two women could hardly have been more different than Maggie McCloskey and Della Rogan. Where Maggie was rounded almost to the point of plumpness, Della was wiry. Where Maggie was dark-haired, Della had started out as a sandy redhead and had gradually bleached out from the sun of the golf course, where she spent at least half of her time, to a yellowish blonde.

And where Maggie was highly emotional, Della was quietly capable, holding herself in check lest Dave who, as a psychiatrist, dealt with emotionally disturbed people all day, come home to the same sort of atmosphere at night.

It was Joe McCloskey Della really felt sorry for, kind, unfailingly courteous, quietly unprepossessing Joe. He'd tried desperately to avoid the divorce, she knew. But Maggie had seemed to take pleasure in flagellating both herself and him, until in the end there had seemed to be no other answer. Since then, Della and Dave had tried to have Joe over for dinner several times to cheer him up. But with her gone so much playing in out-of-town golf tournaments even that hadn't worked out very well. Besides, she was sure Maggie had heard about the invitations and had been all the more unpleasant because of them.

"Hear about Lorrie?" Maggie's voice was already a little slurred.

"Who is it this time?"

"The angel Gabriel—unless he's the flying faggot I think he is."

"Stop clowning, Maggie." Tired as she was and with the alcohol from the drinks not quite into her bloodstream yet, Della's tone was short. "What's with Lorrie?"

"She's kaput. Morte."

"You mean she's dead?"

"That's the general idea."

Startled, Della strangled on her drink and Maggie gleefully gave her a crack on the shoulder blades that jarred her teeth.

"Don't gulp your whiskey, Della girl; it'll last longer if you take it slow. Believe me," she added bitterly, "when you have to live on the lousy pittance Joe McCloskey gives me as alimony, you need to make every drink count."

"What about Lorrie?"

"Mort shot her a few minutes ago—according to the radio and TV. Right through the heart, the man said, though believe me it would have been more appropriate if he'd aimed somewhat lower."

46

Della Rogan felt a cold chill start somewhere in the region of her heart. "Was she . . . ?"

"Alone? I thought you'd ask that." Maggie was getting all the enjoyment she could out of her friend's shock. "Is she ever?"

"For God's sake, Maggie. What do you know?"

"The broadcast said a 'prominent physician' was with Lorrie when Mort drilled her. Whoever he was, he got shot, too—what the lawyers call *flagrante delicto*."

"Who was it?" Cold sweat was breaking out on Della's forehead, though minutes before she had been hot and thirsty. It couldn't be Dave, of course.

Or could it?

"That's what nobody's been able to find out yet. But you can bet a lot of faculty wives have been telephoning each other frantically ever since it happened, wondering whether the man in the case is her husband."

"How do I know you're not making all this up?" Della emptied her glass and shoved it across the bar to the bartender for a refill.

"Threw the fear of God into you, didn't I?" Maggie cackled. "Most of us have been sleeping with each other's husbands for years. Somebody had to get caught sometime."

"Knock it off, Maggie! The bartender's listening."

"Manuel's heard all this before—or he will in the next few days."

"Then it's really true?"

"Ask Manuel, if you don't believe me," Maggie said indignantly. "He heard it too."

Della glanced at the bartender and the cold chill within her deepened when he nodded. "All I know is what was on the radio, Mrs. Rogan," he said. "You see, I keep this little transistor set on when nobody's here."

"Turn it on now!" Della's voice was harsh.

"The manager doesn't like—"

"Turn the damn thing on, Manuel," said Maggie McCloskey. "The male victim could very well be on the board of directors, you know."

"If you ladies say so." Manuel switched on the transistor set just as Grace Hanscombe appeared in the door of the small bar.

"They've got the gory details on the TV set in the Nineteenth Hole—in color," she said, and there was a concerted rush from the small bar to the larger one, where a group of men and women were gathered around the TV set.

"There goes Mort!" Arthur Painter was a lawyer who specialized in estates; he pointed to the screen, on which a chunky man in his shirt-sleeves was being led by a sheriff's deputy to a waiting prowl car. "I wonder if he took out that new policy on Lorrie long enough ago for the company to have to pay it."

"I wrote the policy and we'll never pay it." At thirty, Earl Bieson was already a Life Underwriter and a member of his company's Million Dollar Club—plus suffering from high blood pressure and failing kidneys.

"Don't you two ever think of anything except wills and insurance?" said Della.

"Hello, Della," said Arthur Painter. "Where's Dave?"

A dead silence followed the question, until Maggie said, "A lot of wives are wondering where their husbands are right now, Arthur. I'm glad I don't have—"

"Shut up, Maggie!" Della was straining to get a good look at the TV screen. "Don't forget what will happen to your precious alimony if Joe's been shot."

"The bastard couldn't do that to me." Maggie blanched and gulped the remainder of the drink she carried in her hand. "Could he, Arthur?"

"What are you talking about, Maggie?" The lawyer reluctantly took his attention away from the screen.

"You drew up my divorce settlement—and got enough out of it for yourself. If Joe was knocked off by Mort Dellman, do I lose my alimony?"

"You lose it." At the words Maggie looked as if she was going to be ill. "But Joe's insurance is made out in a trust for you."

"Then I'll get double indemnity—for the accident?" Maggie's

color started to come back as she turned to the insurance man. "You wrote the policy, Earl. Don't I get double?"

"If Joe's the one that was shot and he dies, his estate would collect double indemnity." Even the thought seemed to cause Bieson pain. "They haven't given the name of the man yet but the last I heard he was alive and on the way to the University Hospital."

"It could be Joe," said Maggie. "He was always after Lorrie just like the rest of you—and a lot who aren't here."

A scene familiar to all of them had just come on the TV screen, a house set back among the trees with a curving driveway in front. In Sherwood Ravine, lots had to be an acre in size and the houses a minimum of a hundred feet from the street, so most were set back as much as a hundred and fifty feet.

"Keep the peasants from seeing what goes on among the nobility," had been the motto of old Bob Bieson—Earl's father—when he had built the development. Originally intended to provide space for rich men's houses, the area had now become largely populated with doctors, dentists and lawyers, the new-rich aristocracy of the professions that the postwar world had created so quickly.

On the TV screen, ambulance attendants were wheeling out a stretcher on which lay a still form, covered with a sheet.

"That must be Lorrie," said Della as they lifted the stretcher into the ambulance.

"She's certainly dead," said Maggie. "Or she'd somehow have managed to get rid of that sheet before now."

"You're drunk, Maggie," said Grace Hanscombe. "Come on. I'll take you home."

"Not me. I'm going to stay here until they name the prominent physician who was with Lorrie when Mort gunned him down."

"I'll go with you, Grace," said Della Rogan. "It's almost time for Dave to come home." She stopped suddenly, knowing the hell she saw in the Englishwoman's eyes was mirrored in her own.

"Let's get another drink," said Della. "We both know we're afraid to go home."

"One thing's certain." There was rough burr of cockney in Grace's voice, an accent she usually managed to keep hidden. "This will be the first night in a long time the husbands—and wives—in Sherwood Ravine will all be sleeping in their own beds."

CHAPTER IV

Marisa Feldman was passing through the emergency room from her quarters in the Faculty Apartments across the street, on the way to an early dinner in the hospital cafeteria, when an ambulance, its siren still going, stopped at the ramp outside. As a stretcher was wheeled in hurriedly, she gave a quick glance at the man lying upon it, noting the apparent absence of breathing, the pallor of shock—or death.

"What is this?" she asked, for something about the victim's appearance had rung a warning bell in her brain.

"D.O.A., ma'm—Doctor," said the ambulance attendant, noting the long-skirted white coat she wore because she planned on making ward rounds after dinner.

"Why didn't you take him to the hospital morgue?"

"Nobody's pronounced him, Doctor." Only rarely did hospitals have enough interns to ride ambulances since the impact of Medicare, so she knew the ambulance driver's medical training would have been limited to the brief course in first aid required by law in most states.

"When we put him into the ambulance he was as alive as anybody can be with a bullet in the middle of the chest," the second attendant volunteered. "But he has no pulse now."

"A bullet wound!" Marisa Feldman's mind clicked into action like a computer. "Get him into that cubicle over there! Fast!"

As she spoke, she was reaching for the phone. Dialing the hospital operator, she said urgently, "This is Dr. Feldman, call

'Cardiac Alert' on the paging system, please—emergency room."

When she turned to the cubicle, an orderly was already helping the ambulance attendants lift the wounded man onto an examining-treatment table. And over the loudspeaker she heard the voice of the paging operator, crisp and distinct: "CARDIAC ALERT! ALL STAFF PERSONNEL TO THEIR STATIONS! CARDIAC ALERT—EMERGENCY ROOM."

This was only her second day on the hospital staff, so Marisa Feldman had met only a few of the medical school faculty. But she had learned about the procedure for handling serious cardiac cases—like cessation of the heartbeat—at a briefing session Dr. Hanchmann, Chief of the Medical Services, had given her yesterday. And she approved thoroughly of the routine used here for handling such emergencies.

The two words "Cardiac Alert!" would bring a trained resuscitation team to the emergency room at once, alert the Special Intensive Care Unit to be ready for a new patient, and send to the scene the most experienced doctors in the hospital in every field that might be involved in a cardiac emergency. Marisa wasted no time waiting for them, however, but took immediate command.

"Did you use a respirator?" she asked one of the ambulance men.

"There wasn't time, Doctor."

The words told her only a short period had elapsed since cessation of breathing so there might be some hope that brain damage of any serious degree had not yet occurred. The immediate problem therefore was twofold: first to get the heart started and second to get the patient breathing again, thereby increasing the oxygen level in his blood as rapidly as possible to overcome any temporary damage that might have been done to the brain cells by its brief absence.

"Get an airway in and start the resuscitator," she told the duty intern who, sweating and red-faced, had appeared beside her at the strident summons of the loudspeaker. From where it hung on the wall, Marisa Feldman plucked an obstetrical stethoscope. Its bell was attached to a headband and, with the tips of the soft rubber tubes attached to it in her ears, she was able to lean over and listen to the heart while leaving both hands free for closed-chest resuscitation.

The first step in this new and dramatic method of restarting stopped hearts, which had lessened so sharply the need for the sort of dramatic surgery involved in opening the chest itself and massaging the heart directly, was the determination that cessation of the heartbeat had actually occurred. The precaution was necessary lest the organ be damaged by the somewhat rough treatment given it during the heavy pressure made directly upon the chest in the maneuver of squeezing the heart between the spine and the sternum, or breastbone, just as a surgeon operating under direct view would squeeze it in his hands to stimulate the stopped organ and restore the beat.

Marisa saw the wound when she pulled down the sheet covering the injured man's chest; small and neat, it was just over the cardiac area and a little to the right. Her expert appraising glance also took in the distention of the veins in his neck and the mottled cynosis over his upper chest, neck and face completing the visible clinical picture.

At her side, she heard the intern's voice, shrill with surprise and horror, exclaim: "My God, it's Dr. ———." But the name he spoke was lost to her as she leaned forward to press the stethoscope against the wounded man's chest, shutting away all sound except what came by way of the column of air trapped between the metal bell of the stethoscope, the tubes connecting it to the plastic tips in her ears, and her own auditory canals closed off by her eardrums. Nor would the name necessarily have meant anything to her, since this was only her second day on the faculty of the school.

In the stethoscope, the air column was like an amplifier magnifying every sound within the chest. At first Marisa heard nothing—the sign of death. Then, when her eardrums had adjusted somewhat to the slight change of air pressure, as the metal bell was pressed hard against the pallid skin of the victim's chest wall, she detected a faint rippling sound, like water heard from a great distance as it flowed across a stretch of rocks.

The ripple was without rhythm or pattern but the mere fact that it was audible at all provided the last bit of data needed by the marvelously complex system of memories, impressions and observations that made the human brain a far more complicated and efficient machine than any data-processing system devised by man.

As the ripples of sound had set each of her eardrums into delicately vibrant motion, the first of the three bones of the middle ear, the *malleus,* or hammer, lying against the drum also began to vibrate faintly. This movement was transmitted by mechanical force through two adjoining tiny bones, the anvil and stirrup—medically the *incus* and *stapes*—to a small opening known as the "oval window," separating the middle from the inner ear. Vibrating against the membrane covering of the oval window, the stapes had set up its own faint mechanical ripple in the fluid that filled the semicircular canals of the inner ear.

In rapid sequence, the air wave vibrations of sound falling upon the eardrum from outside the body had been changed to mechanical motion in the middle ear, then back to fluid waves in the semicircular canals of the inner ear. Moving through those canals, the tiny impulses of wave motion stirred delicate hairlike nerve endings in the organs of Corti, sensory terminals for the auditory—hearing—nerve itself, just as the skin of the fingertips forms the organs of sensation for touch, temperature and pain.

In the organ of Corti, the mechanical energy of the fluid wave was once again transformed—in a marvelous and intricate way which even now men were not able entirely to understand—into infinitely small electric impulses traveling along the nerve channels to the center of hearing in the brain cortex. There they were simultaneously interpreted as sound and a picture of this sound sent, through other connecting nerve fibers of the brain, to the centers of memory in the frontal lobes.

Digested, analyzed and compared with other information stored away during years of study in medical school and in hospitals, the whole picture had been subjected in an instant of time and completely without conscious thought to an analysis far more intricate than was possible by any man-made system of electric circuits. Somewhere in the memory and judgment areas of the brain, a complete pattern suddenly formed, like a jigsaw puzzle when the final piece is dropped into position. And once formed, the pattern was flashed to the centers of conscious—rather than unconscious—thought, where it became a concept ready to be voiced.

"Cardiac Tamponade!" Marisa Feldman spoke the diagnosis aloud quite unconsciously, so sudden and explosive was the concept that had taken form in her mind, produced from the stream of data pouring into her brain from every sense.

When she looked up, the shocked look still visible in the eyes of the intern, fumbling with the plastic airway he was sliding between the teeth of the injured man, plus its counterpart upon the face of the graying nurse supervisor, who had appeared at her elbow, told Marisa they had recognized the victim, but that was of no importance to her.

Her first casual glance at the sheeted form on the stretcher had told her something was wrong with the picture, an inconsistency in the clinical pattern of death summed up by the ambulance attendant's casual description of D.O.A.—dead on arrival. The tiny rippling sound heard in the stethoscope had revealed that the dying man's heart, struggling instinctively to preserve life, still fought against the constricting pressure of the blood accumulated in the confined space of its own protective membrane by its desperate attempts to maintain life.

But the tiny and already almost imperceptible movement of the heart would cease, she knew, unless that pressure was relieved in a matter of seconds. And wasting no time, she moved resolutely to do just that.

ii

It was not quite five o'clock when Janet Monroe stepped out upon the small terrace adjoining the cafeteria atop the new surgical wing of the University Hospital, only a few steps away, via an enclosed passage, from the Special Intensive Care Unit where she was nurse-in-charge. She had chosen to have only a quick sandwich and coffee at the snack counter for dinner, rather than the full meal allowed nursing staff members during each eight-hour shift under their contract. That way she had been able to use fifteen of the thirty minutes allowed for dinner to make a quick visit to the Surgical Pediatrics ward several floors below where Jerry was a patient.

The way her son's small face had lit up at the sight of her had tugged at her heart. The terms of the divorce from Cliff Monroe hadn't allowed her much in the way of alimony; he'd still had two years of his residency to go and you couldn't get blood from a turnip. Janet had been left with no choice except to go on working after the divorce, leaving Jerry after three each afternoon in the cooperative nursery maintained by the hospital and medical school in a basement room of the married student housing building for the benefit of working mothers. Most of them were putting their husbands through medical school or residencies or, like herself, working as nurses to support themselves, and often children, after the divorce that ended so many medical student marriages.

What had depressed her wasn't Jerry's appearance; he was bouncingly healthy and obviously the pet of the ward. It was the fact that the hospital staff hadn't yet been able to pin down the cause of the sudden convulsive attack he had suffered two afternoons ago.

Janet had been dressing on her evening off in the small apartment she and Jerry shared—except from 3 to 11 P.M. six days a week—for a date to go with Jeff Long to the pops concert in the new Municipal Amphitheater. Jerry had been playing in the yard and she'd been surprised to see him open the door of the apartment and cross the living room to the bedroom door. Usually he insisted on staying outside in the play yard with the other children until dark, since her day off was the only time he had a chance to play with them in the afternoon.

Turning from the mirror to watch him cross the bedroom to-ward her, she had thought how sturdy and fine he was with his blue eyes, red cheeks and thick mop of dark hair. Boys usually took after their fathers but Jerry leaned toward her family in the genes he had inherited and there was little of Cliff in him to remind her of the past. He was a happy and contented little boy, even though she had to waken him shortly after eleven each evening and carry him the half block between the nursery and her apartment.

Jerry had been halfway across the bedroom when Janet realized that something seemed to be wrong with him. Normally he ran everywhere he went, but today his steps were slow. Once he seemed to stagger, as if his foot had caught in the rug and he was very tired, and when she reached out for him, he stumbled into her arms and put his head against her breast.

"My head hurts." The solidity of his strong little body reas-sured her somewhat, calming the moment of panic she'd experi-enced when he appeared to stumble.

"Mommie will get you a baby aspirin." Half-strength and flavored to taste like candy, the tablets were so attractive that she had to keep the bottle high up on the medicine shelf to keep them away from him. Carrying him—she was still in her slip—Janet went to the bathroom, found the tablets and gave the little boy one.

It was nothing, she had told herself, as he started chewing happily on the tablet. When she gave him a cup of water to wash it down, he seemed to choke a little but that could come from trying to swallow the slightly chalky tablet, she was sure. In fact this whole performance could easily be explained by his wanting her to stay with him, rather than go to the concert. It wouldn't be the first time a slight stomach-ache or even a sniffly nose had suddenly developed when Jerry knew the sitter was coming on her evening off.

"Want to lie down for a little while, darling?" Janet had pressed her cheek against his soft one. "Mrs. Bodey can give you your

57

dinner later." A widow whose small pension was supplemented by baby-sitting chores at night in the neighborhood, Mrs. Bodey lived several doors down the street.

"Aw right, Mommie."

She had carried him over to the crib and placed him in it, then pulled up a chair and sat beside him, crooning a lullaby as she stroked his warm cheek. For a moment she considered calling Jeff Long and canceling their date. After the divorce from Cliff, she hadn't gone out for a whole year, until Jeff had convinced her that she needed to get away occasionally for her own emotional health.

He'd been right, of course, as he was about almost everything. An anesthesiology resident couldn't afford to fail, he'd told her once with the familiar, and by now beloved, grin; in the white glare of the operating-room lights there was no way to cover up his mistake.

She was going to have to make a decision about Jeff soon, Janet had told herself for at least the hundredth time as she sat beside the crib. She'd put it off again and again because she knew only one decision was really fair to Jeff—and she didn't want to make it for purely selfish reasons. However much she'd come to depend on him, and love him, it wasn't fair to saddle Jeff with another man's child, even though Jerry adored him. And it was equally unfair to let Jeff go on loving her without any hope of marriage.

It wasn't that her own unhappy experience had really prejudiced her against marriage; God knew Cliff had never really contributed anything, except the seed that had given Jerry life. Actually the marriage had been a fiasco from the start and Janet had often wondered whether Cliff hadn't married her because she was about to receive her degree in nursing and could support him through medical school, only to be abandoned with a child and a divorce, after he had received his M.D. and was able to earn a living for himself.

Janet had thought Jerry was asleep when the first convulsion came, a seizure that made the little body jerk spasmodically and his eyes roll upward until almost nothing showed except the whites.

It wasn't the first time she had seen the baby in a convulsion; when he'd been about a year old, he'd once had a high fever and a spasm. Even in her natural concern over what was happening, Janet didn't allow herself to panic. Instead she held him close until the jerking stopped, and even had the presence of mind to note that one side of his body seemed to be jerking more than the other. But when the spasm ceased and she saw his eyes rolled back and heard no sound of breathing, her heart seemed to stop.

Fortunately, she'd known exactly what to do. Nothing was to be gained by calling a doctor, with the inevitable delay. The hospital emergency room was only a few blocks away and skilled help was always available there, especially Jeff Long and big, capable Ed Harrison, who was not only the resident on Pediatrics but a friend, too.

Jerry had suddenly started breathing again while she held him in her arms after the convulsion, a stertorous sound like an old person snoring. Placing him in the crib from which she had lifted him during the convulsion, Janet had run to the closet, seized a cotton print dress and pulled it down over her head. Zipping it up she had picked up the keys to the Volvo that was her single extravagance during the two years since the divorce.

Jerry was breathing more normally and his body was relaxed when she lifted him from the crib. He even opened his eyes drowsily and one chubby hand reached up toward her cheek as she moved downstairs with him in her arms.

The Volvo had been parked in the driveway and she had placed the little boy upon the seat, closed the door, and gone around to the side and got in. Even in her anxiety, Janet had retained enough of her normal faculties to realize that this convulsion wasn't like the one Jerry had suffered several years before. For one thing it was more severe; for another, it seemed to be somewhat limited to one side. She didn't have time to think much about that, however, for in less than ten minutes, she was parked at the emergency-room ambulance unloading ramp. She was carrying Jerry into the hospital, when his body began to jerk in her arms with another convulsion.

The rest of that evening seemed almost like a dream now—after seeing Jerry apparently completely his normal self a few minutes ago. The nursing supervisor in the emergency room had put in an immediate call for both Ed Harrison and Jeff Long. And as the competent assured routine of the hospital swiftly meshed into action around her and Jerry, Janet had felt the blind panic she'd experienced at the start of the second convulsion begin to subside.

It had ended as swiftly as the first, even before Ed Harrison could reach the emergency room. Once again the little body had gone through the agonizing period when respiration was arrested by the spasm of the chest muscles and lips and ear lobes started turning blue with the cyanosis of oxygen lack. Then as explosively as with the first spasm, Jerry suddenly began to breathe again and a few moments later looked up to smile at Janet.

That had been two days ago, but Dr. Deemster, Professor of Pediatrics, had decided to wait for a brief period of observation. Ed had explained the reason: "Cases like this are often due to a small hemorrhage into the subarachnoid space around the brain, Janet. If we do a spinal puncture now, we might disturb the pressure relationships and increase the bleeding."

"Isn't there anything you can do?"

"I'll give him some elixir phenobarbital to quiet him down a bit. We'll do a spinal puncture in a couple of days and see what we find. Meanwhile we can make some other tests and have some consultations."

Today was the day; the ward nurse had told her Dr. Rogan was seeing Jerry for a neurological consultation about six and the puncture would probably be done then. Ed had promised to let her know, for on its outcome might well hinge Jerry's future.

Deliberately Janet forced the problems she faced from her mind and looked westward toward the dark range of the Smokies. She'd taught herself to make her mind blank like this every now and then since that day, two years ago, when she'd come home from duty to the small apartment and found Cliff's belongings gone—else she was sure she would have lost her mind. A note on the dresser had said that Jerry was with Mrs. Bodey but Cliff had never come back. Shortly afterward Janet had filed for the divorce he wanted.

Actually, she admitted now as she stubbed out her cigarette preparatory to going back to the Special Intensive Care Unit, Cliff's going had been something of a relief. Certainly her financial status hadn't been any worse, perhaps even better, with the necessity of paying for his tuition, food and cigarettes now removed. To be abandoned by her husband was still a blow to a woman's ego, however, no matter how much of a louse the man was. And for a while she had been numb, until Jeff Long had practically dragged her back into a life outside her work, the apartment and Jerry. Now Jerry's convulsions, with their ominous portent of something serious, threatened to push her back into the state of self-pity and despondency from which she had been only beginning to emerge.

A glance at her watch told her it was five and she stood up, just as the loudspeaker in the cafeteria outside which she had been sitting crackled into its dramatic—and chilling—announcement: "CARDIAC ALERT! ALL STAFF PERSONNEL TO THEIR STATIONS!"

Janet stiffened at the first words of the announcement. Her first thought was of little Jerry, his breathing mechanism stopped by the muscle spasm of another convulsion, his lips and ear lobes dusky with the dread blue tint of cyanosis. Her place of duty was in the Special Intensive Care Unit, according to the standard operating procedure for the most urgent emergency a hospital had to face, the immediacy of a stopped heart. But if it were Jerry whose heart had been stopped by another convulsion, she needed to be at his side, regardless of duty. Torn by indecision and horror, Janet couldn't move one way or the other, until the second part of the announcement released her: "CARDIAC ALERT— EMERGENCY ROOM."

Once more able to breathe, she turned on a run for her station.

iii

It could be Pete, was Amy Brennan's first thought as the numbing news poured from the radio in the announcer's excited voice. Lorrie was completely amoral and had made a play for anything male whenever she felt like it—which was often. Pete was about as male as you could get, she reminded herself, while his wife—busy with her own little plans for personal glory—had been neglecting him shamefully. The thought made her step down hard on the accelerator and the big car leaped forward, while the radio chattered on with more details about the tragedy —except the name she wanted—and was afraid—to hear.

She was turning off the interstate when she noticed the red warning light on the gas gauge and the pointer at "Empty." Disturbed as she was, she had no way of knowing how long it had been there, so she decided not to take a chance on running out of gas before she could get to the hospital. Two service stations were located at the foot of the exit ramp and, pulling into the first one, she drew to a stop beside the pumps.

Two men came from inside the station. One was young and red-haired; the other, gray-haired and stooped.

"Fill it up please—high test," said Amy. "And don't bother with the oil."

While the old man put the nozzle into the tank and started the pump, the younger one began to clean the windshield. He usually chose that job; with the short dresses now in vogue, the view from his position was often spectacular.

Amy's eyes roved restlessly, until she saw the wall pay phone inside the station. Opening the door and stepping out, she fumbled in her purse for a dime but found none, so took out a quarter and handed it to the younger man.

"Some change please—for the phone."

He took the quarter, clicked two dimes and a nickel out of the change counter he wore on his belt and gave them to her. "Charge or cash ma'm?"

"What?"

"For the gas. Do you want me to charge it?"

"Yes." She reached in her purse and handed him her charge card, then moved to the telephone almost on a run. Trembling fingers dialed the hospital number but when the hospital operator answered, she almost hung up, afraid of what she would hear.

"This is Mrs. Brennan," she managed to say. "Would you ring my husband's office?"

"There's a Cardiac Alert on, Mrs. Brennan. We can't ring any phones inside the hospital for outside calls."

"What's a Cardiac Alert?"

"A serious heart case just arrived. The lines have to be kept open until the alert goes off."

"Is—is it one of the staff doctors?"

"I believe so, yes."

"Can you tell—"

"Here's a call now for X-ray. I'll have to handle it."

Numbly, Amy hung up the phone and left the booth. When the younger attendant brought her the small blue plate on which lay the charge slip and her card, she scribbled her name automatically on the slip and dropped the card into her wallet.

"You all right, Mrs. Brennan?" the younger man asked.

"Y-yes. Why?"

"You look like you've seen a ghost."

Amy stared at him, her pupils dilating. Then, with a gasp of horror, she ran to the car, got in and started the engine. Her hands were trembling so much that she could hardly hold the wheel, however, and she put her head down upon it while she fought for control.

"Dear God," she whispered. "Don't let it be Pete."

The act of praying restored her composure enough to drive

out of the station and into the street leading to University Hospital. Watching her, the younger of the two attendants scratched his head thoughtfully.

"You know I'd swear she was prayin' just before she left here," he said.

"Prayin'?" The older man shook his head. "You're imagining things again, Ed."

"Yeah, guess I am at that. I used to service her car when I worked at the big company station downtown. That's Dr. Brennan's wife; he's a big-shot surgeon at the university and she's got everything already. So what would she be prayin' for?"

iv

Maggie McCloskey didn't get to see the rest of the newscast out—neither did Grace Hanscombe. The ambulance on the TV screen had barely disappeared down the street when Maggie suddenly turned green and staggered toward the door leading across the hall to the ladies' lounge. Obviously, she wasn't going to make it without help, and remembering that she was the chairman of the decorating committee for the club and would have to find a cleaner for the carpet in the hall in case of an accident, Grace grabbed Maggie by the shoulder and the belt of her skirt.

Propelling her charge expertly through the door of the Nineteenth Hole, Grace crossed the hall and shot through the lavatory section of the ladies' lounge, kicked open a door and managed to shove Maggie into one of the toilet stalls an instant before the deluge came. She grimaced at the sound of retching from the stall but didn't leave. Even though she was getting pretty disgusted with Maggie McCloskey, Grace wouldn't desert a dog at a time like this.

"Water!" When Maggie's anguished cry came from the stall, Grace took a glass from the shelf over the lavatory basin and filled it from the tap.

"If you feel yourself passing out, dunk your head in the can," she advised as she handed in the glass.

"God damn you, Grace!" Maggie gasped when she finally staggered out of the toilet cubicle and leaned over a basin to splash water on her face. "Do you have to treat me like a pig?"

"You are a pig!" Grace's own fears erupted in a geyser of angry words. "Eating pizza and then swilling down all that liquor."

"It wouldn't have happened if I hadn't gotten upset. I was worried—"

"About Joe?"

"Why not?"

"A little late, aren't you?" Grace's laugh was a bark of anger and disgust. "You aren't worrying about whether or not he's the one that was shot, only whether you can collect double indemnity. And you had to crucify him in a divorce court, just because you weren't able to give him what a man's got a right to expect from the woman he marries."

"You English bitch!" Maggie squalled. "Don't think I didn't know you and Joe slept together at that medical convention the time George and I both passed out. But I bet it wasn't any good."

"For your information, Joe's quite a man—not that it's any of your business, you frigid bitch."

"I'll kill him—telling another woman a thing like that. It's not my fault he was never able to arouse me."

"No?" Grace raised her eyebrows. "Well, he aroused me—and I know something about men."

"I'll bet you do! Everybody says George found you in a barroom but I never believed it. The place he found you in was a London whorehouse."

Grace started for the door, but turned with her hand on the knob. "I was a barmaid in London in '45, Maggie," she said with considerable dignity. "Times were hard then and it's a respectable occupation. But I've made George a good wife and, if you so much as hint at what I just told you, so help me I'll strip the flesh from your body with my bare fingernails layer by layer."

"You can't threaten—"

"Go dry yourself out somewhere before you get the D.T.'s. Then get down on your knees and ask Joe to take you back and teach you how to be a real woman. I don't know why, but he still loves you."

"H-how do you know that?"

"A man usually tells the truth when he's drunk—or making love." Grace grinned crookedly. "Maybe that's why psychoanalysts always have a couch in their offices. Just take my word for it—Joe loves you. If he wasn't the one Mort shot this afternoon —or if he was and gets over it—pray God it isn't too late to go back to him."

She went out, slamming the door behind her. Across the corridor she could see a knot of men and women still gathered around the TV set in the Nineteenth Hole but she was afraid to look. Instead, she examined the carpet in the corridor and was pleased to see that, thanks to her forthright action, Maggie hadn't spilled a drop on it after all.

God what a mess it would have been cleaning up that pizza, she thought as she turned into the women's bar, which was empty now—except for the bartender.

"Double Scotch and soda, Manuel." She took a seat on one of the stools and when the dark eyebrows rose as he reached for the bottle, added, "I'm English, you know. And it's after five o'clock."

As it turned out, though, Grace didn't have time to enjoy her drink. She was barely half finished when Maggie McCloskey came in from the ladies' lounge. She'd washed her face and combed her hair but she still looked green about the gills and held on to one of the chairs grouped around a table to steady herself.

"Any more news?" she asked.

Grace shook her head. "The radio says they've taken the man

in the case to the hospital but they haven't told who he is yet. I heard Arthur Painter tell somebody he'd tried to call the hospital but they've got some sort of an emergency on there and won't accept calls from the outside. Have a drink, Maggie. You look like the wrath of God."

"I'm going to the hospital." Maggie started for the door. "Joe may not have needed me before, but if he was the one with Lorrie, he'll be needing my blood now. We're both B-Rh negative and they're not easy to find."

"Wait for me, you're in no shape to drive." Grace swallowed the rest of her drink in a single gulp. She'd been trying to drum up her own courage to the point of going to the hospital and was happy to find an excuse. As they came out of the small bar, they saw Della Rogan in the door of the Nineteenth Hole.

"Hey, Della!" Grace called. "Want to go with us to the hospital?"

Della hesitated only momentarily. "I'll follow you," she said. "If you get there first, wait for me so we can all go in together."

"We'll wait for each other," Grace agreed. "God knows we all need somebody to lean on."

It couldn't have been Dave with Lorrie, Della assured herself as she hurried across the parking lot to her station wagon. He couldn't do that to her when she was getting ready for the Southern Women's Championship at White Sulphur next month. A scandal would put her so on edge she'd never be able to play her best.

But even as she started the engine, Della Rogan knew in her heart that the man who had been shot could very easily be Dave. Or Pete Brennan. Or Joe McCloskey. Or Paul McGill. Or George Hanscombe. Or Roy Weston.

It could be almost any man in town, for Lorrie had never been caste-conscious in her amours.

CHAPTER V

By the time the paging operator's voice finished the announcement, Janet Monroe had run across the passageway connecting
the Special Intensive Care Unit with the new surgical wing. Her
first move was to glance quickly at the bank of cathode-ray tubes
on the wall above the chart desk; the action was a reflex, part of
the training participated in by the entire hospital staff through
dry runs, until everyone's response was automatic, once the warning was sounded that a human life was in delicate balance due
to the failure of the heart to maintain its function.

The Special Care Unit was used mainly in the treatment of
serious coronary heart attacks. Through electrodes taped to the
body of each patient in the twelve rooms making up the section,
a constant flow of tiny electrical impulses—in reality action cur-
rents pulsing through cardiac muscle with every component of
the heartbeat—was fed to each of the cathode-ray monitor tubes,
where a wavy line traced the pattern of the patient's heart action
across its face. Beneath each tube was a second glass screen, part
of the closed-circuit television system whereby each patient was
kept under constant surveillance, even though no one else was
in the room.

All twelve rooms of the unit equipped with closed TV, continual E.K.G., and piped-in oxygen were in use that afternoon.
There never were enough beds available, for the cost of equipping
and operating a setup like this was fantastic and only those who
needed that kind of constant care were put upon it. Under the
standard operating procedure of the hospital for Cardiac Alert,

however, one of these beds must be made available immediately, even though it meant moving someone to another room at once.

"I got the call on the beeper." Dr. Stirling Kent pushed his head in the doorway of the chart room. A little breathless, he still held in his hand a small apparatus about the size of a cheap transistor radio. Ordinarily carried in the breast pocket of a house officer's white uniform, or the long-skirted coat worn by the teaching staff, this device enabled doctors to be reached at any time—like the men from U.N.C.L.E. When the small monitor beeped out its signal, the bearer went immediately to the nearest telephone to receive the call waiting for him.

"Ran all the way from the soda fountain," he panted. "What's up?"

"I don't know." Janet liked young Kent, for unlike many of the house officers, he wasn't always talking about getting out into practice and starting to rake in the dough. Cliff had talked of little else and even now, nearly two years after the divorce, she couldn't think of him without a twinge of pain and anger. It wasn't just that Cliff had used her, living off what she made nursing while he finished medical school and then dropping her as soon as he was able to support himself and start looking for greener pastures. Rather her anger was directed at herself for falling in love with someone who was unworthy and cheapening herself in her own eyes because of it.

"Help me decide who to move," she said to young Kent. "We'll have to get at it right away."

His eyes went to the bank of TV and cathode-ray monitoring tubes, scanning them as Janet had done when the call first came. The heart patterns portrayed there were about as varied as anything so basically similar could be, lines made up of jagged peaks and valleys as the strength of the electric impulses generated in each heart rose and fell.

"Mrs. Taylor's still fibrillating, so that lets her out," said Kent. "Dignan's P-R interval is twice what it should be and he could go into a ventricular rhythm any time."

"Mrs. Sanborn's still not compensated." Janet took up the account. "And Mr. O'Toole had another small coronary this morning. They all need the kind of close watching we give them with the monitors but the S.O.P. says we've got to clear a room pronto. Dr. Hanscombe will raise hell if he brings an acute coronary up here and we're not ready."

"It's most likely the guy Dellman shot," said Stirling Kent.

"What did you say?"

"I was looking at it on the tube just now in the soda fountain. Dr. Dellman caught a prominent physician with his wife and shot him a few minutes ago. The wife's dead and the man he shot is in the E.R."

"Loretta Dellman? I can't believe it."

"That's what the newscast said."

"I specialed her once, when I was a senior in training. It's hard to think of her as being dead; she loved life so much."

Stirling Kent grinned. "According to the hospital grapevine, she loved a lot of other things, too—even interns and students."

"You know how gossip is." Janet flushed, remembering very well the wild rumors just before her divorce and how true some of them had turned out to be. While he was living on what she had made nursing, Cliff had played the field—she'd learned after the divorce. He'd been another Mike Traynor; there was always one or more in every medical school class. They usually had no trouble finding partners for their amours either—which didn't make her much better than they, Janet thought bitterly, even though she'd had a marriage license.

"If a prominent physician was with Lorrie Dellman, it could be any one of a dozen of the high brass around here," said Kent. "Wonder who's the unlucky one?"

"Mrs. Tatum has the least to lose of anybody here if anything goes wrong." Janet ignored the last remark. "After all, she has an advanced malignancy in addition to the heart."

"Maybe we'll be doing her a favor by taking her off the monitors," said Kent. "I'll explain to her what's up while you get an orderly to help push the bed. I can't wait to see who that prominent physician turns out to be."

ii

Two operations, one of them minor, were in progress in the main operating suite when the call sounded over the muted loud-speaker in the workroom, where two student nurses were putting up treatment trays to be sterilized later in the giant autoclaves. There were no loudspeakers in the operating theaters themselves; surgeons at work needed to concentrate on the job at hand without the continual stream of summons that poured from the paging system all day.

"I'd better tell Miss Straughn," said Millie Cash, the senior student on O.R. duty.

"What does it mean?" asked a second-year student.

"Usually a case of cardiac arrest—stoppage of the heart. We have to get an operating room ready in case they need to open the chest and massage the heart. But with the Pacemaker and this new closed-chest resuscitation thing, they don't do that much any more."

"I bet it's exciting."

"Not so you'd notice it." Millie spoke from the wisdom of two additional years of experience. "The doctors are always on edge with those cases. If they don't get the heart started again within a few minutes, the patient will turn into a vegetable from brain damage due to lack of oxygen. I'd better get in there, or they'll have a patient up here for a thoracotomy before Miss Straughn knows it and I'll catch hell."

Like all the nurses working in the O.R. section, Millie wore a pale green scrub suit. Though unlovely in cut, the sleeveless suits were still much liked by the O.R. nurses. Tied at the waist with a cord, they were comfortable and no slip was needed under them, a fact that an intern or student could quickly recognize. Which was fine, for the less a man figured a girl had on the more likely he was to overlook more visible faults.

Pulling the mask she wore hanging from her neck by its strings over her nose and mouth, Millie stepped through the swinging doors into the adjacent operating theater. A middle-aged surgeon; the surgical resident, Carl Hagstrom; an instrument nurse; a sponge nurse; and the anesthetist, Jeff Long, were grouped around the table upon which the patient lay.

Helen Straughn looked up sharply at the creak of the swinging doors and frowned at Millie Cash. It was bad surgical technique for people to be coming in and out of the O.R. any more than was absolutely necessary. Even though she ran the suite like a military unit, somebody was always breaking technique, forgetting to put covers over their shoes before they came in or a dozen other things that could bring in wayward bacteria. Then days later a wound would pop up infected on one of the wards and the O.R. staff would catch the devil because of it. Helen's years of experience with student nurses had taught her they would seize any opportunity to parade before a group of doctors; when she saw Jeff Long look up and grin at Millie, she moved quickly to where the girl was standing.

"Cardiac Alert, Miss Straughn." Millie spoke before the supervisor could start to bawl her out. "The paging operator just announced it."

Helen Straughn's manner changed at once. "Circulate here while I open the emergency thoracotomy pack in O.R. Four," she directed. "We'll take the sponge nurse off here, if one is needed in a hurry." Lowering her voice to a bare whisper, she added, "Watch Dr. Whetstone's forehead. It's a tough case and he's beginning to sweat."

Millie nodded and took the folded cloth pad Helen Straughn handed her. As she moved close to the table, Dr. Whetstone looked up with a frown. Although the suite was always at the same temperature summer and winter, his face was red and sweat had begun to pop out on his forehead, a sure sign that he was having some difficulty.

"Where's Miss Straughn?" An attending surgeon who operated only occasionally at University Hospital, Whetstone was jealous of the treatment he received there and always insisted upon having the resident assist him and Helen Straughn circulate.

73

"Cardiac Alert, Doctor," said Millie Cash. "Miss Straughn is opening the thoracotomy pack in O.R. Four."

"We've got a new S.O.P. on cardiac arrest cases since Dr. Dieter came, sir," explained Carl Hagstrom. "It's designed to make sure someone familiar with the closed-chest resuscitation procedure will be on the scene at once. But just in case it's necessary to go in and massage the heart, we also prepare an O.R. for thoracotomy."

"Which rarely happens any more, thank God." Jeff Long spoke from behind the wire frame that held the draperies off the patient's face and also marked the barrier between the sterile operative field and the potentially contaminated world just outside it. "It's amazing how often a good hard sock on the chest can bring a dead man back to life."

"Just be sure we don't have to sock this patient, Doctor," said Whetstone testily as Millie stepped in close behind him. Reaching up swiftly with the pad in her hand, she wiped his forehead before he bent over the wound again.

"She's fine, Doctor," Jeff Long said amiably. "Not a bit tired—yet."

Millie Cash almost laughed but choked it back in time and when Jeff Long winked at her, winked back. He was a brash young man and said to be gone on Janet Monroe, but he was also the most capable anesthesiologist the hospital had developed in a long time, with a great future before him.

Even Dr. Dieter preferred Jeff to Dr. Macready, the department head who was getting a bit old for the sort of excitement open-heart surgery always generated. If Monroe didn't have the good sense to nail Jeff, he was fair game. Everybody knew that when he finished his residency next year, he could step into a twenty-thousand-dollar-a-year job without even trying. Which would have made him extremely eligible, even if he hadn't been ruggedly handsome into the bargain.

Busy again in the depths of the incision, the surgeon missed the barb Jeff Long had thrown him but nobody else in the O.R.

did. With the surgical team now relaxed, the operation began to go more smoothly and a few minutes later Dr. Whetstone stepped back from the table.

"Finish the closure, please, Dr. Hagstrom," he directed. "Chromic for the fascia and interrupted silk for the skin."

"Yes, Doctor." Anyone less pontifical than Whetstone would have detected the satirical note in Carl Hagstrom's voice. Telling a man with five years of surgical training since graduation and several hundred operations of his own how to close an incision was a bit like instructing an expert watchmaker about the kind of spring to use in one's watch.

Helen Straughn came back into the O.R. just as the scrub-room door was closing behind Dr. Whetstone. "There's a bullet wound of the heart in the emergency room," she said. "Dr. Dieter's on his way there now. He'll want you for the anesthetic, if he operates, Dr. Long. I've put in a call for a nurse-anesthetist to take over for you."

"As soon as Dr. Hagstrom finishes here, you can change and handle sponges in O.R. Four if we do the thoracotomy, Miss Tyndall," Helen Straughn told the sponge nurse. "An intern will be scrubbing on instruments."

"Who shot who?" Jeff Long asked. With Whetstone out of the room and the incision being closed swiftly and skillfully by Carl Hagstrom, the atmosphere had become normally informal.

"I don't know the last who," said Helen Straughn. "But the first was Dr. Dellman—I hear he found a man with his wife."

"Wow!" Jeff Long whistled. "Anybody we know?"

Which was exactly what Helen Straughn was wondering, too. It could be Pete Brennan—and the thought made her feel cold inside.

iii

As the strident call of the loudspeaker penetrated to every corner of the hospital, those assigned duties in the emergency procedures to be set in motion as part of a Cardiac Alert dropped whatever they were doing and went immediately to their positions.

At the blood bank, located in the basement adjoining the morgue and the pathology laboratory, a technician who had been preparing a batch of the plastic bags, in which blood was stored, for a donor drive among the newly arrived first-year students, dropped her work and moved to the record section. Plucking a stack of punched cards from the drawers of a tall steel filing cabinet, she stacked them into the rack of an IBM machine and, at the touch of a switch, the machine began sorting them into groups and subgroups. Thus almost the instant the blood type of the patient whose life was in danger became known—and a sample for typing would be taken at the earliest moment in the emergency room, to be whisked via pneumatic tube to the blood bank—she would be able to report the number of units of blood available if needed. At the same time she would communicate with the blood bank of Weston's other hospital, St. Michael's, drawing upon them if needed.

Another technician started setting up a preparation of typing serum, ready for the blood sample that might arrive at any moment, while the first now moved to prepare a half-dozen plastic containers of Type O blood and send it to the operating-room suite where it would be ready to charge the so-called heart-lung pump, in case open-heart surgery was necessary. Type O blood had the advantage that in an emergency it could be given to anyone without serious complications, tiding them over until blood of their own type was available.

With the new closed-chest resuscitation technique, in which the heart was rhythmically squeezed between the breastbone and the spine by external pressure on the chest, driving blood into both the lungs and the vitally important blood channels to the brain cells, it was theoretically possible to keep a person alive, even with no spontaneous heart contraction, long enough to open the chest, insert tubes into the heart chambers and let the pump take over. And however unlikely this possibility might be in a single case, it was still a part of the standard procedure to prepare for it when the Cardiac Alert was sounded.

As Janet Monroe and young Kent started to move the bed, with a patient still upon it, out of the room they had selected, an operating-room orderly appeared on the run. Seizing a wheeled cart upon which stood the bulky apparatus of the Cardiac Pacemaker, plus everything necessary to make a small incision in the chest, should the emergency demand direct massage of the heart, he pushed it out of the Special Care Unit toward the nearest elevator bank. There, under another provision of the Alert, an operator was waiting with an empty elevator, ready to carry the cart to the level where it was needed, in this case the ground floor.

Even in the gleaming stainless-steel kitchens preparations for the staff's evening meal had hurriedly to be adjusted, since a considerable portion of the hospital personnel would be locked into their present duties, until the Alert was off, disturbing meal schedules. Secretaries preparing to go off duty at five thirty waited in the offices where they worked, as well as doctors whose presence might conceivably be needed before the emergency was concluded. Teams of house officers trained especially in the chest-heart pressure technique, also moved toward the emergency room, ready to take over if the first team on the scene became exhausted by the strenuous procedure.

In the clinical laboratory that was the heart of the great hospital, technicians moved rapidly to clear the apparatus for evaluating blood gases—oxygen and carbon dioxide—in case the heart-lung machine was utilized. And an electronics technician, whose job it was to keep the delicate monitoring instruments used in many places besides the Special Intensive Care Unit, as well as the Cardiac Pacemaker, in repair, left his shop on the run with his special tool kit bound for the center upon which all activities of the great hospital were now concentrated, the single stretcher table in the emergency room where Marisa Feldman was working swiftly and surely.

iv

The human heart is at once the most protected and most vulnerable part of the body, the very nature of its protection creating its vulnerability. Encased in a tough, fibrous and relatively unyielding sac called the pericardium, the vital pump begins to contract rhythmically when the body is little more than a single cell, with no blood to circulate and no arteries and veins yet in existence through which it can flow.

For centuries, men have argued the question of whether death is a cessation of function in some center of the brain where the soul is concealed, with all body functions slowing to a halt, once the end of man as a person and a personality has occurred. Or whether death occurs only when the heart ceases to function and the blood supply to the brain is cut off, causing the death of the brain cells themselves.

Whatever the mechanism of death, it often occurs when the slender blade of a knife or a tiny leaden bullet, slipping through the soft tissues between the ribs, penetrates the tough muscular wall of the heart, leaving an opening that acts like a valve. With every beat, blood is then pushed through the tiny opening in the heart muscle to accumulate in the pericardial sac, its return being prevented when the pressure in the chambers of the heart falls to minus as they fill for the next beat. Then, with the muscular wall contracting once again, another spurt of blood is forced through the opening into the unyielding sac outside. With no means of escape, it, too, accumulates in the pericardium, increasing in amount with each beat of the heart.

Physical law states that two objects cannot occupy the same space at the same time. One therefore has to yield and this can only be the softer heart which, pumping on in an attempt to maintain the vital circulation, gradually finds itself with less space in which to operate. Thus the blood escaping from its chambers through the small wound with each beat gradually squeezes the heart down, just as it might be constricted by the hand of a deliberate murderer. Finally it can operate no more and comes to a halt—the condition known as *cardiac tamponade*.

Marisa Feldman had recognized the clinical pattern of tamponade at the instant when the evidence accumulating in her brain since she had first glanced down at the still figure upon the stretcher told her what was happening inside the chest of an apparently dead man. The soft murmuring sound she'd heard in the stethoscope could only mean to her trained ears and mind, that, clinically, death had not yet occurred. Therefore the intrinsic control mechanism of the heart, the muscle, the Purkinje fibers, the bundle of His making up a special nervous tissue system of communication within the heart itself to insure that it would continue to beat even though shut away from all nervous control by the brain—all were still trying to keep the pump in action, even though the cardiac muscle had no room now to relax and fill the chambers with blood after contraction.

"Tamponade?" The intern fumbling with the valves of the resuscitator echoed the dread words as Marisa removed the stethoscope from her ears. She met his gaze and read his thoughts, as his brain searched for some bit of information from his studies which for the moment eluded him, but she wasted no time on explanation. More important work must be done at once, if that faint heart action was to be preserved, nurtured and given strength. And it must be done within a matter of seconds before the brain centers were damaged beyond repair from lack of the vital flow of oxygen by way of the bloodstream.

"Fifty cc. syringe! Eighteen-gauge needle!" Marisa's words galvanized the emergency room staff into purposeful movement. The supervisor, a gray-haired wintry nurse whose years of watching men and women at their worst had accustomed her to immediate action, moved swiftly. From a shelf beside the table, she took down a sterile package and opened it quickly.

Without troubling to scrub—infection was the least of the wounded man's troubles today—Marisa picked up the syringe and attached the needle to it. With a single skilled movement, she thrust the point through the skin just to the left of the breastbone—the sternum—about three rib spaces below the collarbone. Guiding the shaft of the needle between the tough cartilages attaching the rib ends to the sternum, she thrust deeper until she felt a click against her hand, as the needle penetrated the tough, tightly distended pericardial sac.

"Aah!" A murmur went up from the small knot of spectators grouped around the entrance to the cubicle, as blood spurted into the barrel of the syringe when the needle broke into the cavity around the heart. Nobody understood exactly how the hospital grapevine worked, but a dramatic case in the emergency room almost a block away from the interns' quarters could bring a half-dozen interested spectators in a matter of moments.

At the head of the table, the intern on emergency-room duty had finished slipping an airway into the wounded man's mouth and throat. A curved plastic tube flattened to make insertion easier, it was designed to hold the tongue forward and provide an open channel to the trachea, the windpipe whereby air entered the lungs. Over the flanged outer end of the airway, he now pressed a mask connected by its flexible tubing to a respirator.

A lifesaving machine of tremendous intricacy, the latter consisted of a tank of oxygen and special valves that allowed pressure to be built up high enough to inflate the lungs thoroughly, then shut themselves off from the tank and simultaneously opened another outlet by which the gas could escape from the lungs as they deflated. By thus alternately filling the lungs with oxygen and then expelling it, the device achieved, far better than any other method was able to do, a very effective simulation of respiration.

While the syringe in Marisa Feldman's hands filled rapidly, the E.R. nurse was opening another. When Marisa separated the needle from the full syringe, the nurse took it from her with one hand and handed her the empty syringe with another. As Marisa was attaching the empty syringe to the needle, the nurse expelled the dark blood from the full one into a sterile basin she had quickly unwrapped, retaining a small amount which she transferred to a test tube, to be whisked to the blood bank for typing.

"Better mix some citrate with that—he may need it for a transfusion." Marisa spoke without taking her eyes off the second syringe, which was now filling rapidly as she maintained the steady pull upon the plunger.

"Tamponade, Dr. Feldman?" The voice was somewhat harsh, with a definite Teutonic accent and, in spite of her intense concentration on the vital job of removing blood from the pericardial sac, Marisa stiffened involuntarily. A solidly built man had moved up to the table as those around it shuffled back respectfully to give him room.

Having heard the voice at the staff conference the evening before, she recognized it as belonging to Dr. Anton Dieter, the brilliant heart and chest surgeon, but the accent still brought memories Marisa had thought exorcised from her mind during the years in England and at Harvard. A refugee from East Germany, Dieter had made a reputation in those fields long before he had been lured to Weston and the University Hospital to beef up the medical school teaching staff.

"I happened to be passing through and recognized the symptoms," she explained.

"*Gut!* You have already injected adrenalin into the heart?"

"Not yet. It seemed more important to remove blood from the pericardium at once."

"Quite right. I will inject the adrenalin. A syringe and long needle please, nurse. And bring the cardiac cart with the Pacemaker."

A smaller syringe with a long slender needle was in Dieter's hand almost before he finished speaking. At the same moment, the nurse placed upon the sterile towel in which it had been wrapped an ampule of adrenalin from a supply kept in alcohol in a jar, so it would be sterile and ready for any emergency. With a small file—also from the jar—Dieter swiftly nicked the neck of the ampule, broke it off with a gauze sponge to prevent possible laceration of his own fingers from the fragments of glass, and began to draw its contents up into the syringe.

81

"Pardon *Fräulei*—Doctor." Dieter's hands moved into the space beside Marisa's, carrying the small syringe filled with the clear adrenalin. The hands, as they plunged the slender needle directly through the chest wall about an inch below where Marisa had placed the first needle, were slender and very facile, the wrists a little stocky and perhaps more hairy than those of most men. They didn't touch Marisa's hands, but she had to fight against recoiling a little, as she carefully disconnected the syringe from the larger needle and handed it to the nurse again, receiving an empty one in its place.

"How much have you aspirated, Doctor?" Dieter asked.

"A hundred and fifty cc."

"We should see some effect soon." Again Dieter's faint Teutonic accent struck Marisa's ears like the clanging of the bell in the prison at Frondheim. "Keep on, please. I shall work around you."

Fully two inches of the smaller needle attached to the syringe in Dieter's hands had now been thrust through the chest wall, quite enough to penetrate into the muscular part of the heart. When he pulled back the plunger of the syringe, no blood spurted into the syringe, showing that the point was in the muscle. Injecting half the contents of the syringe, he pushed the needle on in until the metal shank dimpled the skin and injected the remainder into the chamber of the heart he had penetrated, then removed both needle and syringe with a swift movement.

No one could doubt who was in charge now, as the hospital resident who had accompanied Dieter pushed the wheeled cart loaded with monitoring devices and the electrical stimulator called the Pacemaker close to the table. Marisa experienced an instinctive moment of resentment at having been shoved, so to speak, into the background; after all, it had been she who had recognized that the patient might be saved—even though the ambulance diagnosis was D.O.A.—and had acted accordingly. But the call of "Cardiac Alert" on the hospital loudspeaker had made every available doctor part of the emergency, so she knew she couldn't blame Dieter for appearing. Besides, cardiac surgery was the field in which he was internationally known and if an operation were necessary, it was extremely important that the need should be recognized immediately because of the time element involved.

The deft hands with the tufts of hair on the wrists appeared once again within Marisa's field of vision, this time holding the insulated handles of a pair of electrodes connected to the Cardiac Pacemaker. At the end of each handle was a disk of metal—the electrode itself—from which a wire led to the machine. Taking care not to get in her way, Dieter placed the metal electrodes on the skin of the wounded man's chest, one on either side of the needle Marisa had inserted.

"I think the heart is fibrillating," she said. "I was able to hear a faint sound in the stethoscope but it wasn't rhythmic."

"So? Then we'll give it an extra jolt." Dieter gave rapid-fire instructions for setting the controls of the Pacemaker to the resident who accompanied him. In cases of fibrillation, where the normal rhythmic action of the heart muscle had been lost and a completely disorganized pattern of contraction substituted instead, the sudden sharp jolt of a powerful electric current often literally shocked the muscle back into a normal rhythmic pattern once more.

"Push the button, please," Dieter instructed and the machine hummed momentarily, then as quickly stopped. In that instant, however, an electric current had flowed from the coils, tubes and diodes of the Pacemaker through the wire to one of the electrodes, thence into the heart which lay almost quiescent beneath the chest wall, through the heart muscle and back to the second electrode in the machine, completing the circuit.

In response to the jolting pulse of electricity, the heart leaped like a suddenly roweled horse and Marisa felt it strike the point of the needle penetrating into the pericardial sac, causing a perceptible jolt against her hand as she held the syringe.

"*Gut!*" Dieter's explosive grunt of approval when he saw the

83

syringe move in her hand was pure German, but he lapsed immediately into his slightly accented English. "Switch the Pacemaker to normal rhythm please."

The dials clicked again as the adjustments were made and the machine began to hum, less lively now that the amount of current used was smaller, but nevertheless enough to flow in a steadily rhythmic pulsation.

"I can feel a pulse at the temple," the intern handling the resuscitator reported.

"It means only that we are pumping blood through the circulation," said Dieter. "The heart must take up a rhythm of its own before we can say he is alive."

The issue remained in doubt only a few seconds longer, however. As the artificial Pacemaker stimulated the heart to contract in a steady rhythm, a dramatic change began to take place in the wounded man.

The distention of the neck vessels which had first warned Marisa of what was happening quickly disappeared as the heart, with much of the blood which had literally throttled it in its own pericardial sac now removed, found room to do its work again and the circulation took up its normal activities. And with an adequate supply of oxygen now being pumped into the lungs, where the normal interchange with the blood took place, the mottled blue color of the upper chest, neck and face began to change to the pinker hue of normal oxygenation.

"It's a miracle!" one of the interns who was watching exclaimed.

"Not yet," Dieter corrected him. "His heart contracts; his lungs are inflated and deflated; oxygen even goes into his blood—but we may only be making a corpse go through the movements of liv—"

He broke off speaking when the rhythm of the resuscitator valve suddenly changed. Ever since the intern had started the machine, the steady click-click of the valve, alternately inflating the wounded man's lungs and allowing the air to escape, had not changed. Suddenly now, the interval between the clicks shortened and became irregular, a sure sign that the patient was beginning to breathe of his own accord, the force of his own respiration against the machine changing the rhythm of the valves.

"He breathes! He lives!" Dieter exclaimed. "Congratulations, Dr. Feldman! You have brought about a resurrection!"

CHAPTER VI

Hurrying through the door of the emergency room just as the clock on the wall marked five when he was due to be on duty, Mike Traynor came upon a dramatic scene: the slender woman doctor with the dark hair cut short and the arresting, if somewhat angular, features withdrawing blood from the pericardial sac; the stocky figure of Anton Dieter, holding the electrodes upon the chest of the wounded man; the intern with the mask of the resuscitator over the patient's face, hiding completely the features that would have identified him.

Well, he thought. *For once we're having some excitement around here.*

He didn't doubt for a moment that the patient on the table was the "prominent physician" mentioned in the radio broadcast, and craned his neck over the shoulder of one of the interns to try and see who it was. But the mask of the respirator hid the wounded man's features and Mike was afraid to ask anyone his name. Like many top-notch surgeons Dieter was known to have a quick temper and Mike didn't want to risk incurring his anger.

That newest faculty member wasn't bad, Mike decided when he turned his attention to Marisa Feldman. Of course she could hardly be considered at her best, sweating over the aspiration of blood from the chest of the poor guy on the table. She'd only been on the faculty for two days, but everyone in the school knew that in her field she was considered to be almost as skilled as Dieter was in his. A refugee educated in England, the scuttlebutt said she'd gone into East Germany to help relatives but had

87

been caught there and put in some sort of a concentration camp. Jews weren't liked in that section, even then, and the Russians hated them. But she'd somehow managed to make her escape, finish her education in England, and put in a couple of years as an instructor at Harvard, before coming to Weston with the rank of assistant professor.

The fact that Marisa Feldman was close to thirty didn't bother Mike Traynor at all—or that she was a Jew. He'd always heard Jewish women were passionate and the older any woman was, the more grateful she was likely to be to a younger man who took an interest in her.

Yes, he decided, Dr. Marisa Feldman was definitely worth investigating. The fact that he was a student and she was on the faculty might make things a bit difficult, of course, but it also made the problem more interesting. As a specialist in seduction, Mike liked a challenge and this one looked worthy of his skill.

Just then, the intern handling the resuscitator removed the face mask to adjust the airway and Mike Traynor had a brief glimpse of the wounded man's face that was enough to send him scurrying out of the cubicle. At the door of the emergency room, he met Lew Saunders, his roommate in the intern's quarters.

"Cover for me ten minutes, Lew," he said, seizing the other student by the arm. "I've got to make a telephone call."

"Always chiseling, aren't you, Mike?"

"This is really important. Besides you'll want to see what they're going to do with the heart case over there."

"You're right at that," said Saunders. "But be sure and get back in twenty minutes. I've got a date."

"I promise." Mike was already headed for the locker room, where he'd hung up his coat and put on a white jacket before coming on duty. Thrusting the white coat into the closet space reserved for the students, he grabbed his own jacket and ran down the ramp up which the stretchers were wheeled from the ambulances.

A row of telephone booths was located along the wall directly across from the Snack Bar and he dived into one of them. Fortunately he remembered seeing the name Hilton on the road leading to the cottage where he'd left Elaine McGill about a half hour ago. A quick look in the directory told him there were two numbers listed under Hilton, the second a county exchange which almost certainly meant the cottage. Dropping a dime into the phone, he dialed the second number.

The horny old bastard, he thought as he waited for the phone to ring. Then he began to laugh because it was a rare joke after all.

While he'd been shacked up at the lake cottage with Old Dermatographia's wife, the skin writer had been laying the hottest thing in town.

ii

Elaine McGill was awakened by the sound of the telephone. Still half drugged from the explosive release of long pent-up emotions she'd found in the arms of Mike Traynor the second time, she came groggily from sleep and picked up the phone.

"Mrs. McGill! Elaine!" It sounded like Mike's voice.

"Yes?"

"It's me. Mike Traynor. Have you heard yet?"

"Heard what? I've been asleep."

"You haven't had the TV or the radio on?"

"No. What's this all about?"

"Just the biggest scandal that's ever hit this town. The hospital's trying to get you."

"Why?"

"Your husband was with Mrs. Dellman this afternoon. Dr. Dellman shot them both."

"That's impossible," she said quickly. "Paul couldn't—"

"I saw him in the emergency room with my own eyes, he took a bullet in the chest."

Elaine held on to the bedpost for support. "Will they have to operate?"

"Dieter hadn't decided when I came to call you. Dr. McGill

89

was practically dead with a wound in the heart but a new woman
doctor over at the hospital realized what it was in time to save
him. Don't worry. In Dieter's hands he should be okay. That
guy's a genius when it comes to anything involving the chest or
the heart."

"I'll be there as quickly as I can. Tell them that for me."

"I don't think that would be wise—considering. Do you?"

"No, I suppose not." More than anything else she wanted to
get him off the phone.

"I just thought you ought to know," he said. "And don't
worry. This Dieter is a whiz."

Elaine slammed down the phone and began to dress in frantic
haste. Paul and Lorrie! It was the last thing she would have suspected. With the others, yes. Once at the Dissection Society,
Maggie McCloskey had said they all had one thing in common
—their husbands had slept with Lorrie Dellman.

But if Paul had made it with Lorrie, why did he have so much
trouble with her?

iii

"You can switch to simple oxygen administration now," Dieter
told the intern handling the resuscitator. The resident who had
accompanied the surgeon took the handles of the Pacemaker
electrodes and Dieter picked up the patient's wrist, counting
the pulse by the sweep hand of his watch.

"One-twenty but regular and pretty strong for a man who
was dead a few minutes ago," he reported. "Somebody see what
the blood pressure is."

"That was quick thinking, Dr. Feldman." He turned to Marisa
while the blood pressure cuff was being applied to Paul McGill's
arm. "I'm not quite sure I would have made the diagnosis that
quickly." Coming from Dieter, she knew it was high praise—and
resisted the impulse to be grateful to him for it. "I heard faint
heart sounds with the stethoscope," she explained. "Shall I re-

move the aspiration needle now. The flow seems to have stopped."

"For the time being, yes," said Dieter. "But stay close by, if you will. When his blood pressure rises, he may start pumping blood out through that bullet hole in his ventricle again before we're able to close it with a few sutures. The wound of entry is pretty obvious there at the front of the chest. Did anybody examine his back for a wound of exit?"

"There was hardly time. The ambulance attendants had labeled him a D.O.A. when I happened to see them bringing him into the emergency room and noticed that the veins of his neck were congested."

Dieter's bushy eyebrows rose again. "Then you really did raise him from the dead, Dr. Feldman."

The graying emergency-room supervisor looked from one of them to the other, as she cleared away the syringe and needles from the small table. What could there possibly be between those two? she wondered. The Jewish woman doctor had only been there two days but, looking at them, you could fairly see the sparks of animal magnetism flying.

"He seems to be breathing all right," Dieter observed. "Let's see if he has established a heart rhythm of his own yet."

The resident lifted the electrodes from the chest wall as the nurse clicked off the switch. Dieter kept his fingers upon the pulse for a full minute, while he studied the sweep hand of his watch.

"The beat is pretty fair—and regular," he reported. "I think we can turn him on his side gently to look for a wound of exit."

No sign of any exit wound showed anywhere, and Dieter's expression was grave as they eased the patient back once again.

"Now we'll have to remove the bullet like they do on television," he said. "Wheel him into the X-ray and let's see what we can find. And nurse—"

"Yes, Doctor."

"Bring along the respirator and the Pacemaker just in case we need it. Coming, Dr. Feldman?"

Marisa hesitated only a moment. "I was on the way to dinner —but it can wait."

"Thank you," said Dieter as he pushed the examining table out of the cubicle. "I would like for you to stand by, in case the pericardium starts filling up again."

Some fifteen minutes later, Dieter stood across the X-ray table from Dr. Sam Penfield, the hospital roentgenologist, studying the fluoroscopic screen illuminated by the X rays flooding up through the chest of the patient from the tube beneath the table. A small spot, quite dark, showed against the lighter background of the lungs and the soft tissues of the chest wall. It was located in the shadow of the heart, which could be seen beating regularly.

"*Mein Gott!*" In moments of excitement, Dieter still lapsed into his native tongue. There was good reason for him to be excited now, for the bullet was tumbling slowly within a small restricted area.

"The damn thing's inside the heart!" said the roentgenologist in an awed voice. "Right in the middle of a ventricle, would be my guess."

"No chance that it's outside the chamber—in the pericardium or muscle?" Dieter asked.

"Not the way it's moving," said Penfield. "If it were in the pericardium or the muscle, the shadow would move in rhythm with the heart. But you can see that it seems to be tumbling about in the stream of blood passing through the ventricle, which means it has to be free."

"Take a look at this, Dr. Feldman." Dieter moved aside so Marisa could approach the screen. "You may not ever see anything like this again."

"I never saw anything like it," Penfield volunteered.

"What is his condition?" Dieter asked the intern who was standing at one end of the table, his finger on the temple pulse used by anesthetists to count the heartbeat during operations. A blood pressure cuff had been placed on the patient's arm and a stethoscope strapped against the front of his forearm, so the blood pressure could be taken while he was on the table.

"Very good, sir," said the intern. "Pulse one hundred. Respiration twenty-four. Blood pressure one hundred over seventy."

"The heart seems to have a good stroke," Marisa Feldman observed, watching the beat on the fluoroscopic screen. "There must not be much blood within the pericardium."

"And no more being pumped out through the wound, from the looks of the heart shadow," Penfield agreed.

"What do you say, Dr. Feldman, to lowering the head of the table and dropping the bullet through the aortic valve into the aorta, so it can be pumped out into one of the arteries of the legs?" Dieter asked casually. "All we would need to do then would be to make a short incision over the vessel, open it up and take out the bullet."

"Your reasoning would be sound, Doctor—if the bullet is in the left ventricle." Marisa Feldman's English accent became more clipped. "But if it's in the right, you will be pumping the bullet out into the arterial tree of the lungs, where the vessel caliber gets smaller all the time. Before you knew it, you'd cause a pulmonary embolus and probably death."

"So?" Anton Dieter's tone was slightly amused. "You are logical as well as beautiful, Dr. Feldman."

She stiffened slightly when she realized he'd only been testing her with the question, then relaxed. "I didn't know you were making a joke, Doctor."

"It was no joke; I merely wanted to confirm my own thinking." Dieter turned to the intern. "As Dr. Feldman has pointed out, if the bullet is in the right ventricle and if it accidentally slips out into the pulmonary circulation, we could have a very grave situation on our hands. See that the patient is moved very carefully to the operating room. We don't want that little bullet to start traveling."

"The front office hasn't been able to locate his wife yet, Doctor." The emergency-room nurse had come into the X-ray

93

room. "They've been trying her home but nobody answers and no one else knows where she is."

"Then we'll have to operate without her," said Dieter crisply. "We can't afford to wait any longer."

"A couple of police officers are outside, Dr. Dieter," said the nurse. "Will you have time to speak to them before you go upstairs?"

"Only for a moment. Call Dr. Long please and ask him to order the preoperative medication. If you would accompany the patient to the operating room, Dr. Feldman, I should be very grateful."

iv

Lieutenant Vosges and Sergeant O'Brien rose from the visitor's bench of the emergency room as Anton Dieter approached.

"I have to be in the operating room in a few minutes, gentlemen," the surgeon said briskly. "The nurse said you wanted to see me."

"Does Dr. McGill have a chance, Doctor?" Eric Vosges asked.

"An excellent one—considering that there's a bullet inside his heart."

"Inside his heart?" O'Brien exclaimed. "That's one for the book, isn't it?"

"It's not exactly an everyday occurrence," Dieter agreed. "I haven't had time to get any details of this unfortunate happening. How many shots were fired?"

"Only one." O'Brien grinned. "The bullet went through Mrs. Dellman's heart first, but they were pretty close together at the time, so it wasn't particularly difficult."

"So?" Anton Dieter's eyebrows rose. "Is that all, gentlemen."

"We may want a supplementary report after you finish the operation," Vosges told him.

"Of course." Dieter clicked his heels. "Good day."

Lieutenant Vosges and Sergeant O'Brien had left their car in the parking lot across the street. As they crossed toward it now, they saw four women converging on the emergency-room door from different parts of the lot. All looked worried and one stumbled as she walked between two of the others. None noticed O'Brien, although he lifted his hat politely to them.

"Friends of yours?" Vosges asked with a grin.

"I know them all, but I could hardly blame them for not noticing me at a time like this. My guess is that each of them has heard the broadcast and is hurrying to the hospital to see whether it's her husband who has an acute case of lead poisoning."

He looked back to where the four had come together at the emergency-room door. They appeared to hesitate, waiting for one to be the first to enter. Then Amy Brennan stepped through the door and the others followed.

"There go the wives of four of the most prominent doctors in town," O'Brien added. "All close friends of Lorrie Porter's, too. The things I've heard about some of the parties they have would curl your hair."

"I guess they've got a right to be scared," said Vosges. "Right now each one probably sees her own little world starting to crumble about her."

"Half the time Amy Weston—she's the tall one that came in the white Cadillac—wouldn't give you the time of day," said O'Brien. "Now she's scurrying like the rest to find out who's the loser. Come to think of it, I guess they all are."

"How do you figure that?"

"That group and two or three others pretty much run the society end of town—chairman of this and that fund-raising project, the symphony, Festival of Arts—the whole bit. Amy Brennan is pretty high up in the state medical auxiliary, too, from what I read in the papers. If I know Dellman, he's going to turn heaven and earth to beat this rap, and that means those women and their husbands, plus a few others, will have to help him whether they like it or not." He grinned. "If you ask me this is just about the craziest caper Lorrie Porter ever pulled."

"Why do you say that?"

"When Lorrie was a girl, she was always getting into scrapes. I worked as a security guard in the old Weston Mills before joining the police force, so I had to get her out of a lot of them. Nothing really ornery, mind you—just her idea of fun. When I see all those women scuttling into the hospital to find out which one of them will have to hide her head until this thing blows over, I could almost believe Lorrie planned it that way."

"Can it blow over?"

"Of course."

"You can't just sweep murder under the rug."

"You forget that Weston Mills makes some of the biggest rugs in the world; they'll find one to hide even this particular pile of dirt under. Come on, Eric. We've got to locate this guy's wife and break the news to her."

Lieutenant Vosges saw the car flash through a red light as they were approaching an intersection some ten minutes later. He made a quick left turn to follow, switching on his siren at the same moment, and soon passed the car ahead. But, when he started to swing over toward the curb to slow it down, Sergeant O'Brien said quickly, "Keep ahead of her, Eric, with the siren going."

"What the dev—"

"That's McGill's wife. The one we're looking for."

Vosges stepped on the throttle again as O'Brien leaned out and waved for Elaine McGill to follow them. When she nodded her understanding and fell in behind the police cruiser O'Brien leaned back in his seat.

"You know what would be ironic?" he said.

"This whole damn thing's ironic, if you ask me."

"Suppose the reason nobody could find her was that she was out two-timing the doc with another guy?"

"That would be a switch all right."

O'Brien sat up suddenly. "That's it."

"What?"

"I told you something about this whole thing didn't gee."

96

"I still don't get it."

"Lorrie Dellman was shot *through* the heart and Dr. McGill has a bullet in his, from the front. What does that mean?"

"You tell me."

"Unless Dellman was shooting from under the bed, the positions were switched so when he shot what he thought was a man seducing his wife, it was really his wife seducing a man. Oh I'll bet Lorrie is really cackling over this one—wherever she is."

CHAPTER VII

It was half after five when Dr. David Rogan, psychiatrist for the Faculty Clinic and head of that department in Weston University Medical School, finished dictating a note on the final patient of the day and shut off the Dictaphone. Like everyone in both the clinic and in the hospital, he had been cognizant of the drama being played out across the street in the emergency room. But since he had no assigned duties during a Cardiac Alert, he had resisted the temptation to cross over to the hospital to see what was happening, increasing the press of people who could only hinder the resuscitation team in its work.

That strange communication network called the hospital grapevine had informed him, via his secretary, that Paul McGill had been shot by Mort Dellman "in the very act," to use her phrase. Remembering that he had not yet been able to examine Janet Monroe's little boy in the consultation requested that morning by Dr. Deemster, the Professor of Pediatrics, Dave decided to stop by before going home and took the elevator to the ground floor of the clinic.

Of medium height, he was almost half bald at forty-five, the sparse remaining hair at his temples already two-thirds gray. Golf and yard work over weekends kept his body trim, although he had to watch his weight, both for cholesterol and to avoid what George Hanscombe, the clinic heart and circulation expert, called "creeping inflation of the waistline." Which wasn't easy with Della away so much of the time playing in golf tournaments, and a colored housekeeper whose forte was that gastronomic atom bomb known as "Southern cooking."

Like most psychiatrists, Dave Rogan had the slightly withdrawn look that comes from observing human foibles and peccadillos with an understanding eye, in his case through rimless glasses without which he couldn't read a street sign at ten feet. But right now his normal psychiatrist's calm was diminished by a problem not unusual in husbands—his inability to understand his own wife. It had been two weeks now since Della had gone to Augusta for the Southeastern Women's Open Championship in a huff because he couldn't go with her, but so far he hadn't been able to make any perceptible progress toward arranging a peace.

No quarrel of theirs had ever lasted half this long, he thought as he stepped out of the elevator in the lobby of the clinic, almost deserted now that the tide of ailing humanity surging through the doors every morning at eight had receded for another twenty-four hours. Usually family quarrels in the Rogan household followed the same pattern as with most married couples. There would be a spat, after which Della gave him the silent treatment for a day or two; or if it were a real quarrel, she usually slept in the spare room for one or two nights as a pointed reminder of her displeasure. In the end, though, they'd always made up without the threat of divorce.

This quarrel had started much the same way, but somewhere along the line, particularly after Della had returned from Augusta, the pattern of recovery had failed to develop normally—in fact not at all. He'd made the usual overtures that were expected of him as evidence of his repentance for sins committed—or attributed—but they had accomplished nothing. Each morning, Della marched off to golf, and each evening they sat home in stony silence after dinner until it was time to go to bed. Fortunately, the children were still away at camp; as a psychiatrist he knew very well that marital discord, even the small amount of it that happened between him and Della, could have a shattering effect on developing personalities if long continued.

So there was nothing to do but wait until Della decided to

reveal the as yet unnamed sin of which he had been judged guilty through that strange and tortuous process of reasoning—or unreasoning—called feminine logic. But he was a peace-loving man; after dealing with emotional storms, it had always been a relief to come home to someone who, perhaps largely because she was physically exhausted from playing eighteen holes of golf or more, didn't meet him at the door with a chip on her shoulder. And he wanted nothing so much right now as a cessation of hostilities, however accomplished.

Leaving the clinic, Dave crossed the street and entered the hospital by way of the emergency entrance, a short cut to the Pediatrics ward where he was going to examine little Jerry Monroe. As he passed through the small waiting area outside the white-tiled emergency room, he was surprised to see Della, Grace Hanscombe, Maggie McCloskey and Amy Brennan waiting at the desk and looking uncertain, as people always did when not sure where they should go. The sudden look of relief in Della's eyes when she spied him came as a surprise, after the icebox treatment she'd been giving him for over a week.

"Hello, girls," he said. "If you've come about Paul—"

"Paul!" Amy Brennan gasped. "Then he was the one?"

Dave's eyes moved from one of the women to another, noting the same look of relief Della had shown at the sight of him.

"None of you knew who the man was, did you?" he exclaimed.

"The radio broadcast didn't give the name," Della explained. "We all decided to come and help each other."

"Is Paul going to be all right?" Grace Hanscombe asked.

"I don't know anything except what came over the hospital grapevine," he said. "But I'll talk to the E.R. supervisor and see what I can find out."

He came back in a few moments. "Paul has a bullet in his heart, but seems to have been in good shape when he left here. Dieter has taken him up to the operating room."

"I need a drink." Maggie McCloskey sat down suddenly on a nearby bench.

"I'll get you some water." Going to the cooler in the corner of the waiting room, Grace Hanscombe took down a paper cup from the dispenser and filled it with water. Maggie's hands were trembling so much that she couldn't hold the cup still, so Grace steadied them while she drank.

"Are you going to the operating room, Dave?" Della was hoping he'd be free to go home with her; she was beginning to feel a little shaky herself in reaction to the tension under which they'd all been laboring since the first broadcast had gone on the air.

"I have to see Janet Monroe's little boy in consultation," he explained. "I'm on my way now."

"Is Elaine here?" Grace asked.

"The nurse I talked to said they've been calling her at home but there's no answer."

"Elaine and Paul have been using the Hilton cottage at Lake Tabitha this summer," said Grace. "George and I were out there to supper with them last week."

"I'll tell the operator to try the cottage," he said. "Paul always plays golf on Wednesday and Elaine may have taken someone out to the lake for a swim."

Just then the outside door opened and Elaine McGill came in. She looked at the women, then at Dave. Knowing the question that was on her lips and sensing that she couldn't bring herself to speak the words, he said quickly: "They've taken Paul to the operating room, Elaine. Dr. Dieter thinks he'll be all right but they couldn't wait for you."

"I was at the lake."

"The bullet's in the heart. Dieter is going to go in and take it out." It was a measure of Anton Dieter's reputation and the rapid advance of surgical knowledge that none of them were shocked by the extent or nature of the operative procedure. Open-heart surgery had become so much a part of the hospital's operation since Dieter's coming to Weston that it was almost taken as a matter of course.

"Can I go to Paul?" Elaine asked.

"He's already gone to surgery," said Dave, "but they'll bring him back to the Special Intensive Care Unit afterward. I've got to go to Pediatrics Four for a consultation but it's on my way and I can drop you there."

"Do you want any of us to stay, Elaine?" Grace Hanscombe asked. "I can, if you like."

"So can I," said Della.

"I've got a migraine," said Amy. "But I'll be glad—"

"Please don't." Elaine's tone was grateful. "It will be a long operation, won't it, Dave?"

"Probably. Takes quite a while to get ready for one of these jobs, and after it starts, things can't be rushed."

"I'll be all right," Elaine assured the four women. "Thank you all for coming."

"If there ever was a time to be honest this it is," said Grace. "We really came because we didn't know who the man was and we were all scared stiff."

Dave found himself wishing it had been Della who had spoken, even though the words would have been an admission that she suspected he might have been unfaithful to her. Whatever it was that had shattered the quiet understanding and trust which had been so important a part of their marriage through the years, had apparently come to a climax during that last golf tournament Della had played in at Augusta, the Southeastern Women's Open. He'd been waiting for her to tell him about it, knowing she must unburden her mind of her own accord, if what had been between them was to be restored. But she didn't seem ready yet and he was too good a psychiatrist—and too understanding a husband—to push her.

"You'll be late for dinner, won't you Dave?" Della asked.

"Probably; Ed Harrison is going to do a spinal puncture on Janet Monroe's little boy and I really should stay and see what it shows, if I'm going to make an intelligent diagnosis. You look bushed, hon. Why not go home and lie down until I get there? Then we'll go out to a drive-in or some place and have a bite."

"All right," Della's tone was dull; the animation she'd shown at the sight of him seemed to have vanished.

"I'll try not to be too long," he promised. "Come on, Elaine, I'll drop you off at the Intensive Care Unit."

"How could Elaine be so calm?" Maggie McCloskey said as they were leaving the waiting room. "Our husbands weren't even involved and we were all scared stiff."

"I guess she was numb," said Della.

"If you ask me we're all pretty numb," said Grace. "Where did you hear the news, Amy?"

"What?" So sharp had been Amy's relief at discovering the man in the case wasn't Pete, that she'd been half in a daze while Dave Rogan was speaking to them, listening but barely hearing. Even the migraine had been numbed a little momentarily by her worry over Pete; now it began to throb again.

"I asked where you were when you heard the news," Grace repeated.

"Fifteen or twenty miles west of town on the interstate, coming back from the District Six meeting."

"I'd forgotten about that. How did you come out?"

"I have the pledge of their votes."

"Congratulations! That cinches the election, doesn't it?"

"I think so."

It must be the migraine that made her feel so little satisfaction in announcing her triumph, Amy thought. In fact whatever triumph she remembered feeling had been blasted by the sound of the announcer's excited voice on the radio.

"I wonder what Act Two will be," said Maggie McCloskey.

"What do you mean?" Della's voice was sharp.

"None of us are fools enough to think we've seen the end of the play. This afternoon each of you had to face up to the fact that your marriage might be shot—just as mine already is. I ought to feel triumphant; God knows you all had enough to say about my getting a divorce from Joe. But right now all I can feel is sorrow, for you and even more for myself."

"Let's get the hell out of here," said Grace. "Three of us, at least, have husbands who'll be coming home tonight. We'd better be there to give them hell, just in case they've been thinking about doing a little tomcatting, too."

ii

The Special Intensive Care Unit was located on the top floor of the Medical Building, part of the old section of the hospital. Through the door of the small waiting room, to which Dave Rogan had taken Elaine McGill, she could see the nurses' station, with its banks of electronic monitor tubes and the desk where Janet Monroe was working on charts in the spill of light over the desk, leaving the bank of tubes above in shadow. Elaine hadn't realized she was hungry, until Janet brought her a tray of coffee and buttered toast. Now she was eating mechanically while her mind slowly recovered, in part, from the shock of what Mike Traynor had said when he called her at the cottage on the lake, the still hardly believable fact that Paul had been with Lorrie that afternoon and had been shot by Mort Dellman.

Through the large window of the waiting room, Elaine could see the corner of the new Surgical Building and a bank of windows, one quite large and very brightly lit. She knew enough about the hospital to realize the window marked the location of the main operating suite, but it was still hard to believe that all this wasn't really a nightmare and that, in the room behind it, Paul's life still hung in the balance.

Did she have the right to pray—she wondered—when hardly three hours before she had been in the arms of another man —and as guilty as Paul?

In her favor was the fact that the desperate measure she had adopted was motivated by the purely unselfish desire to bear Paul a child, even though the seed that let it come into being might not be his. At the time, that need had seemed ample justification for the first joining of her body with Mike Traynor's and she had no regrets. But what justification could she possibly find for the second—except Mike's unabashed lust and her own desire for him?

She could have dressed and left the cottage when she awakened; there was no denying that. Instead, she had wakened him earlier than she needed to do in order for him to make his five o'clock assignment at the hospital. Awakened him, she admitted now in a moment of complete honesty, because deep inside her there had been an unanswered question, a doubt whether she was really the woman she thought herself to be, with a woman's ability to respond fully in the physical act of love-making that was such an important part of real marriage.

No, she couldn't blame Paul, when she herself was as guilty as he was. Nor could she really blame Lorrie Dellman, for Lorrie had given them all fair warning at Amy Weston's house over a year ago—during a meeting of the Dissection Society.

They had been playing bridge after Amy's cook, Ethel, had served the peaches flambeau. Lorrie had made a small slam in spades; she was a wild bidder but surprisingly often made the bids anyway. While Amy dealt, Lorrie had begun to make the cards, riffling the deck expertly. . . .

iii

"God, but I'm horny," Lorrie had said, as casually as if she was discussing the weather.

"Contain yourself," said Maggie McCloskey. "Mort's not around."

"Why Mort? Any old port in a storm, you know."

"Don't talk foolishness, Lorrie," Amy said severely.

"With me it isn't foolishness." Lorrie put the made deck beside her on the table and picked up the hand that had been dealt her. "Or maybe one of you gals would like to go upstairs for a little while. I can promise you an interesting—"

"Lorrie!" Amy snapped. "That's going too far—even for you."

"Don't tell me none of you ever thought about it—or tried it."

"Some things you don't talk about," said Maggie. "I bid two hearts."

"Two spades," said Lorrie. "This is the twentieth century, girls.

A hundred years ago a woman wasn't supposed to have any erotic feelings, except when her husband turned her on."

"Like putting a key into a lock," said Grace.

"And only one key was supposed to fit," Maggie added.

"When he got through, she was supposed to be turned off," Elaine had said and remembered again how she had blushed at having inadvertently revealed the truth about her intimate life with Paul. "What I mean is—"

"We all know what you mean, Elaine," Grace Hanscombe said. "It's happened to all of us, I imagine—and more than once."

"Girls!" said Amy. "Let's get back to a pleasant subject."

"I maintain there isn't a more pleasant subject," Lorrie insisted. "The reason a lot of women don't talk about it is because they don't want to admit publicly that they occasionally have the urge to go to bed with some man other than their husband. The truth is, you're all afraid to let yourself go because you think a man gets some sort of power over you for a couple of minutes —at the climax—when you've got to keep going, whether you want to or not."

"Did you ever want not to?" Grace Hanscombe asked.

"What would be the use of getting started in the first place?" said Lorrie. "What you forget is that the man doesn't even have as much control as you—and that makes you the victor."

"Hunh!" Della Rogan exclaimed. "Two minutes of victory and nine months of penance."

"What you have to settle for is a negotiated peace, Della," Grace Hanscombe said with a grin.

"How'd you spell that last word?" Lorrie asked and there'd been a round of laughter.

It was two hands later that Lorrie had dropped the bombshell.

"You know what might be fun," she said.

"Here we go again," said Maggie. "What is it this time?"

"Let's swap husbands."

There was a startled silence, then a burst of laughter—most of it forced.

"Nobody but you would think of such a thing, Lorrie," said Elaine.

"Don't tell me that. You've all thought of it more than once. Come clean now and let your hair down."

A dead silence—a guilty silence—greeted the thrust. Then Amy said harshly, "We're all romantic, else we wouldn't be married, Lorrie. Of course we sometimes dream of being carried off by a Prince Charming. Who hasn't?"

"Only he always turned out to be a dud," said Maggie.

"It takes two, you know, Maggie," said Lorrie.

"Do you know something about Joe?" Maggie had demanded suspiciously.

"No. But since you brought it up, it's not a bad idea. Small men are usually powerful lovers."

"You stay away from him!" Maggie squalled.

"Don't get excited," said Lorrie. "Joe's a urologist and women have more bladder and kidney trouble than anything else. I'll bet a day doesn't pass that a dozen female bottoms aren't turned up for him—"

"If Joe so much as . . ." Maggie had lapsed into incoherence.

"We get together every month anyway, so why not make these sessions more interesting?" said Lorrie. "Think what fun it would be to take on someone else's husband in the interim and report on it every month."

"Lorrie!" It was a chorus of virtuous—and not entirely honest —reproof.

"I mean it. You're all suffering from sexual malnutrition because you have too much of the same diet."

"What do *you* do?" Maggie asked. "Take vitamins?"

"You might call it that. At least I sample an occasional new dish to help me stay young."

"I'll say one thing," Grace Hanscombe volunteered. "Fornication seems to agree with you. I never saw anybody look so damn healthy."

"You can all be the same way," Lorrie assured them. "Now take us: we're seven couples—counting Alice and Roy—and there are seven nights a week, so we can make rounds at least once a month."

"Suppose you're married to a once-a-week man?" Grace asked.

"Maybe the vitamins I prescribe will help him. Who knows?"

"From what I hear, you've got a good start already on this husband-swapping business," said Maggie.

Lorrie grinned. "Wouldn't you like to know?" Waiting for Maggie to splutter into angry incoherence, she continued, "But this time, we'll all start even. What do you say?"

"If this is a joke, Lorrie, it's gone far enough," Amy snapped.

"It isn't a joke and it's going farther."

"What do you mean by that?"

"Our husbands are medical men—at least Mort's practically an M.D. and Roy's the clinic lawyer. When they want to try out a new drug, they run a clinical test, so there's no reason why we can't do the same. Afterward, we'll have a clinic with case histories, like our husbands do when they're discussing whether or not they've made a mistake in treating something."

"You mean a clinical pathological conference, don't you?" said Della.

"What's that?" Since Roy Weston was a lawyer, Alice wasn't familiar with medical terminology.

"It's when the patient's already dead and you're trying to find out what killed him," Della explained.

"We have a few of those, too," Grace agreed.

"I'm betting I can wake up even the dead ones," Lorrie offered.

"Forget it, Lorrie," Amy said sharply.

"Who elected you spokesman, Amy?" Maggie demanded.

"You mean you—?"

"No. But I'm not going to have other people making decisions for me. I say put it to a vote."

Amy shrugged. "Whatever the decision, I'll not have any part of it."

"Maybe Pete will have different ideas, Amy." Lorrie's grin was taunting. "After all, a man who's been chained to an iceberg can't be blamed for getting excited when he sees a palm tree on the horizon."

Amy stiffened, and for a moment Elaine thought she was going to explode.

"Hit you where it hurt, didn't I?" Lorrie chuckled. "Personally I could never see why a full-blooded handsome Irishman like Pete ever married a prude like you anyway."

"Lay off it, Lorrie," said Della Rogan. "Our husbands are close friends and we've all got to live together. It won't help any for us to start scratching each other."

"What about you, Grace?" Lorrie asked. "Aren't you in favor of a little variety?"

"I was seduced by an Irish lance corporal before most of you were wearing bras," said Grace wearily. "When you've had one you've had them all."

"What a terrible thing to say!" Elaine remembered protesting.

"My experience doesn't match Lorrie's, of course," said Maggie McCloskey, "but—"

"Are we going to play bridge or musical chairs?" Grace demanded.

"It sounds more like musical beds to me," said Della.

"Let's take a vote on Lorrie's proposal," said Maggie.

"I vote Yes," Lorrie said promptly.

"No!" Amy said firmly.

"Me, too," said Della.

"I'll abstain," said Grace. "After all, I'm a foreigner."

"I vote No," said Maggie. "So you lose, Lorrie."

"I didn't think you'd have the guts to take me up." Lorrie shrugged. "But I thought I should give you a chance before I put Plan B into effect."

"What's Plan B?"

"Since all of you refuse to be honest, I'm going to make the experiment for you myself. I'll have each of your husbands and if you want any pointers afterward, I'll give them to you."

"At least it would be an expert opinion," said Grace.

"I'm not going to listen to this drivel any more." Amy pushed her cards into the center of the table and got to her feet. "This is my house and I think this party is over."

"You're overlooking a good thing, Amy," Lorrie warned her. "All of us admit to being bored, which means we're tired of our husbands' love-making. I'm willing to do all of you a favor by examining each case thoroughly, making a diagnosis, and recommending a course of treatment—unless the case is beyond hope. Nobody could be a better friend than that."

"You've got a point there," Grace admitted. "But I think my case is beyond hope."

"Maybe you're not using all your ammunition," said Lorrie.

"What does that mean?"

"I don't know how you English manage it, but you age a lot better than we Americans do. I know you're past forty-five, Grace, but you could pass for forty any day—except maybe early in the morning, or when you've gone to bed loaded the night before. Fixed up, you look fine, and so do the rest of us. We just need to work a little harder at being lovers than we're doing at being wives."

"Thanks—for nothing," said Maggie bitterly.

"We're all married to reasonably handsome men—even if some of them are beginning to get a little potbellied. In other words, we're normal lower upper-class prosperous professional American couples. We've got every reason in the world to be happy except one: we're bored stiff with each other and with our husbands—which puts us at the dangerous age."

"That's only supposed to apply to men," said Grace.

"It applies to women, too," said Della Rogan. "Dave sees cases all the time. Lorrie's got us pegged all right. At first we were needed by our husbands and later by our children, so we were kept busy and productive. Now we send the children to camp in summer, and in another five years or so most of them will be going off to boarding school or even to college. We're cut out of our husbands' professional lives and they don't want to play golf or poker with us. Our children don't need us much any more

111

and the maid looks after the house. We're bored at home, so we start having various symptoms."

"I have colitis," said Alice proudly.

"That's a common one—along with a lot of others," said Della.

"But it doesn't have to be," Lorrie interposed. "A woman who's having an exciting love affair isn't bored. She's alive and eager. Her glands are working full speed and she's in high gear."

"Until she runs out of gas," said Grace. "Let's face it, girls. Nothing spoils a love affair like marriage—especially to a good provider."

"Grace!" Amy protested.

"We're all living examples of it—except maybe Lorrie."

"The pill is supposed to keep women young and eager," Maggie protested. "You don't even have to go through the menopause any more."

"Dave still sees cases of involutional melancholia in women at the menopause every day," said Della.

"For God's sake," Maggie groaned. "Can't we talk about something cheerful?"

"I'm cheerful," Lorrie said brightly. "In fact I'm downright excited."

Elaine remembered looking at her and feeling a sudden cold fear clutch her heart as she thought that it would be hard for any man to resist Lorrie when she was like this. In fact, looking back on it now, Elaine didn't doubt that Lorrie had already decided to go through with Plan B, whether the rest of them liked it or not.

But why did she have to begin with Paul? Or had he really been the first?

CHAPTER VIII

Ed Harrison was ready to do the spinal puncture on Jerry Monroe by the time Dave Rogan finished his neurological examination. Dave always welcomed neurological consultations though he would have chosen a different patient if he could, for he was genuinely fond of Janet, who had come down from the ward when the pediatric resident called her, to be with Jerry. Jeff Long would have been there, too, if he hadn't been occupied with preparing for the operation on Paul McGill.

Originally—and often still—neurology and psychiatry were one specialty, termed naturally neuropsychiatry. And reasonably so, since one dealt with the anatomy of the nervous system and with pathological changes in the tissues, while the other was concerned with disturbances of function which were rarely traceable to an anatomical abnormality, except when rarely—now that penicillin cured it—the end results of a syphilitic infection produced insanity. More recently, the two fields had been splitting apart, however, with neurology coming more into the province of medicine, as opposed to surgery; and psychiatry, which occupied practically all of Dave's working time, assuming a category of its own separate from the other two.

Which was absurd, Dave always told his students at the beginning of the course he taught in basic psychiatric principles during the third year of medical school. The mind was a most integral part of the body, and so was the nervous system; how else explain the way a purely emotionally engendered fear or uncertainty could create nervous energy in the form of measurable electrical impulses, which could then travel along the vagus nerve to the stomach and disturb its function so markedly that the organ proceeded to digest itself and form an ulcer. This, in turn, might respond to medication but some cases required the skill of a surgeon, either to close the opening when it digested its way entirely through the stomach wall, spilling highly irritated digestive juices out into the abdominal cavity and creating a grave emergency, or to remove the acid-bearing portion of the stomach in order to save the rest from eating itself up.

"Do you know anything more about Dr. McGill, sir?" Ed Harrison asked Dave as he scrubbed his hands at the tap in the corner of the treatment room of the Pediatrics ward. The little boy was still half asleep from the preliminary medication; the psychiatrist had been forced to awaken him in order to test the reaction of the pupils and the movements of the eyes.

"Dr. Dieter said he was going to have the heart-lung pump ready in case they needed it. That means it will take at least an hour to get ready in the operating room. I hope to look in on the operation before I leave the hospital."

"Did you find anything positive here, Dr. Rogan?" Janet asked.

"Not much. The reflexes may be a little more active on the right side, but you know how hard it is to evaluate something like that in a child."

"Did you think the neck muscles were at all rigid?" Ed Harrison asked.

"I couldn't be sure. He's pretty relaxed now."

Harrison bent over Jerry, who was lying on the treatment table with the ward nurse supervisor beside him, ready to place him in a position for the spinal tap. "Wake up, young man," he said. "You gonna sleep all day?"

The little boy opened his eyes. "Hello, Dr. Ed," he said and, seeing Janet, smiled, "Hi Mommie."

"Hi, darling," she said. "Just do what Dr. Ed tells you and everything will be all right."

"I know, Mommie."

"I want you to lie on your side and the nurse is going to hold you," the resident told the little boy. "You may feel a pin prick in your back, Jerry, but don't move and I'll try not to hurt you. Okay?"

"Okay, Dr. Ed." The long lashes drooped again and Harrison nodded to the nurse, who swung the little body over expertly until the boy was lying on his side, with his head tucked down and his knees up. She put one arm below his knees and the other around his neck so if he tried to straighten out, she could prevent him.

The purpose of the bowed-out position was to separate the vertebrae and widen the spaces between them through which Ed Harrison planned to insert a needle. Penetrating into the spinal canal, the membrane-lined space around the vital nerve cord inside the vertebral column, the needle would allow him to obtain a sample of the fluid that circulated there in communication with a similar space around the brain and also inside it.

Spinal puncture was a vital diagnostic adjunct in any condition involving either the brain, the spinal cord, or the meninges that formed the continuous lining of both. The presence of pus would indicate a fulminating meningitis. Too many lymphocytes usually signified an inflammatory condition of the brain itself known as encephalitis. The appearance of blood in the fluid could have a multitude of causes, ranging from head injury to the brain damage of an apoplectic stroke in older patients.

Putting on sterile gloves, Ed Harrison painted the child's back with a crimson antiseptic in a circle about six inches in diameter, then draped over it a small sheet with a window some two by four inches in size cut into it. Feeling through the cloth for the spinous processes of the vertebrae, the projecting bony points that formed the visible portion of the backbone, he located the first and second lumbar spines and moved the window to expose them. Then with a tiny needle and syringe, he raised a small wheal of novocaine so skillfully that the boy didn't even waken.

From the tray on the table beside him, Ed Harrison now took a flexible needle, through whose center ran a metal wire called a stylette. Centering the point of the long needle in the middle of the small wheal he had made with the novocaine, he pushed it through the skin and deeper into the tissues, continuing until his fingers detected the barely perceptible click inside the spinal canal itself, where the needle penetrated the meningeal layer forming its outer covering.

Carefully, he withdrew the metal stylette from the center of the needle, holding it ready to be replaced should there be any noticeable increase in the fluid pressure. If the spinal fluid pressure was markedly increased, usually from injury or brain tumor, a sudden release of pressure in the lower part of the spinal canal could cause the brain itself to be jammed down against the base of the skull, with serious effects and sometimes death.

No increase in pressure showed, however, only a steady drip-drip from the end of the needle. The fluid was of almost its usual state of clearness but, when Ed Harrison filled a small test tube half full and held it up to the light, the red tinge of blood was distinctly visible.

"Bleeding," he said. "But from where?"

"That's what we've got to find out," said Dave Rogan. "I expect this is about as much as we had better disturb him tonight. You can ask for consultations in the morning with both Neurosurgery and Vascular Surgery."

Ed Harrison nodded. "I'll see to it. Let's hope he doesn't hemorrhage again before we can locate the source of the bleeding."

"Is that likely to happen, Dr. Rogan?" Janet Monroe asked quickly.

"No more than before the puncture," he assured her. "Only a small amount of fluid was removed so the pressure relationships couldn't have been disturbed much."

Ed Harrison plucked out the needle and stuck a small dressing over the spot where it had gone through the skin.

"Is it possible that this may be the end of the trouble?" Janet asked, and the younger doctor looked at Dave Rogan, waiting for him to answer.

"It's possible, yes," the psychiatrist admitted. "But experience with hemorrhage around or in the brain shows that half of them will recur, unless the cause is located and removed."

"But that can be dangerous?"

"There is some danger, I wouldn't try to deceive you. But every time the bleeding recurs, it roughly doubles the difficulty of both finding the cause and removing it. That's why we need to go on with some diagnostic studies, even though Jerry seems to be all right now."

"I understand," she said. "What's the next step?"

"Dr. Brennan and Dr. Dieter will have to decide that. My guess would be a radioactive brain scan and possibly a cerebral arteriogram." Dave Rogan picked up the small case in which he kept the instruments for neurological examinations—an ophthalmoscope for studying the eye grounds, a reflex hammer, a small brush for testing skin sensation, a needle for evaluating the response to pain, a tuning fork for testing the vibratory sense, and other similar tools. "But try not to worry; just be glad we discovered the hemorrhage before it becomes really severe."

Dave Rogan left the ward on that note. Angiography, the injection of a chemical that was opaque to X rays directly into the arteries going to the brain, so they could be visualized, was a valuable tool, but not without danger. More important: If an X ray of the cerebral arterial tree, the multiple network of branches by which blood was carried to every part of the brain, confirmed the diagnosis that was beginning to take form in his mind, the outlook for the life of little Jerry Monroe was no better than 50 per cent. There was no point in telling Janet that just now, however. She was troubled enough already as it was.

Crossing from the old building to the new, where the operating rooms were located, Dave took the elevator up to the floor above the main surgical theater level. Halfway down the corridor, he opened the rear door of the glass-fronted observation gallery, where operations could be watched by as many as a dozen people, both through the glass and also by means of a closed-circuit television camera pointed directly at the surgical incision. Thus even though the surgeons were working in the depths of a wound in the skull or the heart, the closest details could be brought directly into the visual range of those watching in the observation gallery.

The brightly lit operating theater was the scene of bustling activity as preparations went on for the major drama that would be played out shortly on the tiled stage below. The technicians had not yet finished charging the heart pump with blood, Dave saw, so the actual surgery might not start for another half hour or even longer. Knowing he could be of no help to Paul McGill as long as he was in the expert hands of Anton Dieter, Dave left the gallery and took the elevator down to the ground floor and the door leading outside.

I hope Mort doesn't plead temporary insanity, he thought as he entered the door of the Faculty Clinic on the way to his office. Decisions like that were always hard for a psychiatrist to make and, knowing Mort, he doubted whether the biochemist had ever done anything without a clearly thought-out purpose and procedure.

All of which made it difficult to understand why Mort had almost killed a friend that afternoon, when he could have had ample opportunities on other occasions to select someone else as a target.

ii

"Damn Joe McCloskey!" Maggie fumed as she and Della Rogan were leaving the hospital.

"What are you so mad at Joe for?" Della was so relieved to discover the man Mort Dellman had shot wasn't Dave, she couldn't even be short with Maggie.

"Why couldn't it have been Joe instead of Paul McGill? After I knocked myself out getting here to give him blood."

"Just now you were mourning about losing your alimony if it were Joe; now you wish it had been. What sort of woman are you, Maggie?"

"I didn't mean I wanted him shot. But Joe could at least be grateful for me wanting to give him blood."

"Why don't you go tell him?"

"And let him know—"

"What?"

"Nothing," she said sullenly.

"That you still love him?"

"For Christ's sake. Just because Dave's a psychiatrist, do you always have to be psychoanalyzing people, Della? Before you start running other people's lives, take a hard look at your own."

"What are you talking about?" Della stopped short at the entrance to the parking lot.

"I drink—you play golf. What's the difference?"

"I play golf because I like it."

"Yeah? And I drink because I love the stuff. Besides, don't think Dave stays home every night while you're off playing in tournaments."

"I don't expect him to."

"Must be nice having so much confidence in your husband. All those stories you hear about golf widows—you can't tell me the same thing doesn't apply to golf widowers."

"What do you know?" Della demanded.

"Nothing at all." Maggie shrugged. "But I bet you won't be quite as comfortable the next time you go away to play in a tournament."

Della didn't answer, for Maggie's random shot had hit her where it hurt—badly. But it all wouldn't have happened, she reminded herself, if Dave hadn't been tied up with that court case and unable—or unwilling—to go with her to the Southeastern Women's Open at Augusta two weeks ago.

It was the first time they hadn't been together on their wedding anniversary since they were married. The tournament couldn't be changed because of that, of course, but why did Dave have to be so damned honest that he couldn't claim he wasn't able to testify at that particular time? Roy Weston would have postponed the trial. After all Roy was a friend and a member of the Faculty Clinic Corporation, too.

They'd quarreled bitterly over Dave's not being able to go,

though. And even though just before she left for Augusta he had given her the golf bag she'd wanted so badly as an anniversary present she'd gone off in a huff, not even letting him drive her to the airport but taking her station wagon and parking it there in the lot.

Her anger hadn't kept her from playing well, though. She'd come in three strokes ahead of the field and within one stroke of the course record for that particular tournament. Naturally the victory had excited her and she'd called Dave to tell him, but hadn't been able to reach him. When she'd gotten back, he'd said he'd gone to see Elizabeth Taylor and Richard Burton in *Who's Afraid of Virginia Woolf?* that night—Della didn't particularly like movies and, knowing Dave did, she had no real reason to think he wasn't telling the truth.

That night in Augusta, she hadn't been moved by love for Dave, however, or by the consideration that he, too, might have been lonesome, with the children away at school and her at Augusta. And when her night flight home had been canceled because of bad weather, she'd even blamed him for that too, irrational though she'd known it to be even then.

She'd been crossing the lobby from the hotel transportation desk, after learning she couldn't get a flight back to Weston before early morning, when Eve Post, the girl she'd beaten that afternoon for the Women's Southeastern, had corralled her. Della liked Eve; they'd been opponents before. And when Eve insisted that, since she wasn't leaving, she join a celebration party with the rest of the tournament crowd in one of the hotel suites, she'd been just irritated enough with Dave for not being at home and for everything else, to accept.

It wasn't as if she hadn't known what champagne did to her either; at home she never drank it except with Dave. But the congratulations on her victory had called for several toasts and there hadn't seemed to be any harm in having dinner with a half-dozen people she knew from professional tournaments, particularly the handsome professional from Pebble Beach, who had been her dinner date. What she hadn't figured on was the way the effect of the champagne and the rest of the drinks she'd had would hit her all at once. Or that there really was something to the old belief that, if you drank a glass of water after taking on considerable champagne, you'd get high all over again.

It had been an exciting evening—as much of it as she was able to remember. But there hadn't been much doubt about the broad picture of what had really happened, not when you woke up at dawn in bed with a man you'd just met the night before—who wasn't your husband.

The whole thing, she told herself now for the dozenth time, had been Dave's fault. If he'd gone with her to Augusta, as he should have done with such an important tournament—and on her anniversary, too—none of it would have happened. Or if he'd been home when, bubbling over with the excitement of winning and nearly equaling the course record for women, she'd called to tell him of her victory, she would have gone on to bed and her conscience wouldn't be driving her crazy now.

What had happened this afternoon piled on top of everything, had been too much. And even though Dave had extended the olive branch just now and she had tentatively accepted it, she wasn't going to let him off that easy. The thing to do was break the damn thing and throw it in his face to show him what happened to husbands who neglected their wives.

"So that's what goes on at a golf tournament." Maggie's voice snapped Della out of her reverie.

"What d'you mean?" Feeling her cheeks burn, Della knew she'd never fool Maggie.

"You're no good at hiding your sins, Della. Your eyes give you away and you're blushing like a schoolgirl caught in the hay. What was he like?"

"Don't be absurd."

"I won't tell Dave, if that's what is worrying you. After all, we women have to stick together where those things are concerned."

"Where do you want me to drop you?" Della's voice was sharp as she started across the lot.

"If you're going to be so damn high and mighty," said Maggie, "I'll get a cab back to the club. Thanks—for nothing."

When Maggie headed for one of the telephone booths against the wall of the hospital, Della started to call her back and apologize. Then she shrugged and went on to where she had left her own car in the lot.

Why couldn't Dave have come home with her? she thought resentfully. It was after five o'clock already and the clinic was closed. Besides he wasn't a pediatrician and Ed Harrison was perfectly capable of looking after that nurse's child. Dave's big fault was that he always thought of other people before he did his own family—like now, when he was more concerned over a patient than over the fact that his wife was upset. He was a psychiatrist, so he should have seen how disturbed she was in the waiting room and come on home with her when she asked him.

By the time she got home, Della was thoroughly angry with Dave and sorry for herself into the bargain. Pouring a glass of milk and making a sandwich, she ate morosely at the kitchen table. Then, after scribbling a note telling him there was sandwich meat, bread and mayonnaise in the refrigerator and that she was going to bed with a headache, she climbed the stairs to the children's room and closed the door, a pointed reminder that she didn't want to be bothered.

iii

In front of the clubhouse, Maggie McCloskey paid the driver and got out of the cab. Her own car was still in the lot and for a moment she considered getting it and driving away from the city, away from everything that reminded her of the happiness she'd known in Weston, before her whole life had started coming apart.

When she and Joe had been courting, they'd driven along the river on many an evening like this to a restaurant located high up on the side of the mountain that marked the western border of the valley in which the city lay on the banks of Rogue River and the lake formed by the dam downstream. Right now, she would have given anything she possessed to recapture, if only briefly, just one of the moments when they'd parked the car at the edge of an overlook in the summer twilight to watch the pattern of the lights take form in the lowlands spread out below them.

But something had gone wrong along the way. And though in this moment of self-analysis brought on by her depressed spirits, the absence of alcohol, and the tragedy of Lorrie's death, Maggie faced the fact that the fault was largely hers, she wasn't able to pin down the point at which her marriage had actually begun to fall apart.

Certainly it hadn't been in those first several years when she'd kept on working as Dave Rogan's secretary, while Joe was busy organizing the Urology Department of the medical school. They'd had only his salary then and the house in Sherwood Ravine. They'd bought it before they could really afford the payments, but it had been so perfect, sitting there at the head of the glen looking down the wooded ravine to the slope of the highest hill in Weston, perhaps a half-mile away, that they hadn't been able to resist it.

With the monthly payments on the house so large, Maggie had done the decorating herself after finishing work each day at the clinic. She'd always loved that sort of thing and had wanted to go to Pace Institute in New York to take up decorating at the end of her second year of college. But her father had died suddenly that summer and she'd barely had enough money left after the funeral to finance a year at the Katherine Gibbs School, preparing herself for a job as a medical secretary.

Assigned one day from the secretarial pool shortly after she came to Weston to fill in for Joe McCloskey's regular secretary, she'd found the innate courtliness and obvious gentility of the bantam-sized urologist infinitely attractive. The two of them had hit it off from the start and they'd been supremely happy, even on Joe's salary, for a while. Then Mort Dellman and Pete Brennan had come up with the idea of an automated diagnostic clinic staffed by faculty members of Weston Medical School, with a substantial part of the professional fees collected there going to the staff of the clinic.

Fearing that the quality of teaching in the school would suffer, the trustees of the medical school hadn't been in favor of the change. In the end, they'd had no choice, unless the school was to lose their best teachers. For with the income of doctors in private practice beginning to skyrocket in the fifties, making an extra source of income available to much of the faculty had been the only way to keep from losing most of them to other schools, where the rules about outside private practice were somewhat less strict. And as it had turned out, the quality of teaching had not suffered at all. Instead it had improved, for Weston had been able to lure important men in many fields to the staff because the phenomenally increasing reputation of the Faculty Clinic drew them there.

The clinic setup had worked out especially well for the six who had come there together from Korea—Joe McCloskey, Dave Rogan, Pete Brennan, Paul McGill, George Hanscombe, and Mort Dellman who, as Director of Laboratories, had ridden herd on what envious doctors in the surrounding area called a "medical production line." Patients loved the clinic, too, because it could accomplish in two days at most what would take a week of running from one specialist to another. Of course the doctors had been forced to work harder than before and their home life had been sharply curtailed. But the prosperity that went with being on the clinic staff more than made up for that.

Or had it? Maggie wondered now.

Take herself—she'd been busy and happy as a secretary. Even after they'd moved to Sherwood Ravine, she'd done much of her own housework, decorating the home, digging in the garden, hiking with Joe in the early evenings before dinner along the trails that circled the ravine or watching the trout dart in the rocky pools of the brook that tumbled down through the gorge below the house in a succession of small waterfalls. But soon the demands of both teaching and the clinic had begun to keep Joe from getting home in time for the afternoon walks—though he'd still found time, she remembered with a flash of resentment, for the weekly golf game with some of the others and the twice-monthly poker games.

At first Maggie hadn't resented that part of Joe's life, for having been together in Korea before they came to Weston and working together during the day, the six men—plus Roy Weston—were a close-knit group. But time, and a mounting discontent, had changed her viewpoint.

She hadn't really needed a full-time maid, particularly after she stopped work at the clinic; after all, she'd done all the housework herself in the early years, except for a woman to clean one day and iron another. But Joe's income had doubled almost overnight, and when Della, Grace and Elaine had gotten theirs—Amy Weston of course had live-in servants she'd inherited from her mother and so did Lorrie and Alice—Maggie couldn't very well go on doing her own housework and hold up her head in the level of society that successful doctors moved into from the very beginning. With almost nothing to do at home and no real purpose any more, there'd been more time to spend at the club—and the bar.

The story of my life, she thought bitterly. *And what do I have before me? Nothing.*

Getting out of the car she slammed the door, and started across to the pro shop entrance, the shortest way to the Ladies' Bar, where soft-voiced Manuel would listen to her—if nobody else would.

CHAPTER IX

On Wednesday afternoons Pete Brennan usually played golf with Paul McGill, Joe McCloskey and whoever they could find to make out the foursome. Sometimes it was Arthur Painter, who did most of the legal work for the Faculty Clinic Corporation. Roy Weston was a member of the corporation, since it was he who had persuaded the doctors to come to Weston, but he was also district attorney for the county and aiming for the job of attorney general of the state the next year, so it hadn't seemed best for him to handle the clinic's legal affairs.

That particular Wednesday, Pete had begged off from the golf game. Taking his Porsche from the parking lot, he'd driven along River Road until he came to the Rogue River dam, about ten miles downstream from Weston. He'd left the car in the parking area of a marina near the dam and descended the slope to the boat sheds and dock at the edge of the lake.

Rogue Lake being a power project, boating was allowed, and the whole area had become aquatic-minded, with water skiing a major sport in summer and fishing in the dozen of coves created when the river valley filled, attracting people the year around. Pete kept an eighteen-foot outboard at the marina for pulling the kids on skiis, for overnight camping and for fishing trips, whenever he was able to take them.

At the boat sheds near the water level, he had his outboard runabout put into the water from dry storage where it was kept, except when Michael and Terry were home in summer and using it every day. Filling the tank with gasoline at the marina pump and adding the necessary oil, he pushed the button to start the motor and was pleased when it roared into life on the second turnover, even though he hadn't used it more than a half-dozen times all summer.

With the clinic running full blast, plus his duties as president of the Faculty Clinic Corporation, Pete didn't get much time off any more, missing at least half of the Wednesday afternoon golf sessions. This afternoon he had been moved by more than just the urge to feel the wind in his face and the surge of the motor at the stern of the boat when he opened the throttle. More than ever before he needed time alone to think. And since he wasn't expecting Amy back until tomorrow, this had seemed the best time to do it.

There wasn't any use denying it any longer, he admitted as he put the engine in reverse and backed away from the marina dock —things just weren't going right between him and Amy. Lately, this business of getting to the top in the state medical auxiliary had become an obsession with her, until it was almost as if the two of them were engaged in a battle to the death for supremacy.

Actually, Pete felt no overpowering urge to become president of the state medical association. The position would come to him in time and meanwhile there was plenty to occupy him besides medical politics. The clinic was growing so fast that they were going to have to consider putting up a new building before long, one somewhat better adapted to the production-line type of diagnostic study, for which the organization was already becoming famous far beyond its normal patient drawing area.

At the last meeting of the A.M.A., Pete had seen one of the twelve-channel sequential multiple analyzers that could make thirty different laboratory blood analyses an hour. Such an apparatus would be fine for the clinic, he had realized at once, but they would need more room to accommodate it and the increased stream of patients that would be pouring through when the laboratory test rate was stepped up. X-ray, too, needed more space, as did the radiation laboratory, the record room with its new data-processing equipment, the insurance office that was twice as busy now with Medicare, as well as new offices for additional clinic doctors.

Pete could handle all that with the help of Mort Dellman's undeniable genius in that field, even though Mort had been more surly than usual lately and more insistent on building up clinic income sometimes to the detriment of professional efficiency. Dave Rogan and Joe McCloskey had both spoken to Pete about that recently, and he knew that, with the pressure of discontent building up, there was bound to be a showdown at one of the corporation meetings soon. Being a biochemist, not a physician, Mort's point of view was bound to be different from theirs, but his obvious commercialism was beginning to get on Pete's nerves, too—as if he didn't already have enough to worry about with Amy and his rapidly disintegrating marriage.

Putting the gear lever into "Forward" Pete opened the throttle and steadied the wheel as the boat began to plane over the smooth surface of the lake. The vibration of the motor settled into his muscles and his nerves, acting as something of a cathartic and washing away the petty troubles that had accumulated since his last golf game had given him the much needed weekly release of tension.

Clinic problems, as well as the purely professional decisions arising in his own practice of neurosurgery, were something he knew how to handle. But when it came to doing something about what was happening between him and Amy, he felt himself baffled.

Looking back on it now, it was almost as though she had been seized by a fever, a disease that had slowly changed her in the past several years into a driving, relentlessly ambitious woman who was completely different from the girl with whom he had fallen in love that night at Weston Country Club when Roy had introduced them. That night—and for a long time afterward—Amy had seemed to be the wife he'd always dreamed he would have one day—tall, assured, handsome rather than delicately lovely, the bearing of her New England heritage apparent in her face and in her carriage. She had stirred a fire within him that night which still continued to glow, but lately she seemed to be intent upon destroying it, for reasons he could not understand.

He'd recognized the aggressive streak in her even before they were married, but then it had only seemed to complement his own capacity to work hard for what he wanted. She'd been disappointed, he knew, by his decision not to become Professor of Surgery, when the post had been vacant some five years ago. Having always had money and accepted it as a matter of course, Amy hadn't been able to understand how Pete could turn down the prestige that went with the full-time professorship and what it would have meant to her for a mere clinical teaching position, even with the opportunities for money-making afforded by the clinic. The task of getting the clinic organized and into successful operation had been a real challenge at the time and now that it had become an undoubted success, his judgment had been proved correct. But he sometimes thought Amy still considered the clinic itself as an enemy.

At first, he had been pleased when she had turned her tremendous energy to medical auxiliary work, but that, too, had quickly become a tooth-and-claw affair. Now she literally ate, slept and dreamed political maneuvering. And while she seemed completely oblivious of it, he knew that even her own circle of friends —represented most closely by the members of the Dissection Society—had begun to draw away from her.

Guiding the boat into a secluded cove, he broke out a spinning rod and some lures, and began to cast into the edge of the weeds, not so much hoping to catch anything as to give his hands something to do while his thoughts ranged and he sought to grapple with his dilemma.

The trouble wasn't sex, he was sure; actually that had almost disappeared from their relationship these past eight to twelve months while Amy had been engaged in her relentless campaign to become state president of the auxiliary. Sex was always in plentiful supply around a hospital, the major part of whose personnel was composed of women, and he'd had no trouble finding all the release he needed there.

Perhaps the simplest thing would have been to establish a completely outside relationship—as Roy Weston had done. At least Alice seemed content. But deep inside him somewhere, Pete's Irish ancestry carried with it a streak of conformity, perhaps due to the Catholic teachings of his childhood, although when he'd married Amy, he'd joined the Episcopal Church, to which her family had belonged for generations. In any event his conscience wouldn't let him be satisfied with the sort of unresponsive wife and passionate mistress setup the French seemed to accept as a matter of course and which existed to a high degree in the levels of Weston society where all of them moved.

A divorce would rock their small world but not destroy it, although it might well destroy Amy by cutting away at one stroke her connection with medical politics and wounding her fierce New England pride. Lots of doctors got divorces at his age, it was true; he could name a half dozen on the medical school faculty. Most of them soon married younger women—the secretaries, nurses, technicians with whom they were thrown in daily contact. And the new wives often brought to these second marriages an understanding and love that had largely disappeared from the old.

But Pete loved his children and he loved the girl he had married, if there were only some way to bring her back and spare her the shame of the sort of scandal that had happened many times in even so small a city as Weston, when husbands started looking abroad for the easily found solace they no longer found with their wives.

It was almost six o'clock when Pete Brennan finally nudged the outboard runabout to a berth at the marina dock and tied it up. The attendants would take care of hoisting it from the water with the giant hydraulic cradle and putting it on a wheeled dolly for dry storage. As he was passing the office, the manager came to the door.

"All hell's broke loose in town, Dr. Brennan," he said. "It's been all over the radio and TV."

"What's that?"

"A doctor—Dellman, I think it is—shot his wife and another

doctor who was with her this afternoon. The woman was killed and the man's in the hospital—not expected to live."

Mort Dellman and Lorrie! It was hard to believe, not that Mort wasn't capable of it; there was a hard, vicious, cold, calculating streak in him that Pete had recognized long ago and avoided in his contacts with the brilliant biochemist. But Mort must have known of Lorrie's penchant for hopping in and out of beds; she'd certainly made no secret of it. And knowing it, Mort should have had better sense than to destroy the gold mine represented by his marriage to Jake Porter's heir.

"Who was the man?" he asked.

"They didn't give his name for a while, but it was announced just now," said the manager. "It's Dr. McGill. He's got a boat out here and a nicer quieter fellow you couldn't find anywhere. Who would have thought—?"

Pete was already on the way to his car. His first thought was that with Amy still away at the auxiliary meeting, Elaine would need all the help he could give her—Paul, too, poor devil. And God only knew what it would do to the Faculty Clinic.

ii

George Hanscombe came through the front door of the clinic just as Dave Rogan started inside to put away his neurological kit and get his hat before leaving for home. Older than the psychiatrist by some ten years, Hanscombe was tall, with the well-clipped and groomed look of the upper-echelon executive or professional man, even to the small brush of mustache on his upper lip. His hair was still dark—rumor said by courtesy of a masculine rinse that had zoomed into popularity recently. Nobody kidded him about it, however; almost completely devoid of humor, George Hanscombe was the epitome of brisk efficiency and expected everyone else to be the same.

"Thought you were playing golf, George," said Dave, standing aside for the internist to come through.

"I was on the way to the club when a call came from Sam Portola's wife. She thought she was having a heart attack, so what could I do?"

"Nothing—except go," Dave agreed. Portola was the head of the syndicate that now owned Weston Mills, a millionaire and, with his family, among the most important patients of the Faculty Clinic group. "Was it a coronary?"

George Hanscombe shook his head; since he wore his hair rather long, the effect was somewhat that of a slightly peeved lion. "Nothing but gas. She insists on eating all that rich Italian food. I had to spend the afternoon working with her until she could erupt in a good solid belch."

"The old Five-F syndrome?"

"What's that?"

"Have you forgotten your medical school days? Fair, fat, forty and full of flatus." Then Dave's face grew serious. "You heard about Paul and Lorrie, didn't you?"

"Yes. I came by the hospital just now." The internist grew even more sour than before. "They tell me Paul's in the hands of the Great God Dieter, so I guess the kraut will pull off another of his miracles—or at least claim one."

"Anton's got plenty of evidence to back up his claims," said Dave. "Too bad about Lorrie."

"And Mort. After all he only did what any red-blooded—"

"Come off it, George. Mort's a louse and we all know it, but Lorrie was one of the most completely normal people I ever knew."

"Normal!" George Hanscombe exploded. "I suppose that's some of your Freudian business?"

"I think Freud would have approved of her. Most of the troubles we psychiatrists see come from people butting their more primitive instincts against the stone walls of their inhibitions. Lorrie just let hers go."

"Adultery is adultery."

"You sound like Gertrude Stein," Dave said with a grin. "With that sort of reasoning, all of us would be guilty—including you. It isn't as if Lorrie hadn't given us all fair warning of what she was going to do, either."

"What do you mean by that?"

"Don't you remember what she told us that night at the club, when she came into the game room during the orchestra intermission?"

"I'm not sure."

"You, Joe, Paul, Roy and I were playing poker."

"Got no time to remember anything now," said George. "Grace will be home from the club by the time I get home and dinner will be ready. She's been so damned irritable lately, I never know when she's going to take my head off."

"Go on then. Glad to see I'm not the only one who's in the doghouse."

At the newsrack in front of the clinic, Dave dropped in a dime and took out a copy of the final edition, rushed on the streets with news of the afternoon's events. A picture of Lorrie Dellman occupied the center of the front page, with the story in black type all around it. . . . Seeing her smiling at him from the newspaper, Dave found himself remembering even more clearly the incident he had mentioned to George. In fact the dress she was wearing in the newspaper picture was the same one she'd worn the night of the dance, as usual cut rather daringly low to emphasize the fact that she was well endowed by nature.

"Mind if I sit in?" Lorrie had asked when she came into the game room where they were playing, a half-filled glass in her hand. Mort Dellman had been away that night, inspecting some new automation equipment they planned to buy for the clinic and so had Pete Brennan, Lorrie had come with Roy and Alice Weston and, like most everybody at the dance, she was already a little high.

"This is a man's game." George Hanscombe was losing and that always made his temper even shorter than usual. "Go play with the women, Lorrie."

"They're afraid of me," she said with that gamin grin of hers that always preceded some salty observation.

"Why?" Roy asked.

"I had a heart-to-heart talk with all of your wives at Amy's house yesterday," Lorrie informed them. "I made them a proposition and now they're worried that I really meant what I said."

"Did you?" Dave asked.

"Of course. I don't lie—not even to myself."

"That's asking a lot of anybody," Dave remembered saying.

"Stop gabbing." George had lost again. "Let's get on with the game."

"By the way, George," said Lorrie. "How long has it been since you put on a tuxedo and took Grace to a fine restaurant or a night club?"

"A couple of years ago—at the convention."

"I'm not talking about conventions," she said. "A lot of people get drunk and wind up in somebody else's room then. I mean how long has it been since you made a date with Grace and took her out for an evening of wining, dining and dancing."

"What the hell does that have to do with playing poker?"

"Maybe if you paid more attention to Grace and less to poker and golf—the stock market too—she wouldn't always be talking about going back to England." Lorrie's voice had suddenly taken on a cutting edge.

"That's going too far, even for you, Lorrie," Roy Weston had protested.

"Let her talk," Dave remembered saying. "Maybe she's saying something we all need to hear. Go on, Lorrie."

"I'm not going to listen to such drivel." George threw down his cards and stood up. "After a man has worked all day to make enough money so his wife can drive a Cadillac, have a full-time maid, play golf and get drunk at the club, he shouldn't have to play gigolo just because she doesn't have enough to do to keep her happy."

"Hear! Hear!" said Lorrie and this time there had been a real cutting edge to her voice. "Spoken like a true American husband—the dullest guys in the world."

"What's this proposition you were talking about?" Roy asked with a grin, as George Hanscombe left for the bar in a dudgeon.

"Now that I see you together, I'm not sure you aren't all beyond help," said Lorrie. "But I'm willing to do whatever I can."

"Which is?"

"The other day I told your wives I'd go to bed with each of you, then report back on your particular cases and prescribe treat—"

"Good God, Lorrie!" Paul McGill exclaimed. "Do you realize what you're saying?"

"Sure." Lorrie grinned impudently. "I'm offering to make a legitimate experiment out of something we've all been experimenting with illegitimately anyway. One thing's sure: you're all lousy lovers, or your wives wouldn't be so dissatisfied with the status quo. Because you're all my friends, I'm willing to put my years of experience on the line to help you out."

"Just how do you propose to institute treatment?" Dave asked.

"At first I thought it would be enough to report back to your wives, like in a clinic," said Lorrie. "But now I've decided both husband and wife should be given the diagnosis together and treatment discussed. You see it would really be a purely clinical procedure."

"Maybe clinical," Dave remembered interjecting. "But hardly pure—by most people's standards."

"I'm not using most people's standards, just my own," said Lorrie. "Do any of you doubt my credentials for carrying out the experiment? I don't have to remind you that most of you have good reason to know."

Nobody had answered until Paul McGill said: "Really, Lorrie. If this is your idea of a joke."

"Who's joking?" She looked from one to the other but got no answer. "Come on; who's going to be the first test case?"

Still nobody answered.

"Then I'll just have to sneak up on each of you," she said. "Good night, boys."

They hadn't felt much like playing poker after that, for none of them had been sure whether or not Lorrie was joking.

Now it appeared that she wasn't.

iii

Mike Traynor was working in the emergency room, sewing up a kid who had fallen while on skates, when Pete Brennan came in from the parking lot.

"Know anything about Dr. McGill?" Pete asked him.

"He's in surgery, Dr. Brennan. Dr. Dieter's getting ready to take a bullet out of his heart."

"What about Mrs. McGill?"

"I saw her talking to Dr. Rogan and several doctors' wives in the waiting room a little while ago," said the E.R. nurse supervisor, who had come over when she saw Pete. "I think they said Dr. McGill would be taken to the Special Intensive Care Unit after surgery. That's probably where she is now."

"Mrs. Brennan was with them, but I believe she's left already," the nurse added as Pete was going out the door.

Pete wheeled at the door. "My wife?"

"Yes sir."

"But that's impossible. She's out of town."

"I saw her, Dr. Brennan. She must have gotten back early."

It didn't make sense, Pete told himself as he headed for the elevator. Amy had said she would spent the night so her enemies —that had been her own word—couldn't work behind the scenes after the meeting to gain an advantage.

Janet Monroe looked up from the desk of the Special Intensive Care Unit when Pete Brennan came in. "Dr. McGill's still in surgery, Dr. Brennan," she said. "Mrs. McGill is in the waiting room."

"How's she taking it?"

"Very well, sir."

Elaine managed to smile when Pete sat down beside her and took her hands in his. "Everything will be all right," he assured her. "Dieter is a whiz."

"Dave came by just now. He says Paul's chances are good."

"Have they started the operation yet?"

"He said they're getting the heart-lung machine—whatever you call it—ready."

"That takes time. I'll go up and watch."

"You'd better go home to Amy, Pete."

"Then she really was here?"

"She heard the broadcast like the others—and didn't know who the man was. The girls all came together but Amy still looked upset when I left them downstairs. She needs you more than Paul does, Pete."

The idea of Amy needing him seemed so unlikely that Pete found himself wondering. Still it must have been something of a shock to Amy to think he might have been the man with Lorrie. And that could certainly account for her being upset.

"Sure you don't want me to stay with you?" he asked Elaine.

"I'm all right now, Mrs. Monroe is looking after me."

"Be sure to call me if you want me."

"I will—and thanks for coming, Pete."

"I was out on my boat on the lake all afternoon. Only learned what happened a few minutes ago."

As a clinical professor, Pete had a small office in the hospital, as well as his more elaborate suite across the street in the Faculty Clinic. Going directly to his hospital office, he dialed his home telephone number.

iv

Amy was halfway home, driving mechanically and still half in shock from the headlong race there and the sudden rush of relief at discovering Pete hadn't been in danger after all, when the pounding agony of the migraine reminded her forcibly of what she had been going to the hopsital for when she'd heard the first broadcast. Briefly she considered turning back, until she saw by the dashboard clock that George Hanscombe's office would have closed half an hour ago. She could always go to the emergency room for an injection, of course, but that would mean an explanation to the intern on duty, who would naturally be suspicious of anyone asking for a hypodermic that included a narcotic.

Pete wasn't in the hospital; she'd learned that from the operator when she stopped by the switchboard on the way out. Rather than turn back now she decided to go on home, hoping he might be there by now and could give her something out of the emergency medical case he kept at home for night calls. Her plans for the evening had been shot away, first by Lorrie's death and now by the migraine. But there was certain to be something in the refrigerator she could use to make Pete a sandwich for his dinner. As for herself, right now food was the farthest thing from her mind.

At the house, Amy fumbled a little with the key; the pounding of the migraine was already blurring her vision, as it always did until she got relief. Finally, she managed to open the door and make her way into the kitchen. Grasping at the first thing that might help relieve the pain, she took a bottle of bourbon from the store of liquor in the small cabinet behind the built-in bar that opened to the family room. Pouring some into a glass without stopping to measure it out carefully, she filled the rest of the glass with ginger ale from a bottle in the refrigerator and drank down half of it in one shuddering swallow.

Carrying the glass, she climbed the stairs to the master bedroom and finished the drink. Since her stomach was empty, the alcohol was absorbed almost immediately and she could feel its warmth begin to pervade her body, though the throbbing pain of the migraine still continued. Just then the phone rang and, putting down the empty glass, she picked it up.

"Amy?" It was Pete's voice.

"Yes."

"I was out in the boat and got to the hospital just after you left. Elaine said you seemed to be upset. Are you all right?"

"It's a headache." The whiskey was already slurring her voice a little.

"I'm getting ready to leave for home. Do you want me to bring anything?"

"Ethel's off and I don't feel like making dinner."

"I'll stop by that fried chicken place and bring a couple of boxes. Anything else?"

"No. That will be fine."

"See you in about half an hour then."

"'Bye." She hung up the phone, half blind still from the migraine, in spite of the powerful jolt of whiskey she had drunk. Stumbling toward the bed, she started to lie down, until her eyes fell on Pete's small medicine case. He sometimes made calls at night, when a close friend became ill and worried, and to save trouble, kept a small kit ready with drugs and some dressings that might come in handy in an emergency.

There ought to be something in that bag she could take for the migraine, Amy thought, perhaps an ampule or two of Demerol. Of course she couldn't inject it without a sterile syringe but even taken by mouth it still might be effective if she took two ampules at once.

Going to the closet, she took down the small case and opened it but saw no Demerol, the drug she had been looking for. In a small pocket inside the case, however, she discovered about a dozen tiny tubes, each with a needle covered by a plastic guard attached.

"Morphine sulphate one-fourth grain," she read, and recognized at once what the small tubes were. Called syrettes, each contained a quarter-grain dose of morphine in a tiny collapsible tube, like the little toothpaste samples the kids sometimes brought home from school, though smaller.

Having taken a first-aid course given by the PTA as part of the civil defense disaster training program, Amy knew how to use them. Sponging off her arm with cotton and alcohol from the medicine cabinet, she took one of the syrettes, removed the small plastic cover from the needle and, jamming it into her flesh, squeezed the small tube empty, forcing the drug solution under her skin.

As she massaged the skin where she'd made the injection with the cotton pledget to hasten the absorption of the drug by the blood vessels in the tissue beneath it, she felt the powerful dose of morphine begin to take effect in a feeling of languor that seemed to spread outward from the site of the injection. The throbbing in her temple soon lessened, too, and the effect of the drug, combined with the drink she'd already had, was somewhat like that of floating on a cloud. She resisted the desire to lie down and fall asleep, however, determined to enjoy to the fullest this marvelous state of nirvana into which she had literally injected herself by squeezing the tiny tube of the morphine syrette.

As she started to undress for her bath, Amy noticed the small case from which she'd taken the morphine still lying on the bed where she'd left it when she'd gone into the bathroom to get alcohol and cotton from the medicine cabinet. She started to close the case but, moved by a sudden impulse, took out nine of the tiny syrette tubes and put them into a drawer of her dressing table beneath the lining paper. Then, closing the small case, she put it back where it had been on the closet shelf.

The migraine attacks, she knew from experience, could come on at any time and the relief she had already obtained from the morphine was far greater than from the piddling injections of Demerol and ergotamine George Hanscombe always gave her. This way, she could take care of herself without being a bother to George when the attacks came.

By the time Amy finished undressing and stepped into the shower the pain was entirely gone and she was all but walking on air. She showered quickly, and then, hoping to wash away some of the drowsiness, turned the needle spray on "Cold" for a moment, so her body was all rosy when she stepped out of the shower and began to dry herself with a nubby towel. She was admiring the glow of her skin in the pier glass mirror on the door of her bathroom when Pete came into the bedroom.

"Well!" He gave a whistle of appreciation. "This is a pleasant surprise."

Amy's first impulse was to hide behind the towel. An instinctive prudery had always kept her from letting Pete see her nude, if she could help it; even when they made love, she'd always insisted that the room be dark. But the combination of morphine and whiskey had removed most of these inhibitions, so she made no move to cover her naked loveliness.

"I didn't hear you come in," she said as she went on drying herself with the towel.

"Maybe I should try coming home like this more often," he said with a grin.

Amy walked over to the closet, warmly conscious that Pete's eyes were following her every movement and thankful that she'd kept her figure. Riffling through the hangers, she started to take down a gown and robe combination, such as she usually wore at night, then removed from another hanger a somewhat filmy negligee instead. Wrapping it about her, she went over to her dressing table and began to brush her hair, quite conscious that every movement of her arm with the brush accentuated the fullness of her breasts under the thin fabric.

In the mirror, she saw Pete come up behind her before she felt his hands on her shoulders. The contact sent a tingling feeling through her, somewhat like the way she remembered feeling when he'd first taken her in his arms on their honeymoon, but also a bit like the sensation she'd experienced when the hypodermic began to take effect just now. Dropping the brush, she reached up to take his hands and leaned backward as he lowered his head to kiss her throat, turning her head so he could find her lips.

It had been a long time since they had kissed like that and, when his hands slipped down to push the robe from her shoulders and bare her breasts, she didn't resist. Instead, her hands moved along his temples, holding his head between her palms as she kissed him eagerly. When his hands caressed her breasts and the warm flesh beneath them, she stood up and turned in his arms, freeing the thin robe from her shoulders and letting it fall to her feet.

Lying on the bed, watching Pete as he undressed quickly, Amy suddenly began to laugh.

"I'm not that funny-looking," he said in mock anger. "What's the joke?"

"The chicken will get cold—and I don't give a damn."

CHAPTER X

Looking down from the glass-walled observation gallery, Marisa Feldman found herself less than ten feet away from the operating table occupying the center of the theater. Upon it lay Paul Mc-Gill, his entire chest and abdomen bare, as well as the right groin. The two concave lights above the operating table, focus of all the activity in the room, were so placed that those working there did not cast a shadow. When the body of one of them came between the light and the operative area, the other lamp would still flood it with illumination. Sterilized handles were attached to the center of the lights so the surgeon could reach up and adjust either or both of them to his exact requirements during the operation without contaminating his sterile gloves.

Anton Dieter had not yet appeared, but the scene below was a beehive of activity. At one side, three technicians worked over a machine of shining metal, glass and tubing. Its central portion consisted of a large plastic tube about three feet long and perhaps four to five inches in diameter containing more than a dozen metal disks attached to a central spindle by which they could be rotated.

Now motionless, the complex of disks and spindle, the very heart of the apparatus that could take over the function of both heart and lungs, would begin to revolve at the flick of a switch. Each rotation would expose to an atmosphere of pure oxygen in the long tube a thin film of the blood mixture filling the lower part of the horizontal cylinder as it was picked up by the revolving disks. The mixture itself, called the perfusate, was composed of roughly three-fourths blood from the hospital blood bank and one fourth a solution of saline, plus a small amount of heparin to keep it from clotting.

The observation gallery was almost filled with students and interns. They discussed the scene below in muted tones, though no sound from the gallery itself could reach the operating room.

"That long gadget is called the oxygenator," an intern was explaining to several first-year students. "As the blood is picked up in the form of a film on those metal disks, the oxygen that fills the tube is absorbed by the hemoglobin in the red blood cells, and the carbon dioxide is given off into the space there at the same time."

"Why is that?" a student asked.

"The atmosphere in the tube is practically pure O_2. With a high O_2 in the tube and a low concentration in the red cells, oxygen is absorbed by the hemoglobin and carried to the rest of the body. At the same time, with a high CO_2 in the blood and a low concentration in the top part of the tube, where the O_2 is, the blood gives off its CO_2."

"Just like in the lungs?"

"Except that the machine—it's really called a pump-oxygenator —takes the place of both the heart and the lungs. That way the surgeon can open the heart, if he has to, and work inside it, replacing valves or patching abnormal openings while the circulation goes on without the heart or lungs being involved at all."

"How long can he do that?" the student asked.

"The longest I ever saw a patient on bypass—the whole procedure is called a cardio-pulmonary bypass—was three hours. But Dieter's a slick operator; he rarely keeps one on it more than an hour and a half."

"What happens to the heart during that time?" another student asked. "Doesn't it move at all?"

"If Dr. Dieter uses the bypass tonight, you'll see that Dr. McGill's heart will contract only slightly. With nothing much to do, it sort of lays down on the job."

146

"Gee!" said another student. "This is just like Ben Casey, isn't it?"

"Actually, the blood is cooled and the patient's temperature lowered at the same time," the intern explained. "Once they've cooled, the tissues don't need much oxygen so everything operates at a low tempo. The heart doesn't have to do much work and it's protected that way, along with the brain."

The students filling the front row had left a little space on either side of Marisa Feldman. Now a dark-haired and brashly handsome fellow in a white coat came in and pushed himself to the front, taking the space next to her and forcing her to slide over a little.

"My name's Traynor, Dr. Feldman," he said. "Mike Traynor. I saw that job you did down there in the dispensary with the tamponade. It was great! Just great!"

"Nothing so spectacular as that." Marisa had been in America long enough to recognize what the students called a "brown-nose" job.

"Is this the first operation you've seen Dr. Dieter do?"

"Yes. I was on a month's vacation before I arrived here yesterday."

"From Harvard?"

"I've been on a fellowship there for two years since finishing my clerkship in England." She gave it the English pronunciation, as if the word were spelled "clark" instead of "clerk."

"That's like an internship over here, isn't it? Or a residency?"

"Roughly, yes."

In the center of the operating theater below, an assistant had begun to paint the patient's abdomen with a brilliant-colored antiseptic solution. Almost at the same moment, a somewhat stocky figure in the usual green scrub suit, cap and mask appeared from the door leading to the scrub room.

"That's Dieter!" The intern who spoke uttered his name in much the same tone he might have used for a visiting king. "Now you'll really see something."

ii

The appearance of the surgeon galvanized both the observation gallery and the theater itself into a state of stepped-up tension. Those in the gallery leaned forward to watch, even though Dieter was only putting on his gown and gloves. Marisa found herself tensing with the rest, not even noticing that Mike Traynor's shoulder pressed against hers rather more than was justified by even the packed state of the gallery. A beautiful woman got used to that sort of thing, particularly when she lived in a world populated largely by men, as the medical one was.

On the floor below, Dieter had finished putting on his gown and gloves. He looked up to the glass-walled gallery and his eyes moved along the row of students and interns until they found Marisa's in the very center of the group. With the contact, she felt the impact of his personality across the space, even through the plate glass of the viewing window, just as she'd felt it downstairs in the emergency room something over an hour ago.

Being a realist, she didn't deny the attraction she had felt the first time she'd come in contact with Dieter. Yet at the same time, something deep inside her was strongly urged to resist that attraction, an inner antagonism triggered by the rough burr of his German accent, when he'd spoken to her downstairs.

That Anton Dieter would seek to enlarge upon their initial meeting, Marisa did not doubt, just as she knew from the feel of Mike Traynor's shoulder against her own that he would like nothing better than an invitation to her apartment. That, too, was part of the sixth sense any woman possessed, the instinctive knowledge that a man was interested in her, moved by the animal urge to sexual contact which was, after all, the vital force underlying all relationships between men and women, no matter what the circumstances of their meeting.

As to what she would do about Mike Traynor's bumptious aggressiveness and a distinctly unsubtle pass, when his hand slid off his own knee and touched her leg, she had no doubts. Romantic

148

relationships between faculty and students could never cause anything except trouble; and besides, for all his dark handsomeness and pure animal energy, she felt no attraction toward Mike Traynor.

Anton Dieter was another matter altogether, she admitted, as she watched him going purposefully about the business of preparing for an important surgical procedure. What had sprung into being between them downstairs was a complicated force of attraction and repulsion, a force that could go much deeper than any casual sexual encounter and indeed could probably not be kept at such a level, if she wished. Yet, as she watched the somewhat stocky figure that had taken over the center stage below, just as he'd taken it over in the emergency room earlier, she no more doubted that she would be faced with such a choice than that Anton Dieter would shortly perform another of the surgical miracles which had sent his reputation zooming upward like a rocket in flight.

What troubled her most was that the decision might be forced upon her before she was ready for it, either emotionally or—most important of all—physically.

At the latter thought, Marisa was gripped by the old fear, the horror she had hoped was shut behind her by the gates of Frondheim prison, but which, she knew, she must shortly battle once more. Moved by a sudden urge to flee, to postpone for a little while at least the start of the ultimate conflict, with its now familiar and traumatic ending, she half started to rise in her seat and leave the observation gallery. But just then, one of the circulating nurses on the operating-theater floor below plugged the microphone cord trailing from beneath Dieter's gown into a receptacle in the floor and his voice, booming out of the loud speakers at each end of the gallery, rooted her to her seat.

"Dr. Hagstrom, resident surgeon, is assisting me," Dieter announced. "Dr. Jeff Long, resident in anesthesiology, has charge of that most important part of our activities. The apparatus you see beside the operating table is a disk-oxygenator, commonly referred to in the lay press as a heart-lung pump. We hope we shall not have to use it but we must be ready in case we do."

"A Weston-Dieter Production," an intern in the back of the gallery intoned in a remarkably close imitation of the surgeon's voice. "Photographed in gorgeous Medicolor."

Marisa found herself relaxing as a wave of laughter swept through the gallery. Dieter's manner was a bit theatrical, it was true, but she knew that many great teachers deliberately dramatized in order to seize the attention of their students.

The first assistant had now finished painting the entire exposed portion of the patient's abdomen and groin with a reddish-brown antiseptic. As he finished one area the intern acting as second assistant painted on a second coat of the solution designed to kill the skin bacteria that were always present. The painting completed, both men stepped back and Helen Straughn approached the table with an aerosol spray can in her hand. Moving up and down in even strokes, she covered the whole exposed area of skin with a liberal coating of spray from the can.

"Miss Straughn is applying an adhesive compound," Dieter explained through the microphone resting against his chest beneath his gown. "In a moment, we will cover the entire field with a transparent plastic sheet, cutting down the number of draperies that will be needed and expediting our work."

Jeff Long had been busy while Dieter was speaking, skillfully inserting a laryngoscope into the patient's mouth and throat. A metal tube with a light at the end, the instrument enabled him to slide a rubber tube with a small balloon rubber cuff at the end directly down through the patient's larynx into the trachea, or windpipe. Removing the laryngoscope and leaving the tube in place, he quickly inflated the small cuff around the end of it—now located deep in the patient's trachea—to form an airtight seal. In this way air could only enter and leave the lungs through the intratracheal tube and pressure could be maintained inside the chest after it had been opened surgically.

Dieter now moved up to the table to take one side of a sheet of thin plastic from the sponge nurse. Carl Hagstrom took the other and they unrolled it, laying it upon the brilliantly painted skin of the wounded man and smoothing it over the abdomen and the groin where it was held in place by the adhesive Helen Straughn had sprayed upon it. Around the plastic-covered area, they now draped sterile towels and sheets, tinted a pale green like the scrub suits of the doctors and nurses, the draperies and gowns, in order to ease the strain upon the eyes from the bright lights of the operating room.

"This is a case of a bullet wound of the heart." Dieter looked up to the observation gallery once again. "X-ray shows the bullet still inside the heart; judging from the position of the wound of entry it would appear to be in the right ventricle." Here he pointed to a reddish spot on Paul McGill's chest, a little to the right of the midline and almost on a line with the nipple of his right breast.

On the wall of the operating room across from the observation gallery, a window of frosted glass was illuminated when Helen Straughn tripped a small switch. Drawn there in bold strokes with a black wax pencil were the outlines of a human heart with the various chambers clearly marked. Beside it, another ground-glass window containing the X-rays also glowed, the white image of the bullet clearly distinguishable within the somewhat dimmer shadow of the heart and the much lighter pattern of the lungs surrounding it.

"As best we are able to re-create the path of the bullet, it came somewhat from the right," Anton Dieter continued. "Such a path would take it into the right side of the heart but the fact that it passed through another body first and therefore may have been deflected makes it possible that the bullet could have entered from almost any angle."

"Two with one shot," said a student admiringly. "Where I come from that's some shooting."

A burst of laughter, unheard below, rocketed through the observation gallery, but subsided when Dieter continued: "We hope the use of the disk-oxygenator will not be necessary, but we will first expose the femoral artery so it may be opened and cannulated, allowing it to be connected to the oxygenator and afford a return of arterial blood to the body, should we have to resort to its use."

He was working as he talked, his hands moving swiftly like— Marisa Feldman thought—those of a master pianist. The operating team, too, functioned smoothly as a small incision was made in the right groin and hemostatic clamps caught small bleeding vessels which were quickly tied off. It was much easier to see what was going on than would have been the case if the incision had been surrounded by towels, as in older operative techniques. Besides, the plastic sheet glued to the skin not only removed the possibility of contamination of the wound itself from bacteria on the surface but materially increased visibility of the operative area, both for the surgeons and for the observers.

From where she sat, Marisa Feldman could watch Dieter's hands probing swiftly with a curved pair of blunt-ended scissors in the depths of the small groin wound. After a few moments, he put down the scissors and picked up a curved forcep which he slid under the femoral artery, a whitish-looking tube perhaps the size of one's little finger, visible now as it pulsated in the depths of the wound. An assistant slipped the end of a piece of cotton tape between the jaws of the clamp and Dieter closed them shut, pulling the tape beneath the artery and isolating it where it could be reached quickly. A few more quick strokes exposed a vein, thin-walled and blue, nearby. This, too, he isolated with a piece of tape and, leaving the intern who was handling instruments to cover the groin wound with a moist cotton pad, Dieter and Carl Hagstrom moved up to the chest.

"We will expose the heart through a median sternotomy incision by splitting the breastbone," the surgeon explained into the microphone, using the lay term for the flat, thin bone forming the front of the chest cage in deference to the presence of first-year students in the gallery, who had not yet begun the study of anatomy. "This incision gives free access to the heart itself and allows us to investigate both the right and left sides."

Dieter's hands were moving as he spoke, laying open with the scalpel that seemed an extension of his living flesh the skin in the midline directly over the sternum. The knife went down to the bone in one swift stroke and for a moment the wound itself was hidden as Dieter and the assistants moved swiftly, clamping off bleeding vessels and tying them with fine catgut ligatures drawn from metal spools. The upper end of the incision had halted some two or three inches short of the hollow of the neck; now he extended it both to the right and the left for several inches, giving the appearance of a Y.

"The major drawback to a median sternotomy incision is that thick scars called keloids tend to form when it heals," Dieter explained as he worked. "For this reason, we form a Y at the upper end so the scar will not show above the collar."

He moved now to the lower end of the sternum and extended the incision a short distance downward through the outer layers of the abdominal wall there. "The entire sternum must be exposed, too, else we should not be able to split it widely and thus gain the exposure we need."

"That Dieter's an artist," Mike Traynor said but Marisa Feldman hardly heard him, so engrossed was she in the rhythmic movements of the surgeon that were like a stylized ballet. For a moment she was even able to forget that the chief player in the drama was a German, from the race that had destroyed her parents and forced her to undergo the ultimate degradation.

Dieter was now splitting the outer covering of the sternum, the periosteum, with a single scalpel stroke down its center. Picking up a chisel-like instrument bent at a right angle near its lower end—known as a periosteal elevator—he began to scrape the periosteum back from the midline on either side, exposing the bare bone for the entire length of the sternum.

"Oscillating saw, please." The intern handling instruments gave him a heavy object covered with a sterile sleeve. At its end, a metal spindle projected through an opening closed with a drawstring at the end of the sleeve. Bolted to the spindle projecting from the body of the motor hidden by the protecting sterile cover was an oddly shaped sawblade, the toothed edge being an arc of about an eighth of a circle, like a wedge cut out of a completely circular saw.

"We shall use the oscillating saw to cut almost all the way through the sternum." Dieter stepped upon a switch placed close to his right foot beside the operating table and the cutting section of the saw began to vibrate with a high-pitched whine. When he lowered it to touch the sternum, a fine spray of bone dust was sent in either direction as the saw bit into the bone. On the other side of the table, Carl Hagstrom was directing a steady stream of sterile water from a syringe upon the blade to keep it cool.

As cleanly as if it were cutting a board, the saw cut into the breastbone for its entire length. Handing it to a waiting nurse, Dieter next accepted an oddly shaped tool which the instrument nurse was holding ready for him. It had a small blunt foot with a blade just above it about two inches long but sharp on only one side. Just above the blade the shank of the instrument was thick for a short distance, thinning out again for perhaps a foot to end with a cross-handle upon the top.

"It is possible to cut completely through the sternum with the oscillating saw—at the risk of sawing into the heart," the surgeon told the observers. "In order to be absolutely safe we will cut the inner part of the sternum with the Lebsche knife."

With the words, he slid the foot of the knife over the top end of the sternum, setting the cutting edge firmly into the slot cut by the saw. Carl Hagstrom picked up a metal mallet and at Dieter's nod began to tap upon the thickened portion of the knife just above the cutting edge, moving the blade down along the course already charted by the saw to split the sternum neatly for its entire length.

Behind the blade of the Lebsche knife, the intern and the sponge nurse worked rapidly, smearing the cut edges of the bone with wax to close off the spongy marrow forming its middle and stop the ooze of blood from it. When Dieter removed the instrument from the incision at its lower end, he, and the assistant also, took wax and worked upward until the entire exposed surface of the marrow was closed off and all bleeding stopped.

Using two retractors, rake-like instruments with handles about a foot long, the intern now held the cut edges of the sternum separate so Dieter could examine the posterior, or inner, layer of periosteum covering the back of the sternum, searching for bleeding vessels which might interfere later with the operation.

The heart itself was already visible within its pericardial sac through the opening in the bone, beating steadily and strongly.

Using a gauze sponge held between the jaws of a forcep, Dieter gently pushed away the tissues beneath the upper end of the now divided sternum, exposing a tough fibrous band extending across the space thus opened. When he slipped a curved forcep underneath the band and cut it through, the split in the breastbone widened suddenly.

"I have just cut the interclavicular ligament," he explained. Using his gloved finger, he was pushing the pericardium away from the underside of the sternum as he spoke, moving down on either side until it was well separated away.

"Rib spreader, please."

An instrument with heavy blunt prongs was now inserted between the cut surfaces of the bone. A ratchet drive on the instrument enabled the jaws to be separated. And, as the space between the cut halves of the sternum widened appreciably, the heart in its enveloping pericardial membrane was more fully exposed. A blood-tinged fluid could be seen within the pericardium and a small amount of it leaked out into the space through the opening made by the bullet.

"Another advantage of the median sternotomy incision," Dieter said, as he finished twisting the ratcheted screw of the rib spreader, "is that in most cases the plural cavities surrounding the lungs need not be opened. However, should we open either cavity intentionally or inadvertently, no lung collapse would result because Dr. Long has prudently put in an intratracheal tube and the patient is now receiving positive pressure anesthesia."

From the instrument table, he picked up a slender pair of

thumb forceps, toothed at the end. With them, he was able to tent up a section of the pericardium and, when the resident caught it on his side with a forcep, nick the membrane with a knife. Placing a small clamp on each side of the marrow opening, so the whole thing could be lifted well away from the heart, Dieter slit the pericardium widely, exposing the heart muscle beneath it.

"You will note, Dr. Feldman, that there has been no further leak from the ventricle wall since you released the heart from strangulation by tamponade." Dieter looked up to meet her eyes through the glass wall of the observation gallery and, realizing that the all-male audience in the observation gallery had transferred its attention from the operation to her, Marisa blushed. "Heart wounds often close themselves, once enough blood is accumulated in the pericardial cavity to decrease the movement of the heart markedly. The danger is that the accumulation will throttle the heart and kill the patient. Only Dr. Feldman's prompt action prevented this from happening to Dr. McGill.

"Here is the wound of entry." His eyes on the operative field once more, Dieter indicated a dark spot on the heart surface where a small amount of hemorrhage into the muscle had occurred. "Presumably the bullet is in the right ventricle but we cannot be sure with the wound of entry where it is; the bullet could have gone through the septum between the ventricles and now be located on the left side. Before we make any attempt to find out where it is, therefore, we must expose the pulmonary artery so we can block it and prevent the bullet from escaping into the lung circulation where—as Dr. Feldman pointed out in the X-ray room—it could cause a fatal embolism by blocking the blood supply to a large portion of the lung."

Using a slender thumb forcep and a curved pair of dissecting scissors, the surgeon began to separate the tissues at the upper part of the heart between the pulmonary artery supplying the lungs and the aorta, the giant channel that carried blood to the rest of the body. A hush fell over the observation gallery as he worked, for even the greenest student there knew a false step could lead to a hemorrhage which might be uncontrollable. Dieter, however, acted as if he had no knowledge of the dreadful consequences of even a slight misstep, working as calmly as if he were separating a toenail from its bed.

"That guy must have ice water in his veins," one of the students in the gallery said in awed tones.

"Brennan's just as good when it comes to the brain," said an intern.

"Or McCloskey in the bladder," another agreed. "This place is lousy with good surgeons—internists, too."

Dieter was working a curved forcep behind the pulmonary artery. When it appeared on the other side, he seized the end of a piece of tape between the metal jaws and drew it back through, clamping the two ends together and lifting the artery up so the students could see where it took its origin from the right ventricle.

"Since we can now prevent the bullet from being accidentally dislodged into the lung circulation, we are ready to explore," Dieter announced. "Purse-string suture, please."

Just to the right of the visible portion of the ventricle could be seen the thin-walled upper chamber for that side of the heart, called the atrium, with the giant veins, the superior and inferior vena cavae, bringing blood to it from the entire body, except the lungs. On the thin wall of the atrium, Dieter began to sew a circular pattern, roughly an inch and a half in diameter, thrusting the needle completely through the wall of the chamber with each stitch.

"The purse-string I am placing can serve two purposes," he explained to the gallery. "First it will enable me to insert a finger into the right side of the heart and determine whether or not the bullet is there."

Putting down the needle and its holder, with which he had been placing the suture pattern, Dieter pointed toward the diagram on the ground-glass view box against the wall.

"On the other hand, if the bullet went through to the left side, we shall have to put the patient on the oxygenator, allowing us to open the heart widely, remove it and repair the wound where it penetrated the septum between the ventricles so as to prevent an abnormal communication from forming there later on. Fortunately, if we have to use the cardiopulmonary bypass, we will be able to insert plastic tubes directly into both the inferior and superior vena cavae through this purse-string area and thus provide a route by which blood from the entire body will pass through to the oxygenator."

The purse-string suture was now in place, ready to be drawn together in much the same way an old-fashioned tobacco or powder pouch was drawn shut, to close the opening he would make in the center of the circle encompassed by its stitches. Carl Hagstrom held up the two ends of the suture, lifting the wall of the atrium as Dieter picked up a sharp pointed knife with his left hand, holding his right index finger ready.

With a swift movement, he stabbed the blade into the center of the circular pattern he had sewn in the wall of the atrium. Blood spurted out as the knife blade entered the heart, but an instant later his finger had plunged into the opening. As Carl Hagstrom tightened the purse-string, the wall of the atrium was drawn snugly about the surgeon's finger, shutting off the flow of blood around it.

"I am able to feel the inside of the atrium and the tricuspid valve between it and the ventricle." Dieter described his findings as he moved his exploring finger about within the heart itself. "The valve does not seem to be damaged."

As he pushed deeper into the heart, the thin wall of the atrium, held snugly around his finger with the purse-string, was carried along with it, much as one might push in the side of a paper bag.

"Now my finger is in the ventricle touching the bullet," he said, and the air in the operating-theater room was suddenly filled with a tension that could be felt even in the gallery.

"The bullet is loose in the ventricle as we suspected. Tighten the tape around the pulmonary artery please, Dr. Hagstrom."

The resident lifted the ends of the tape beneath the vessel and crossed them so as to prevent any flow of blood through it. "It's tight, sir," he reported.

"We can block the circulation to the lungs for only a few seconds without severe danger," Dieter said, and Marisa Feldman found herself leaning forward, waiting tensely, her heart pulsing in her throat. "I hope to work the bullet back through the wound of entry."

"Christ A'mighty!" one of the students said hoarsely. "My heart won't stand much more of this."

"I have the bullet against the wall of the ventricle now." With the fingers of his left hand, Dieter supported the spot on the outside where it had gone through into the heart, separating his fingers so as to leave the wound itself free. "The nose of the bullet is entering the wound from inside the ventricle and I am now pushing it through the wall."

Another "Aah" went up from the gallery when a glint of metal appeared suddenly on the surface of the heart, growing larger as Dieter's finger pushed it through from the inside. Gingerly, Carl Hagstrom seized the steel-jacketed bullet with a forcep whose jaws contained a number of delicate teeth interlocking together. When he drew the projectile out, a spurt of blood gushed up from the reopened wound, but stopped at once when Dieter plugged it with his left index finger.

"Release the pulmonary artery, please, Dr. Hagstrom." Even in the gallery, the onlookers could sense the exultation in the German surgeon's voice over a truly remarkable surgical maneuver. "Then please to place some sutures in the ventricle around my finger in order to close the wound of entry."

The sutures were quickly placed, biting into the muscular wall of the heart on either side of the tiny opening through which the bullet had both entered and been withdrawn. When Carl Hagstrom drew the strands snug, Dieter removed his finger. Only a faint drop of blood appeared between the two sutures.

"One more should do it," he said, and separated the long ends of the two sutures which had already been put in place so Hagstrom could place another between them. With three sutures tied, no blood oozed from the ventricle.

"We were very fortunate," Dieter said to the gallery. "Since it was not necessary to open the heart, except to explore it through the soft wall of the atrium, it will not be necessary to place the patient upon the disk-oxygenator after all. If you will hold the purse-string please, Dr. Hagstrom, I shall remove my finger from the atrium."

Only a small gush of blood occurred before Carl Hagstrom could draw the purse-string tight, after Dieter withdrew his right index finger from within the heart. With that suture tied and several others reinforcing it, the small wound in the atrium was also closed.

"What is his condition, Dr. Long?" Dieter asked.

"Fine, Doctor. Pressure one hundred ten over seventy. Pulse one hundred."

"No sign of shock?"

"None."

"Good. We will not transfuse; no need to expose him to the hepatitis virus. And since the wound is dry, it should not be necessary to drain."

The closure went rapidly. Marisa Feldman left the gallery as the wires designed to pull the two halves of the sternum back together and hold them in place were being put in by means of a stout awl pushed through the outer layer of the flat bone. A glance at the clock on the wall at the back of the gallery told her the operation had taken an hour and a half, but caught up in the tense scene, it had hardly seemed half that long.

It was hard to believe now that only a little over two hours ago, she had looked down at the still form on the ambulance stretcher and heard the attendant dismiss Dr. Paul McGill as a D.O.A.

CHAPTER XI

It was almost six o'clock before Alice Weston began to recover from the bout of gripping agony that had seized her when Jake Porter had called her, looking for Roy. There was an extension phone in the bathroom, so she had managed to call George Hanscombe's office at the clinic. By then it was closed, but the staff doctor on night duty was familiar with her condition and ordered a refill of the prescription she took from time to time when she was having colon trouble, delivered to the house from a nearby pharmacy. Since her last checkup had been more than a year before, he also suggested that she come to the clinic early the next morning.

When the medicine came—a green solution with what looked like ground-up leaves in the bottom—Alice took a double dose. By the time the pain began to subside, she had listened to the six o'clock local TV broadcast—breaking her rule never to listen to the news—and knew that Paul McGill had been shot by Mort Dellman. Shortly afterward, Roy's office called to say he would be tied up with business connected with the arrest of Dr. Dellman and wouldn't be home for dinner.

Alice had already prepared Roy's martini and her own before he called. She drank hers and ate a bowl of soup she warmed up on the stove, fumbling with the controls, for it was the first time in months she had touched the stove. On Wednesdays, when the maid was off, she and Roy usually went to the club for dinner after the ritual martinis.

In her disturbed emotional condition, Alice had forgotten to dilute her own drink. When the hot soup stirred up the circulation in her upper digestive tract, the alcohol was quickly absorbed, filling her with a warm glow she hadn't dared to let herself feel for a long time—not since she was a senior in high school and Lorrie had come home from college that first Christmas.

Jake Porter had been away on business the night Lorrie arrived. When Lorrie dared Alice, they started drinking before dinner and took the bottle upstairs when they went to bed. Lorrie had talked Alice into taking a last drink at bedtime and, by the time she'd finished undressing, the younger girl was half drunk.

When Lorrie came into her room from the connecting bath they shared, rubbing her hair dry with a towel after her shower, Alice was already in her somewhat prim muslin gown. Brushing her hair at the dressing table, she hadn't been able to turn her eyes from the reflection of Lorrie's nude body in the mirror as the other girl crossed the room to sit on the bed.

"You ever been with a boy, Al?" Lorrie had asked.

Alice shook her head, blushing, her eyes still on Lorrie's golden body. "H-how did you get the tan all over?"

"I use a sunlamp in winter."

"N-naked?"

"Sure. Why not?" Lorrie's eyes had a bright gleam in them that made Alice feel all funny inside. "Stand up, Al."

When Alice obeyed, Lorrie stooped and, taking the hem of the muslin gown, lifted it over the younger girl's head, leaving her standing naked on the rug beside the bed, her skin all pink and white, in the reflection of herself in the mirror, where Lorrie was brown—and blonde where Lorrie was dark.

"You've grown up, Al." Lorrie's voice had taken on a new note, a tension that hadn't been there before. "You've filled out here." She touched the already full breasts. "And here."

Alice had felt a hot flush all over when Lorrie's hand rested casually on her waist, just above the swell of her hips, then moved down across her smooth round belly. She knew she should turn away, but she had no strength—or desire—to do so.

With one swift movement, Lorrie had crossed the room then, turned the key in the lock, and reached up to flip the light switch beside it, leaving only the light over the dressing table burning. She was back in an instant and, with one sweep of her hand, pulled down the sheet on the bed.

"Want another drink, Al?" she asked.

Alice shook her head; already the room was going around in a dizzy circle, like one of those swings at the county fair.

"What are we waiting for then?"

Alice had gone to sleep in Lorrie's arms afterward, warm and surfeited with love. When she'd awakened in the middle of the night to feel Lorrie's hand caressing her warm flesh, the now familiar excitement had risen again, demanding the satisfaction Lorrie was so expert in giving—and receiving at Alice's own grateful, loving hands.

That Christmas had been the happiest in Alice's memory—until Lorrie went back to Sweet Briar. The following summer, Lorrie had gone to Europe and, when she'd come home at Christmas a year later, she'd had a crush on a French count who had followed her to the States. She'd had no time for Alice, and right after that, Alice had started going with Roy, who'd cut a dashing figure in his uniform of an officer in the R.O.T.C. at college.

Seized with a desperate loneliness now, Alice stumbled to the phone and dialed a number. "Corinne?" she asked when a woman's voice answered in a deep contralto.

"Yes, dear." Corinne Marchant often sat with the children during the school year, whenever Alice and Roy were going out. She also stayed with Alice during Roy's increasingly frequent absences on political matters.

"Roy's tied up at the office and I've had a colon attack, Corinne," said Alice. "I've taken some medicine for it, but could you possibly come by and stay with me until I get to sleep."

"Of course, dear. You say he'll be late?"

"His secretary phoned to say he wouldn't be home until midnight or maybe afterward. Something about that Mort Dellman business. I'll leave the door on the latch, Corinne."

"I'll be there in ten minutes."

As Alice was putting the butter dish she'd used for her crackers back in the refrigerator, she noticed Roy's martini on the shelf. Picking it up she drank it down before she could have a second thought. Then, leaving the door on the latch, as she'd promised Corinne, she went upstairs to put on her filmiest nightgown, the martini already heightening the feeling of anticipation stirring within her.

ii

"You've been drinking too much again, Grace," were George Hanscombe's first words when he came into the living room after his ritual evening visit to the bathroom following dinner. Located on a lane leading off Sherwood Ravine, the lot was spacious and the house comfortable and large, like all houses in this area.

Crossing to the family room, where a small bar occupied one corner, he poured a generous measure of Scotch, his favorite drink, splashed soda into it and stirred it with a glass rod. He had formed the habit of taking his drinks without ice while in England, one of the few English customs of which he approved.

"Why shouldn't I drink? You do." Grace was tired and cross. Coping with Maggie McCloskey at the club and bringing her to the hospital, plus the worry about whether or not George had been shot, was more than any woman should have to put up with in a single afternoon.

"Now Grace, you know you have diabetes." George's calm tone infuriated her even more than the words, which she'd heard him speak in exactly that same reproving tone a thousand times. She didn't have a severe case; in fact she hadn't shown sugar now for at least a year.

"Does that mean I have to be a zombie?" she demanded angrily. "I might as well be dead."

"Now Grace." Still the same tolerant note. "You have a lovely home here, with the club and your service work to keep you busy."

Twice weekly, she put on a slate blue uniform and cap to push a cart containing magazines, candy and immediate necessities like writing paper, envelopes and ball-point pens from ward to ward, selling them to patients. It was part of the activities of the Hospitality Shop located on the first floor of the hospital. The proceeds went toward scholarships for student nurses at the university.

"I'd rather be a barmaid again," she flared, knowing she could always strike a nerve that way. Whenever she got high enough to mention it in public, George always corrected her by saying she had been hostess in a restaurant, which was actually a bit closer to the truth. What she'd really done was entertain guests in a very high-class London pub, helping out when the regular bar girls were too busy to serve everybody quickly.

"You were never a barmaid, Grace," George said—just as she'd known he would. Picking up a magazine, he crossed to the lounge chair before the TV. Fifteen minutes after the first program began, he would be asleep snoring softly, with his mouth open.

"Would you be ashamed of me if I had been one?" Grace demanded.

"I don't know." He opened the magazine. "I've never considered the idea."

"You weren't ashamed before we were married," she snapped. "I remember how anxious you were to get me in the hay—"

George went on reading his magazine as if he hadn't heard.

"Tell me the truth, George. Were you ever with Lorrie Dellman?"

He looked up. "Did you say something, dear?"

"I asked whether you ever slept with Lorrie Dellman."

"Of course not. Whatever gave you that idea?"

"All your friends did. Why not you, George?"

"Don't speak disrespectfully of the dead, Grace," he said severely.

"I'm not disrespectful; I even admire Lorrie. After all she did what she wanted to—whenever she wanted to do it."

He shrugged and went on reading without answering.

"You're about the same age as Paul McGill, but he's a better man than you are, George," said Grace.

"Why do you say that?"

"Paul made it on a Wednesday. You're no good except Saturday night—and not much then."

"Don't be vulgar, Grace. What the hell's gotten into you?"

She had reached him at last, she thought with a vast satisfaction. Men didn't relish being told they were less anything than others, particularly when it came to sex.

"I'm tired of the same thing day after day and night after night, that's what." The words broke through at last and surged up in an uncontrollable flood. "I'm tired of being only a mild diabetic; why can't I have the real thing or nothing? I'm tired of sitting home nights waiting for you to come home from medical meetings. And still sitting home nights when you're here, not even getting a word through to you because you're snoring in front of that damn TV set. I'm tired of playing golf and bridge at the club, tired of the same old faces, the same old affairs."

He'd gone back to the magazine, so she let him have a shot amidships.

"Why couldn't it have been you with Lorrie this afternoon, George?" she demanded.

"What?"

"Was it because it's Wednesday instead of Saturday? Do your testicles only function for an hour every Saturday night?"

"For God's sake, Grace. What's gotten into you?"

"You and I are getting old, George. Life is passing us by. What happened to all those promises you made in England? The ones you used to get me into bed with you."

"As I remember it, you didn't need much persuasion," he snapped.

"We don't have much time left, George." She was half crying now. "Why can't we spend some of our money, go on a cruise, take a trip to Eng—?"

"Now Grace. We've been into that."

"To Rio then? The International Congress of Cardiology is

meeting there next month. A travel agent sent us a folder on it."

"You know I have responsibilities, Grace—and classes."

"The others go to a lot of medical meetings. You've got some men on your staff who could teach your classes. They'd be glad to get the chance."

"That's out of the question," he said shortly.

"That's why you never take a vacation, isn't it—except to play golf and bridge in the summertime at some place like Deerslayer Lodge when classes aren't on? You're afraid one of those bright young men will turn out to be a better doctor than you, George. Everybody in the hospital knows you don't give them a fair shake."

"Grace," he said stiffly. "I refuse to listen to such drivel."

"You've got to listen, George. We're married for better or for worse—and God knows it couldn't get much worse." She had really begun to cry now. But when, not knowing what to do, he tried patting her on the shoulder, she threw his hand off.

"Why don't you talk to Dave Rogan, dear?" he suggested, but when her shoulders stiffened, added hastily, "or Jack Hagen. After all, the meno—"

"Women don't have the menopause any more. You're a hell of a doctor if you don't know that. Gynecologists give them hormones and they grow old gracefully—no hot flashes, no thin bones, nothing. It's the Fountain of Youth, George. Women can stay young forever. Only men get old."

"Now you're talking foolishness again."

"I read about it in a column by a doctor. He says there's no male menopause either, that it's all in your mind. So why can't you make it Wednesday, like Paul McGill did? Oh God, how I envy Elaine." She jumped from the sofa and ran to the stairs leading up to the bedrooms. "Good night— No, damn it! There's nothing good about it."

She was asleep when he came up, exactly at ten as always. Nor did she waken when he got in on the other side of the double bed.

iii

Pete and Amy Brennan were lying in bed smoking and watching TV about eight thirty, when the telephone rang.

"Don't answer," Amy said quickly. "I—I'm still in the mood."

"How can I make it a second time with that damn thing ringing?"

"Take it off the hook."

"And have the operator hear us panting. She'd figure it was an emergency and send the cops."

"Answer it then—but don't go 'way."

He picked up the phone and put the receiver to his ear. "Dr. Brennan."

"Pete!" It was Roy Weston.

"What is it, Roy?"

"You'd better come down here to the jail. Mort Dellman wants you—and so do I."

"What good can I do Mort? He needs a lawyer."

"Mort doesn't want a lawyer—at least not right now. He insists on talking to you."

"Can't it wait 'til morning?"

"If you don't get down here and quiet Mort down, he's going to spill his guts to the newspapers. You know what that will do to the clinic—and half the men in town."

"All right," said Pete resignedly. "I'll see what I can do to cool him down."

"Hurry, Pete. I can't keep the lid on this thing much longer."

Pete looked across the bed at Amy, naked as an houri under the pale blue sheet. What a time to have to be thinking about a louse like Mort when, after ten years of perfunctory love-making, your wife suddenly sheds all her inhibitions.

"All right, Roy," he said into the phone. "I'll be there right away."

"What's wrong with Roy?" Amy asked as he hung up.

"Mort Dellman wants to see me. Roy says I'd better come or

168

Mort's going to blow the whole story of Lorrie's affairs—starting with Roy himself, I gather—to the newspapers."

"But that was a long time ago."

"It could still ruin Roy's chances in the election. Abner Townsend is always lecturing on morality. Think what he could make of this in the campaign, when Roy runs against him."

"I don't want to think about Mort, or Roy, or Lorrie right now. I want to think about us." Amy's voice was slurred a little from the morphine but Pete was too disturbed by what Mort Dellman could do to the clinic to notice.

"Take a nap while I'm gone, darling." He kissed her, then slid out of the bed and began to dress. "It will help you gain strength —for when I get back."

"You're the one who'll need the strength, lover." Amy giggled. "Better put the chicken in the refrigerator as you go through the kitchen. We can have it for breakfast."

iv

From where she was sitting in the small waiting room just off the Special Intensive Care Unit, Elaine McGill saw the stretcher move past. Jeff Long walked at the head of it and smiled encouragingly at her but Paul was surrounded with so much apparatus—the tubing and bottles of two intravenous sets being carried by the operating-room nurses who had come with the stretcher, the connections for the electrocardiograph, the blankets covering his body—that she couldn't see his face at all. It was almost as frightening as the waiting had been, but she didn't try to go to his room, knowing everyone was much too busy there to be bothered with her. A few minutes later, Anton Dieter stopped at the door of the waiting room.

"I'm Dr. Dieter, Mrs. McGill," he said. "We met last year during a reception at Dr. Hanscombe's."

"I remember. It was shortly after you came to Weston."

"Your husband is fine. We were able to remove the bullet fairly easily." From his pocket he took the shiny, steel-jacketed missile and held it in his palm for her to see. "Of course, the authorities will want it."

"I certainly don't." Elaine shivered. "How soon will Paul be awake?"

"That depends on several things. Your husband was clinically dead for a period of time, Mrs. McGill—without respiration or a perceptible pulse. We don't know how long that period was, but there is no doubt that the brain cells were without oxygen for a while."

"Then he could still—?" She stopped as a case she'd read about came into her mind, a patient whose heart had ceased to beat, during an operation. Though finally revived, he had never regained consciousness and had lived on for years in a state of stupor. "Then he could still have trouble?"

"After Dr. Feldman recognized the condition and instituted emergency treatment, your husband came back remarkably quickly, so there is every reason to believe he may recover completely," Dieter assured her.

"But you can't be sure?"

"I'm afraid not."

When Dieter left, Elaine groped her way to a chair in the small waiting room. Until now, everything had centered about the dramatic operation and she hadn't even thought of the possibility that the greatest damage might have been done before the surgery was even started, damage which might well be irreparable, in spite of all the medical facilities of a great hospital which had been marshaled to save Paul's life. No one could tell just how long it would be before they knew whether his brain was damaged because they had no way of knowing themselves, until he either regained consciousness or continued in a state of stupor.

Until then, she could only wait—and pray.

She was still sitting in the small waiting room when Jeff Long came out of Paul's room. From her chair, she could see the closed-TV picture of the room on one of the monitor tubes, and beneath it, the flashing line marking the picture of Paul's heart action as recorded by the electrocardiograph. Janet Monroe had

explained to her how the system worked and that it was better for
her not to remain in Paul's room, where the nurses and interns
would be busy watching his postoperative condition, but that
she could see him anytime she wished by glancing at the monitor
tube.

Jeff Long had been introduced to her as the anesthesiologist.
He paused briefly at the nursing station, then came over and sat
down beside Elaine.

"Jan—Mrs. Monroe—tells me you're worried about Dr. McGill,"
he said. "You needn't be; he's doing fine, though he may not become conscious for several hours."

"Dr. Dieter says you won't know until then whether—whether
he'll have all of his faculties."

"Why not cross that bridge when we get to it—if we have to?"
he said cheerfully. "The important thing now is that he's come
through the operation safely."

"Why are they giving him oxygen and doing all those other
things, if Dr. Dieter successfully removed the bullet?"

"They're only protective measures," he explained. "The bullet
went into the right side of the heart—perhaps you could understand better if I made a diagram."

"I'm sure I could."

He went to the chart desk and returned with a blank sheet of
paper and one of the metal chart clipboards. With swift strokes,
he drew a rough diagram of the heart, the four chambers separated by the central partition called the septum.

"Fortunately the bullet didn't hit anything solid in its course,
like a rib or even a metal button," he explained. "Otherwise it
might have mushroomed and made a much worse wound than it
did. Actually the hole where the bullet entered the heart was
very small and only a few sutures were required to close it."

"Wasn't that hard to do?"

Jeff Long smiled. "Not for Dr. Dieter. He operates on hearts
like most surgeons do on the appendix, but we still leave as little
as we can to chance. We're injecting heparin into Dr. McGill's
bloodstream to keep clots from forming where the wound in the

muscle was closed. And we're also watching to make sure the communication system in the heart isn't interrupted by swelling or hemorrhage."

"I'm afraid I don't understand."

On the diagram he'd made of the heart chambers, Jeff Long outlined with a pencil what looked like the branches of a tree, spreading out through the muscle of the four heart chambers. A central trunk ran through the septum, of which he had spoken, separating the right side from the left.

"These might be called the telephone circuits of the heart," he explained, pointing to the treelike pattern he had drawn in. "Each beat originates in a center located up here in the right auricle—the small upper chamber. It spreads through these branches I've drawn and causes both auricles to contract, filling the ventricles with blood during the first half of the heartbeat. At the same time, the electrical impulse of the heartbeat has been traveling along this trunk of tissue I've drawn through the septum"—here he indicated the single trunk—"before spreading out through the ventricles and causing them to beat."

"It's all pretty complicated, isn't it?"

"The first time you see it, yes. Actually it's really no more complicated than your telephone—maybe not as much." He turned back to the drawing. "Because the main channel for the nerve impulse of the heartbeat to the ventricles passes through the septum, it's a pretty vulnerable area and swelling or hemorrhage in such a narrow space can press on the nervous tissue carrying the impulse and shut off the message."

"Causing death?" she asked quickly.

"Possibly—if we aren't prepared for it. Usually the ventricles immediately take up a separate rhythm of their own, though one that's slower than the impulses sent out from the auricles for the normal heartbeat. But in case they don't start doing their own work immediately, everyone who works in the Intensive Unit knows how to operate the Pacemaker."

"Pacemaker?" she frowned.

"It's a device to stimulate the heart from outside by passing a small electric current through the muscle. Dr. Dieter used it in the emergency room when your husband was brought in—"

"I thought the woman doctor took care of him there."

"Dr. Feldman no doubt saved your husband's life by withdrawing blood from the space around his heart. Dr. Dieter arrived shortly afterward and got the heart started functioning again with the Pacemaker."

"Is this liable to happen—this swelling you spoke of?"

"We think not. Certainly there's no sign of it now and, as I said, we take no chances. The oxygen he's getting will take a load off his heart, the heparin will prevent clotting, and we're ready in case there's a block."

"I guess you anticipate everything."

"Most everything. Dr. McGill is in excellent condition now and there's no reason why you should stay here—though you're free to if you wish."

"You'd rather I didn't, wouldn't you?" Elaine hadn't missed the brief pause or its significance.

"That depends on how you feel about what happened this afternoon."

"What do you mean?"

"My concern is for your husband, Mrs. McGill; he's my responsibility until he recovers completely from the effects of the anesthetic. So far everything is going well, but the balance in cases like this can be weighted easily against the patient by something so apparently trivial as an emotional disturbance."

"Are you worried about my making a scene?"

"I want to be sure you don't—at least not until there's no likelihood of its crippling his heart."

"All I want is for my husband to be well again, Dr. Long. I'd like to be here to tell him so when he regains consciousness."

"Then we both have the same goal." Jeff Long smiled. "There's a couch in the small room at the end of the corridor; the intern on duty sleeps there when we have a critical case. Why don't you lie down and get some rest?"

"Could I ask you one more question?"

"Of course."

"I've heard that the students call my husband Old Dermatographia. Could you tell me why?"

"It's a term of affection. Dr. McGill is an unusually perceptive and wise physician. He teaches us that the skin reflects the whole state of the body, including the emotional balance. If I hadn't wanted more than anything else to become an anesthesiologist, I'm sure I would have applied for a residency on his service."

"Thank you, Dr. Long. I guess that's about the highest compliment you could pay him, isn't it?"

"It certainly is. Now you'd better get some rest so you'll be ready to see him when he becomes conscious."

"I don't think I could sleep. Not after so much has happened."

"I can take care of that, too," he assured her. "Mrs. Monroe will give you a Nembutal."

"If you're sure it will be all right."

"It's just what this doctor ordered," he said cheerfully. "Leave everything to us. We're professionals at this business, you know."

If she only could really leave it to them, Elaine thought as she lay on the narrow cot in the small room, waiting for the yellow capsule to take effect. Until this afternoon, she had left almost every major decision up to Paul, as he preferred. But now she had not only to think of her own life, and his, but also the child who was still only the single cell formed less than five hours ago within her body.

Briefly she wondered whether she should tell Paul about that afternoon, but put the thought away at once. Paul was a proud man and nothing could break a man's pride more quickly or more effectively than the knowledge that his wife had been unfaithful to him. She felt no actual guilt herself; what she'd done had been merely part of her own biological need to bear a child without which no woman was really fulfilled. But she knew she couldn't expect Paul to see it that way.

Nor did the fact that Paul had been caught *flagrante delicto* with Lorrie Dellman and the scandal his action would make for them both really make any difference. Man, though monogamous

by custom and even by law, was not really a monogamous creature and nature had obviously not intended for him to be—else
why were there more females in the human species than males.

Knowing Lorrie, and remembering the bet she had tried to
make with them all that afternoon at Amy's, Elaine was not at
all certain that Paul had even been the aggressor this afternoon.
To Lorrie, he'd no doubt represented a conquest she'd never been
able to make before; Elaine herself had seen to that by keeping
him away from the others at medical conventions and avoiding
the pattern of heavy drinking that characterized so many in their
own circle. Somehow, she was certain, Lorrie had managed to
inveigle Paul into coming to her house that afternoon and from
that point on he'd been a sitting duck.

It was too bad that Mort had chosen that particular time to
go hunting.

CHAPTER XII

The Weston County jail was the most modern in the state, occupying the top floor of the new courthouse. Pete Brennan was taken up in a special elevator by an armed guard.

"Mr. Weston's down the hall in the interrogation—I mean the conference room," the officer said.

The door to the big room was open and Pete went inside. A number of offices opened out from it, somewhat like the setup of a newspaper city room. Roy Weston, his collar open, his face red with anger and irritation, was pacing the floor in one of them, tongue-lashing a younger man whom Pete recognized as Jimmy Lastfogel, the assistant district attorney for Weston County. When he saw Pete, Roy came out and motioned for the surgeon to follow him into another office.

"Thank God you were home when I called, Pete," he said. "The reporters have been badgering me for the last two hours. I've been able to stave them off so far with a lot of malarkey about the dangers of pretrial publicity and the need to guard the prisoner's rights against self-incrimination."

"It sounded like an open and shut case from the radio broadcast," said Pete. "I was out on the lake in my boat this afternoon, but when I got back to the dock and heard about it, I rushed back to the hospital. I called Uncle Jake, but he said he'd already made funeral arrangements and wanted as little fanfare about the whole thing as possible."

"That's what we all want—but that bird-brained assistant of mine had to gum the works."

"How?"

"I wasn't available when Mort was brought in and Jim O'Brien was busy looking for Elaine. Seems like she was at the Hiltons' lake cottage this afternoon and didn't hear anything about all this until somebody thought to call her there."

"The same thing happened to me out on the lake."

"A lot of us were too busy to listen this afternoon, it seems. Jim O'Brien and Eric Vosges sent Mort to jail in a prowl car when they finished investigating the case on the ground at Mort's house. They went to the hospital to see about Paul and talked to Dieter briefly just before he took Paul up to the operating room, then went out to look for Elaine. But instead of letting things wait until I was available, Jimmy Lastfogel started quizzing Mort —you know, the enterprising TV prosecutor grilling the suspect and getting him to confess the crime." He banged the desk with his fist. "You'd think any first-year law student would know better, since the Supreme Court decided the Escobedo case the way it did. Confessions aren't allowed as evidence any more."

"What did Mort say?"

"What didn't he say? First he insisted that Jimmy get a court reporter in. Then he proceeded to tell the whole story—for the record. So what do I have?—a confession covering everything about this case I might have been able to dig up for myself and use as evidence. Now all I can do with it is shove it."

"It's still open and shut, isn't it?"

"Not when it gives Abner Townsend just what he needs to torpedo my candidacy for state attorney general."

"Maybe I'm a little dumb about legal matters, but—"

"If I don't go after Mort hammer and tongs and try to get a conviction, Abner will claim I'm protecting him because I'm a member of the clinic corporation. Personally, I'd like to see Mort burn for killing Lorrie. She may have liked sex—but who doesn't? And she never hurt anybody. Now this damn confession has nullified all the evidence I might introduce."

Roy sat on the desk and lit a cigarette with fingers that still shook from anger. "I think Mort planned it this way, knowing

178

damn well that if he confessed to everything I might use against him, then repudiated the confession, I wouldn't be able to introduce any of it in evidence if I brought him to trial. He's smart enough—and unprincipled enough—to do it."

"How did you happen to get wind of it?" Pete asked.

"Jim O'Brien knew where to find me; he knows everything that goes on in this town. When he came back to headquarters after locating Elaine McGill and discovered what was going on, he called me. But by the time I got here, the whole thing was in the reporter's stenotype machine. And you know what a scandal there'd be if I tried to bribe a court reporter to tear up her notes."

"Did Mort repudiate his confession?"

"That's why I called you. Mort sent for me just now and, cool as you please, said he'd been interrogated without being warned of his rights while he was under a great emotional strain because of the death of his wife. He claims he doesn't know what he told Jimmy Lastfogel and the reporter but that whatever it was, he now denies everything."

"Did he sign the statement?"

"No. But that wouldn't make any difference under the Escobedo ruling. The confession would be thrown out if he wanted it to be, even if he'd sworn to it on a stack of Bibles."

"Mind telling me what he confessed to? Or is that forbidden, too?"

"I don't see why not. As soon as Mort beats the rap, he'll probably sell the whole story to a magazine for a fortune. I SHOT MY WIFE AND HER LOVER—believe me it would make a story to beat anything on the best-seller list. According to Mort, as long as Lorrie kept her amours in the family, so to speak, he didn't particularly mind. The way he looked at it—and he's pretty close to the truth there—a lot of us have been sleeping with each other's wives for years, probably providing the variety that's kept several marriages from breaking up."

"I don't imagine many marriage counselors would agree with that kind of therapy," Pete said with a grin. "But you may have a point."

"Anyway Mort admitted that Lorrie was too much for him, so he didn't mind her extracurricular activities, as long as she confined them to members of the club. Lately though she'd been putting out to a student."

"A medical student?"

"A curly-haired and curly-tailed senior named Mike Traynor—"

"I know him—got a nurse in trouble a couple of years ago. We almost booted him out."

"Too bad you didn't."

"Turned out the nurse was almost as bad as he was."

"Anyway, Mort suspected what was happening—or Lorrie may have even told him. It would have been her idea of a good joke. Mort's had her watched for some time now and his watchdog discovered that the guy was coming around on Wednesday afternoons, when most of you play golf."

"He couldn't have chosen a better time."

"Mort decided to use this Traynor as an object lesson to scare the hell out of Lorrie and make her go back to the club. I guess he also planned to put the fear of God into some others we could name, too, but the main purpose apparently was to scare Lorrie into laying off medical students."

"It was a clever plan."

"Just the sort of thing Mort would think up—and go through with," Roy agreed. "The trouble was, it was pretty dark in the bedroom they were in. Mort's a crack shot but apparently he didn't figure on Lorrie being on top."

"What?"

"Jim O'Brien and Eric Vosges checked the angles and directions the bullet must have taken. They both say it couldn't have been any other way. But who would have thought Paul McGill would be the one that was with her?"

"I would have bet Paul was a virgin when he married Elaine—and hadn't looked at another woman since," Pete agreed.

"Chances are, Lorrie lured Paul out to the house this afternoon some way—maybe it was connected with that crazy bet she made with the girls."

"Wait a minute. What's this about a bet?"

"You mean Amy didn't tell you?"

"Not a word."

"It was over a year ago. They were all at a meeting of that sewing circle they have—"

"The Dissection Society?"

"Yeah. Alice told me about it then. It seems that Lorrie started analyzing our marriages. I gather she told the girls they weren't getting what they were entitled to. She offered to make a study of each of us men in bed—and report on her findings."

"You don't mean they took her up?"

"Of course not—that's probably why Amy never mentioned it to you. As for Alice, she couldn't care less; half the time when I board her she's asleep before I get through. Anyway, none of them would take Lorrie up, so she told them she'd do it anyway—and apparently did."

"So that's why Lorrie tried to get me out in a car with her at the club dance last year," said Pete.

"You mean you didn't go?"

"I happen to love your sister, with all her faults—though I don't know how I can stand them much longer."

"I've been wondering about that, too," said Roy. "Ever since she was a little girl, Amy's always had to be boss. I guess it was because Mama was always running over Dad. The only way I could ever get the best of Amy when we were kids was to knock the daylights out of her, so it looks like you'd better start doing the same thing. But getting back to Mort. After he repudiated his confession, he demanded to see you, so I called you."

"Guess I'd better talk to him then."

"Do me a favor, Pete. See if you can get him to plead temporary insanity."

"Will that get you off the hook with Abner Townsend?"

"It's my only chance. And maybe Mort's too."

"Do you think he'll do it?"

"It's either that or take his chances with the so-called unwritten law—and you can never tell how a jury is going to react to that."

"If Mort's figured this thing out the way you think he has, he's probably covered that angle, too."

"Then make him understand that it's the closest to a sure-fire bet he can have for acquittal. A man comes home and finds his wife in bed with another guy and shoots him in a fit of rage— that makes him not responsible for his actions, as far as most people are concerned. No jury in this part of the country would convict him if he claims he went mentally berserk. In fact I might even keep it from coming to trial at all, if Mort will cooperate."

"How?"

"We've got a grand jury sitting now. If I can get this case before them and have a psychiatrist—"

"Not Dave Rogan!" Pete exclaimed.

"Dave's the last one I would want," said Roy. "In the first place he probably wouldn't certify Mort as insane. And, whether he did or not, Abner Townsend could still claim it was all rigged. I'll get a psychiatrist from Atlanta or Asheville. With the right kind of testimony, we can sweep this whole thing under a rug and Abner Townsend won't be able to do a damn thing about it."

"What happens to Mort? I've got to know that before I can advise him."

"He'll have to leave town in any event—this way it won't be in a coffin."

"Have you suggested this to him?"

"I'm the district attorney, Pete! I'm supposed to do my best to hang Mort and I would try if he hadn't beaten me to the draw. Now we've got to get out of it the best way we can."

"I still don't see how you can keep the lid on this scandal, if Mort insists on making news out of it."

"We can't—if he insists. If we can get him to let me bring the case before the grand jury with a plea of temporary insanity, the proceedings will be secret and we can probably keep them that way. But we've got to move fast."

"Can I talk to Mort privately now?"

"Of course. I'll have him brought down here. Tell him not to worry about the place being bugged. The last thing we want right now is another confession."

ii

Pete Brennan had never particularly liked Mort Dellman, and under other circumstances would hardly have chosen the stocky clinical pathologist as an intimate associate. Like the others of the small group of doctors forming the nucleus of the Faculty Clinic, he'd been thrown with Mort for two years in the Army general hospital in Korea where they'd all been working. When the rest had applied for faculty positions in the new Weston University Medical School fifteen years before, at Roy's suggestion, Mort had applied, too—on his own.

Mort's credentials as a biochemist and a skilled laboratory director were beyond reproach, whether any of them liked him or not. All of them, plus the Board of Trustees of the medical school, had recognized his genius in his field so he'd won a faculty position. When they decided to open the Faculty Clinic for their private practice—outside their teaching work—Mort had made valuable suggestions for automation and increased efficiency, so they'd naturally made him director of the clinical laboratories. Busy primarily with medical work, too, they'd been happy to hand him the job of setting up the administrative organization of the clinic—all of which he had done exceptionally well.

It had been Mort who had developed the automated techniques that let the Faculty Clinic process twice as many patients a day as any other group of the same size in the country, except perhaps several in California that were using the same techniques. In fact, Pete suspected that the Faculty Clinic was patterned very closely after some of those California organizations, since Mort had been working for one of them when his reserve commission had suddenly dragged him into the army and the Korean war.

When computers first came into prominence, Mort had seen their possibilities for storing and retrieving medical data rapidly and had scored a clean beat on most medical groups in the country by persuading the others to invest in a computer. Recognizing the potentialities of the clinic as far as publicity was concerned, he had also invited magazine writers to witness its methods of operation and write them up in the sort of pseudoscientific general reports that were fully acceptable ethically, yet managed to be a very effective form of medical advertising.

Roy had left the door to the small office open. When Pete saw a turnkey ushering Mort Dellman through it, he came around the desk and shook hands. "Have they been giving you a bad time, Mort?" he asked.

The biochemist dropped into a chair and accepted the cigarette and light Pete gave him. He was of medium height with a somewhat beefy face, deep-set shrewd eyes, and a shock of graying hair. His clothes were rather rumpled and his eyes somewhat bloodshot.

"I've been giving myself a bad time, but I'm all right now," he said. "Lorrie's dead and I can't help her, so I've got to get out of this thing the best way I can."

"Maybe you'd better not talk until you get a lawyer—"

"I'm building my own defense right now. You know how Lorrie was, Pete. If you didn't get your share like the rest, it was your own fault. I'm sure you had plenty of opportunities."

Pete made no comment, since none seemed to be indicated.

"As long as Lorrie kept her activities in the family, I didn't particularly mind. A man gets tired even of a special dish, if it's put before him too often. I don't mind admitting she was too much for me alone and letting my professional confreres dally with my wife occasionally gave me a hold over them I might not have had otherwise. I don't flatter myself that many of the people around here like me and frankly I don't give a damn—except where you're concerned."

"Why me?" Pete asked, startled.

"I admire you more than any of the others, though Dave Rogan has always treated me squarely, too. Maybe it's because of that Irish charm of yours." He grinned wolfishly. "Or I could be a latent homosexual—like one or two I could name."

"Get on with your story."

"Roy probably told you about that confession his eager-beaver assistant trapped me into making," Mort said with a knowing grin, and Pete was sure now that Roy Weston's surmise about the purpose of the confession had been correct. "I could forgive Lorrie most anything except shaming me by having an affair with a medical student. Can you imagine what sort of a story that would make in the intern's lounge?"

"Not a very pretty one, I'm sure."

"This guy had been coming around on Wednesday afternoons so I figured to use him to scare the hell out of Lorrie and maybe put the fear of God into some other people."

"Are you saying you went out there this afternoon planning to shoot this—what's his name?"

"Traynor? Hell no! I only intended to wing him a little. But who would have thought Paul McGill would have been there instead?"

"He'd never been with Lorrie before?"

"Not that I know of—and the man I hired kept pretty good records. How is Paul, by the way?"

"He'll live. Anton Dieter took your bullet out of his heart."

"Good! I always thought Paul was a fuddy-duddy, but I wouldn't want to hurt him."

"Do you have any idea how Paul got mixed up with Lorrie?"

"All he had to do was to go to the house. You know that."

"But why would he go?"

"Lorrie must have asked him to stop by; I remember her saying something about a skin irritation when I left this morning. Or was it yesterday morning? Anyway our house is right on Paul's way to the club where he usually plays golf on Wednesday afternoons, so he wouldn't suspect anything. Or maybe Lorrie was expecting the medical student and he didn't show up, so she settled for Paul. Anyway you couldn't expect him to resist much, with her jaybirding around."

"Jaybirding?"

"She read about it in a magazine; I think it may have been

Time. It seems that a lot of nutty women have started doing their housework at home in the altogether. They call it jaybirding—I suppose because they're as naked as jaybirds."

"You must be kidding."

"Get the article for yourself, if you don't believe me. The weather's been hot and the children were at camp, so Lorrie took it up this summer. She says it's wonderful and I'll say one thing, she certainly had me going home to lunch for a while."

"Too bad you didn't go home today," Pete said dryly.

"Wasn't it? The way I figure it, once Lorrie got Paul in the house, he was caught in a situation where even a stone statue wouldn't have been able to resist. It was just his luck that I decided to make an example of that damn medical student today."

"Roy can chew you up in court, if you admit that you deliberately went home this afternoon to shoot Traynor. Particularly when you knew he'd been with Lorrie before."

"You don't think I'm that dumb, do you? My defense is going to be the unwritten law. I shot defending my home and my marriage; no jury would convict a man for that."

"What about temporary insanity? It would fit into that defense and strengthen it a lot."

"Not a chance! With a rap like that pinned on me, I might escape the electric chair. But they'd sure as hell send me to a state hospital for maybe a couple of years—until some dumb bunny of a hack psychiatrist decided I was normal. And even then they could try me again. No, I'm going to beat this rap all the way—my way."

"Why did you send for me then?"

"I'm going to need a lawyer—maybe somebody like Percy Foreman. It's up to you and the rest of the boys to pay for him."

Pete gave him a startled look. "How do you figure that?"

"You've got to save me to preserve the standing of the Faculty Clinic and the reputation of the ones Lorrie had already gotten to with that crazy bet—"

"You knew about that?"

"She thought it was a good joke. I guess the joke's on her now."

"Would you believe I never heard of the bet until Roy told me about it just now?"

"I'd believe anything you tell me, Pete. That's why I sent for you—that and because you're president of the clinic corporation."

"What does the corporation have to do with it?"

"I'll have to get off the faculty—which means the clinic, too— so I'm willing to sell out to the rest of you for money to finance my defense."

"Under the unwritten law?"

"Yeah. I'll take the chance that a jury may convict me of manslaughter or unpremeditated murder—with maybe two to ten years in prison. Even if they do, I'll still walk out in a year or so with a hundred thousand dollars in the bank."

"How do you figure that?"

"I'm asking a hundred thousand for my share of the clinic— and its future."

"You're dreaming!"

"If I am, it's a nightmare—for the rest of you, not me."

"But we don't have a hundred grand, Mort."

"Maybe not in cash—but your credit's good. Each of you takes better than fifty thousand a year out of the clinic, plus your university salary. If you, George Hanscombe, Dave Rogan, Joe McCloskey, and Paul McGill each take ten thousand a year out of that fifty, you can pay back a hundred-thousand-dollar loan in two years—with maybe another year to take care of the interest."

"You seem to have it all figured out," said Pete.

"I'm not exactly stupid; you ought to know that. A hundred thousand dollars isn't nearly as much as I would make from the clinic in the next few years, but I'm getting sort of tired of the place anyway. With Lorrie gone, I can take that hundred thousand and enjoy myself."

"Where?"

"They're crying for medical personnel in South Africa and a lot of other places. Biochemists trained as clinical pathologists aren't a dime a dozen either."

"But a hundred thousand—"

"Think about it and you'll find it's a cheap price to pay. After all I automated the clinic and made more than that for the rest of you in the past five years."

"None of us would deny that," Pete admitted.

"What do you say then?"

"I can't say anything until I talk to the others—and Paul McGill isn't in shape to decide anything right now. Give me a week."

"Too long. I don't like jails. If Roy doesn't spring me in a day or two, I'm going to throw a *habeas corpus* at him."

"Five days?"

"Three. If Paul's in as good shape as you say, you can talk to him by day after tomorrow. But you'd better be persuasive, Pete. It's my neck I'm risking and I won't give an inch."

iii

Roy Weston came into the small office after Mort Dellman had been ushered out by the turnkey. "You look like you've seen a ghost, Pete," he said.

"I have. Is there anything to drink around here?"

"In a jail?" Roy grinned and opened a desk drawer, taking out a bottle of bourbon. Pete took a stiff jolt and lit a cigarette with fingers that shook a little.

"He's a cheeky bastard," said Roy. "I'd really like to sink my teeth into him in a courtroom."

"Forget it. Any good that might do you in gaining votes would be more than lost because of the way the newspapers would handle the scandal."

"That's why I wanted you to talk him into pleading temporary insanity."

"He won't buy it, Roy."

"Why?"

"The way Mort figures it, he'd be shoved into a state hospital; and he doesn't have any more confidence in the staffs of most of those places than I do. He thinks he might not get out for a couple of years."

"It's better than the rope."

"Mort doesn't figure to get the rope. Just to be sure, he's gonna get a high-powered lawyer—somebody like Percy Foreman."

Roy Weston whistled. "They come high."

"Mort isn't worrying about that. He intends for George, Dave, Joe, Paul and myself to pay the bill. We're to buy him out of the clinic for a hundred thousand."

"A hundred thousand dollars!"

"His share's worth that. I can't argue with him about it."

"So?"

"I'm going to talk to the others tomorrow and make arrangements for the money."

"Don't forget that I'm a member of the clinic corporation. I'll pay my share."

"Not on your life. This is our baby and we're stuck with it. Besides, think what Abner Townsend could do with that information in the next campaign."

Amy was asleep when Pete got home. She'd pulled the pale blue top sheet up under her chin and was sprawled out on the bed like a child. The light over the bed was still on and she looked lovelier in the spill of the light than he'd remembered seeing her for a long time.

How could he have ever considered divorce, he wondered? But then he had to admit that for more than five years now there hadn't been anything between them like the brief period tonight, when they had once again been two young lovers finding new rapture in each other.

Where does it go?—that youthful rapture—he wondered as he undressed. What happens to two people who love each other? What invisible wall rises between them over the years—for no real reason?

In their own case, he'd put most of the blame on Amy's ambition. But in all fairness to her he had to admit that he'd known about that before they were married. The clinic had occupied much of his time these past five years but the real trouble, he decided now, must have been his own desire for money—money he'd made with his own hands and not the fortune that was Amy's, most of it safely invested in high-yield bonds with the interest going into a trust for the children.

He had been a fool, he admitted as he faced the possibility of all he'd worked for being blasted into nothingness by the scandal Mort Dellman could create. A fool to let anything threaten what he and Amy'd had together in the beginning. If they'd only spent a little more time working at their marriage, each giving in a little to the other's weaknesses and recognizing the other's strengths without resenting them, the years when they'd gradually drifted apart could have been an entirely different story altogether.

Amy didn't move when he got into bed and switched off the light. Her face was against the pillow, so he didn't notice the pupils of her eyes. Had he done so, the tight constriction from the dose of morphine she'd given herself just before his arrival earlier that evening might have told him something was wrong, something so dreadful that he'd never even considered it a possibility.

But then, some other things he'd never considered possible had happened today, too. It was a long time before he finally got to sleep.

iv

It was after nine o'clock and Maggie was alone in the small Ladies' Bar, nursing a bourbon and ginger ale morosely, when Manuel, the bartender, touched her elbow.

"We're about to close up, Mrs. McCloskey," he said in his soft Cuban accent. "You want me to call you a taxi?"

"Taxi?" Maggie shook her head to clear her vision but his features remained blurred. "My car's in the lot."

"A taxi would be better, Mrs. McCloskey. You can leave your car in the lot."

"All right. Call one for me, while I finish this."

"Wouldn't you rather have a cup of coffee? I've made some for myself."

"Okay." Maggie was too tired and depressed to argue. With Manuel's coaxing, she managed to get down two cups of coffee by the time the taxi came. He helped her from the now deserted club into the cab and closed the door.

"3501 Sherwood Ravine Drive," she murmured and sank back against the cushions. At her home, she got out of the taxi and paid the driver.

"You all by yourself ma'm?" he asked.

Maggie swayed and held on to the cab for support. "Do I look like twins?"

"I'll just keep the lights on the door until you get inside," he suggested.

"Thank you." Maggie stumbled up the drive and, after some fumbling, managed to fit the key into the keyhole. She opened the door and, reaching inside, brought her hand down across the bank of light switches beside the door, flooding not only the house itself—a rambling one-story structure of old brick with wide eaves to which floodlights were attached at the corners—but also the yard.

The coffee had stimulated her enough to lessen somewhat the torpor induced by the alcohol, though not enough to clear her foggy mental processes. More than anything else at the moment, she wanted to escape from the reality of her own blank future into the nirvana of sleep, but she'd had just enough coffee to make it elude her.

The master bedroom with its empty twin to her own bed depressed her even more, as she stripped off her clothes, letting them fall where they dropped, and put on a nightgown. In the bathroom, she opened the door to the medicine closet, not knowing exactly what she was looking for—until she saw the bottle half filled with small yellow capsules. Unscrewing the top from the bottle, she dribbled four of them into her palm and, turning on the tap, filled the plastic cup from the toothbrush rack at one side with water.

With the capsules halfway to her mouth, she stopped and frowned in concentration, trying to remember something Joe had told her about them. But the memory refused to come, so she swallowed the capsules, washing them down with water. She'd taken four before—that much she could remember—so there was no reason why she couldn't now.

Back in the bedroom, she started to turn down the covers of her bed but the emptiness of the second one and the feeling of loneliness it always gave her was enough to make her turn to the adjoining room and throw herself down upon the spotless counterpane.

There, tears finally came and with them, at last, oblivion.

CHAPTER XIII

The operation on Paul McGill had been almost finished and only the closure remained, when Marisa Feldman left the glassed-in observation gallery, with its dramatic view of the brilliantly lit scene encompassing the operating table with the patient upon it, the team of surgeons and assistants gathered around it and, in the penumbra of lesser illumination, the circulating nurses, the electronic monitors that kept watch upon heart action, blood pressure, respiration and other vital functions and, ready as always while heart surgery was going on, the pump that could take over completely the function of both circulation and breathing in an emergency.

The hospital cafeteria was closed at this time of night, she knew, although it opened briefly after ten o'clock to provide coffee and sandwiches for the nurses who came on duty for the night shift at eleven and for members of the medical house staff working late with emergencies. Conscious of being quite hungry— it was eight hours now since she'd had lunch—Marisa left the hospital and crossed the street to the brightly lit Snack Bar.

The small gleaming restaurant was only half filled and she selected a red cushioned booth in the corner. The menu in the rack beside the napkin dispenser was apparently prepared for children; the dishes offered were pictured in gleaming color.

Mabel, the buxom blonde waitress, put a glass of water before her and waited for the order.

"Everything looks so good," Marisa said with a smile. "Just bring me what's best."

"Tender-medium, Abe. Easy on the oil for the hash browns, French for the salad." Mabel ticked off the order as she inscribed it upon a small check pad, circling the abbreviations for the various items. "Coffee now, Dr. Feldman?"

"How did you know my name?" Marisa wasn't wearing the uniform that subtly distinguished different classes of hospital personnel: long-skirted white coat for the teaching staff, white duck jackets and pants for the house officers, rumpled whites for the orderlies, and nylon for nurses, maids and attendants—with their distinctive caps setting the nurses apart.

"Being new here you wouldn't know about the hospital grapevine, but it knows about you, Dr. Feldman," Mabel said with a smile. "We've got a special connection over here with the hospital, the medical school and the Faculty Clinic. Want to hear a sample of what's come over the grapevine about you?"

"Y-yes. If it isn't too critical."

"You get a good report." Mabel went to the big gleaming urn with its three glass tubes, one clear for hot water and two dark brown with coffee. She drew a cup, and leaning over the narrow lower counter in the booth section, placed it on the table before Marisa.

"You're Dr. Marisa Feldman—lovely name, Marisa, by the way—and you're an Assistant Professor of Medicine." Mabel had been working expertly at the big refrigerator while she talked over her shoulder. Now she set a brown plastic bowl of salad before Marisa and expertly arranged a knife and fork on a napkin beside it. The spoon had arrived on the saucer with the cup of coffee. "They tell me you're real good."

"Who tells you?"

"The grapevine. A secretary in the personnel office says one thing, a technician in the laboratory, another. Two interns were discussing you last night at supper. Put it all together and before you know it, there's a full dossi—what's the word? I heard it once on 'The Man from U.N.C.L.E.'"

"Dossier?"

"That's it. Pretty soon you've got a full dossier."

The coffee was delicious, so was the salad. Marisa was enjoying them both when the door behind her opened, letting in a blast of warm air from outside to dilute the air-conditioned coolness of the interior. From the corner of her eye she saw Mike Traynor come in. When he saw her at the booth, he took a step in her direction; the booths were all occupied. Marisa looked away quickly, so as to give him no encouragement. And, after hesitating a moment, he shrugged and moved down the row of booths to the end, where a rangy blonde girl was sitting alone, reading a paperback.

"Mind if I sit here?" Marisa heard him ask, and when the blonde smiled and put her book aside, spoke a silent prayer of thanksgiving that she had been spared the chore of being rude. The last thing she wanted tonight was to joust with an amorous young male.

"Dr. Dieter!" Marisa heard Mabel exclaim warmly when the door opened a second time, letting in another gust of humid air from outside. She stiffened involuntarily at the name, but forced herself to relax, lest he notice the effect it had upon her.

"They tell me you saved Dr. McGill," Mabel was saying to Dieter. "He's such a nice man."

"How do you do it, Mabel?" The surgeon and the waitress seemed to be on the best of terms, an American characteristic which Marisa, even after two years in the United States, found somewhat hard to accept. "I just finished the operation, yet you know all about it already."

Mabel laughed. "This is the crossroads of Weston, Doctor—like that place at Times Square and 42nd Street they used to call the Crossroads of the World."

"I bet you know everything that goes on across the street."

"Just about."

"Then you already know Dr. McGill was really saved by Dr. Feldman here." Marisa looked up from her salad as Dieter paused before her booth.

"May I join you, Doctor?" he asked. "Everything else seems to be filled."

"Of course." By then she'd had time to control her instinctive reaction to the Teutonic burr in his voice, and the unpleasant memories it brought. "R.H.I.P."

Dieter looked blank. "I'm afraid I don't—"

"An Americanism I picked up at Harvard." Having shown her superior knowledge, at least in the sphere of slang, Marisa decided to be gracious. "Rank has its privileges, you know."

"I'm not pulling rank, as the Americans say," he assured her. "If you'd rather—?"

"Please sit down. I was just trying to be funny and not succeeding very well, I'm afraid. It's my English background."

"What are you having?" Anton Dieter asked as he slid onto the other side of the booth facing her.

"A tender-medium—whatever that is."

"An excellent choice. I'll have the same, Mabel. That other fine dressing of yours—the remoulade—for the salad, please. And light on the croutons."

"I know just how you like it, Doctor." Mabel obviously adored him.

"I had hoped you wouldn't leave the operating suite before I could thank you properly for saving Dr. McGill's life this afternoon," Dieter said to Marisa. "He's a very fine person."

Prepared to dislike the surgeon, Marisa found herself warming under his praise instead—and steeled herself against it.

"I couldn't have taken the bullet out of his heart," she reminded him.

"I'm not so sure of that." Dieter stirred sugar into his coffee. "I suspect that you are a very resourceful person. But since there will be no fee, suppose we share the credit."

"The approach is certainly original," Marisa said a bit tartly, but Dieter only grinned. Apparently he wasn't easy to insult.

"And the purpose?" he inquired. "Have you decided that?"

"The usual, I imagine."

He shook his head. "I have a feeling that nothing about you is quite what you call the usual, Dr. Feldman—and I hope the same can be said of me. Then we understand each other?"

"Perfectly."

"Good. That saves a lot of trouble—and time."

"Don't be too sure of that."

"We avoid two words in medicine—always and never. I maintain the same rule in my personal life."

Marisa's steak had come by then. It was small but thick and tender, with the potatoes beautifully browned and a toasted bun spread with butter.

"Please eat your dinner," Dieter urged her. "Your food will get cold."

Like the salad and coffee, the steak, potatoes and bun were delicious—and cooked perfectly. "It's a lot better than the English food I grew up on," Marisa admitted.

"The same goes for German sauerbraten or *bigos*." He saw the sudden pain in her eyes at the mention of a favorite Polish dish and said quickly, "Forgive me if I have offended."

"My family were Polish Jews; they're all dead now."

"I didn't know."

"My older brother was a lieutenant in the Polish army. The Nazis executed him."

"So that's why you were antagonistic to me?"

"Were, Doctor?"

"Perhaps I did take too much for granted, particularly on such short acquaintance. Mabel finds me irresistible and I was hoping you would, too. Anyway we have plenty of time, since we're to be professional colleagues. How do you like Weston?"

"Very much—so far."

"I am a very direct man, perhaps too direct." He hadn't missed the inflection in her voice. "But I suspect you are direct, too, so we shall get along, I am sure."

Dieter's food arrived and he started wolfing it down, then forced himself to eat more slowly. "You must pardon my table manners," he said. "We were so long with too little food in East Germany that even now in America, where there is plenty, I cannot help eating like an animal."

The word struck Marisa's senses like a warning bell, reminding

her of human animals who spoke the same language this man
had learned to speak as a child.

"My father was a professor in the university at Frankfurt, but
we were never Nazis," he continued. "I was not old enough to be
taken into the army when the war began and because I wanted to
become a doctor, the Nazis let me attend the gymnasium and the
university. When the Russians took over East Germany, my father
was lucky enough to find among the officers in the occupying
Russian troops, a friend who had been a professor before the war.
He saw to it that I was allowed to finish my medical education
and was given a chance to work in the vascular surgery clinic of
Moscow University."

He emptied his coffee cup, but Mabel was there immediately
to refill them both. "Would you care for dessert? They have a
delicacy here called Black Bottom Pie."

"I shouldn't, but—"

"Surely you don't need to worry about calories—or cholesterol.
Two orders please, Mabel."

The pie was everything he'd said it was, rich, delicious and
filled with chocolate. Comfortably fed, Marisa found that she
needed all her will to resist Dieter's powerful masculine charm
and remind herself that he was a German. Or to remember the
reasons why she hated them as a race.

"You know, I'm sure," he said, "that the Russians were per-
forming all kinds of far-advanced experimental surgical procedures
in the laboratories of Pavlov during the reign of the czars."

"I studied about Pavlov's experiments in England."

"Recently they developed a wonderful machine for suturing
blood vessels together during vascular surgery. I managed to smug-
gle one out when I escaped."

"If you were doing what you wanted to do in Russia, why did
you leave?" she asked. "I thought the Russians gave considerable
freedom to scientists."

"I was relatively free—for Russia. But we occasionally saw American medical journals and, when I realized they were moving much
faster over here in my field than the Russians were, I decided to

escape to West Germany and come to America. It was relatively easy before the Berlin Wall was built."

"I remember very well what it was like in East Germany," Marisa said, making no attempt to hide the bitterness in her voice.

"Your accent is English. How did you happen to be there?"

"I was a little girl in Poland when the Ger— the Nazis came. My brother was killed but my mother and I escaped to England with the Polish freedom forces. She died there but my father remained in Germany in prison." Marisa's voice became bitter in spite of her resolve to try to be pleasant. "You were safe in school, so you can't have any idea what it was like for a girl in those concentration camps—a Jewish girl."

"In a hospital in Russia I saw some of those who were freed by the Russians when they invaded Germany. Please don't talk about it, if it causes you pain."

"The hate that has been bottled up inside me for so long makes it difficult even now to speak of it," she admitted.

"Especially to a German."

"Yes."

"But we're both Americans now. That's behind us."

"All but the memories."

"With happiness they will fade in time. You're doing what you want to do—as I am. That's the most important thing."

"I'm afraid you don't have as much to forget." She couldn't have told why she was speaking to him of things she hadn't put into words for a long, long time. But somehow she felt that she had to—and that he would understand.

"At first, I didn't know my father was alive," she continued. "When I learned that he was—after I'd studied medicine in England—I went back to East Germany to try to bring him out, but they took me prisoner. Father had an advanced case of angina pectoris and the Germans wouldn't give him nitroglycerine to relieve it—so I bought the drug myself."

"In prison?" His eyes didn't leave hers.

"Yes—with the only currency available to me then."

Intent upon their conversation, neither of them noticed the gasp from Mabel, who had managed to listen even while moving briskly back and forth behind the counter, serving the few customers in the sandwich shop now.

"No wonder you hate Germans," he said softly.

"I had no right to cry on your shoulder. Excuse me, please." Marisa rose suddenly in her seat.

"It's there—any time you need it." He stood up, too, and when she fumbled in her purse, said quickly, "Please let me—"

"No." Her voice was taut. "I'm perfectly capable of looking after myself."

He stood back to let her pass him to the cash register, where Mabel was adding up the check. "Of course, you are," he said gently. "Good night, Dr. Feldman, I'm sorry if I upset you."

"Good night." She paid the check and almost ran from the lighted interior of the Snack Bar into the darkness of the street outside.

It had been a long time since she had cried—not since the night she'd stumbled back to the dormitory of the prison after her first visit to the quarters of the commandant.

"She's a very lovely girl," Mabel said as she made Dieter's change.

"Very lovely—and very troubled." Dieter moved back to the booth and left a liberal tip. "Troubled by things you here in America can't even conceive of. But I think she may be groping her way back."

"With your help?"

"With my help—if she will let me. Good night, Mabel."

ii

"Don't believe I've seen you around here before," Mike Traynor had said as he eased himself into the other side of the booth from the blonde at the end of the Snack Bar. "My name's Mike Traynor. I'm a senior over there"—he nodded toward the building across the street—"substituting this summer as an intern."

"Sibyl Carter," said the blonde. "My roommate and I took an apartment down the street a week ago. She's a private duty nurse, but she's on night duty now, and I didn't want to eat alone."

Whether the blonde had intended to or not—and being worldly-wise, he suspected that she did—she'd told him a lot.

"Are you a nurse, too?" Mike asked.

"I'm a graduate student in sociology at the university; finished at Vassar last June. I work part-time with the social service department of the hospital, so it's more convenient to live in this section of town."

"Sociology, eh? That should be interesting."

"I'm working on a research project, interviewing unmarried mothers in the O.B. clinic and putting their stories on tape."

"Bet you get some real ones."

"You should hear some of them." When the girl accepted the gambit, Mike was sure he was home safe.

"I'd like to." He glanced at the booth where Dieter and Marisa Feldman were engaged in earnest conversation and felt a deep burn of resentment surge within him. The damned Jewish bitch! Snubbing him one minute and making up to Dieter the next like a teen-ager on her first date. It was disgusting.

Mabel put Mike's hamburger before him and he bit into it savagely before turning back to the blonde. "How about tonight?" he asked.

"I don't know. My roommate's on three-to-eleven."

"We've got two hours. Unless you have other plans."

"Oh, no."

"Give me a minute to eat this and we'll be on our way." He finished wolfing his hamburger and drank his coffee, while the blonde was paying her own check. Paying his, he followed her out.

She had a white Mustang and, as he got into it, he saw Marisa Feldman walking toward the Faculty Apartments. When she passed under the street light, he got a glimpse of her face and was sure that she had been crying.

So she and Dieter had quarreled. When he got around to it, he'd try that Feldman again. One of the most exciting things about women was that you never knew when they would change their minds.

When Mike came in shortly before midnight, Lew Saunders, his roommate, was looking at television in the room they shared in the interns' quarters, where Mike was living while substituting that summer.

"You cut it close as usual." Saunders looked at his watch. "You're supposed to be on emergency call after midnight, you know."

"I'm here—with time to get a quick shower," said Mike. "And believe me, I need it."

"Who was it this time?"

"A graduate student in sociology—with her own apartment." Lew Saunders gave a low whistle. "And a roommate?"

"A graduate nurse—on three-to-eleven. I saw her picture in the apartment and she might interest you, when she changes shifts next week."

"Aren't graduate students in sociology a bit intellectual for you, Mike?"

"This baby was—at the start." Mike grinned as he started to the shower. "She's got a tape recorder and puts everything on the record."

"Everything?" Lew Saunders raised his eyebrows.

"Damnedest thing you ever heard. How would you like to be trying to make the grade while this New England accent was dictating through her nose: 'Erogenous zones responding to stimulation. Clitoridal erection becoming marked. Introitus now receptive to phallus. Penetration maximal. Pre-orgasmic excitement beginning. Increasing rapidly. O-o-orgasm!"

"Sounds exciting!" Lew Saunders bellowed with laughter.

"Strangely enough, it was. We had a playback right afterward but she got so worked up, she forgot to turn on the recorder that time. I left her moaning because she didn't have a complete record."

"I don't see how you do it, Mike. How many times does that make today?"

"Four. And you'd never guess who I was with this afternoon."

"The waitress across the street in the Snack Bar?"

"For God's sake, Lew! Mabel's old enough to be my mother. Besides she doesn't like me. Would you believe Old Dermatographia's wife?"

"No."

"Take it or leave it." Mike shrugged as he stepped through the bathroom door and reached in to turn on the shower. "I can tell you this much—Old Dermo was writing on the wrong skin this afternoon. He's been neglecting his homework."

iii

A great hospital at night is like a sleeping city, its resident population safely tucked away well before the change of shifts at eleven. Yet a continuous bustle of rubber-soled activity, a constant, though muted, obbligato hums always just underneath the hush that lies over the buildings, the corridors, the dimly lit wards, the brightly illuminated chart rooms, utility areas and ward diet kitchens, where a coffeepot always boils after midnight to help those on duty keep awake during the long, lonely hours until dawn.

Backs, irritated from the day's stay in bed, have long since been rubbed with fragrant, stimulating alcohol and glycerine. Evening medications have been given: a narcotic for pain, a mild barbiturate for sleeping. All necessary treatments for the day are finished —unless the patient's condition necessitates continuous medication—to be resumed with the bustle of awakening at 6 A.M.

Here a white-coated intern or resident, dressed in rumpled white duck, heads for the house staff's quarters, shoulders drooping with weariness after a day of work that may have been all of eighteen hours or even longer. On the way, he exchanges hurried greetings with an assistant resident in obstetrics, coat freshly starched, on his way to an emergency delivery.

In the basement of the hospital, the night work shift is busy preparing for the activities of the day. Rubber-wheeled trucks piled high with treatment trays, dressings, green-tinted linen for the operating rooms, and hundreds of other supplies requiring sterilization, move through the silent corridors below ground toward the giant autoclaves.

In the power plant at one corner of the hospital quadrangle, connected to the main building by a maze of subterranean conduits carrying water, heat, steam, electricity—the very lifeblood that must continue to course through the arteries of the hospital, whether day or night—an engineer is always on duty, a boiler is always stoked and fired, producing steam for the autoclaves, scalding hot water for sterilizing utensils in the utility rooms and the diet kitchen sinks.

Through the almost silent corridors connecting the wards, an electrician, tools hanging from his belt, hurries to repair an overloaded circuit breaker, turning his eyes away when he meets a silently moving stretcher upon which lies what was only a few moments before a living human, the face now covered with a sheet as the body is wheeled to the morgue. There it will be placed in one of the compartments of a huge refrigerator, to await the revealing knife of the pathologist in the morning.

In one of the obstetrical delivery rooms, the first cry of a newborn is like the notes of a flute in the midst of the symphony of life that forms the musical theme of a hospital. In one of the Intensive Care rooms the steady click-click of a respirator, inflating and deflating lungs which, for one reason or another, no longer function of their own accord, sets the rhythm for the drums, while the clang of a falling metal pan occasionally adds the touch of the cymbals' clash. The hum of a suction machine, removing life-threatening mucus fluid from a severely decompensated heart case, is like the throaty note of a cello.

The grunting motor of a milk truck leaving the main kitchen delivery area after unloading its cargo of milk, provides the deep vibrato of the tuba. An ambulance, approaching the emergency-room entrance, sounds a high-pitched note like a trumpet's wail. And the sound of cars, impatient to be on their way after being stopped by the traffic light at the corner, floats through open windows like the melodious tones of French horns and the deeper blast of trombones. Even the violins are there in the plaintive cry of a schizophrenic in the locked psychiatric ward, endlessly repeated like some mad motif that seizes hold of the melody and will not be silenced.

Ordinarily, the symphony of the sleeping hospital was a music Janet Monroe loved to hear; often as she traversed the corridors on the way off duty, she would stop to listen, entranced by some hitherto unheard note and seeking to learn its source. Tonight, however, she had hurriedly given her report to the night supervisor of the Special Intensive Care Unit and was on her way to take a look at Jerry before going home for the night. Troubled by the implications of the reddish tinge in the small tube of spinal fluid Ed Harrison had drawn from Jerry's body, Janet heard none of the hospital's symphony tonight.

The small light burning beneath Jerry's crib gave just enough light for her to see that he was sleeping quietly. She did not wake him but leaned over to kiss him lightly, before turning back to the chart room. A glance at his chart told her there had been no change since she'd been with him earlier when Ed Harrison had done the spinal puncture and Dave Rogan the neurological examination. Pulse, respiration and temperature were all normal and, looking at the chart alone—or even at Jerry sleeping in the crib—it was hard to believe anything was threatening his life.

But threat there was in Ed Harrison's terse note about the color of the spinal fluid; in Dave Rogan's request for neurosurgical and vascular consultation; as well as the order for a radioisotope scan that had proved so valuable in revealing hard-to-identify conditions.

Janet was putting Jerry's chart back on the rack when Jeff Long came into the chart room. "Just missed you on Intensive," he said. "Figured I'd find you here."

"I wanted to look in on Jerry before I went home."

"I came down after we brought Dr. McGill from the O.R. but Jerry was already asleep by then."

"He still is, but I'm worried, Jeff. What does it all mean?"

"I missed my dinner." He took her arm. "Come on. I'll walk you as far as the Snack Bar."

"I couldn't eat—"

"You'll feel differently with one of Mabel's waffles under your belt and a cup of coffee. Come on before I drop dead of starvation at your feet."

In the Snack Bar, Mabel greeted them with a smile and ushered them into one of the red-cushioned booths. "How's your little boy, Mrs. Monroe?" she asked.

"Not so good," said Janet. "I brought him into the hospital two days ago with convulsions."

"Is that nice Dr. Harrison taking care of him?"

"Yes—and Dr. Rogan."

"He couldn't be in better hands." Mabel's confidence in Weston University Hospital and the Faculty Clinic was sublime. "Let me get you some coffee while you're deciding what you'll have. It will perk you both up."

When Mabel had taken their orders, Janet reached blindly across the table to Jeff and he covered her slender hand with his strong one, knowing she needed the support of his own strength. "That blood in Jerry's spinal fluid, Jeff. It means something really bad, doesn't it?"

"Not necessarily." He knew his voice wasn't convincing—but then he wasn't convincing himself.

"Just what does it mean?"

"I'm out of my field there."

"Tell me the truth, Jeff. Anything is better than this uncertainty."

"I talked to Ed about it when I came to see Jerry earlier," Jeff admitted. "All anybody can tell at the moment is that it probably means something congenital."

"Something I gave him?" It was a cry of guilt.

"You're mixing hereditary conditions with congenital ones, Jan. People inherit a defect, probably because it's been handed down in the family from generation to generation—like color blindness, or hemophilia. Congenital only means something you're born with, it has nothing whatever to do with the parents."

"But it's still bad?"

"They won't know until all the reports are in. Right now the bleeding seems to have stopped, or Jerry would be having more convulsions."

"But it can start again?"

Mabel came just then with their food, but Janet didn't touch hers at once. "It could, couldn't it?" she insisted.

"That's what is bothering us all," Jeff Long admitted. "But you mustn't look at only the worst that could happen. The chances are Jerry was born with some little defect in the circulation around the brain, or the meninges covering it. What we've got to find out now is just where that defect is and cure it."

"But can they cure it? Is he going to be like—like one of those spastic children Dr. Rogan examines sometimes?"

"Spastics usually have brain damage when they're born," he explained. "Except for the small amount of bleeding in the spinal fluid when Ed did the tap just now, both he and Dr. Rogan said they could find very little abnormal."

"Maybe if I'd stayed at home and not worked when I was carrying him things would have been different," said Janet. "But we always needed money for Cliff's tuition and other expenses."

"Your working or not working wouldn't have made a minute's difference, darling," he assured her. "Eat your waffle and stop blaming yourself for something you couldn't possibly have had anything to do with."

"They're a nice young couple," Mabel said to Abe Fescue as she was clearing away the dishes after Jeff and Janet left. "Too bad about her little boy."

"Didn't I hear her tell you the headshrinker is looking after the child?"

"If you mean Dr. Rogan, yes. He's a fine doctor."

"You been to him yet?"

"Of course not. There's nothing wrong with my brain."

"You never can tell." Abe grinned. "I had a wife once had

asthma. One of them headshrinkers claimed it was due to nerves but I always figured she was born with ice water in her veins instead of blood. Coldest natured woman I ever saw; wouldn't let me get in the bed with her until I'd taken a hot bath that left me limp as a dishrag. I tell you that woman was always either wheezing or freezing."

"Oh you!" Mabel leaned on the counter and looked across the street at the new Surgical Building. "I sure wish I could have seen Dr. Dieter take that bullet out of Dr. McGill's heart."

"Yeah," said Abe. "It must have been exciting—but not half as much as having the husband come in with a gun just when you're—"

"Don't be crude! Dr. McGill's a very nice gentleman."

"Gentleman, shentleman! He was still bangin' another guy's wife. Why don't you feel sorry for this guy Dellman?"

"Because nobody likes him. Everybody knows he only married Lorrie Porter for her money."

"So now he's got it?"

"Unh-unh! She wouldn't have gotten it until Mr. Jake Porter died—and he's still very much alive."

"It looks like Dellman killed the goose before she could lay the golden egg," said Abe. "With all the money old man Porter's got, Dellman could have had himself a ball in this town."

"The way I hear it he did anyway. So what right has he got to shoot his wife and that nice Dr. McGill?"

"Better ask the D.A. the next time he comes in here," Abe advised. "You claim to know his wife so well; maybe you and Mrs. Weston could get together and figure it all out from those soap operas you both look at on TV."

iv

Grace Hanscombe awakened a little after four in the morning with a headache—as she often did. George was heavier than he should be and his weight caused his side of the bed to sink. As a result she slept on an incline and had to prop herself with a pillow to keep from rolling down against him. During the night, the pillow usually gave way, though. And since she didn't always wake up, the unconscious attempt to stay on her side of the bed created a tension that kept her from sleeping well and gave her the headache.

It was not that she was repulsed by George. In her way she supposed she loved him as much as the average wife loved her husband after fifteen years of marriage—which wasn't necessarily very much. She'd always had a healthy interest in love-making too, and enjoyed it still, even after seventeen years of marriage and what had gone before. But when it was over, she was feminine enough to like her privacy, without being forced to sleep jammed up against a man who had been sweating for ten or fifteen minutes and whose skin, whenever she happened to touch it—which she tried not to do—felt sticky.

Grace had suggested a long time ago that they have separate beds instead of the old-fashioned double one George liked. She would even have settled for one of the new-type twins that could be jammed together to form a king-size double bed, letting her have her own springs and mattress. But George liked for her to be where he could reach over and pat her when he came back to bed, after getting up in the middle of the night.

One of these days Joe McCloskey was going to have to take out George's prostate and she shuddered to think what that would do to his ego. Maggie had told her Joe said a lot of men lost their potency altogether after a prostate operation and she knew George well enough to know what a blow that would be to his self-esteem.

Not that his loss would trouble her much. After all, she was older than Amy and the others and had already begun to experience some of the sudden flashes of heat that threatened to suffocate her, even in winter. She'd had to give up sweets, too, when the semiannual checkup at the Faculty Clinic had shown a low sugar tolerance, indicating a mild case of diabetes.

Having grown up in England where there were plenty of puddings and other rich foods, Grace didn't think giving up sex could be much worse than the rigorous limitation of sugar George had insisted upon when the mild diabetes was discovered. And even if George wasn't able to make it very often, she was still attractive to men, as had been proved several times at medical conventions and elsewhere.

Grace knew she shouldn't have gotten so upset with George last evening. He was really very sweet—except about a few things, like that business of patting her fanny and waking her up in the middle of the night. Surely a doctor ought to know a man had no business doing things like that unless he had ideas—which George never had at that time of night.

The memory of yesterday afternoon and the terrible hour until they'd reached the hospital and learned the truth brought on one of the hot flashes and, slipping from beneath the covers, Grace went to the open window. The cool night air quickly brought relief but she made a mental note to talk to Jack Hagen about stepping up the dose of hormones. Jack said a woman really didn't need to have any symptoms of the menopause, if she didn't want to, but deep in her heart, Grace knew her trouble wasn't just hormones. She was bored, bored to the very marrow of her bones—with George, with the club, with her friends, with Amy Brennan's constant pushing in that medical auxiliary business, with Weston.

God but she'd like to be in England again. Back in an English pub, where you could joke over a pint of ale with a costermonger or an earl, and pitch your skill with darts against the men. No need to worry about sugar there; if you got diabetes the National Health Service took care of you.

George had even refused to consider going back to England, however. Nearly five years of it during the war, he'd said, was enough to last him the rest of his life. Actually Grace had felt much the same way when they'd left England, all torn and bruised from the war. She knew it wouldn't ever again be as she remembered it from her childhood; time had a way of dulling memories—even of love. But she needed something badly and England was far enough away to offer a change from the deadening monotony of her life in Weston, perhaps even a chance to find a meaning she hadn't found here.

The mornings were cool in early September here close to the Great Smokies and, suddenly starting to shiver, Grace crept back into bed. She didn't prop herself with a pillow but moved close to George, seeking comfort in her moment of deep depression. His body was warm and she felt a sudden rush of affection for him when he reached over and patted her bare thigh where her nightgown had slipped up. His hand lingered against her skin, causing her pulse to quicken for a moment in the old way. But then it slid off and he gave a gentle puffing snore, telling her he'd actually been asleep all the time and the movement only a reflex.

Oh God! she thought. *I'm married to an old man. And I'm getting old myself, while any sort of meaningful life is passing me by.*

CHAPTER XIV

Elaine McGill was awakened by a gentle tug at her elbow. She sat up quickly on the narrow couch, where she'd slept soundly since taking the capsule Janet Monroe had given her last night on Jeff Long's orders.

"Is my husband—?"

"Dr. McGill's fine." The nurse who had awakened her was smiling and she saw now that the room was illuminated by daylight. "It's six o'clock and he's asking for you."

Elaine's hand went instinctively to her hair. "Give me a minute."

"Of course. The lavatory is down the hall. Do you have everything you need, Mrs. McGill? Lipstick? Comb?"

"They're in my handbag. You're sure he's all right?"

"We've discontinued the oxygen. His pulse rate and E.K.G. tracing are normal."

Paul was propped up slightly in bed when Elaine came in about fifteen minutes later. He was pale but managed to smile and she was glad she'd taken time to wash her face in cold water, comb her hair, put on lipstick and rouge and freshen up her dress as much as she could.

Before he could speak, she moved quickly across the room and kissed him warmly on the mouth. "I'm so glad you're all right, darling," she said.

"You mean you don't blame—?"

"Of course not."

"But the scandal?"

"We'll weather that together."

"Then you do forgive me?"

"Don't say any more." She put her finger across his lips. "I love you; that's the only important thing."

"What a relief!" He took a deep breath and she knew she'd handled it exactly right. "I was afraid I'd lose you."

"If you ever two-time me again, you might," she said lightly. "But not this time."

"I really didn't intend to—"

"Hush." She put her finger to his lips again. "It's done and over with. The important thing is that you're all right."

"The nurse said Anton Dieter took a bullet out of my heart."

"Yes. I saw it."

"It's too bad about Lorrie."

"She's dead, Paul. The whole thing's over and done with. We don't even have to speak of it again ever."

"Everything all right in here?" The nurse had poked her head into the door. "Your E.K.G. wave just kicked up a storm for a beat or two."

"That was from relief." Paul managed to laugh. "Everything's fine!"

"I'd probably better not stay any longer," said Elaine. "You need your rest, Paul."

"And you need sleep," he agreed. "Thank you again, darling— for being an understanding wife. And most of all for being you."

Outside the hospital, the city was already beginning its daytime life with the movement of early traffic along the streets. The Snack Bar was almost empty, when Elaine crossed to it and went inside. Taking a stool at the counter, she ordered scrambled eggs, toast and coffee.

While the cook was preparing them skillfully at the grill, she was conscious of admiring glances from a couple of truck drivers having coffee at the other end of the counter. The knowledge that men she didn't know found her attractive at this time of the morning, after what she'd been through in the past twelve hours,

was almost as stimulating as the strong black coffee the counter-
man served her before starting to cook her breakfast, and she ate
slowly, enjoying the food.

Elaine was crossing the parking lot to her car when she saw
Mike Traynor come out of the emergency entrance of the hospital and head for the Snack Bar. He saw her at the same moment
and changed direction so as to intercept her. She tried to ignore
him, but when he called to her she turned slowly.

"Were you speaking to me?" she asked.

"How is Dr. McGill?"

"Fine, thank you. I left him a few minutes ago."

"Surely you're not going to take him back."

"That doesn't happen to be any of your business, Mr. Traynor."

She had kept her voice low but he couldn't fail to hear. And
when she saw him flush angrily, she knew he understood her
meaning.

"Look here! If you think you can use me—"

"Mr. Traynor!" The icy coldness with which she pronounced his
name cut off the flow of angry words. "You have another year of
medical school, I believe?"

"Yes. But what's that got to do—?"

"My husband is a member of the faculty. If I mention to him
that you accosted me here, I doubt if you would be allowed to
finish and get your degree."

He started to speak again as she got into the car, then thought
better of it. From her tone he didn't doubt that she would do just
what she had threatened to do. And after that business with the
nurse—who hadn't had the good sense to take the pill or even
carry a suppository—he certainly couldn't afford any trouble over
the wife of a faculty member.

Women! He'd never understand them—which maybe was just
as well. Most of the time it wasn't worth the effort—in Mike
Traynor's world.

ii

It was six thirty when Della Rogan woke up in the children's bedroom of her home in Sherwood Ravine. She'd taken a Nembutal after shutting herself up in the bedroom and had almost immediately gone to sleep, not even hearing Dave when he came in. Going to the window, she saw that the sun was already up and the weather looked fine for golf. The idea really didn't generate much enthusiasm within her; she would much rather have gone back to bed. But the way her game had been falling apart since she'd come back from Augusta, she needed the practice, if she were going to make any sort of showing at all for the club championship next week.

Her clothes were in her closet and dressing room off the master bedroom, where Dave would be asleep. Tiptoeing along the hall, she looked in and saw that he was lying on his right side, facing away from her, with the pillow bunched up under his head.

For a moment she was tempted to wake him and apologize for making him get his own dinner last night, then decided against it. He'd refused to come home with her from the hospital, even though he couldn't have helped seeing how disturbed she'd been, so he deserved to be punished awhile longer. She would just slip out of the house to the club for an early round of golf before it got hot, leaving him to get his breakfast at the hospital; he often did that anyway when he had scheduled early morning ward rounds.

Moving as softly as she could, Della took fresh lingerie from her dresser drawer and went into the bathroom to sponge and dress. The brassiere she'd picked out of the drawer had a broken strap and she came out of the bathroom to get another, wearing only a pair of sheer nylon briefs. Dave turned over and yawned hugely.

"Hello, honey." Reaching for the pillow she would have used had she slept in the same bed, he shoved it under his head to prop himself up. "What're you doing up so early?"

"My game's off. Thought I'd get in an early round."

"Alone?"

"Got some shots I need to work out." She was fumbling in the drawer, looking for a bra. "Somebody else will be out early and I can probably get in eighteen holes before lunch. Then if I take a nap afterward, maybe Grace or one of the girls will go round with me in the afternoon."

She slid her arms through the straps of a fresh brassiere and reached around for the hook, but had trouble locating it.

"Come over here and I'll do it for you," Dave offered.

She couldn't very well refuse, for she'd been grateful for the quick warmth that had come into his eyes when he awakened to see her, nude for all the covering afforded by the sheer nylon briefs he liked for her to wear. Crossing the room, she moved over to the bed and waited for him to hook the bra. But when his hands lingered on her bare back, she moved away quickly and began to look for her skirt and blouse in the closet.

"Do you really need all that much practice?" he asked.

"Of course. The club championship tournament starts next week."

"You could use a little practice in some other things," he said casually. "As a psychiatrist, I usually see the worst side of women, but this morning I can certainly see the best side of you. What we need is a second honeymoon."

"We played golf on our honeymoon."

"So you remember?"

"Of course I remember!" Della snapped. "It wasn't that long ago."

"Only fifteen years, close to a fifth of the three score and ten allowed to us. Anyway you look at it, we've got nearly four of those decades behind us, Della."

"You're the one who's getting fat and old—not me." She was laving her face with protective cream; the sun could be very bright in September and Paul McGill was always warning her against too much exposure to it. Already she was troubled with little places of thickened skin which he had to treat with the liquid nitrogen that didn't leave a scar like the electric needle did.

"You've still got a great shape on you, honey," Dave said with a grin. "Maybe what we need is another child."

"Two are enough. We agreed on that years ago."

"That was when the kids were small, but in a few years they'll be gone off to prep school and college. It would be pretty wonderful to have somebody little around the house then."

"Is that another way of saying I don't stay home enough?" she demanded angrily. Since Augusta, her nagging conscience had kept reminding her that she ought to spend more time at home. Now, with one of the perverse quirks that so often characterize feminine logic, she found reason to shift the blame to him. For if he had gone with her to Augusta, as he should have done, none of it would have happened and her guilty conscience wouldn't be driving her mad.

"I've never objected to your being away." Dave hadn't missed her immediate reaction, and being familiar with most of the many faces of guilt, was troubled by it. "It's just that I've seen so many marriages where people began to drift apart after the children left for coll—"

"Ours are still far from that."

"Not as far as we want to think. Or from marriage either, considering the way college students are marrying these days. Maybe I'm selfish but I'm thinking of the time when I may be alone a lot while you're away winning those national golf championships. It would be pretty wonderful to have somebody little to tuck into the crib that's up in the attic."

He'd struck the nerve again, and her reaction was instinctive, the same sort of lashing out that makes a child who feels itself shamed strike even those who would help it.

"You don't want me to excel at anything," she stormed. "You sit up there in that office of yours at the clinic and think you're managing everybody's lives, when the truth is, you can't even manage ours."

"You may be right at that," he admitted. "Everybody knows doctors' families get the poorest medical care of any group."

"So you admit you can't fix everything?"

He grinned. "If you'll tell me what I'm guilty of, dear, I'll know how to plead."

"There you go, making jokes! You never take me seriously, Mr. God."

Dave's face sobered. "There's where you're wrong, Della. Maybe I neglect some of your emotional needs; even a psychiatrist has a hard time understanding women, and most doctors don't understand their wives. It's a price we have to pay for being so closely involved in the lives of others all day long. If you'll just tell me what I've done wrong this time, I'll try to make it up to you."

She turned away quickly, but not before he saw the sudden hell in her eyes and the flush of guilt in her cheeks. Something had happened in Augusta, he was sure now, something he was completely powerless to do anything about, unless she broke down and told him about it. And he was pretty sure now that she wasn't going to do that.

The realization brought a sense of futility and an even greater sense of pain. Della, he knew, was an unusually level-headed woman. She'd been a rock throughout the years when he came home at night, exhausted from coping with the emotional problems and crises of his patients—until golf had started taking her away so much.

A natural instinct told him another man was involved. He was enough of a realist to know, too, that occasional sexual infidelity was in no sense an absolute barrier to the successful continuation of a marriage. In fact, as a psychiatrist he could have made a convincing case for the negative, if he'd cared to debate the question. But it still hurt to think that Della had given herself to another man. What was worse, whenever she was away for any time playing in a tournament from now on, he wouldn't be able to help wondering just what might be happening.

At the door she turned and lashed out at him again. "You're

just like the rest of the men; you want a wife always at your heel like a dog." Then, with one of those sudden switches of mood that make women the delightful creatures they are, she said: "Can you get your breakfast at the hospital?"

"Sure. I've got to see Janet Monroe's little boy before office hours anyway."

"The one you stayed to see last night?"

"Yes."

"Was anything wrong with him?"

"I'm afraid so. He's had convulsions and there's blood in the spinal fluid."

Della remembered enough from her days as an X-ray technician to know something of the significance of the finding. But she was too tense right now to feel anything except irritation that Dave had mentioned it and caused her to feel guilty about the way she had reacted to his staying at the hospital yesterday afternoon to examine the child.

"It's probably just something temporary," she said.

"I hope so. I didn't wake you up when I went to the hospital last night, did I?"

"You went to the hospital?" She turned in the doorway, startled by the question.

"About one o'clock. Maggie McCloskey tried to commit suicide."

Della leaned against the doorframe when her legs suddenly felt as if they were turning to water. "How . . . how did it happen?"

"The usual—barbiturate and alcohol. Lucky for Maggie Jeff Long was there. He kept her going with a respirator until they could wash the drug out of her system with intravenous fluid. She's on my private ward."

"Maggie's not crazy."

"You could get two opinions about that this morning—one, I suspect, from Maggie herself. Actually she's on my service because all attempted suicides go there." He gave her a keen look. "You all right, hon? You're as white as a sheet."

"It's just the shock. Tell Maggie I'll do anything I can to help."

"She's the only one who can help now. If she's finally willing to admit that, maybe we can get somewhere. Have a good game."

Della didn't answer but plunged through the door. Why does he always have to be so damned understanding with everyone else and never understand me? she thought resentfully as she went down the stairs. He could forbid me to play and ask me to stay home more. That was the trouble with being married to a psychiatrist, they understood you too well.

Or did they?

If Dave understood her, why didn't he know that if he put his foot down about her golf, she wouldn't be able to play so much and she'd have an alibi when she started losing tournaments. Instead, he let her go on knocking herself out trying to beat everybody else, when all she really wanted to do was enjoy the game a little. Enjoy it the way she and Dave had done before he'd got too busy with the clinic making his fifty thousand a year to play with her and she'd been left with a feeling of having no real part in his life any more.

It would almost be better, she thought, to have a mild case of diabetes like Grace; and, remembering that George Hanscombe usually left early for the hospital, she turned into the Hanscombe driveway, when she came to it about a quarter mile down the ravine. Sure enough, George's car was already out of the garage, so Della parked hers in the driveway and went around to the back door.

Inside she could see Grace wearing a housecoat and drinking coffee, while she watched the "Today" show on television. When Della rang the doorbell, Grace came to the window and looked out, then went to open the door.

"Come in and have a cup of coffee," she said. "I need cheering up this morning—I feel like a walking corpse."

"I don't feel so hot myself." Della dropped into a chair at the kitchen table while Grace poured the coffee. "Dave was helping me dress to play golf."

"That can hold things up," Grace said with a grin. "But why

play golf if that sort of exercise is available at home—without having to bother about dressing?"

"In the morning?"

"Take my advice, dear, and strike whenever the iron is hot. There'll come a day—and all too soon—when it doesn't get hot very often and even then you usually have to settle for lukewarm."

"Can't you talk of anything but sex, Grace? You're as bad as the men—or Lorrie."

"Poor Lorrie. I'm going to miss her," said Grace. "She was in a class all by herself—a completely honest woman. Why did that bastard have to shoot her anyway? He's done worse than she ever did."

"Dave wants me to have another baby," Della changed the subject.

"You've still got the figure for it and you're still young enough. Why don't you?"

"A lot of right you've got to talk," Della said furiously. "Why don't you have one yourself?"

Grace looked away quickly so Della wouldn't see the pain in her eyes. She and George didn't have any children and she knew the reason—though George didn't. Jack Hagen had laid it on the line; that attack of what was called appendicitis she'd had in the early months of the war hadn't really been appendicitis at all, he'd told her. Salpingitis—an inflammation of the tubes leading from the uterus to the ovaries that often left those vital channels sealed off beyond any repair by surgery—had been the real diagnosis.

In the early days of the war when the boys, so handsome and young, had been marching off to battle, it had been the patriotic thing to do. Only how was she to know that one of those gallant brave young men would leave her a sinister legacy that would keep her from bearing children ever after?

"Did I say something wrong, Grace?" Della was really fond of the Englishwoman.

Grace smiled crookedly. "Just an old skeleton walking over my grave."

"How about some golf this morning?"

"Not today. I bawled George out last night because it wasn't him with Lorrie. Now I've got the willies. Can you remember back when you were poor, Della?"

"Of course. Why?"

"Weren't we all happier then?"

"I . . . I guess so."

"What happened to all of us, Della? You're miserable; I'm miserable; Amy's killing her marriage to Pete trying to keep ahead of him. Elaine had to go through hell last night wondering whether Paul was going to die; Lorrie's already dead. The only one of the group I know that's really happy is Alice—with her soap operas. Maybe she's got more sense than any of us."

iii

Pete Brennan was still asleep when Amy woke up and was startled to find that she had slept all night nude, something she hadn't even done on her honeymoon. As she groped her way back through the fog that still hung over her brain, she began to remember something of what had happened before Pete had been called away and she'd fallen asleep.

She wished now he'd awakened her when he'd come back to bed; perhaps if he had, they could have held on a little while longer to the precious rapture they'd shared with such abandon and such delight. But it was lost this morning, lost with the waning effects of the morphine, as her body went about the business of destroying the drug, just as it did any alien substance.

For a moment, she considered injecting another of the tiny syrettes, seeking to escape from the reality of the day, but put the thought from her. She was strong enough not to need any crutch, she reminded herself firmly, except when the sickening throb of the migraine began.

Slipping from the bed, she went into the bathroom to take a shower and try to wash away some of the fuzziness that still clung to her brain. She came out of the shower wrapped in a voluminous

223

terry-cloth robe; the way she felt this morning, the last thing she wanted was to stimulate Pete into a repetition of last night. But he was in the shower of his own bathroom, singing his college alma mater as he'd done practically every morning since they'd been married.

While Pete was bathing, Amy dressed quickly in tailored slacks and a blouse; she'd made it a rule at the beginning of their marriage never to pad about the house mornings in an old bathrobe with curlers on her head and cream on her face like so many women did. Briefly she debated telling Pete about her success at the District Six meeting, but discarded the idea. There would be other—and better—times, now that she'd discovered the magic key that opened the world she'd almost forgotten existed since the days of their courtship and honeymoon.

"Good morning, dear." Pete came out of the shower, a towel wrapped around his middle like a skirt. He smelled of shaving lotion and hair tonic as he bent over to kiss her. Though he was forty-two, his body was only a little heavier than it had been in his college days—thanks to golf and regular workouts in the small gymnasium and swimming pool in the basement of the Faculty Apartments. His hair was dark and curly with only a faint sprinkling of gray at the temples. And his eyes could still dance, as they did now when he rested his hands upon her shoulders.

"We had us quite a time last night, Shug." How long had it been, she wondered, since he'd called her by that pet name? "We should do that more often."

"Maybe we will," she forced herself to say.

"What got into you anyway?"

"I remember pouring a drink downstairs—the migraine was pretty bad by the time I got home from the hospital. I guess by the time you got here I was loaded."

"Whatever it was, I'm for it." He went over to the chest of drawers and took out a pair of shorts, dropping the towel and stepping into them. Amy felt a sudden moment of panic at the thought of what he would say if he knew what really had loosened the normally tight hold she maintained upon her impulses.

Last night had been an isolated incident, she assured herself. If she'd been able to reach George Hanscombe's office yesterday afternoon and had gotten the injection for migraine, she wouldn't have had to take the morphine. And even while one part of her body was busy remembering how much more relief she'd gotten from the tiny syrette than from her usual injection, another and sterner part was telling her she mustn't ever do it again.

"What was it you had to go out for last night?" she asked as Pete was putting on his pants.

"Something important, you can bet on that. Wild horses couldn't have dragged me away from you otherwise." He grinned. "If you were loaded, you may not remember, but you were really something—the sort of thing only Mohammedans are supposed to dream about."

"Was it an emergency?"

"Of a sort. Roy called to say Mort Dellman wanted to see me."

"What did he want?"

"I'll tell you about it at breakfast." He'd finished dressing now and put his arm around her waist as they crossed the room to the door. "Ethel must have it about ready; I smell bacon from downstairs. I've got to see Arthur Painter this morning, so I'll have to eat in a hurry."

"Is . . . is Mort going to make trouble?" she asked, as he pulled out her chair at the table. It was only set for two, since the children were still at camp.

"No." He took the coffee cup she filled for him from the silver urn. "But he'll have to go away when he gets out of this trouble—"

"Can he—get out, I mean?"

"He thinks so—and Roy does, too. Being in the position he's in, though, Roy can't say so in words. Mort wants to sell the rest of us his share in the clinic—for a hundred thousand dollars."

"It's worth that much, isn't it?" Having always had plenty of money, the amount didn't startle Amy.

"More, in fact. I'm calling a meeting with the others today at lunch. Some of 'em will squawk, of course, until they realize they don't have a choice."

Amy's fingers had just closed about the handle of her coffee cup but, at his words, the cup began to rattle so much in the saucer that part of the coffee spilled over on the snowy white tablecloth.

"What's the matter?" Pete's tone was concerned.

"Nervous, I guess." She tried to smile and knew she wasn't doing a very convincing job of it.

"That's not like you."

"Too much unaccustomed activity last night, maybe." She forced a laugh which sounded equally hollow.

"You'd better start getting accustomed to it again."

"What did you mean by not having any choice?"

"Let's face it. Mort could tell some pretty tall tales if he got started—most of 'em true."

"But not about you—and Lorrie?"

"You know better than that. Oh, I sampled her once or twice, before we were married—every new man who came to town did. But not since."

Amy breathed more easily. It didn't occur to her to doubt him. Pete had never failed to tell her the truth.

"We'll have to buy Mort out and it's up to me to find some way to raise the money," he continued. "Not many of us have that kind of dough lying around."

"I could lend it to you." She knew better by now than to say "give."

"Thanks." He was busy eating. "But all the members of the Faculty Clinic Corporation will have to be in on this deal, except maybe Paul McGill. I don't think there'll be any difficulty in getting the loan, but you can do me a favor, if you will."

"Whatever you want."

"I called Uncle Jake last night from the hospital but he just wanted to be left alone then. Would you go over and see him this morning and find out what we can do for him—about Lorrie?"

"Of course." Amy was glad of the opportunity to be doing

something for Pete, postponing for a while, at least, the time when she would have to tell him she was going to be president of the state medical auxiliary a year before he became head of the medical association.

iv

Grace Hanscombe had saved a morning urine specimen, as she'd done ever since her blood sugar test had shown a high curve a year ago. After Della left, she tested it automatically, hardly noticing what she was doing, until the color of the solution suddenly changed to a deep orange.

Shocked—it was the first time she'd ever seen any change at all—she repeated the test, but the result was the same. Going to the phone, she dialed the clinic number with trembling fingers and asked for George's office, knowing he always went there to dictate letters and reports before starting morning rounds in the hospital. Recognizing the urgency in Grace's voice the secretary put her through to him at once.

"I have only a minute, Grace," he said.

"I showed sugar this morning, George."

"What color?" His voice changed and became crisp and incisive.

"Orange. It's quite a lot, George."

"You've had breakfast, haven't you?"

"Yes—with you, George."

"Of course. Come to the clinic as soon as you can get dressed. Go directly to the lab. I'll phone them before I start rounds."

"Wh—what will you do?"

"We'll start with a sugar tolerance curve. You were upset last night over Lorrie and that could give you the sugar. And Grace—"

"Yes, George."

"I may not know much about women, but I do know a lot about diabetes." She knew it was his way of apologizing and reassuring her and was grateful for it.

"I'm sorry about last night, George," she said. "I was upset

about Lorrie and I'd had trouble at the club with Maggie Mc-
Closkey. She was drunk."

"Maggie was brought to the emergency room last night about
midnight, Grace. Tried to commit suicide."

For a moment, Grace couldn't believe what she heard. "Did
you say tried?" she asked finally.

"She didn't quite make it. They pumped her out and Dave
Rogan has her on one of his wards. Take your time coming down
to the clinic, dear; there's no need to drive fast. You can wait in
my office after the tests are finished. They'll phone me the results."

Grace hung up the phone and went upstairs to dress. How
many more, she wondered, would Mort Dellman's single bullet
bring down? It had killed Lorrie, almost killed Paul McGill, and
from what George said had come almost as near getting Maggie
McCloskey. It had thrown her into a severe diabetic attack and
certainly Della hadn't been herself this morning, when she'd
stopped by the house.

As for Elaine McGill, she remembered now the strange way
Elaine had reacted yesterday, when she had offered to stay at the
hospital. She'd always been pretty fond of Elaine and Paul; since
Paul was about George's age, the two of them had been somewhat closer than the rest of the boys. Elaine had been strangely
calm yesterday afternoon, for someone whose husband might be
dying. Perhaps it had been with relief at learning that Paul wasn't
dead. At least she hadn't seemed to blame him at all.

Which was pretty logical, Grace decided as she started to dress.
After all, Lorrie had taken on all their husbands at one time or another anyway.

As she finished dressing and went out to the Mercedes George
had given her for Christmas, Grace decided that Alice Weston
was the only one of the Dissection Society who hadn't been
affected by Lorrie's sudden death. They were cousins of a sort
but Lorrie had always been pretty contemptuous of Alice, so
there couldn't have been much love lost between them.

As she was parking the Mercedes at the hospital parking lot, Grace saw Alice hurrying into the clinic, bent over a little as if her stomach was hurting her. And she knew then that Mort Dellman's bullet had gotten Alice, too.

CHAPTER XV

Alice Weston was going through the Faculty Clinic, as the duty officer had suggested when he'd phoned the prescription to the drugstore for her the night before. Since more than a year had elapsed since her last checkup, she was following what was called the "routine medical check."

At the desk where she registered, she was given a clipboard to which was attached a digest of her previous record in the clinic, condensed and abbreviated so it could be punched on IBM cards. With it was a blank sheet on which to write her present symptoms and a sheaf of cards for the examinations to be done that day. As she was entering the long corridor behind the appointment desk she saw Grace cross the reception room to register but there was no opportunity for them to speak to each other.

In a small cubicle at one side of the corridor, Alice removed her clothing, except shoes and briefs, putting on one of the disposable paper examining gowns that turned clinic patients into duplicates of each other whose very souls, it seemed, could be punched into the proper spaces on the IBM cards of the clinic record. The paper gowns were much better than the old cloth ones, though. The nurses made some attempt to select one that was nearly your size so you, at least, didn't look as if you were walking around inside a tent.

Alice had come to the clinic without breakfast, so she went first to the laboratory. Built under Mort Dellman's personal direction, this heart of any large clinic was constructed to attain the highest possible degree of efficiency and mobility in carrying out the necessary examinations. On both sides of the central corridor were small cubicles, barely large enough for the patient to sit erect in a chair with an arm board attached and for the technician to stand beside her while drawing blood.

Alice always dreaded the needle, but the girl in the crisp white uniform this morning was very skillful and the pain was hardly more than the prick of a brier. From a rack on the wall of the cubicle, the technician drew a tiny strip of adhesive which she fastened expertly over the small red spot on Alice's arm where the needle had penetrated the skin and vein in one quick single thrust. The specimen of blood she had drawn in the syringe would be divided up for all the various examinations to be made in the laboratory.

Outside in the hall the technician pulled a paper cup from a dispenser on the wall and drew it full of a yellowish liquid from an adjacent container. "Drink it all," she commanded. "It prepares you for—but you've been here before, haven't you, Mrs. Weston?"

Alice nodded and emptied the cup. The liquid had the familiar sweet taste, a little tart with lemon flavoring. The combination of glucose and carbonated water would be absorbed from her empty stomach into her blood rather quickly; about an hour later, at a station farther along the examining line, another blood sample would be drawn.

Just exactly what all this meant, Alice didn't understand, except that somehow the information from the first blood test and the second, fed into a data-processing machine to be compared with her previous examinations, would come out with a diagnosis of a normal blood sugar or diabetes. When the technician stamped the time on one of the half-dozen data-processing cards clipped to the board Alice was carrying, she saw that the blood-test part of the examinations had taken exactly four minutes.

A few yards farther along the corridor, Alice stepped into Station 6, stamped in red on her routing card, and lay down on a table. Another faceless figure in white—to Alice they all looked alike—expertly strapped a battery of metal electrodes to her wrist and ankles, connecting them by rubber insulated wires to a panel of knobs and dials on the wall. She dozed while the machine buzzed away, recording an electric tracing of her heartbeat on sensitized paper, until the technician put one of the electrodes over her breast and she shivered at the contact with the cool metal.

"We're almost through, Mrs. Weston," the girl said. "I just have to do this lead, and then record the heart sounds."

"Doesn't a doctor do that?"

"You haven't been through the clinic lately, have you?"

"Not for over a year."

"We use a phonocardiograph now and make a tape recording of your heart sounds." She showed Alice a small metal box which could be slid into another apparatus standing in the corner of the room. "The tape is in this box, and after we make the recording, it is sent along with your electrocardiogram. When the cardiologist reads the E.K.G. he can also listen to the tape and study a six-foot X-ray film of your chest that tells him the size of your heart. This way, the doctor can do a complete heart examination and never lay a hand on you. Next year, they hope to do the whole thing by computer and maybe we can do away with doctors altogether."

Alice laughed dutifully at the joke. But remembering what examinations had been like in the old days, before the Faculty Clinic had been automated, the technician's attempt at humor began to sound more and more like a prediction of the future.

Another of the cards on the clipboard was punched as she left Station 6, and she saw that she had been inside that cubicle exactly eight minutes. As she went out, a door opened across the hall and she recognized Grace Hanscombe getting on another table over there, an exact duplicate of the one she had just vacated.

At the next station, Alice's pulse and blood pressure were recorded by another technician—she still hadn't seen a doctor and knew she wouldn't until the end of the examination. One step farther along drops were put into one of her eyes, dilating the pupil so the inside of the eyeball—the eye grounds, it was called

233

in medical terminology—could be photographed in color on TV videotape, where it could be studied later by an ophthalmologist. The tension of her eyeballs was also tested for glaucoma, an insidious disease which, if undetected, could cause blindness before the victim knew what was happening.

At another station, the capacity of her lungs to contain air was measured. A lessening of ventilation, as it was called, would indicate emphysema, another insidious killer that needed to be recognized early. At the next, her chest was X-rayed almost as rapidly as she could pass in front of the machine. And at another, her weight and height were recorded, along with a lot of other measurements, of whose significance she had no idea.

The next stop was for the smear of the Pap test, which helped to discover cancer of the female reproductive organs. All of this, Alice knew from hearing the doctors talk shop at cocktail parties, combined to give as complete a picture of the whole patient as it was possible to get by every mechanical device which could be used to lessen the need for expert medical personnel— the hardest quantity to find, she knew, in the whole clinic setup.

At the last stop before she was to see a doctor, a technician drew a second blood sample from Alice's arm. A glance at her watch told her exactly an hour had elapsed since she'd drunk the flavored glucose mixture after the first blood sample had been taken. Here, she was also directed to void a specimen of urine into a numbered container, completing the laboratory examinations.

Alice was tired by the time she was ushered into a somewhat sparsely furnished office. An X-ray view box was on the wall and the examining room next door contained the familiar table which could be put into a dozen positions for internal examinations. She had just finished writing an account of last night's attack on the blank white sheet of the clipboard—she'd been so busy earlier that she hadn't had a chance to make those notations—when the door opened and a young woman came in wearing the long white coat of a doctor.

"Good morning, Mrs. Weston." The faint English accent was pleasing. "I'm Dr. Feldman."

"The new woman doctor?"

Marisa Feldman smiled. "I'm a woman, I'm a doctor, and this is my third day in Weston—so I suppose you're right."

"I didn't mean to be rude," Alice said quickly, feeling an instinctive liking for the slender young woman doctor with the high cheekbones and the brilliant arresting eyes.

"I'm sure you didn't." Marisa Feldman took the chair behind the desk. "I may be new here but I'm not new at treating conditions such as you have, Mrs. Weston. Dr. Hanscombe spoke to me about you this morning."

Marisa didn't tell Alice that George Hanscombe's words had been: "Alice Weston's got her gut in a spasm again. Please see her for me and try to get her relaxed."

"May I have your record, please," Marisa asked.

Alice handed over the clipboard and Marisa Feldman began to study it. After a moment she reached over to a small console with numbered keys and punched a few of them. After a brief interval during which she seemed absorbed in what Alice had written about her most recent attack, the machine began to click and several of the familiar punched cards dropped out of a slot.

Alice knew this was a part of her previous record, as well as a report on the examinations which had already been finished. Marisa Feldman glanced at them, stacked them beside the blotter pad on her desk and continued reading.

"You seem to have had a pretty rough time last night," she said finally.

"It was terrible—until I took the green medicine the clinic duty officer prescribed. I've taken it before but my bottle was empty and I'd been doing so well that I hadn't had it refilled. Last night I had to take a second dose before I could get relief."

"The green medicine—as you call it—is an old-fashioned but still very effective remedy, belladonna, phenobarbital and peppermint water. We used a lot of it in Boston; up there we called it the 'Magic Elixir.' Do you feel better this morning?"

"Much better, thank you."

"Suppose we finish the examination then. Will you go into the next room and lie down on the table?"

Marisa Feldman's hands were gentle and knowing. They found the tender spot, low down on the left side of the abdomen, but there was none of the sudden pain that always occurred when George Hanscombe pressed there. As the gently probing fingers kneaded the spot, Alice could feel herself relaxing.

"There, that's better," said Marisa Feldman. "You had quite a spastic area here but it's relaxing now."

Even the instrument examination, which Alice had always dreaded, was almost pleasant in the hands of this handsome woman doctor with the facile fingers and pleasant manner. It was finished almost before Alice realized it had started.

"You still have some spasm and a mild infection of the lining membrane of the colon," Marisa told Alice as she was wrapping the paper gown about herself once more. "Did anything occur recently that might have caused the attack last night?"

"My cousin was killed."

"Mrs. Dellman?"

"Yes. We grew up together and were very close." It wasn't the truth, for she and Lorrie hadn't gotten along at all well lately, but Alice didn't want the new doctor to think she was neurotic. George Hanscombe had called her that once and she'd never entirely forgiven him for it.

"The shock could easily have caused the attack," Marisa assured her. "I think you should be a little careful of your diet for perhaps a week, Mrs. Weston. Stick to bland foods; you've been on a low-residue diet before, so you know what is allowed. And take the eli—the mixture as before. If you have any more trouble just call me. Dr. Hanscombe feels that I should have charge of your case from now on. I hope you don't mind."

"Oh no." Alice blushed. "I'm glad."

"I would like to see you in about three weeks—just for a visit. You're in excellent condition except for this little trouble and I think we can control that."

"Thank you, Dr. Feldman," Alice said gratefully. "My husband is a member of the clinic corporation, so we'll probably be seeing you socially."

"I hope so. Good-bye."

Alice departed in a warm glow, her abdominal discomfort quite forgotten. The new doctor was wonderful; she could hardly wait to tell the girls about her at the next meeting. But then she wondered whether there would be a next meeting of the Dissection Society—with Lorrie dead.

She wasn't going to feel sad about Lorrie, though. After all it was Lorrie's fault for running after men—when Alice herself had longed to give her all the love anybody could desire.

In her office, Marisa Feldman jotted down a few notes on a slip of paper and attached it to one of the IBM cards with Alice's record. The salient facts would be punched in later by the punchcard operators, so they could be retrieved quickly by the computer when needed in the future.

One note Marisa didn't make, but her face was thoughtful as she put the record into the slot where it would be carried by a continuous belt to the central record storage section. It had taken her only a few moments to realize that Alice Weston was a Lesbian; there'd been too many of them in the prison at Frondheim for the telltale signs to be missed by a trained observer. Knowing this, she couldn't help wondering what Alice's husband was like, and what sort of married life they could possibly have together.

ii

After Pete left for the hospital, Amy changed into a linen dress—slacks hardly seemed appropriate for visiting a father who had just lost his only daughter. The Weston house—it was still called that in the town, although Amy had occupied it as Mrs. Peter Brennan for some fifteen years now—was located on a knoll overlooking the river several miles from the newer development in Sherwood Ravine where most of the other doctors' wives lived.

Jake Porter's home was about a half mile away from Amy's on another rise, with a shallow ravine between them.

The Westons had moved south from New England after the Civil War when land could be bought for a song and labor was almost as cheap as it had been under the slave system. By applying New England thrift and know-how to rug and fabric weaving, Amy's grandfather had made a fortune and established himself as the leading citizen in that part of the state. Jake Porter had been younger, a foreman at first in Weston Mills, but with a genius for management that had shortly put him into a position of authority and eventually part ownership.

Amy's own father hadn't been the businessman her grandfather had been, but Jake Porter was managing the mill by then and building his own fortune with massive investments in timberland and industrial property. It had been Jake who had negotiated the sale of Weston Mills to the Portola interests at the time of the second New England textile migration from the union-dominated, high-cost labor markets of the North to the huge unorganized pool of cheap and largely ignorant labor in the South.

As a result, though actually no relation, Amy and Roy had grown up thinking of Jake Porter as their uncle. When Roy married Alice, Jake's ward, the ties had been cemented even more closely. Amy, Alice and Lorrie had grown up almost like sisters, until finishing school and college had separated them for a while. Then marriage had brought them all back together again, when Mort Dellman and Pete Brennan had come with Roy and the others from Korea to become members of the faculty of Weston University Medical School. Now everything was in danger of being blasted by the single shot from Mort Dellman's pistol—unless Pete could find the hundred thousand dollars Mort demanded for his share of the clinic.

Amy didn't doubt that Pete would be able to arrange a loan to buy out Mort, however. The real danger was that, if Roy put pressure on Mort because of his own political ambitions, their tight little world would be blown apart by a scandal that could force the trustees of the medical school—who were not too happy about the success of the Faculty Clinic anyway—to take action and demand the resignations of those involved from the faculty. That, of course, would be very bad for the clinic, necessitating a change of name and perhaps endangering the solid reputation it had built as one of the finest organizations of its kind in the entire Southeast.

Amy had decided to walk to Jake Porter's rambling, cypress-shingled home, where she'd spent so many happy hours when she was a little girl. She was hoping to recapture, if only for a little while, that now almost forgotten period when Weston had been small and she, as daughter of the most important man in town, the most envied and eligible girl in it. Halfway to the house, she was sorry she hadn't taken her air-conditioned Cadillac out of the garage, for the day was hot and she could feel the thin summer dress beginning to stick to her perspiration-wet skin across the shoulders.

High up on the slope of the mountain to the west, she saw the sun glint off metal and knew the source was the antenna at the top of the system of microwave relay towers that carried telephone conversations and TV images across the crest of the mountain range. The tower stood beside a road leading down to a pocket in the mountains where Deerslayer Lodge was located, and she wondered whether—once the nightmare of yesterday and the next few days was over—she might be able to talk Pete into going up there for a week. They'd spent their honeymoon at Deerslayer Lodge and, with the help of the tiny syrettes she had cached in her dresser drawer, they might find again some of the bliss they'd shared there—but which they had seemed to have lost until last night.

Jake Porter was sitting on the porch in a rocking chair when Amy came up the steps. He occupied the big old house alone, cared for by a pair of colored servants who lived in an apartment over the garage.

"Good morning, Uncle Jake." Amy leaned down to kiss the old man's leathery cheek. "I guess you know how sorry we all are about what happened."

"Sit down, Amy." The old man sounded tired. "It was nice of you to come."

"Pete wondered whether there's anything we can do to help with the funeral arrangements."

"It's all taken care of, Amy. I called the funeral parlor and told them to give her a decent burial. Dr. Potter's out of town, but the canon from the cathedral across town will hold a graveside service." Potter was the minister of the largest Episcopalian church in Weston, to which most of those among the higher levels of society in the town belonged.

"Lorrie wouldn't want anything elaborate," Amy agreed. "Will the children be here?"

"I sent Jasper to bring them from the camps they're in up near Asheville," said Jake Porter. "They would have been coming home Tuesday anyway to start school."

Jasper was the colored chauffeur-houseman who helped look after Jake Porter. Amy's children were in the same camp.

"Lorrie always had her own mind," the old man added. "I hope the man she was with lives."

"Dr. Dieter took the bullet out of Paul McGill's heart last night," Amy told him. "Pete says he should be all right."

"What about Dellman?"

"They've got him in jail. He's offered to sell his share of the clinic to the others in the corporation."

"For how much?"

"A hundred thousand dollars."

"That means he expects to get off—probably on the unwritten law. I'll be glad to see the last of him, too. Don't see why he had to kill her, though—unless he thought Lorrie had something to do with my changing my will."

Amy had been listening with only half her mind. "What did you say, Uncle Jake?" she asked.

"I couldn't stand the idea of Dellman getting hold of my money after I died, so I changed my will about a month ago. Left everything in trust for Lorrie's kids, with the bank as trustee. Good thing I did, too, the way things turned out."

"Lorrie loved the children. She'll be glad they're going to be taken care of."

"They will be—you can count on that." There was an odd intensity in the old man's voice but half bemused as she was, Amy didn't notice it. "Dellman isn't going to make any trouble for your husband and the others, is he, Amy?"

"What do you mean, Uncle Jake?"

"You know what I'm talking about."

"Pete says Mort's going to leave Weston as soon as the court decides what to do with him."

"It will be good riddance—for everybody. Lorrie wasn't really bad. She loved the children and she may even have loved Dellman—at first. But she couldn't do without men any more than a wino can leave the bottle. I guess you could call it a disease with her and now it's killed her, just like any other disease. Maybe it's my fault for letting her run loose so much when she was young. Or maybe she got her ways from me; I haven't exactly been a monk, you know."

Not knowing what to say, Amy said nothing.

"Not that I regret what I've done any more than Lorrie did; it's just the way we were made. Tell that fine husband of yours to come to see me. I want to talk to him about this whole thing."

"Maybe he can come over this evening."

"You've got a good man there, Amy, a fine human sort of a man. Sometimes he's going to do things you don't like; after all, you take a lot after that rock-bound New England branch of your family. But go easy, girl. A good marriage is about the most precious thing in the world. Lorrie's mother and I had it, so I know what I'm talking about."

"Pete and I are doing fine, Uncle Jake."

"I hope so—but there's been talk. Some people even say they think he won't be able to stand your driving much longer and you'll end up with a divorce."

The words hit Amy between the eyes like a blow with a cudgel. Pete divorce her? It was unthinkable.

"You're smart, Amy, and you're ambitious like any other

woman." Jake Porter had apparently not noticed the effect of his words upon her. "Just don't let your own ambitions wreck your marriage."

"I won't, Uncle Jake." She got up quickly and moved down the steps, stumbling a little from the shock of what she had just heard.

"Thank you for stopping by," he called after her, but she didn't even hear.

By the time she reached the corner, Amy was able to regain some control of herself. When she looked back, Jake Porter was still sitting in the rocking chair on the porch of the house, with his chin dropped forward on his chest as if he were dozing. It was hard to believe he had just rocked Amy Brennan's snug little world to its very foundations.

iii

The worst thing about drinking was waking from the stupor brought on by alcohol, but this time it was different. Maggie Mc-Closkey floated for a long time between consciousness and unconsciousness, trying to sleep while, it seemed, the whole world was seeking to keep her awake. Somewhere in between, there was a torturer who choked her, burned her throat with a hot rod, and pricked her with needles, like the drawings of Dante's Inferno she remembered studying in college. Finally, she awoke, to find herself in unfamiliar surroundings, the antiseptic whiteness of a hospital room.

Her head throbbed, her throat was sore, and her face felt as if someone had been beating her. Her arm hurt, too, but when she tried to move it, she saw that it was strapped to a bandage-covered board, from which a small plastic tube dangled. And when she turned her head to follow the course of the tube, she could see that it was connected to a flask hanging from a stand, a flask half-filled with a yellowish-colored liquid.

The movement of her head brought a window within her range of vision. When she saw the distant slope of the mountains through it, she knew she was still in Weston, probably at the

University Hospital. The outside, too, was bright with midday sunlight, which meant that she must have been out for a long time.

"Awake?" a fresh young voice asked and a student nurse with short red hair and freckles moved into her range of vision.

"Wh-what time is it?"

"Almost noon. You're having lunch."

"How long have I been here?" It was an effort to talk, partly from the languor that still beckoned to her and partly from the strange soreness in her throat.

"You were admitted to the emergency room around midnight, but they didn't bring you to this ward until nearly five o'clock this morning."

Maggie tried to make sense out of the figures. She'd gone home about ten—that much she remembered. Midnight was two hours later, so she must have passed out. What about the period from midnight to 5 A.M.? The effort was too much, however, and finally she gave up and went back to sleep.

When she woke again, her head was much clearer. The bottle of fluid hanging from the stand had been changed; it was now a brilliant red color and the shadows upon the mountain visible through the window told her it must be afternoon.

"Lunch was yellow." The hoarseness of her own voice startled her. "Dinner's red."

She began to laugh, but the laughter soon changed to sobs, sobs she wasn't able to control for a long time. When finally they stopped, she lay staring blankly at the white ceiling of the new private wing—the old ceilings were fly-specked—staring at the nothing that was her life.

CHAPTER XVI

Pete Brennan had called a meeting of the Executive Committee of the Faculty Clinic for lunch, in a small private dining room off the staff lounge on the top floor of the clinic. Most of the staff ate the noonday meal across the street at the hospital cafeteria. In order to save time, however, the small dining room had been placed adjacent to the lounge for the convenience of the medical staff in holding lunchtime conferences. Everybody was there except Mort Dellman and Paul McGill, neither of whom, under the circumstances, could have been expected to participate.

"Lock the door please, Dave," Pete said to the psychiatrist, when the food had been served and the waitress had left. "You're the nearest to it."

Dave Rogan locked the door and sat down again. Nobody asked the reason for the secrecy; more than enough had happened in the past twenty-four hours to justify it.

In a few succinct words, Pete told of his conversation last night with Mort Dellman. When he finished, the stricken looks on the faces of most of the men gathered at the table reflected his own feelings after leaving the jail last night. Since then, however, he'd had time to do some thinking and to make at least some preliminary plans for salvaging what they could out of the difficulty in which they found themselves.

"Mort hasn't got anything on me," George Hanscombe blustered. "I never—"

"He's had a detective watching Lorrie for a long time, George," Pete warned. "Better be sure you're pure."

"Sure you're pure!" Dave Rogan laughed mirthlessly. "If it wasn't so darn true, Pete, that would be funny. It must have been a Freudian slip."

George Hanscombe opened his mouth to speak, then shut it without saying any more.

"It would take a louse like Mort to put a private eye on his wife." Joe McCloskey was chubby and his hair was thinning, but he was one of the most solid and dependable members of the group, as well as a highly skilled specialist in his field, and everybody in the clinic respected him. "What I can't understand is why he did it. After all, he must have known Lorrie had been sleeping around for years."

"Shooting Lorrie was an accident," Pete explained. "She'd been laying this medical student and Mort planned to make an example of him."

"Mort knew Lorrie was bound to get herself mixed up in a scandal someday," said Dave Rogan. "My guess is that he put the detective on her so he'd have a stick to hold over Jake Porter's head, if it came to a divorce. Jake worships those grandchildren and would have put up a pretty large settlement to keep his daughter's sex life from becoming known to them."

"It looks like Mort has us dead to rights," Joe McCloskey admitted.

"But why would he do that to us?" George Hanscombe protested. "After all, we cut him in on this clinic when we didn't have to do it."

"Mort cut himself in by becoming a member of the medical school faculty originally," Pete reminded them all. "Let's not kid ourselves that a lot of the Faculty Clinic's success hasn't been due to him."

"Actually, Mort stole the automation idea from those clinics out in California that started it," Dave Rogan pointed out. "Though I doubt that the rest of us would have realized its possibilities, if he hadn't sold us on the computer."

"So we buy him off?" Joe McCloskey asked.

"At a hundred thousand?" George Hanscombe's voice was a little shrill. "Are you crazy, Joe?"

"I didn't ask you here just to scream because you've been hit," Pete said sharply. "How many of you would sell out today for a hundred thousand?"

There was no answer.

"Then what we need to do now is to decide how to go about arranging the deal."

"I don't have that kind of money," George Hanscombe protested.

"You've got your stocks with Merrill Lynch," Joe McCloskey reminded him.

"You're crazy if you think I'm going to tie them up."

"You make as much as the rest of us, George," Pete said pointedly.

"But you've got Amy's—"

"Shut up, George," Dave Rogan said wearily. "You know Pete has paid his own way ever since he came here."

"Thanks, Dave," said Pete. "My guess is that, counting lawyer's fees and the like, it will cost us maybe from twenty-five to thirty thousand apiece—including the interest."

George Hanscombe opened his mouth to protest again, then apparently thought better of it.

"One thing worries me," said Joe McCloskey. "How can we be sure Mort won't take our money and then sell us out? For the kind of story he'd build up out of what's been going on in a town like Weston, some magazine would probably give him another fifty grand. Or he could always write one of those 'as told to' books."

"What's been happening here goes on in practically any town this size—even without a university," said Dave Rogan. "We're a very close-knit community within a larger one and things sort of build up."

"Until they explode—like now," said Pete.

"We're still in a jam," Joe McCloskey insisted. "All your psycho-analyzing isn't going to change that, Dave."

"It can still make us take a long look at our own lives to see how we got into this mess," said the psychiatrist. "Maybe twenty-five thousand is a cheap price to pay for a little self-analysis."

George Hanscombe's snort was an explosive comment. "You can talk, Dave. You're not on a big margin in the stock market, with the Dow Jones touching bottom."

"But look at all you made when it was touching top, George."

Pete Brennan held up his hand for silence. "We all have excellent financial statements and good prospects, so we're A-1 credit risks. I say we borrow what we need, paying it back to the bank just like we would any other loan. It may cramp some of us, but like Dave said, it might be worth it in the end."

"You still haven't answered my question about how we can be sure Mort won't double-cross us," Joe McCloskey reminded him.

"I'm not sure he doesn't have something like that in mind," Pete admitted. "Last night he told me what really happened, yesterday afternoon. You see he expected to find this medical student with Lorrie and planned to crease him, as a warning. This morning I wrote down all Mort told me—"

"Not to your secretary, I hope," said Joe McCloskey.

"I'm not that big a fool, Joe. It would have been all over the clinic in half an hour and across town by noon. I wrote it down by hand and the document's right here." He took a long envelope from his pocket. "I'm going to mail it to myself by registered mail this afternoon and leave it in my safe-deposit box unopened when it's delivered. That will establish the time it was written."

"That's damn clever, Pete," said George Hanscombe.

"Writers do it all the time to protect manuscripts; a patient told me about it once. By sending themselves a carbon copy of whatever they want to protect, they automatically have proof that it was written before a certain date."

"Then Mort can only double-cross us by putting the noose around his own neck with the admission that he actually went out there intending to shoot the student," said Dave Rogan. "That should hold him."

"What about Paul McGill?" Joe McCloskey asked. "Where does he come in on this?"

"Paul's got nothing to gain by making any deal with Mort, so I think he should be left out," said Pete. "I take it we're all agreed that we should form a group and borrow the hundred thousand we need. Mort sells us his share of the clinic legally for that amount and, if I know Arthur Painter, he'll figure out some way to make it all a business expense. Give me a show of hands."

Three hands went up at once; George Hanscombe finally raised his, making it unanimous.

"I'll have Arthur get the papers and consult the bank," said Pete. "Is there anything else?"

Nobody broached a new subject, so the meeting broke up. Dave Rogan stayed behind after the others had gone.

"I've been thinking about this mess we've got ourselves into, Pete," he said. "Got a minute to talk about it?"

"Sure. Let's have another cup of coffee and a cigarette."

The waitress had left a glass Silex container bubbling on a hot-plate in the corner. Pete filled two fresh coffee cups and brought them over to the table where Dave Rogan was sitting. He was very fond of the psychiatrist, and in the beginning of their association they'd spent many pleasant hours in bull sessions. Lately, though, they'd both been too busy with teaching duties and the demands of the clinic to leave much time for anything else.

"I guess you know I've got Maggie McCloskey on one of my wards, Pete."

"Joe told me. Will she be all right?"

"She's safe this time, but maybe not the next."

"Why would she do it?"

"Maggie still loves Joe. She was at the club yesterday afternoon when the news came that Mort had shot Lorrie. The first reports didn't mention Paul's name, only that a prominent physician was also involved. Maggie, Della, and Grace Hanscombe came tearing over here—each wondering whether her husband was the man in the case."

"Amy was here, too. And last night—" Pete stopped suddenly as a possible explanation of Amy's behavior came to him.

"You were going to say?"

"Amy was—you might say—more affectionate than usual, when I got home."

"That early broadcast put the fear of God into all of them," said the psychiatrist. "George told me just before lunch that Grace showed a heavy spilling of sugar this morning for the first time in a year. Her glucose tolerance curve is all shot to hell, so he's put her into the hospital because he's afraid she might go into a diabetic coma."

"That must have been what was eating George just now. He's not usually as stubborn as he was this morning."

"I guess any one of us would be shaken up, if his wife spilled sugar into the urine to prove she still loved him. Grace's diabetes will quiet down in time; she was only a mild case before. It's Maggie and Joe I'm worried about. Did you know he's been paying the bartender at the club to persuade her not to drive home when she's stoned—which is practically every night?"

"No."

"After she left the hospital yesterday, Maggie went back to the club and stayed there until the bartender sent her home in a taxi. Evidently she was too much disturbed to go to sleep, so she took some barbiturate capsules that were in the medicine chest. Joe's been driving by the house late every night to see whether she was all right. Fortunately, he suspected something was wrong when he saw the whole place lit up last night and took her to the hospital. Jeff Long was on duty and put an intratracheal catheter into her windpipe, so he could pump oxygen into her. Then he gave her an intravenous drip with a psychic energizer to jolt her brain and she began to come around early this morning."

"Sounds like it was close."

"Too close. When Maggie wakes up, I'm going to try and scare her into taking the cure."

"Most alcoholics don't, do they?"

"No. But I think I've got something I can hold over Maggie this time. Her rushing to the hospital yesterday afternoon proves she still loves Joe, and we both know he's been eating his heart out for her ever since the divorce. Maybe I can parlay those facts into getting her straightened out."

Pete Brennan stared at the white tablecloth and the smudge of ashes that had fallen on it from his cigarette. He was remembering Amy's relatively wanton—for her—actions last night, and seeing them now as a symptom of something disturbing. Because no matter how much it had pleased him at the time, that kind of behavior wasn't typical of Amy.

"What's happened to all of us, Dave?" he asked. "Where did we go wrong?"

"A psychiatrist doesn't have any hard and fast rules for distinguishing right from wrong, Pete."

"I mean how did we get our lives into such turmoil? Most of us have been sleeping around for years—Lorrie was . . . just honest about hers. But what did it get us?"

"Pleasure?"

"Maybe at the moment. But how long does it last? And how much is it worth?"

"It lasts only a moment—and it isn't worth a damn thing."

"Then why do we do it? Surely that kind of behavior can't be considered normal."

"That's another term psychiatrists try not to use, but I know what you mean. Maggie drinks too much. Grace Hanscombe has a sudden flare-up in what was a mild diabetes. My Della plays too much golf. Amy has migraine. Alice Weston has spastic colitis. I guess Elaine McGill is the only real balanced one in the crowd, but she's sterile and can't find a reason for it."

"Who's to blame—or what?"

"We husbands aren't quite what you'd call normal either. We work too hard for our own good, and our wives don't get the understanding they should from us. Take George Hanscombe for example. He's darn near paranoic in many ways, like a lot of so-called normal people. Voted for Goldwater, belongs to the John Birch Society, may even be a Klansman for all I know—he's certainly rabid enough on the subject of segregation. Grace is a warm, fairly intelligent English girl who would have been supremely happy married to the owner of a middle-class English pub. She really was a barmaid, you know. Instead she marries George, tries to be worthy of him, and does a fine job—with damn little help from him. The wonder is that she hasn't had diabetes—or something else—before."

"I'm not going to ask you to analyze me." Pete managed to grin. "You're too penetrating this morning for comfort."

"All of this is really elementary," Dave Rogan assured him. "Actually, I'm no better able to cope with my own wife's problems than the rest of you are. You don't think Della's a golf champion only because she loves the game, do you?"

"But—"

"Because I'm a psychiatrist, Della's got the conviction that she's intellectually inferior to me—which doesn't happen to be true. As long as she was busy with the children, she didn't have time to brood on it; nothing builds a woman's ego like having handsome children who need her. But the thought of them going away to prep school and college has already started eating away at her self-esteem. So she becomes a golf champion to prove she's physically superior to me—which she is."

"What are you going to do?"

Dave grinned. "Get her pregnant again, if I can ever pin her down that long. But it looks like I'll have to substitute lactose tablets for those birth control pills she takes; the damn things don't leave anything to chance."

"What I still don't understand is how we all got so mixed up, when none of us is really very far from what's ordinarily considered normal," Pete insisted. "There are maybe a hundred members of the medical school faculty and we must have thirty of them on the staff of the clinic. Are we the only abnormal ones?"

"Watch out for that word 'abnormal,'" Dave Rogan warned. "The main trouble is that we're very much alike in income, social level, the way we live—which makes us a pretty inbred group by any standard you could imagine."

"Inbred?"

"You, Joe, George, Paul, Mort, myself—and Roy—sort of drifted together in Korea, but not just by chance. In many ways, we're very much alike. We're intelligent, ambitious, with lots of drive. We're go-getters, the kind of men who succeed, no matter what field they're in. In Korea we came together out of the whole hospital staff by a process of natural selection. An accident of fate—the opening of the medical school here—threw us all together after the war in Korea was over. We married women from different walks of life but the pressure of circumstances started squeezing them into the same mold."

"Like what?"

"The pattern of conformity—for one thing. We all live in the same sort of house. We belong to the same club. We drink the same liquor. Pretty soon we were all leading more or less the same sex life. So who cares if we change about a little?"

"You make us sound like guinea pigs in some sort of a diabolic experiment."

"Maybe that's what life really is—the devil testing us out to see whether we're eligible for hell."

"I don't buy that," Pete protested. "It would mean being in hell twice."

"Most people are."

"What's the answer then?"

"For men it's the sort of friendly competition we have here in the clinic every day. We're so busy we don't have time to build aggressions that might be channeled into physical symptoms or emotional disturbances. With the women we marry, though, it's different. At first they have jobs to do—helping us get started, making a home, raising small children, the things a woman knows she's better at than any man could ever hope to be."

"Having a nice home, a beautiful wife and children have always been pretty attractive to me," Pete protested.

"They are to all of us—until we start taking them for granted. Happiness—in marriage, in your work, in your living—isn't just something you can drift along with. If you do, you'll find pretty soon that you've lost it. Happiness has to be worked at, making a house, raising children—"

253

"Maggie and Grace don't have any kids," Pete protested. "That doesn't stack up very well with this theory of yours."

"Why do you suppose they're more seriously ill than the others?"

"And Amy?"

"Sure you want my opinion?" Dave asked.

"I would appreciate it."

"I'm not sure Amy isn't in more danger than the others, Pete. That's one reason why I wanted to talk to you today."

"Surely she hasn't consulted you."

"Neither have the others—except Maggie who was automatically put on my service because she's a potential suicide. Amy's ambition worries me. Surely you've noticed it—particularly lately."

Pete nodded soberly. "At first it wasn't so intense. She already had a position here, she was independently rich, and she could help a doctor-husband get started. She did, too, I don't deny that. We had some battles in the beginning, mainly because I insisted that we live on my salary. But then the clinic got going and I suddenly began to earn as good an income on my own as her father ever had."

"Think clearly now," Dave Rogan interrupted. "Was that when she began to be interested in the medical auxiliary?"

"About the same time, yes. I think it was just after I turned down the post of Professor of Surgery across the street."

"Didn't she have her first migraine attack then?"

"Come to think of it, yes."

"Ever wonder why?"

"Are you saying that was when Amy began to think I didn't need her any more?"

"At least the unconscious doubt must have been there," said Dave. "Amy's always been independent and ambitious. She's been a leader in every community activity a woman can get into in Weston, and now she's spreading her sphere to include the state. But she's paying a price for it already—though so far only in migraine."

"Are you implying that it could get worse?"

"Who can tell? For one thing, Amy's no longer sure of you. None of our wives are, or they wouldn't have been so upset when they heard on the radio that a doctor was with Lorrie yesterday afternoon."

Pete filled his coffee cup again and lit another cigarette. He wasn't surprised to discover that his hand was shaking so much he had difficulty controlling the lighter.

Had it been fear that had changed Amy so much, he wondered? Or relief at learning he wasn't hurt? Somehow neither answer fitted the picture, yet he had no other clue. And you could hardly ask even a close friend like Dave why your wife—who had become almost frigid these past several years—would suddenly start behaving like a wanton.

"Like I said before"—Dave's voice brought him back to the present—"I think the trouble with our little group is what I call inbreeding. We men are together here all day at work and our wives are together at the golf course, the club bar, or with that group of Amy's you named the Dissection Society. Even when we socialize, it's mainly together, and we usually attend the state medical conventions in a body. It's a case of familiarity breeding something more than contempt, a sort of letting down of barriers that's like a game of musical chairs."

"Maybe it would be more appropriate to call it musical beds," said Pete. "Do you think we'll change—after what's just happened?"

Dave Rogan shook his head. "We're all forty or thereabouts—and some beyond that—so the damage is already done. What we've got to do now is learn to live with ourselves and make the best of what we've got." He squashed out his cigarette in the saucer of his coffee cup and stood up. "I've spent all the time philosophizing I can afford to right now. Have you had a chance to see Janet Monroe's little boy?"

"Not yet," said Pete. "I was planning to do it after we finished here but I've got to talk to Arthur Painter on the phone and start him to work on the deal with Mort—and the loan. Got any idea of what may be the trouble with the kid?"

"My guess would be a congenital aneurysm in the Circle of Willis that's been leaking a little. Anton Dieter is going to see the child this afternoon and Ed Harrison is setting up a radioscan for tomorrow morning."

Radioscanning was a relatively new method of locating tumors within the body through the tendency of malignant tissue to absorb certain radioactive isotopes—in this case usually a mercury salt. Using a sensitive instrument related to a Geiger counter that reacted to the presence of radioactivity, it was often possible to outline the presence, and even the shape, of a growth deep within the body by recording on an X-ray film the increased degree of radiation emanating from the tumor cells.

"That's about all you can do at the moment," Pete Brennan agreed. "I'll see the boy before I leave this afternoon. Janet's a fine girl who's had a tough break. She deserves some good fortune—like getting the kid well and marrying Jeff Long. I hope we can bring it off."

But as he took the elevator upstairs to his office and for the talk with Arthur Painter about the loan, the neurosurgeon knew that if Dave's tentative diagnosis was correct, the odds against success were very great indeed.

ii

"Why did you do it?"

The question startled Maggie McCloskey into answering without stopping to think—as Dave Rogan had intended it to do—an eruption of truth from the preconscious portion of her mind, where it had no chance to be colored by emotion.

"I wanted to give Joe my blood—but he didn't need it." Her eyes filled with tears. "He used to need me—but he doesn't any more. Nobody does."

Suddenly Maggie realized what she was saying, the truth she hadn't admitted previously to anyone—hardly even to herself.

"Damn you, Dave Rogan!" she exploded as the psychiatrist came into view. "How did you get in this room without me hearing you?"

"You were too busy feeling sorry for yourself. Besides, I wanted to startle you into giving me an honest answer."

"How can you be so sure?" She was already beginning to recover a little of her old composure.

"Because it was the answer I expected. The feeling of not being needed is a basic cause, as well as a symptom, of the Doctor's Wife syndrome."

"Doctor's wife what?"

"It's a well-known condition—Doctor's Wife disease, if you don't remember the meaning of syndrome. That's a collection of symptoms by the way, denoting a specific disease pattern."

"You're kidding."

"I was never more serious. Della has it—only her symptom is golf, not suicide."

Maggie stared at him, her eyes dilating slowly with horror. "You think I tried to—?"

"Didn't you?"

"Christ no! Why would I want to do that?"

"Because you think you're no longer needed. You just admitted it."

"You caught me with my pants—my defenses—down."

"You told me the truth, the first time. Now you're covering up." Dave took a seat at the foot of the bed and began to fill his pipe. "Exactly what did happen last night, Maggie?"

"Della and Grace and I were at the club having some drinks when the news about Mort shooting Lorrie came over the TV. How is Paul?"

"He'll live. Keep on about yourself."

"Why should I?"

"You're my patient. This is my service."

"Psychiatry?"

"The same. Tell me your story! I haven't got all day. Some other doctors' wives—and a lot of people in general—have the same disease you have."

"I still don't believe it."

"My time is valuable and you're getting it free," he told her bluntly. "Get on with your story."

"I was sick yesterday afternoon at the club after I first heard the broadcast. Then I remembered Joe's a Type B-Rh negative like me and they're hard to find, so I started for the hospital."

"Were you still sick?"

"Was I?" Maggie blanched a little at the memory. "Grace drove me and Della followed us."

"So even though you were sick, you still started for the hospital to help Joe? What's next?"

"You know. It was Paul that was shot—not Joe."

"So?"

"After we saw you downstairs, I had an argument with Della in the parking lot. Did you really mean that about golf being her symptom?"

"Yes. But we're talking about you."

"I took a taxi back to the club and got drunk as usual. Manuel got me a taxi when they closed the bar a little before ten o'clock. I left my car in the lot." A spasm of pain crossed her face. "I've gone home that way before—lots of times."

"Why were the lights all on at the house?"

"I guess I must have hit the bank of switches by the door with my hand when I turned the front lights on. I remember the driver kept his headlights on until I could find the keyhole." She started to laugh, with a touch of hysteria.

"None of that," Dave Rogan said sharply. "Keep on with your story."

"I was drunk but not sleepy—Manuel had given me some coffee at the club. I guess it was the sight of the bed that really upset me."

"What bed?"

"Joe's—the other twin; it's empty. I found some capsules in the medicine cabinet, so I took some of 'em."

"How many?"

"Three or four. I've taken that many before."

"But not when you were already drunk."

Her eyes opened wide. "I was trying to remember something about those capsules before I took 'em, something Joe once told me. He said you don't ever take 'em when you've been drinking. Was that what put me out?"

"The combination of pentobarbital and whiskey can be lethal," he told her. "You weren't even breathing when you were brought to the emergency room. Fortunately a very smart young doctor happened to be on duty and recognized the condition at once."

"Did they wash out my stomach? Is that why my throat's sore?"

"You'd had the pentobarbital for two hours, long enough for most of it to be absorbed. The first thing Jeff Long did was to put an intratracheal tube down your windpipe, so he could attach you to a respirator and pump oxygen into you. He also put a small nasal catheter into your stomach, but there wasn't much there."

Maggie shivered. "Do you have to talk about me like I was an animal—something you were using for an experiment?"

"Animals don't try to kill themselves, Maggie. They've got better sense."

"I told you it was an accident," she flared.

"And I don't believe you." Dave took a lighter from his pocket and lit the pipe again.

"Why?"

"You've been trying to destroy yourself ever since you started drinking so heavily, long before you and Joe broke up. Alcoholism is a form of suicide, Maggie. When you add barbiturate poisoning—"

"I told you that was an accident."

"And I say it wasn't. Just now you had no trouble remembering that Joe had told you never to mix the drug with alcohol. Yet you claim that last night you couldn't remember."

"I was drunk," she said sullenly.

"But not drunk enough to go to sleep without help. And not

drunk enough so you couldn't find the capsules and count them out."

"I just wanted to sleep."

"I'm sure you did—permanently. Hollywood actresses who take barbiturates in so-called suicide attempts usually manage to telephone a friend or somebody at the last moment. But you made no attempt to call."

"How do you know?"

"The phone was still on the hook when they found you. You'd undressed, put on a nightgown, and were lying on the bed in the next room. I wondered about that, until you told me just now about the twin bed."

She turned her face away from him. "I couldn't bear the thought of Joe knowing."

"Now we're beginning to get somewhere," Dave said briskly and moved from his seat at the foot of the bed to knock out his pipe in the ash tray on the bedside table.

"I don't see how."

"You've finally admitted that you tried to kill yourself because you feel Joe doesn't need you any more. You wouldn't finish the job in the room you'd shared with him because you were ashamed of what you were doing. And you're afraid now that you may get to the point where you'll try it again—and succeed."

"Who are you? God—or somebody?"

"I could have told you all those things when I came in here just now. I see this pattern often—and not just in doctors' wives. It's also fairly common where men rise rapidly in a profession like law, insurance or even in business and their wives aren't able to keep up with them—or think they can't. The important thing was for you to admit all this to yourself."

"Then you've only been leading me on?"

"That's what a psychiatrist really does, Maggie—lead people on until they see the truth about themselves. Fortunately you're not too far gone to face the facts and you're intelligent. That puts us halfway on the road back."

She wondered if she dared believe him, or if he were only saying it to encourage her. "How do you figure that?"

"The most important force in any woman's life is the knowledge that she's wanted and needed. Her whole physical and emotional make-up is geared to that one drive and losing that knowledge can be as crippling physically as a severe heart attack, or ulcer. Or if she's lucky, the kind of mild colitis or cystitis that sends so many women to doctors. Mentally, the mildest reaction is psychoneurosis; the most severe is some form of real mental disease."

"Or suicide?"

"Yes."

Maggie took a deep breath. She was almost afraid to ask the question that was on the tip of her tongue, yet it had to be asked —and answered. "Just now you said I was halfway back. But to what?"

"Joe needs you, whether you know it or not."

"If he does, why did he shack up with that slut in Greenville?"

"Do you really want the answer? I'll have to be brutal."

"Y-yes."

"Because he wasn't getting what he had a right to get at home."

"I never denied him," she flared. "He lied if he told you that."

"Joe didn't tell me anything; I've seen too many cases like yours not to know the pattern by heart. Besides, what right do you have to be so damn virtuous, after that convention of the Southern Medical in New Orleans?"

The impact of his words struck her like a punch in the solar plexus. When her stomach suddenly tied up in a knot, she groped for an enameled basin beside the bed, but Dave Rogan beat her to it.

"Don't start puking on me because you can't face your own guilt," he snapped. "A lot of husbands and wives didn't sleep in their own beds that night—or a lot of nights before and since. When a man isn't able to satisfy his wife, even though he seems to be potent, he begins to wonder whether it's his fault. There's only one way to find out—another woman."

"Was he all right—with her?"

"How in the hell would I know? Intelligent and educated people don't go around talking about things like that. There's one way you can reassure him though—and don't ask me to draw a diagram for you." He picked up her chart folder from the foot of the bed. "I've got to go now. Feel like some real food?"

"I could use a bowl of soup with some crackers. And a cup of coffee."

"Good girl. I'll order the intravenous discontinued and see you in the morning. We'll talk some more."

He was at the door when she called, "Dave."

"Yes."

"You said just now that Joe needs me. How do you know, if he hasn't talked to you about us?"

"Because of Joe you're here and able to ask for soup and coffee, instead of being on a slab beside Lorrie Dellman. Since the divorce, he's been driving up to the turnaround in front of your house every night about midnight, to see if you're all right. Last night when he saw all the lights on he went inside.

"It was Joe that brought you to the hospital, Maggie. And if you've got half the sense I think you have, you'll thank God for him in your prayers tonight. I'll have my secretary send up an article on the Doctor's Wife disease. Since you were once a medical secretary yourself, you'll be able to understand the terms. I think you'll find it very interesting reading."

CHAPTER XVII

Janet Monroe got up at eight, stopped by the Snack Bar for breakfast, and came to Jerry's ward a little after nine. The chart said he had slept all night, and when she came into the room he stood up in the crib and held out his arms to her.

"You have to stay in bed, darling," she told him. "Dr. Ed wants you to."

"Can we go home today, Mommie?"

"I don't think so. We'll have to wait and see what Dr. Ed says."

"But you'll stay with me, won't you?"

"Until lunch. Then I'll have to go home and put on my uniform. Some sick people upstairs need me."

Dave Rogan and Ed Harrison came by about a half-hour later making rounds. The older doctor made a quick neurological examination, then put the instruments he had used back into the pocket of his long-skirted white coat.

"Everything's normal this morning," he reported. "Have you remembered anything else about the convulsions that might help us, Janet?"

"I'm not sure—it all happened so suddenly. The muscles of the right side may have been more involved than the left." When she saw a quick glance pass between the two doctors, she added quickly, "Does that mean anything?"

"It could help us localize the cause," Dave Rogan told her. "We need all the information we can get."

Ed Harrison stayed in the room after the psychiatrist left.

"We're going to be doing a few things today, Janet," he said. "I thought I'd warn you so you wouldn't be disturbed."

"Like what?"

"There'll be a neurosurgical consultation with Dr. Brennan. And I've asked Dr. Dieter to see Jerry, too. We don't know yet but Dr. Dieter will probably want to do a cerebral angiogram."

Janet was familiar with the procedure—and its significance.

"You still think it's something serious, don't you?" she asked.

"I'm afraid so. The fact that Jerry hasn't had any more convulsions is in his favor, of course. The bleeding we discovered with the puncture last night seems to have stopped—for the time being at least. But we want to stay ahead of it by finding the cause before another flare-up of hemorrhage can complicate the picture." At the door, he stopped with his hand on the knob. "Have you seen Jeff this morning?"

"No. The nurses say he hasn't been around."

"Mrs. McCloskey tired to commit suicide last night. Jeff was up until five, keeping her alive."

"How awful!" Janet exclaimed. "What did she take?"

"Alcohol and sleeping pills. Fortunately Dr. McCloskey found her in time."

"They—they're divorced, aren't they?"

"Yes. But he's still carrying a torch for her."

"At least she has that much. I came pretty near it once or twice myself, so I know what she must have felt."

Ed Harrison glanced at the little boy, who was standing in the crib with his elbows on the rail and his thumb in his mouth. If the presumptive diagnosis proves correct, he thought, Janet was in for something even worse than her divorce from Cliff Monroe —at least a 50 per cent chance that her baby wouldn't survive. Only the need to care for little Jerry had kept her from a serious emotional breakdown when Cliff Monroe had moved out, he knew. And if something happened to Jerry now, it would be even worse for her than before.

Janet came back to the hospital about two o'clock, this time in uniform, planning to spend a half-hour or so with Jerry before she went on duty at three in the Special Intensive Care Unit. As she came into the ward, one of the nurses was putting Jerry into a wheelchair.

"He's going up to Dr. Dieter's office for examination," she said. "I believe Dr. Brennan is going to see him up there, too."

"I'll take him up," Janet offered. "If they don't finish before I go on duty at three, I'll ask Dr. Dieter's nurse to call you when he's ready to come back."

Jerry enjoyed the ride through the busy corridors and up in the elevator to the office suite in the new surgical wing. There Janet turned him over to Dr. Dieter's nurse who put him on the examining table. Dieter came in just then and shook hands.

"This is a fine young lad you have here, Mrs. Monroe," he said with his faint Teutonic burr. "Dr. Brennan is coming over from the clinic, so I'll go ahead with my own examination while he's getting here."

Watching the way the vascular surgeon went about the examination and his gentleness with Jerry, Janet felt a little better. As for the little boy, he took to Dieter from the start, laughing uproariously as the doctor stroked his belly to test the reflexes of the abdominal muscles. Maybe there won't be any more bleeding or convulsions, Janet told herself. Things like that did clear up sometimes of their own accord, with no one ever discovering the cause.

At least the thought was something to hang on to, something far better than the diagnosis of brain tumor that had been her first thought, when she'd seen Jerry's body start to jerk with the initial convulsion.

ii

Pete Brennan came into Dieter's examining room just as the vascular surgeon finished examining Jerry Monroe's eyes with an ophthalmoscope.

"I have just finished, Doctor, if you would like to make your own examination." Dieter still used some of the Old World formalities. "The eye grounds seem to be normal."

Pete made a quick neurological examination; he'd already seen a summary of Dave Rogan's tests on the consultation sheet sent to him from Pediatrics.

"You can take him back to the room, Mrs. Monroe," he told Janet when he finished. "Dr. Dieter and I will discuss the case and let you know our recommendations later."

In Dieter's office, Pete sank gratefully into a comfortable chair and lit a cigarette. "I've really been running today," he said.

"The business of Dr. Dellman?"

"That—plus a lot of other things. Mort's offered to sell his share of the Faculty Clinic for a rather large sum, which he needs quickly. A lot of details are involved and, as president of the corporation, most of them wind up in my lap."

"Will the authorities release him?"

"Nobody knows—until he's brought before the grand jury."

"In Europe such cases are recognized as being in a special category," said Dieter. "The French call it a *crime passionnel*—which is as good a description as any."

"What do you think of Mort Dellman, Anton?"

If he was surprised by the question, Dieter didn't show it. "I would say that he is a very smart man, an excellent technician and administrator. But he would never make a good doctor."

"Why?"

"A doctor must have a greatness of heart, if he is to be a real physician. Dellman doesn't have it. I think it may be best for your clinic that he is getting out before he becomes—how do you say it over here?—the rotten apple that spoiled the barrel."

It was an apt description of Mort Dellman, one of the best Pete had ever heard. "What do you think of the child?" he asked.

"Convulsions are more in your field," Dieter demurred. "Perhaps you should make your guess first."

"It can't be much more than an educated guess at this stage," Pete Brennan admitted. "The skull X-rays showed nothing, but I wouldn't expect them to. Last night Dave Rogan thought per-

haps the reflexes might be more active on the right side, which
certainly fits in with the right-sided convulsion the mother described, but she was undoubtedly excited at the time and could
have been wrong. As of now I see nothing to suggest a brain
tumor. We should know definitely tomorrow when the brain scan
is finished, but I think it will be negative."

Dieter nodded. "Those are my conclusions, too. Which leaves
the most likely possibility an aneurysm in the region of the
Circle of Willis, with an intermittent leak of blood."

"Can you do the angiogram tomorrow, after the scan is finished?" Pete asked. "I have to go to Lorrie Dellman's funeral in
the morning, but I should be back by lunch."

"I will schedule it in the morning." With a skilled vascular surgeon on the staff, the tricky job of injecting a dye that was opaque
to the X-ray and would therefore show the pattern of the brain's
blood vessels had been turned over to Dieter. Cerebral angiography—literally photographing the blood vessels of the brain—
was an important technical advance that was yielding valuable
dividends in evaluating and treating strokes and other conditions
affecting the brain circulation, offering the possibility of help to
many cases for which there had been no treatment before.

"Are you thinking what I am thinking?" Pete asked.

"That this may be a case for using the California technique of
aneurysm thrombosis with iron sludge?"

"Yes."

"We shall see after the angiogram is done tomorrow. If the
technique proves suitable for this case and we succeed, it will be
a fine thing for the mother and the child."

Pete heaved himself reluctantly out of the chair. "I've got to
look in on Paul McGill. He's a good man and a friend; thanks
for saving him for us."

"It was Dr. Feldman who saved him." Dieter's eyes twinkled.
"I expect to see her soon and will give her your thanks."

So that's the way the wind blows, Pete thought as he took the
elevator to the Special Intensive Care Unit. Only in America
could a Polish Jew and an East German strike up a romantic

attachment in the three short days since Marisa Feldman had joined the staff.

Paul McGill was out of bed in a chair when Pete Brennan stopped by his room after leaving Dieter's office. Pete had always liked the dermatologist, even though their personalities were completely different. Where Pete was extroverted, with a typical Irish enthusiasm for life and living, Paul was more introspective and reserved. Both were intelligent and skilled in their field of work, however, and each respected the other.

"How's it going, Paul?" Pete asked.

"Not bad as long as I don't cough," said the dermatologist. "Then it feels like the place where Dieter split my sternum is going to come apart. But I'm so glad to be alive, I can stand that."

"Anton Dieter says if that new Jewish girl from Harvard hadn't recognized what was happening, you would have been another mortality statistic. How's Elaine taking it?"

"Like a trouper." Paul McGill's eyes warmed. "She came to the hospital as soon as she heard about the shooting and stayed here last night."

"Elaine's a fine girl. Amy's very fond of her, and so am I."

"I guess none of us know what our wives are really like until something like this comes along. I was scared to death that Elaine would leave me."

"I hope you asked her to forgive you."

"I did have that much sense." Paul's face was sober. "But I'm not so sure about the members of the corporation. Have I damaged the clinic, Pete?"

"If you have it will get over it." Pete grinned. "My guess is that whatever patients we might lose for various reasons, will be more than compensated for by the women who will want to see you."

"I'm really not a Don Juan, you know."

"Neither are the men these women are married to. I think they'll be tolerant."

"I've been trying to decide all day whether to submit my resignation."

"You can be sure we wouldn't accept it if you did. We had a meeting today at lunch but that didn't even come up so you can be sure the others feel as I do. Mort Dellman has offered to sell us his share of the corporation stock—for a hundred thousand dollars."

"That's quite a profit—considering that he only put in ten thousand at the start like the rest of us. What did you decide?"

"We're going to buy. I've asked Arthur Painter to make the arrangements—and borrow the hundred thousand from the bank. We agreed that you shouldn't be liable for this extra debt, Paul."

"But I insist on it."

"You've suffered enough in this business already. Nobody thinks you should be penalized any more."

"I'm responsible for the whole thing," the dermatologist protested. "Actually I'm the one who should pay the hundred thousand and give the stock to the rest of you."

"We wouldn't hear of that." Pete debated briefly whether to tell Paul that his being the object of Mort Dellman's marksmanship had been wholly accidental, but decided against it. Not only did he feel an obligation not to reveal what Mort had told him in confidence, but he was male enough to sense that the revelation might depress the wounded man at a time when he still needed his strength to recover as rapidly as possible.

"I still insist on being responsible for my share of the debt like the rest of you," Paul said.

"All right—if you want it that way."

"I do, and I'm sure Elaine will, too. Anyway I'll speak for her."

"When the papers are ready, I'll bring them by for you to sign," Pete promised. "Anything else I can do for you?"

"No. I just thank God that you had the foresight to lure Anton Dieter here—and Dr. Feldman."

When Pete Brennan had left, Paul pressed the call button

beside the bed. "Please ask Dr. Rogan to come by whenever he has a chance," he told the nurse who answered on the small speaker at the head of the bed. "There's no rush."

His conversation with Pete had settled one thing that had been troubling him, but another question still needed answering. Only Dave could do that—if anybody could.

iv

It was after four o'clock that afternoon when Marisa Feldman stopped in to see Grace Hanscombe. The day had been something of a blur for Grace since George, looking more disturbed than she'd ever seen him, had plucked her out of the clinic line, shortly after the first blood sugar specimen had been taken, and hustled her into the hospital without even giving her time to go home for her clothes. She hadn't realized how rotten she felt, until she was settled into bed in Marfield, the exclusive private ward section reserved for staff members, their families, and V.I.P.'s. Since then nurses and interns had been poking needles into her until she felt like a pin cushion.

"I'm Dr. Feldman," Marisa said with a smile. "Dr. Hanscombe is tied up with a heart case and asked me to come by on my way to dinner and check up on you."

"Is it that late?" Grace asked.

"Hospital dinner hours are earlier than others. How do you feel?"

"Lousy. But just hearing your English accent has made me feel better."

"You're English, too?"

"Was. Dr. Hanscombe and I were married during the war. I've been over here nearly twenty years. How about you?"

"I was born and grew up in Poland, but we managed to escape when war broke out—that is my mother and I did. I went to school in England but was in prison in East Germany for a while afterward. Later I came over here and took a fellowship at Harvard. But I still love England."

"So do I—what I remember of it. I'm going back as soon as I can get straightened out from this." It was the first time Grace had put in words the decision that had come to her sometime during the night, perhaps when she'd tried to get close to George for warmth and he'd remained asleep.

Marisa opened the chart folder she carried in her left hand and glanced at the laboratory report sheet. "You're coming around nicely," she said. "Your last blood sugar was almost normal."

"Could this possibly have happened the way it has? I mean, could my whole system suddenly go blooey just like that?"

"It has probably been happening gradually over several days," said Marisa. "Have you been testing your urine every day?"

"Yes. No. I didn't test it yesterday, I remember—or the day before." She grinned. "I was mad with my husband."

"And since he was making you test it, you got back at him by not doing it?"

"You don't happen to be a psychiatrist, by any chance?"

"No. But I treat a lot of digestive-tract disturbances and they're closely related to emotional tension. Do you have any idea what might have set you off this time?"

"I *know* what it was," said Grace. "I was mad at Geor—at Dr. Hanscombe—because he wasn't the one Mort Dellman shot."

"I'm afraid I don't understand."

"You have to have been married for twenty years to a man who thinks God created sex on Saturday night to understand. I take it you've never been married?"

"No."

"Take my advice and don't. Stay single and play hard to get—but not too hard, mind you."

Marisa Feldman smiled. "I understand that part."

"Make the men in your life want you because you're an attractive woman and they know damn well somebody else will get you if they don't. Not just because you run a comfortable house, see that their clothes are washed, their food is properly cooked and served, and because you're there between the sheets whenever they're ready."

Marisa changed the subject somewhat abruptly. "I saw a friend of yours in the clinic this morning—Mrs. Weston."

"Alice?"

"Yes."

"I suppose her gut is in a gripe again—probably over this Mort Dellman business like the rest of us. But I wouldn't have guessed it made that much difference to Alice whether Roy shacked up with Lorrie or not. God knows he's had enough women in this town over the past fifteen years, but this was pretty close to home so I guess Alice was afraid of having her nice warm little world disturbed. When you know her better, you'll find that she lives in a world of her own that's largely make-believe, like a little girl playing dolls."

"Your world is certainly real enough."

Grace looked at her sharply. "Why do you say that?"

"Only that you have a very realistic attitude toward it, Mrs. Hanscombe. After all, Mrs. Weston had a mild colon spasm, but you almost went into diabetic coma."

Grace looked away, her face suddenly drawn. "It's not so much that my world is realistic, Dr. Feldman, but that most of it has long since passed me by. And what little I do have is all shot to hell."

"You'll feel better tomorrow, when your blood sugar gets back to normal," Marisa assured her.

"Do you think it will by morning?"

"I'm sure of it. Why?"

"I may not see my husband this evening; he'll probably forget I'm here and go home. Will you tell him I'd like to get away from the hospital long enough in the morning to go to Lor—, to Mrs. Dellman's funeral? She was one of the few people I know who was completely honest and I always liked her."

"I shall leave the order for a pass myself," Marisa promised. "And I'm sure you're more honest than you give yourself credit for being."

Grace looked startled, then grinned. "You're nobody's fool, are you?" She held out her hand and Marisa took it. "We might become friends at that—even though you're young and pretty and you'll be working closely with my husband. After all, we English ought to stick together."

v

Paul McGill was back in bed when Dave Rogan came in and pulled a chair up beside him.

"What a day," the psychiatrist said. "From the way you look, Paul, I think Mort's bullet wounded a lot of people worse than it did you."

"Why do you say that?"

"Grace Hanscombe's in the hospital one jump ahead of diabetic coma, though she didn't even have to take insulin before. Maggie McCloskey mixed alcohol and barbiturate last night and we barely got her pumped out in time."

"I guess I caused a lot of trouble."

"It had to come someday. When a group of people get their lives as intertwined as most of ours have been for years, you wind up with a powder keg that eventually has to blow itself up, and everything else around it."

"Will the parts ever settle back together?"

"Not in the same pattern, I hope. But that happens more often than you'd think, too. People's lives start repeating themselves as soon as they take off diapers; the way they behave under stress is pretty well determined in childhood. Given a similar situation later on, they'll usually repeat the same reaction."

"Not me," Paul McGill said firmly. "This was my first and last slip."

"I had an idea it was the first," Dave said. "Did you send for me to get that off your chest?"

"Not entirely. Something's troubling me."

Dave Rogan leaned back in the chair and lit his pipe. "Let's have it then."

"I . . . I don't even talk to Elaine about intimate things," Paul admitted. "Does that mean I'm repressed?"

"In the true sense of the word, perhaps yes," said the psychiatrist. "Freud made the word popular—or maybe I should say unpopular—but few people really understand what he meant. Freud saw repression as an unconscious mechanism whereby an individual denies certain impulses access to conscious thought, leaving their emotional energy—perhaps that's as simple a term as any—to appear later in the form of physical disease, the various mental symptom patterns of neuroses, or even the more serious illness that we call psychosis. But most of us still have a lot of repressions that never bother us."

Paul McGill started to speak, then hesitated, obviously embarrassed.

"What happened to you could have happened to anybody, Paul," said Dave, hoping to get him started on what he had to say without too much delay. "The musical beds game is being played around this town often enough for almost anybody to have been in the position you were in the other afternoon, and the same could be said for practically any other town regardless of size. People behave according to the same basic drives, whether they're rich or poor and whether they're in Terre Haute or Timbuktu. The pattern of human behavior hasn't changed appreciably that I've been able to see since the time of Pithecanthropus erectus."

"Maybe so, but I still can't figure out how I got into this mess. I love Elaine and she loves me. Neither of us have had anything to do with the hanky-panky that goes on around town."

Dave Rogan grinned. "You just dated yourself, Paul."

"How?"

"With that expression 'hanky-panky.' They're calling it by its real name now—and not only in books."

"I'm afraid I don't even know the words," the dermatologist confessed.

Dave Rogan glanced covertly at his watch. Paul McGill was his friend and he wanted to help him if he could. But Della would be starting dinner soon; they'd long ago formed the habit of making the evening meal with the children a discussion period in which everyone was free to have his say. And even though the children were in camp, he was still hoping to have a quiet talk with Della during the meal. She liked to have it on schedule, though, and so did he. An early dinner made for a long evening and he loved the quiet period after the children had gone to bed, when he and Della could read or talk together without interruption—except that lately their lines of communication seemed to have been breaking down.

"You sent for me, Paul," he reminded the dermatologist. "Was there anything in particular you wanted to talk about."

"It . . . it's pretty personal."

"A man shouldn't have any secrets from his confessor—or his psychiatrist."

"I guess you're wondering how I happened to be at Mort Dellman's house the other afternoon."

"I figured that was your business—and Lorrie's."

"I was getting ready to play golf; you know I always play on Wednesday afternoons. Lorrie had been having a skin eruption that she said was bothering her. I'd given her some drug samples when she was in the clinic last week and she called me Wednesday afternoon early to say she was out of the samples and asked me to drop some more by the house on my way to the club. I didn't think anything about it, so I took the samples with me and went by there."

"I suppose she was alone when you arrived."

"You're not implying that—"

"You were snared by one of the oldest ploys in the world, Paul."

"Why me?"

"I suspect you were the only one in our particular group that Lorrie hadn't gone to bed with. I remember Della saying once that Lorrie had bragged during a bridge game about how she could seduce any one of us, if she really tried."

"But I never—"

"I'll take your word for that. What happened when you got to the house?"

"She wanted me to take a look at a place on her back. She was wearing some sort of a negligee—pretty thin."

"And nothing under it, I suppose."

"Well, no."

"Quite a lot of women have taken up what they call jaybirding lately, particularly in hot weather. During the day when they're alone in the house, they like to pad around the house naked. They claim it makes them feel free, but I've got a hunch it's another form of the latent tendency to exhibitionism that underlies the psychology of most women."

"Elaine's not like that."

"She likes to wear low-cut evening dresses when she goes out formal, doesn't she?"

"Yes."

"Then she's the same as every other woman. Before the new styles came around they'd make a fetish of keeping their knees covered when they sat down, yet think nothing of wearing a bikini on the beach that was even smaller than the briefs and bra they wear as undergarments. What happened next?"

Paul McGill blushed. "It was so fast after that, I'm not real sure myself."

"My guess is that you sort of got raped. Did you resist?"

The other man's flush deepened. "No."

"Good for you. Your repressions aren't as deep as I was afraid they might be. So you and Lorrie were pretty busy when Mort came in and fired the shot."

"Well . . . yes."

"I'm sorry to tell you, Paul, but under the circumstances you didn't have any more chance of resisting than Mark Antony had when Cleopatra went after him. You can at least satisfy your conscience with that assurance—if it needs any satisfying."

"That's not what I wanted to talk to you about," Paul protested. "I've already confessed the whole thing to Elaine and she forgives me, so there's no need for it to be on my conscience."

"Are you bothered because you enjoyed it?"

"No."

"Then what's the beef?"

"I . . . I'm what you might call hasty with Elaine."

"Premature ejaculation?"

"Yes—but I wasn't with Lorrie. The thing that bothers me is how can I love my wife as much as I do and not be a real man with her, when I was able to be with another woman?"

"Lorrie wasn't just another woman; you were seduced by an expert." Dave Rogan got to his feet. "I think I know the answer to your question, but it will take a little more time than I've got this afternoon to make it clear to you. Think about the problem tonight; I'll drop by tomorrow and we'll talk about it some more. I may be able to show you the answer and help you into the bargain."

vi

Della Rogan came into the Ladies' Grill at the club and went up to the bar for a drink. She was tired to her very bones and, worst of all, she'd played a lousy game all day.

"Gin and tonic, Manuel," she said. "Where's everybody?"

"I heard some of the ladies saying Mrs. McCloskey and Mrs. Hanscombe are in the hospital, Mrs. Rogan. Didn't you know?"

"I knew about Mrs. McCloskey but I've been on the course all day. Did Mrs. Hanscombe have an accident?"

"Not that I know of. There wasn't anything about it in the news."

Della sipped her drink, wondering why it tasted like the quinine her mother used to dose her with in the springtime down in southern Georgia to keep off malaria. Grace had complained of feeling lousy that morning but she hadn't seemed to be really sick so it must have been something sudden. Right now she'd be almost willing to have something sudden herself, Della admitted, rather than face the thought of a golf ball sitting nice and quiet on its tee tomorrow, waiting for her to slice it into the rough the way she'd been doing all day.

Leaving her glass half-emptied, she went to the telephone and rang the hospital, asking for Dave.

"Dr. Rogan's office thinks he's with Dr. McGill, but the line to Intensive Care is busy," the clinic operator told her. "Is it something urgent, Mrs. Rogan?"

"No. It can wait until he comes home."

"If I hear anything from him, I'll tell him you called."

"No, please don't," Della said quickly. "I wouldn't want to bother him."

If Janet Monroe's child and Paul McGill were more important to Dave than his own wife, Della thought resentfully as she went back for another drink, he deserved to eat a TV dinner when he got home. And to see the Thursday Night Movie, no matter how old it was.

Then a happy thought struck her. Tomorrow was Lorrie's funeral and she had a perfectly good excuse not to play golf.

CHAPTER XVIII

It was after five o'clock Thursday evening before Marisa Feldman finished seeing the patients George Hanscombe had asked her to visit on the private wards. It had been a long day and she was tired, so she decided to have an early dinner at the hospital cafeteria and go to her apartment for a quiet evening of reading and television.

As she was placing her tray on a table in the corner of the cafeteria, Janet Monroe stopped beside it. Janet, too, had been planning to eat alone, but when she saw the slender woman doctor with the arresting features and the lovely dark hair, some impulse she could not have named made her take her tray to Marisa's table.

"Dr. Feldman?" she asked.

"Yes." Marisa looked up from the table where she was arranging the dishes she had chosen.

"My name is Janet Monroe. I'm the nursing supervisor on the Special Intensive Care Unit."

"Oh yes. Dr. McGill is your patient."

"He doesn't need much nursing any more. Dr. Dieter says he'll be able to go home early next week."

Marisa hoped the warmth that rose in her cheeks at the mention of Anton Dieter's name wasn't apparent to the nurse.

"Do you mind if I share your table?" Janet asked. "I'd like to talk to you about something."

"Of course not." Marisa gestured toward the empty chair. "I'm afraid I have a lot of dishes. I was in prison in East Germany for a while and when I see all this food, I almost go berserk."

Janet arranged the salad, pie and coffee she'd chosen on the table and transferred both their trays to a nearby cart.

"I read in the hospital bulletin that you had come here from Harvard," she said, as she pulled out the chair across from Marisa and sat down. "I was wondering whether medical school and hospital life is different there from what it is here in the South."

"In what way?"

"I mean about medical school marriages. I've been divorced about two years—from a student who graduated that spring."

Marisa didn't miss the sudden bitterness in the nurse's voice as she continued: "It was one of those meal-ticket marriages. I worked and put my husband through medical school, then he left me for another woman—with money."

"I'm sorry. Actually though, you may be better off."

"How can you say that?"

"Forgive me. I have no right to tell you what is good—or not good—for you. This is a very personal thing."

"I'd still like to know what you meant."

"A friend of mine at Harvard recently published a paper on medical school marriages," Marisa explained. "The divorce rate among them is very high."

"Who knows that better than I do? But why?"

"For one thing there's never been a time when young doctors could make so much money right after they finish their residencies. In most cities, too, their income puts them immediately into a social—how do you say it over here?"

"Bracket?"

"Yes. A social bracket considerably higher than they would normally reach for many years. Many of them married young, often in college. The girl sacrificed her own education to help her husband complete his residency, then children came and the wife was left behind. Divorce—or worse—resulted."

"Worse?" She saw the shocked look in the young girl's eyes. "What could be worse?"

280

"Alcoholism, drug addiction, mental illness. It's not a pretty picture."

"Maybe I'm better off than I think," Janet admitted. "I was very bitter at first. But when I look back on everything, I can see that part of what caused the break with Cliff was my fault."

"My friend who wrote the study found there was usually reason to blame both partners in the marriages that failed," Marisa agreed.

"I'm sure of that—now."

When she saw Janet Monroe's eyes suddenly fill with tears, Marisa knew she had accidentally stumbled upon the real reason why the nurse had joined her for dinner.

"I've never had a child, Mrs. Monroe, but I'm a doctor and a woman," she said. "Do you want to tell me about it?"

The girl hesitated momentarily, then the words began to tumble out: "Soon after our marriage, I realized that Cliff had only wanted me because I could work and put him through medical school. He—he started staying away from home and running after other women. I was hurt and angry—I guess I wasn't thinking straight."

"Women in love rarely do."

"I decided to get back at him and make him settle down—with me—by having a baby. Only it didn't work. When he found out I was pregnant, he beat and kicked me. I almost had a miscarriage." She stopped suddenly, then hurried on: "Now my little boy has some sort of congenital condition that's causing convulsions."

"And you blame yourself?"

"Y-yes."

"How could you possibly feel guilty about what happened?"

"When Cliff beat me, couldn't that have caused the cells in the embryo not to develop properly?"

"That's possible, of course. But even if prenatal trauma was a factor in causing your son's condition, it was your husband that was to blame, not you."

"No, the fault was really mine."

"How can you say that?"

"Before we married, I agreed that I wasn't to get pregnant until after he was out in practice and we could afford children."

Marisa smiled. "Pregnancy can't always be prevented that easily."

"With the pill it can—almost a hundred per cent. But I deliberately stopped taking it, so Cliff had a right to be angry."

"And you blame yourself?"

"It's been driving me crazy. You see, I tricked Cliff, thinking that if I had a child I could hold him. I thought the breakup of my marriage was punishment enough. But now my baby may die, too."

"Are you a religious person, Mrs. Monroe?"

"I was—I guess I still am."

"Then you believe in God?"

"Oh, yes."

"Do you honestly believe God would punish you for your misdeeds—even if you were guilty—by crippling your child?"

"I—I don't know."

"He wouldn't be much of a god if he did, would he? Not the sort you could respect and love."

"When you put it that way, I suppose not."

"Even in the Old Testament, the Shema we Jews recite at our services instructs us to love God."

"I never thought of it that way." Janet felt a great load suddenly lift from her shoulders. "I guess I've been pretty much of a fool, Dr. Feldman. Jeff—Dr. Long—told me the same thing, but he wants me to marry him, so I thought he was only rationalizing."

"Dr. Long is a fine young man; I've heard nothing but good about him. Are you going to marry him?"

"I don't think so—at least not for a while, if ever. One experience with marriage was enough for me."

"Forgive me, but is Dr. Long pressing you?"

"Not really. He has to give two years to the Army, after he finishes this last year of residency. If we do marry, both of us want to start with at least an even chance of making a success of it. And we don't think being separated right at the start would be good for our marriage."

"I'm sure it wouldn't," Marisa agreed.

"You're so lovely—and capable. I'm surprised you've never married," Janet said as she stood up to go. "Or maybe you haven't met Mr. Right—as they say in a teen-age romantic magazine?"

"I've never read one of those, but it could be true. Good night, Mrs. Monroe."

"Good night, Doctor. And thank you for being so helpful."

As she watched the girl in the crisp white uniform move across the cafeteria to the door leading to the walkway connecting it with the building where the Special Intensive Care Unit was located, Marisa felt a surge of the old melancholy begin to oppress her.

She was beginning to be at least half certain that she might at last have found Mr. Right—as Janet had called him. The trouble was that she was wrong—wrong in a way she had long since decided could never be corrected.

ii

Pete Brennan had finished up for the day a little after five, when Arthur Painter called.

"I've got to go to Atlanta in the morning, Pete," the lawyer said. "But I've made a rough draft of the Dellman papers and if you want to go over them with me tonight, I'll stay here at the office until we finish. Then my secretary can type them first thing in the morning and you can get them signed tomorrow."

"I was just going home to dinner," said Pete. "Let me call Amy and see what the situation is."

"Arthur Painter wants me to work with him on the sale of Mort's share of the clinic tonight," Pete said, when Amy answered the telephone. "What are your plans?"

"I have to go to the medical auxiliary fashion show at the YWCA," she said. "Didn't I tell you about it this morning?"

"You may have, but I've had trouble remembering things since last night."

"I don't even remember much of that. Next time I'll watch how much I pour into a glass before I add the ginger ale."

"I'll sneak a bigger shot glass into the bar cabinet if you do," he told her. "Since you're tied up this evening, I'll go work with Arthur. Okay?"

"Of course, darling. See you later."

"Sounds fine."

When she hung up, Amy stood looking at the telephone thoughtfully for a long moment. Her innate honesty and sense of fairness made her hesitate to do what her mind was urging her to do. She'd never checked up on Pete before, not even during the past year, when he'd spent more and more evenings at the hospital for staff conferences—or so he had said. But her conversation with Jake Porter that morning had shaken her more than she would admit to anyone except herself. And faced with the bleak future of a life without Pete, she was willing to do anything that needed to be done to hold him.

Picking up the phone, she rang Arthur Painter's office. The lawyer himself answered. "Is Pete there yet, Arthur?" she asked.

"He called just now to say he was grabbing a sandwich and would be right over," the lawyer told her. "We've got a lot of work to do tonight, if we're to put the Mort Dellman deal through in the three days Pete's given me to do it. Did you want him to call you?"

"No. Just give him a message, please." Amy felt a little giddy with relief at discovering that Pete had been telling the truth about spending the evening with the lawyer. "I have to go to a fashion show that's being put on at the YWCA by the medical auxiliary and I forgot to tell Pete I'll probably be as late as ten thirty getting home."

"I'll give him the message, Amy. Anything else?"

"About the loan for buying out Mort, Arthur. Are you likely to have any trouble raising the money?"

"Not a bit," he assured her. "Any bank in town would lend

your husband a hundred thousand tomorrow on his personal note
—without endorsement. That's how much the businessmen of
Weston respect him."

"Don't tell him I asked, please."

"Of course. I understand your position, Amy. After all, I'm your
lawyer, too. Good night."

"Good night, Arthur."

Amy was singing as she went to take her shower before dressing
for the fashion show. Uncle Jake Porter had been disturbed this
morning, or he never would have relayed what was obviously a
baseless piece of gossip.

Pete couldn't possibly be considering divorcing her. After all,
she was the perfect doctor's wife.

iii

Arthur Painter looked at Pete Brennan over the tops of his
unifocals and drummed his fingers on the blue cover of the
topmost of a sheaf of legal documents lying on the blotter of his
desk.

"You sure you want to do this, Pete?" he asked once again.

"Yes." Pete tried to keep impatience out of his voice. Arthur
was a good lawyer and a friend, as well as a trustee of the in-
denture by which a large part of Amy's fortune was tied up in
trust for the kids. The income tax on the returns was thus paid
at the children's lower rate, so Amy's income wouldn't be added
to the top of his already substantial one, putting them into a
ruinously high income tax bracket.

"What about the others?"

"As members of the corporation, they'll have to sign it, too.
But I told you we all agreed to it."

"The papers are all here," Painter told him. "You read the
carbon copy and I'll make the notes for my secretary on the
originals."

"Good. Mort wants this thing settled before Roy takes the case
to the grand jury."

"That shouldn't be for a couple of days at least. Lorrie's funeral isn't until tomorrow morning."

"It's still the way Mort wants it, Arthur. How soon can we close the whole deal?"

"As soon as all of you—and Dellman—sign. Two sets of documents will be necessary; one is a straight sale and purchase agreement between the members of the Faculty Clinic Corporation and Mort Dellman, whereby he sells you his share in the clinic for a hundred thousand dollars. The other is a note for the hundred thousand to the First National Bank of Weston."

"The bank didn't quibble?"

The lawyer permitted himself a wintry smile. "Roy Weston is a director and so is George Hanscombe. Your wives will sign, too, of course."

"I take it there's no way out of that?"

"State law requires it. Surely you don't think Amy would object?"

"No. She offered to lend us the whole amount herself."

"You were wise not to accept, both as an individual and as her husband. What about Paul McGill?"

"He and Elaine insist on being a part of this. I gave him a chance not to be in it, but he refused."

"How about the insurance policies?" Pete asked when they'd finished going over the documents.

"Earl Bieson is working on that but there shouldn't be any trouble," the lawyer told him. "Twenty thousand additional on each of your lives under the clinic's group policy, assigned to the bank until the note is paid off, is all that's needed. The whole thing's ironclad."

"Then I'll see that the others and their wives sign these papers tomorrow and get them back to you." Pete got to his feet. "Anything else?"

"Mort Dellman is still getting the best end of this deal. I could almost believe he planned it that way. He gets rid of an unfaithful wife and makes three hundred thousand for himself—"

"One hundred thousand, Arthur."

"A hundred thousand." The lawyer corrected himself hastily. "Plus a chance to leave a community where nobody likes him much anyway—all with one bullet. I'd say that was an exceptional day's shooting."

"Not if his neck is stretched."

"It won't be. I heard this afternoon that Douglas Turner is going to defend him, if the grand jury returns an indictment."

Pete looked startled. "When did all this happen?" Turner was the most successful defense lawyer in a dozen states, a flamboyant old-school type who boasted that no client of his had ever been executed.

"This morning, apparently."

"I don't see Mort putting out that kind of money—even to save his neck."

"Mort isn't paying it. Jake Porter is."

"But Jake hates Mort's guts."

"So do a lot of other people. But Jake loves those grandchildren and he isn't going to see them have the knowledge that their father was hung left as a black mark against them for the rest of their lives."

A bell rang in Pete Brennan's mind. "Just now you said three hundred thousand—"

"A slip of the tongue," Painter said quickly.

"Was it? Tell me the truth, Arthur."

Painter shrugged. "This is in strict confidence—especially as far as the others in the clinic organization are concerned."

"Of course."

"If they knew, they might squawk about signing your agreement. They aren't as well off as you are, Pete."

"I agreed that it was confidential." Pete was beginning to be irritated by the lawyer's fussiness.

"His interest in the clinic isn't all your friend Dellman is selling." Painter picked up the blue-folded legal documents. "Jake's giving Mort two hundred thousand to leave the country and never communicate with his children again—payable to him by deposit in a Swiss bank he's been sticking money into for several years."

So that had been at the back of Mort's mind last night, Pete thought. With three hundred thousand dollars as a nest egg and the sort of salary a man of his undeniable ability in the clinical laboratory and medical administrative field could demand in a dozen parts of the world besides South Africa, which he had mentioned, Mort would be far better off than he'd been in Weston. And he'd be rid of the embarrassment of Lorrie's amours into the bargain.

Pete wondered whether he should tell Roy Weston about what Arthur Painter had said. The story Mort had told him the other night about only wanting to crease the backside of that medical student—whatever his name was—could have been something Mort had dreamed up as part of an elaborate scheme to get rid of Lorrie and fatten his own pockets at the same time. And knowing Mort as he did, Pete didn't put it beyond him.

"Like I said"—Arthur Painter seemed to be reading Pete's thoughts—"you could almost believe Mort Dellman planned it all this way. He's certainly smart enough—and unscrupulous enough. But I guess we're all lucky to be getting rid of him as cheaply as we are."

Outside the lawyer's office, Pete got into his Porsche. The dashboard clock told him it was only eight thirty, which meant that Amy probably wouldn't be home for another couple of hours according to the message Arthur Painter had given him. He toyed with the idea of killing time in a movie but couldn't remember the name of anything decent playing in town, so he finally turned the car southward along River Road. In front of an apartment house set back from the river, he parked and got out.

The elevator took him to the sixth floor. Halfway down the corridor, he stopped and punched a bell. He could hear the staccato sounds of guns firing in a television Western inside, but they softened immediately and moments later the door opened.

Helen Straughn stood in the doorway, looking quite different—in mint green slacks and a yellow blouse, with a matching green

band about her flaming red hair—from the way she did as supervisor of the operating-room suite at the University Hospital.

"Come in, stranger," she said. "I was beginning to think Mort
Dellman had got you, too—with that famous bullet of his."

iv

George Hanscombe met Joe McCloskey at the front door of
the clinic as they were both leaving for the day. Being taller,
George pushed the door open for Joe to go through first. Outside,
they stood somewhat awkwardly under the marquee, each hesitating to ask the other the question that was on his mind.

"Where are you eating, George?" Joe asked.

"I don't know. I didn't want to eat at home alone so I phoned
the maid to go on."

"How about the Snack Bar then?"

George glanced toward the gleaming chrome and glass structure at the corner of the parking lot. "I suppose it will do as well
as anywhere else. I'm going to see Grace later."

"Let's give it a try then."

When the two men came through the door, Mabel looked up
from the counter and smiled warmly. "Good evening, Dr. Mc-
Closkey. Dr. Hanscombe," she said. "Take the booth at the corner; the air conditioning doesn't blow right on you there. I'll
bring you some coffee."

The two men slid into the red-cushioned seats, facing each
other. The restaurant hadn't yet begun to fill with the six o'clock
crowd, so there were only a few customers. They ordered and
George Hanscombe took his saccharine bottle from his pocket
and put it on the table between them.

"What's it like, being alone, Joe?" he asked.

"Hell!" said the urologist. "Pure hell! But why should that
bother you? Grace is out of danger, isn't she?"

"She didn't go into coma, but she probably would have in another twenty-four hours if she hadn't discovered the sugar this
morning."

"That's something to be thankful for, at least."

"Grace isn't a severe diabetic, Joe. Why would her blood sugar control system suddenly go haywire?"

"Didn't you test your urine for sugar and albumin when you were taking final exams as a medical student?"

"Sure. That's routine."

"How many in the class showed sugar—or albumin?"

"About half, as I remember it. Are you saying this sudden flare-up was psychosomatic?"

"What does Dave Rogan say?"

"I haven't asked him. He's been pretty busy—"

"I know."

"Joe." The internist's face was suddenly concerned. "I didn't mean—"

"Let's face it, George," said the pudgy urologist. "Mort Dellman might as well have shot all of us, when he got Lorrie and Paul. That bullet blew our nice orderly little world apart—not that mine wasn't shot to hell already."

"Maggie came through last night O.K., didn't she?"

"Yes. Dave Rogan even thinks he may be able to make some progress with her now—unless she gets mad with him and takes herself out of the hospital."

Their food came just then and they gave their attention to it, so there was a hiatus in the conversation. Over the second cup of coffee, George Hanscombe said: "Our wives have everything a woman could desire: plenty of money, time to enjoy themselves, servants, nice homes, charge accounts, a position in the community. Good God! What else do they want?"

"Maggie seems to want to drink herself to death."

"And Grace keeps harping on going back to England."

"Think she'll go?"

"After today it looks like that—or a severe case of diabetes."

"Let her go, George. That way at least you'll have some chance of getting her back—if you want her."

"Of course I want her."

"Have you told her so lately?"

"I tell her every night. With this prostate of mine, I can't last more than four hours before getting up. A thing like that is a constant reminder that you're getting old, and after I get back in bed I usually reach over and touch Grace. She's always warm and soft—you know how a woman feels in the dark. Just knowing she's there used to give me the assurance that I'd have somebody to grow old with, somebody I love. I've never admitted this to anybody before, Joe, but the reason I've always refused to let Grace go back to England was because I wasn't sure she would ever come back."

"I know how that is," Joe McCloskey agreed. "Last night when I went in the house and found Maggie stretched out on the bed, barely breathing, I thought she'd be gone for good before I could get her to the emergency room. The worst hour I ever spent in my life was that one—until Jeff Long got her breathing again."

"You've been divorced for six months. Surely that makes a difference."

"It only makes things worse. How do you think I feel while I'm driving by the house every half hour after ten o'clock, when they close the bar at the club, until I'm sure Maggie's safe at home? Since last night I've been saying a prayer of thanksgiving that she's still alive for me to be that close to her."

"Do you have any idea what's behind the whole thing? Her drinking, I mean—and last night?"

"No more than you have."

"That's none at all."

"Dave Rogan insists that it's all mixed up with Maggie's childhood, with her feeling that she came from the wrong side of the tracks. But why should that make any difference?"

"I don't know," George Hanscombe admitted. "I grew up on a tobacco farm in North Carolina and worked my way through college and medical school. None of my ancestors ever owned a slave and I was the first in my entire family even to go to college. Grace's family have been solid Welsh tavern-keepers for generations, so she's got no reason to feel inferior to me. Yet she's always throwing that business of having been a barmaid at me."

"Dave Rogan's got a theory about practically everything and half the time I don't agree with him, but he may be right about the Doctor's Wife disease. Dave claims that the trouble with doctors' wives as a group is that so many of them come from middle-class people, the kind who study nursing, or learn to become technicians or secretaries."

"Why in the hell would that make any difference? My family weren't even middle-class; during the Depression we were as poor as Job's turkey."

"Apparently that isn't where the sore spot develops. No matter what a doctor's background is, he still has to go to college in order to get into medical school. A lot of people think that having gone through both places automatically makes him an intellectual."

"Doesn't it?"

"Hell no, George. Taken as a group, doctors are about the narrowest-minded educated people you could think of. We've fought against every major social advance since Herbert Hoover was President."

"But socialism must be stamped—"

"That's a bunch of crap, George, and you'd know it if you ever stopped to really think. The world's changing every day and the social order with it. This country is never going back to all that States' rights guff and the sacred cow of purest private enterprise you so-called conversatives worship. This is a changing world and you've got to change with it—or be left behind."

"I don't quite agree," George said stiffly.

"I'm not asking you to. I'm just pointing out a few of the forces that make so many doctors' wives crack up—mentally, physically, or both—about the time their husbands reach the peak of their success. Take your own case. You came from a dirt-farmer family, but you're as highly regarded in this town as anybody I know because you're the best internist. You're on the board of the largest bank. You're a Senior Warden in the Episcopal church. And you're on the board of the Weston Country Club. You can look Amy Brennan in the eye any day and nobody would know you started at the bottom while she was born at the top. But how did you get there?"

"Mainly by hard work—and sacrifice."

"That's only part of it—maybe not even the most important part. You got where you are because the M.D. after your name automatically makes you the social equal of a Weston—or anybody else. Look at Sam Portola. He's got money enough to buy the whole town, but socially he never made it to where you are right now—and he never will."

"You make it sound logical," George admitted. "But—"

"Take my own case," said the urologist. "My family came to eastern North Carolina in the days of the lord proprietors. We've even produced a couple of Episcopal bishops—which is about as good proof of a deep-seated case of dry rot in a family as you can possibly get. But if it hadn't been for the sulfa drugs and penicillin, I'd be nothing but a high-class clap doctor, like urologists were in the old days, and you'd be looking down on me."

"You're exaggerating, Joe."

"Only to prove my point that a doctor who's worth his salt not only gets rich—unless he's a complete dope—but also winds up at the top of the social ladder, too—if he wants to be there. The trouble is that lots of times the women we marry aren't ready to go up that fast. Or they tell themselves they aren't—which is even worse."

"You may have a point there," George Hanscombe admitted. "We spend most of our time making decisions people live or die by, so we've got to be right a good portion of the time. It's the women who have time to be uncertain."

"Uncertainty can drain away a person's self-esteem faster than almost anything else," Joe McCloskey agreed. "I don't have to tell you that feeling sorry for yourself can get you in the heart, the stomach, or the bladder. Why do you think I see so many women with cystitis?"

"The glucose regulatory function of the liver and pancreas are just as vulnerable," George Hanscombe agreed glumly. "To say nothing of Alice Weston's colon. Sometimes I wonder why it is that when women get psychosomatic complaints, an excretory function is so often involved."

"Because that's the way they're made. Why else?"

George Hanscombe laughed, and absorbed in their conversation, neither of them heard Mabel's gasp of indignation. The Snack Bar was still almost empty and she'd been plying them with fresh coffee all through the conversation, so she'd hardly missed a word.

"I guess the Lord must have had doctors in mind when he made women," George agreed; then he sobered. "So what do we do about Grace and Maggie?"

"Dave doesn't want me to see Maggie for a while so I'm playing it his way. I have a lot of respect for Dave, and besides, I don't know anything else to do."

George Hanscombe slid out of the booth and reached into his pocket for his wallet. "I guess I'll have to let Grace go back to England—and hope it will be only for a visit. Sometimes lately, when she was giving me hell more than usual, I even envied you, Joe. But I guess we're really in the same boat."

"Up the creek without a paddle," the urologist agreed.

"You certainly got an earful that time, Mabel," said Abe Fescue, when the two doctors had paid their bills and left the restaurant. "But you know there's a lot in what the little fellow said."

"Aw go race your horses!" Mabel said in disgust and began to clear off the table.

Abe grinned. "From the way it riled you, I'd say they must have come pretty close to the truth."

"Truth!" Mabel snapped. "They were so busy feeling sorry for themselves, they didn't even leave a tip. A couple of big shots they are. Better I should serve interns—or even students."

CHAPTER XIX

Twilight was beginning to fall when Marisa Feldman crossed the street to the Faculty Apartments and took the elevator up to her one-bedroom corner apartment. She didn't pause in the tastefully furnished living room but walked through it to the small balcony that opened upon it. Pulling up an aluminum porch lounge, she stretched out on it and lit a cigarette, smoking it slowly while she watched darkness settle over the city.

The apartment was located high up in the central tower of the building, so she had a good view of nearly half the city from the balcony. Southward, the rolling terrain was mostly green pineland, with here and there the regular geometric pattern of a cornfield, the stalks, fodder, and ears already turning brown with the approach of autumn.

To the west, the hills rose steadily toward the dark line of the mountain range, some fifty miles away at this point, she had been told. When she looked toward the river, she could see that the water was already taking on the darker hues of approaching night. And though she could hear the staccato roar of a motorboat, she was barely able to distinguish the curving V of its wake in the swiftly falling darkness.

It was the part of the day Marisa had always liked best. In Cambridge, where she'd had an apartment close to the Harvard Yard, she had often gone walking through the center of the great university in the early evening, absorbing the peace that seemed to characterize the pursuit of learning. When she had first come to Weston, she'd thought that much the same quiet atmosphere prevailed here—and it still might on the university campus at the end of town for all she knew, since she hadn't had a chance to go there yet. But here at Weston Boulevard and North Avenue, where the medical school and hospital were located, the lavalike turbulence of emotional conflict boiled continually, just as it did wherever any group of humans, be they only two in number, came together.

Somehow, it reminded Marisa of a scene she'd witnessed in Yellowstone National Park, when she'd taken a three weeks' bus trip westward from Boston the first summer after her arrival there from England two years ago. The Devil's Garden—she remembered the guide calling the area that came to mind—was a place where the fires of volcanic energy kept popping to the surface from deep within the earth, roiling the thin outer crust until a particularly violent burst of energy sent a towering spurt of steam and scalding water hurtling upward, losing its energy before subsiding to leave the area once again smooth and peaceful—until another geyser broke through.

She had heard enough of hospital gossip in the brief period since she'd arrived at Weston to know that more than one geyser had already erupted here in connection with the shooting of Dr. Mortimer Dellman's wife yesterday. And she had gained the impression that much of the hospital and medical school personnel were waiting to see where the next explosion would occur—hoping to be there to watch it.

Below her, in the faculty parking lot, the floodlights suddenly flared into brilliance, turned on by an automatic clock. The sudden burst of light bathing the rectangle of concrete, caught Marisa with her defenses against memory down, thrusting her backward some six years—into another place and another time.

ii

The prison compound at Frondheim had been bathed in just such a brilliance that night, when she had started across the open quadrangle from the long dormitory building in which she and the other women prisoners slept, packed closely together like sardines in a can, toward the hospital building on the opposite side. Marisa hadn't been able to keep from shivering with dread at the tangible menace in the rifle barrels of the guards aimed down at the compound from sentry booths along the top of the wall.

This was the moment for which she had taken the chance of crossing over into East Germany and risking the arrest which had occurred almost as soon as she set foot on the border. But even though she'd been warned by British authorities of what would happen if she tried to find her father in an East German prison and bring him out to freedom, she could not control a sense of satisfaction that at last she was near to him.

This was the first time she'd been allowed to visit her father since she was brought to the prison, although she had made application for visiting privileges as soon as she had been transferred to Frondheim, where Elijah Feldman had been in prison for some time. When she'd come into the prison ward, he was only a frail body lying upon a cot, his eyes closed, the hands upon the blanket that covered him almost transparent, so thin and pale had he become.

"Papa! Papa!" Marisa had cried out with the pain of seeing her once strong and laughing father reduced to a creature in whom life itself seemed barely present.

"Marisa! *Liebchen!*" The old man opened his eyes at the sound of her voice. Seeing her and realizing that she was actually there, he tried to rise upon his elbows, but gasped suddenly with the effort, his face contorted with pain as he fall back upon the pillow.

"What is it, Papa?" she cried.

"*Der Schmerz!*"

"*Wo ist es?*"

"*In das Herz, und der Arm.*" A gasp of pain broke off the words but Marisa understood their meaning. "Pain in the heart and in the arm" could be only one thing—angina pectoris.

"Nurse!" she had called out although she had seen no nurse since she had come into the ward, only the single balding orderly, who had leered at her when he took the pass she gave him. Receiving no answer to her call, she ran back to the small room at the end of the ward where the attendant had been when she'd come in. He was still there, sitting in a chair reading a lurid-covered magazine, and had grinned up at her with the same look in his eyes.

"My father is having an anginal attack!" she cried. "An attack!" she repeated when he showed no sign of comprehension. "He needs medicine—nitroglycerin—at once."

"There is no nurse here, *gnädige Fräulein*."

"Then let me get it from the medicine cabinet. I am a doctor."

"A woman doctor?"

"Yes! Where are the medicines?"

"Up there." He nodded toward a cupboard above his head. But when she reached up to open the closed wooden doors, he seized her around the waist.

"Not so fast, *Fräulein Doktor*. You are still a prisoner, are you not?"

"Of course."

His little eyes gleamed. "If I let you have the medicine, what will you pay?"

"I have no money."

"Money? Who has money? Now for a kiss, I might not look when you get the medicine you want."

She hesitated only a moment. "All right. But the medicine first."

He shook his head. "First the kiss, then the medicine." His hands slipped up along her body as he rose from the chair with an agility rather surprising for one of his bulk. His fingers squeezed her breasts, as he bent to kiss her, and the smell of sauerkraut and cheap wine on his breath almost nauseated her.

Steeling herself against the almost overwhelming impulse to flee, she let him kiss her, his thick lips slobbering over her face and down her neck. Nor did she resist when his fingers began to unbutton the neck of the cheap cotton uniform she wore and started fumbling for her breasts, since her own hands were busy opening the cabinet above his head and searching frantically there for the nitroglycerin bottle.

She saw it just as the orderly broke the left shoulder strap of her brassiere and, with a cry of triumph, scooped her left breast from the cotton fabric cup. By then, she had managed to seize the nitroglycerin bottle and, when he bent his head to thrust the nipple into his mouth, buried her elbow into his right eye socket, bringing a cry of pain.

As he staggered back, clutching his face in his hands, she darted from the room and ran down the space between the row of beds, hiding her half-exposed breast as best she could with her left arm. Beside her father's bed, she hastily opened the bottle, shook out one of the tablets, and gave it to him. Elijah Feldman needed no instruction to place it beneath his tongue. And, as the nitroglycerin—absorbed into the body as rapidly from that spot as it might have been had it been given by hypodermic—began to exert its dilating effect upon the coronary arteries of the heart, the pain started to fade and his tortured features relaxed.

Quickly, Marisa slid the bottle, with perhaps a dozen tablets still in it, beneath his pillow. Then hurriedly she did what she could to repair the damage to her uniform and her person caused by the guard's pawing so her father wouldn't see it and realize how she had managed to get the nitroglycerin.

"*Gott sei dank!*" The sick man opened his eyes again. "Until a week ago they let me have the tablets whenever there was pain but since then they have given me no more. I have prayed for death to free me from the agony, but even that has been denied me."

"I hid the bottle under your pillow," she told him. "Keep it there and use it whenever you need it."

"But how did you—?"

She put her fingers over his lips, for the orderly was only a few steps away, his face red with anger. "Tell no one you have it," she warned her father. "I will come to see you again when I can."

"*Fräulein Doktor!*" The orderly's eye was already beginning to swell. "Your visiting pass has expired. You must leave at once."

Marisa made no objection. Getting up quickly, she was through a nearby door and out into the brightly lit compound before the orderly could stop her. Stifling the impulse to flee to the haven of the women's quarters, as poor as that was, she walked slowly lest one of the guards in the sentry towers along the walls think she was escaping and shoot her down, even though she had gone to the hospital with an official pass signed by the commandant, Colonel Wilhelm Geitz. Such things, she knew, had happened, so little value did her captors place upon the lives of those they guarded.

A woman warden with a flashlight directed Marisa to her pallet in the long dormitory. She saw the woman's eyes on the disarray at the neck of her uniform where the orderly had torn two of the buttonholes in his eagerness. But when she gave no explanation, the warden went back to her post at the end of the long room.

Lying on her pallet in the darkness, Marisa sobbed silently in desperation, not only for herself, but for her father. Her training in medicine—she had already graduated from medical school in England—had taught her how agonizing the pain of angina could be without the relief of nitroglycerin, to say nothing of the feeling of impending death that accompanied it, a sensation that some sufferers described as being even worse than the pain.

The medicine she'd managed to obtain would relieve Elijah Feldman for a while, if the hospital orderly hadn't found it and taken it away. But in her father's condition, it couldn't last very long—about a week at most. And once the tablets were used up, there seemed to be no way she could get more for him.

As it had happened, however, her problem was soon solved; Zelda, the girl who occupied the pallet next to her, revealed the way as they were working in the prison factory the next day. Under the other girl's prodding questions, Marisa recounted what had happened the night before and her fear for her father, when the agonizing pain came once again and there was no relief.

"Why don't you buy the tablets for him?" Zelda asked.

"I have no money."

"You're rich," said Zelda.

"With what?"

"You're pretty. You have a figure like Sophia Loren. And you're Jewish."

"What's that got to do with it?"

"German men think Jewish women are passionate. Make a deal with them."

"Who do you mean?"

"How about the orderly to start with—the one who tried to rape you in the hospital ward?"

"Not him." Marisa shuddered. "I couldn't go through with that."

"You'll be surprised what you can go through with after you've been in one of these places for a while," said Zelda. "But I guess you're right. With what you've got, you might as well aim for the top."

"Colonel Geitz?"

"No less. Some of the girls have been getting extra food and cigarettes for visiting him occasionally. You ought to be able to write your own ticket—as the Americans say."

Marisa hadn't taken Zelda's suggestion seriously until, on the third day after her visit to her father, the hospital orderly from the ward had fallen into step beside her as the women were marching to their dormitory from the mess hall.

"We found the tablets you gave your father the other night, *Fräulein Doktor,*" he said. "The old man has been having a lot of pain, but I could fix it so he could get more medicine, if you'd cooperate."

"How?"

"One of the women attendants is paid to let some of the girls out of the barracks at night, so they can visit the guards' quarters and enjoy themselves. After all, it isn't right for so much beauty to go to waste. You could be one of them." Seeing her hesitation, he added, "With such pain as your father has been having, I don't think he will live very long without the medicine."

The next morning, Marisa made formal application to see the commandant—on personal business. The word "personal" seemed to be the open-sesame to his presence, for she was pulled out of the work line that afternoon and sent to the administrative offices of the prison, where she shortly found herself in the presence of the commandant himself.

Looking at Colonel Geitz, sitting in a reclining chair behind his desk, Marisa wasn't sure he was much to be preferred to the orderly, except that he was probably clean. About fifty, she judged, he was somewhat portly, red-faced and wheezed a little.

"What did you wish to see me about, *Fräulein?*" he asked.

"I'm ready to make a bargain with you, Colonel."

"You're hardly in a position to bargain."

"On the contrary, I'm in an excellent position." Unbuttoning her uniform, she stepped out of it. Beneath it she wore only the brassiere and shorts that were undergarments for the women prisoners; when the rate and intensity of Colonel Geitz's wheezing began to increase, she knew she was winning.

"The rest, please." His voice was hoarse. "I'm not yet convinced."

As calmly as if she were preparing to take a shower in the dormitory washroom, Marisa unbuttoned her brassiere and took it off, then stepped out of the shorts, holding both garments in her hand. The Colonel's face was twice as red now as it had been when she'd come in and he seemed to be having trouble getting his breath.

"Turn around, please," he ordered, and she turned, like a statue upon a pedestal, until she faced him again.

"As you say, your bargaining position is excellent, *Fräulein,*" he admitted. "Perhaps after a demonstration of your capabilities—"

Without answering, Marisa stepped into her shorts, put on her brassiere and buttoned it, then donned the uniform and buttoned it, too—all the way to the top.

"What are your terms, *Fräulein?*" It was capitulation, complete and absolute, but she felt no elation. After all, she had never doubted the outcome.

"I'm a doctor, Colonel Geitz. My father is a patient in the

prison hospital with a serious case of angina pectoris. He needs nitroglycerin tablets from time to time because of agonizing pain, but you have chosen not to make them available to him. Appoint me medical supervisor of my father's ward, with free access to whatever medication he needs, and I will spend one night a week in your quarters."

"Two."

Marisa shrugged. "It doesn't matter. Is it a bargain?"

"I accept. You will come to my quarters tonight."

"Only after I've made sure my father has an ample supply of nitroglycerin."

"Agreed." He scribbled an order on a piece of paper and handed it to her. "This will assign you as nursing supervisor of your father's ward."

"Good day, Colonel."

"Until tonight, *Fräulein Doktor.*"

Outside the building, Marisa leaned against the post until she stopped trembling. But when she came to Colonel Geitz's quarters that night, she had been able to prove a conviction for which there was perhaps no true medical explanation, namely that, with a sufficient exercise of will, a woman could so control her body that no feeling existed in her generative tract, not even pain, and no nerve impulses at all would reach the brain to involve the emotions.

Elijah Feldman lived nearly six months in comfort. By that time, Marisa was physician for the entire prison hospital and most of the staff had forgotten she was actually a prisoner. Thus one day when she was sent to East Berlin to vaccinate a new group of prisoners about to be transferred to Frondheim, she had managed to slip across the border into West Berlin.

The British consul there had arranged for her return to England, where she had obtained a clinical clerkship in internal medicine without difficulty. Even then, young British doctors were fleeing in droves from the country rather than submit to the steady encroachment of the National Health Service upon their cherished professional freedom. Several years later, Marisa had followed the same course, by way of a two-year clinical teaching fellowship at Harvard Medical School.

There she had learned a distressing physiological fact: her success in divorcing herself of all feeling during the time she'd spent with Colonel Geitz had been too complete. In doing so, it seemed, she had succeeded in depriving her reproductive tract of all feeling —presumably forever.

iii

Janet Monroe was leaving the Pediatrics ward where Jerry was a patient when the telephone rang in the chart room. The charge nurse answered, then handed the receiver to her.

"Janet?" It was Jeff's voice.

"Yes."

"I was trying to get up there before you went off duty, but got stuck with a pentothal in the emergency room for a shoulder reduction and just finished it. Can you meet me across the street at the Snack Bar?"

"I think so—yes. Jerry's already asleep."

"Good. See you in a few minutes."

He was waiting for her, tall and ruggedly handsome in his crisp white ducks, when she crossed the street. The restaurant was almost filled with the eleven o'clock rush of interns, nurses and students, but they found a booth in the corner.

"What's so important?" Janet asked, when Mabel had taken their order and brought them coffee.

"A proposal."

It would be so easy—for both her and Jerry—to say yes, Janet thought. Jeff Long was everything a girl in her right mind could want; handsome, talented, kind. Jerry adored him and he was even independent financially, since he came from a wealthy Georgia family. But then she'd thought many of the same things about Cliff—and how wrong she had been. In her heart, she knew it wasn't really fair to compare Cliff and Jeff; and she was fond of him in a way she'd never felt about her former husband. But something she couldn't put into words at the moment still held her back.

"Please, Jeff," she said. "I need to be free for a while—especially with Jerry sick."

"You've been brooding too much," he protested. "Marriage doesn't have to be like what you had with Cliff."

"What about Mrs. Dellman? And the others—Dr. Hanscombe's wife and Mrs. McCloskey? Their husbands are at the top, but look what it got them. One's dead and another would be, if you hadn't been there when she was brought in last night. They tell me Mrs. Hanscombe almost went into coma, too."

"We're not like them," he protested.

"I'm not so sure, Jeff. I imagine all those couples loved each other, maybe they still do. I've been divorced, so I know something of what Mrs. McCloskey must have felt to bring her to—"

"That could have been an accident. Not many people know how dangerous it is to mix alcohol and barbiturates."

"Does Dr. Rogan think it was?"

"No," he admitted.

"See what I mean? A lot of medical marriages—particularly where the doctor is very successful, as you're bound to be—suffer from some sort of a sickness later on. I was talking to Dr. Feldman about it at dinner."

"She's an old maid!"

"What an awful thing to say about somebody so lovely and nice!" Janet cried indignantly. "She was telling me about a study of student marriages a friend of hers made at Harvard. A lot of them cracked up, just like mine did."

"We've been over all this before," he reminded her.

"What happened yesterday to Mrs. Dellman only makes what I'm saying more true." She reached across the table to squeeze his long, skillful fingers in a gesture of trust and affection. "Please, Jeff. I'm very fond of you and so is Jerry. Can't we just be good friends?"

"I hope we'll always be friends—but there's another alternative."

She gave him a startled look. "Are you suggesting—"

"Of course not. You know me better than that, Janet."

"I thought I did. What's this mysterious alternative you're talking about?"

"Lately I've been doing a lot of thinking about us—and the future. Dr. McCready is going to retire in another five years or so and Dieter practically came right out the other day and said he would boost me for the job of head of the Anesthesiology Department."

"That would be wonderful for you, Jeff."

"I'm not so sure—if it means your turning me down because you're afraid of what success could do to our marriage."

"That's not fair," she protested. "You're trying to put the burden of knowing I had cut you out of the chance here on my conscience."

"Not so fast," he said with a grin. "I didn't say I wanted to take the job."

"But—"

"I asked you over here tonight and let you make all your old arguments first, just so I could cut the ground from under your feet."

"What in the world are you talking about?"

"After I finish my residency next July, I've got to give two years to the Army. With my training, I'm sure to be sent to a big general hospital like Walter Reed or Brooke, which wouldn't really be much different from working right here."

"That's what you want, isn't it?"

"I had been thinking a lot about what I really want—even before this Dellman business came up. It wasn't any secret around here that a lot of top-brass marriages were in trouble—Brennan's, for one. And the McCloskeys already had their divorce."

"That's what scares me."

"About a month ago I saw a squib in the A.M.A. *Journal* about a project one of the big foundations is working on to start a top-flight medical school at Saigon in South Vietnam. It was intimated that young doctors willing to teach there would have the time they spent credited on their military service."

"Something like the Peace Corps?"

"I guess so. As I understand it, the whole thing is a private venture in partnership with government. Anyway I wrote them several weeks ago and today I had an answer. If I want it, the job will be mine next July when I finish here—chief anesthesiologist for the hospital and Professor of Anesthesiology in the medical school."

"That's wonderful, Jeff."

"It's a real challenge, but don't get the idea that this is some grandiose project. They're starting small and it will be an uphill fight to train really competent doctors. One thing's sure; there's not much money in it. I won't even make as much as if I were in the Army, but fortunately that doesn't make an awful lot of difference."

"Think of the good you'll do. And the satisfaction you'll get out of doing it. You're going to take the job, aren't you?"

"I wired them my acceptance this afternoon. This thing's been cooking for several weeks, but I haven't mentioned it to you because I figured it wasn't fair to tell you about it until I was definitely committed."

"Why?"

"Just now you accused me of putting pressure on your conscience," he reminded her. "No matter what happens, I'm going to Vietnam for two years, Janet, maybe longer. They're going to need teachers badly in their School of Nursing. I hope you'll decide to go, too—as my wife. And we shouldn't have any trouble finding a native amah—or whatever it is they call them—for Jerry."

"Suppose Jerry doesn't come through this trouble he has?" She finally put into words the fear that was tormenting her. "Or is left an invalid?"

"You'll need me more than ever." He didn't try to minimize the gravity of Jerry's condition. She was too intelligent—and too good a nurse—for that.

Janet felt her defenses crumbling. As Jeff had said, her own arguments had been largely destroyed before she could make them. In fact the only reason to refuse him now would be that she didn't love him enough.

"You don't have to decide right away," he said. "I've already committed myself, but you could sign up at any time. I think we could do important work out there, Janet. Most important of all we'd be happy."

Looking at him across the table of the small booth, Janet was tempted strongly to say yes—and fought against it, knowing that this time she had to be absolutely sure. If she married Jeff and the marriage failed, she would never be given another chance at real happiness—of that she was convinced. Once the pattern of marriage and divorce was established, it was easier to make the break each time and tell yourself you could start again, when in actual fact the odds against success went higher with every failure.

Deep in her heart something told her the affection she felt for Jeff Long, built upon a solid foundation of mutual interest, warm admiration, and the satisfaction of work shared, was a far more solid basis for a successful marriage than had been the largely physical passion that had brought her and Cliff together—and later torn them apart. But she needed time to be sure, to think out her fears and recognize them for the groundless worries she was already half convinced they really were. And particularly to see what happened to Jerry.

"For a start, why don't you get assigned to seven-to-three duty," Jeff suggested. "That way we can spend a lot of time together this winter taking a night French course I'm signing up for at the university."

"Do they speak French in Vietnam?"

"Educated people do. The medical school classes will be conducted in French; they once ruled the country, you know. There will be a lot of concerts and things we can go to this winter here in Weston, too. I'm off three evenings a week and every other weekend."

"I've been thinking about making the duty change, anyway,"

said Janet. When she'd come back to work after the divorce, she'd been forced to take the three-to-eleven shift because nothing else was available at the salary she needed to support herself and Jerry. A seven-to-three shift was opening soon and she could have it if she wished, but she'd held off, thinking of the long evenings in the apartment, after Jerry was asleep.

"You don't need to work any more, just so you'll be occupied evenings," said Jeff.

"How did you know that?"

"I was in love with you before you married Cliff—remember? And I probably know nearly as much about what makes you tick as you do yourself."

"How could I ever have any mystery for you, if you know me so well?"

"There'll always be the mystery of how anything as nice as you could happen to me," he assured her.

"I'll make a bargain with you, Jeff," she said impulsively.

"Name it."

"I'll change duty hours to seven-to-three. And I'll take the French lessons with you; I always loved the language anyway and Mrs. Bodey can sit with Jerry."

"That sounds like complete capitulation to me. What's the catch?"

"You must promise not to ask me to marry you for six months."

"Accepted." He held out his hand with a grin. "As long as you don't try to limit my thoughts. And when the six months are over?"

"If I can't make up my mind by then, you wouldn't want me anyway."

As they shook hands, Janet glanced at her watch. "Goodness! It's almost midnight. Do you know what Jerry's program is for tomorrow? I didn't get to see Ed Harrison tonight."

"Dieter has tentatively scheduled a cerebral angiography on him for eleven, if the radioscan is negative." He didn't add "for brain tumor"; there was no point in troubling Janet any more than she was troubled already.

CHAPTER XX

The medical journal Dave Rogan had promised to send Maggie McCloskey arrived Friday morning. The article he had marked was a paper presented at a meeting of the American Psychiatric Association. After she finished her breakfast, Maggie started to read; before she'd gone very far, however, she began to be acutely uncomfortable.

"Frequent admissions of physicians' wives to a private psychiatric hospital raised the question of a possible relationship between the husband's occupation and the occurrence and manifestation of illnesses in the wives," said the opening paragraph.

The study, she saw, was of fifty cases, carried out in a prestigious private psychiatric hospital. Seven of the wives in the report had participated actively in the husband's practice early in marriage, as Maggie herself had done in the work of the Faculty Clinic during the years when she had been Dave Rogan's secretary. But when their husbands took on other nursing and office help, they had soon begun to feel left out and unneeded, an almost exact statement of Maggie's own state of mind for nearly a decade.

She'd been busy and happy during the first five years after she and Joe had first been married, even though she had continued to work as Dave's secretary most of that time. After they bought the house in Sherwood Ravine, she had been busy decorating and landscaping it, but once the clinic was operating freely, it hadn't seemed right for the wife of a doctor making over $25,000 a year to be without a full-time maid.

Maggie was intelligent enough to know the breakup of a

marriage couldn't be blamed simply on the fact that the wife had a maid and therefore little to do. Her own trouble went deeper than that; in fact warning signs—if she had only known how to recognize them—had appeared during the first weeks of her marriage to Joe.

In only nine of the fifty couples, the article said, had "frequent and mutually satisfying sexual relations" existed throughout the marriage. The rest listed much variation while, in thirteen, sex as a meaningful part of their lives was "very infrequent or mutually unsatisfactory."

On the honeymoon Maggie had attributed her lack of response to Joe's love-making to physical discomfort during the act; later she'd blamed it on him. When she continued not to reach a climax, except on rare occasions when she'd been drinking heavily at parties or conventions—she'd gone to Jack Hagen on the pretext of having a Pap test. But Jack had pronounced her perfectly normal and she'd been ashamed to confess to him the real reason for her visit.

She should have consulted Dave Rogan then, she realized now. But she'd been brought up by her mother to be very reticent about such things; in fact, she was sure her parents had stopped sleeping together long before her father died, for they'd had separate rooms as far back as she could remember. Now she found herself wondering whether that could have had anything to do with her frigidity. The word itself repelled her, however, and she turned back to the medical journal.

"A family history of emotional disturbance was present in thirty-one of the wives' families," the article said. "In eighteen of these families, there was a history in parents or siblings of psychiatric hospitalization, suicide, or psychotic illness."

So that had been the real nature of her mother's "nervous breakdown." Mother had blamed Father for it, railing against him for being ineffectual and afraid to ask for a raise or a more important job. Maggie had accepted her mother's accusations at face value, too, knowing her father to be easygoing and not inclined to argue back. But Joe was very much like that, too, yet she knew Pete Brennan and the other doctors in the Faculty Clinic had a tremendous respect for him. And the students had twice voted him their favorite teacher.

The most frequently cited characteristics of the mothers of the doctors' wives who had required institutional psychiatric care, she read on, were "domineering," "distant," "rejecting attitude toward the patient," "moody," "demanding," and "rigid."

That was Mother, Maggie admitted wryly, then sobered when she remembered the same thing could be said about her own attitude toward Joe much of these past ten years.

"Fathers were most often seen as having a close relationship with the patient, as being shy or retiring, easygoing, strict and dependent," she read, but by now the tabulation of symptoms and facts had begun to depress her. For the first time since she'd finally regained complete consciousness yesterday afternoon, she felt the need for a drink. But there was no chance of getting one in the hospital, and after night before last, she was afraid to ask for a barbiturate.

Maggie was intelligent enough to realize that most of the rising sense of anxiety she felt came from the almost uncanny similarity of the symptoms enumerated in the psychiatric article to those which had characterized her own family life as a child—plus the undeniable fact that in her own marriage, she had tended to imitate almost exactly the story of her parents' difficulties. It was no wonder, she thought, that her father had died early of a heart attack and her mother had been a querulous, demanding invalid for so much of her life.

The next paragraph in the report was labeled "Symptomatology." Maggie hesitated a moment before going on, sensing what she would find: "anxiety and muscle spasms"; "depression and excessive drinking"; "overuse of drugs or alcohol"; "suspiciousness"; "suicidal attempt"; "persistent pain"; "hostility"; "agitation"; "feelings of rejection"—they were all there, like ghosts come to haunt her.

Most chilling of all was a paragraph that said: "Seven patients had sufficiently long-standing histories of overconsumption of al-

cohol to warrant a secondary diagnosis of alcoholism. A secondary
diagnosis of drug addiction was made in the case of eleven patients, while eleven others had histories of using addictive drugs
to the point of psychological and physiological dependence."

That she was physiologically dependent on alcohol—the real
test of an alcoholic—Maggie was already convinced; by now her
nerves were fairly screaming for the solace of a drink. She almost
put the article aside at that point, but the morbid fascination of
looking at herself, as it were, through a microscope, made her
go on.

In discussing the fifty cases, the reporting psychiatrist said of
some four-fifths of the women: "Nevertheless, prior to illness,
they had been quite successful. They were well educated and
pursued a variety of intellectual and cultural activities in their
leisure moments. They were able to marry men with high
sociocultural standing. As a group they had successfully weathered
the difficult years of their husband's medical and specialty training
and the early years of practice. Only after an average of almost
thirteen years of marriage was an overt illness manifested.

"By the time of admission, these women had raised families
averaging almost three children, and participated in community
activities and had furthered their social aims. Most patients in
this group possessed enough ego strength prior to illness to
achieve a superior level of social adaptation."

Maggie laid down the article and turned her eyes to the smooth
white blankness of the ceiling. She hadn't really started going to
the club very often until she'd gotten a full-time maid and was no
longer responsible for any real duties about the house. Like many
others she knew—and not all them doctors' wives—she'd become
at about that same time what the psychiatrist making the report
had characterized as "overly dependent upon the environment for
reinforcement of her self concept."

"With a mean age spread between husband and wife of
5.6 years," the report continued, "the peak age for onset of illness
[early 30's] occurred at the time when most physicians, including
the husbands of these women, were established and in their peak

years [late 30's] of active practice. Underscoring the possibility of a relationship here is the prevalence of complaints about the increasing absence of the husband at the time when the wife's personal involvement in her husband's work is decreasing."

"Sexual incompatibility," she noted, had existed "in at least seventy-five per cent of the cases."

"Marriage to an older man, whose vocation may have been unconsciously associated with omnipotent, understanding, protective attributes," the article said, "may be interpreted as an attempt by many of the patients to resolve persisting Oedipal conflicts. Illness developed when the equilibrium of the adjustment was disrupted by such reality factors as the increasing involvement of the doctor in his work, or a conflict between his personality characteristics and the idealized expectations of his wife.

"Despite the broad variety of diagnostic categories, three symptomatic themes tend to recur: depression, drug addiction and somatization [physical complaints]. As the doctor became increasingly involved in his work, depression was precipitated by the physiological loss, which intensified the wife's ambivalent feelings. In addition, the wife, previously an active participant in her husband's career, was faced with the loss of this role. The secondary symptomatic theme, the use of drugs, is specifically related to the husband's profession by virtue of ready accessibility of medications. Thus the patient unconsciously symbolized her dependency needs through the use of one of the most fundamental and gratifying resources the physician has to offer—drugs used to relieve pain.

"The third theme, frequently interwoven with the previous two, appears in the history of somatic [physical] symptomatology, particularly of pain. This symptom also points to the hostile-dependent aspects of the husband-wife relationship. Pain brings a patient to the attention of the physician, who, in turn, directs his energy to the alleviation of that pain. Nothing can be more frustrating, confusing or embarrassing to the physician than pain of undiagnosed etiology which he cannot relieve. It is a symptom which professionally cannot be ignored or left unattended; it must receive that attention which, in his wife's view, the doctor devotes to his patients, perhaps to the exclusion of his wife's needs.

"The recorded comments of family, patients and therapists gave a number of indications that the husbands had contributed to some extent to the illnesses of their wives, a participation which extended beyond the doctor's preoccupation with his work. The physician, secure in his omnipotent roles with patients who are frankly dependent upon his professional capabilities, rejected his wife's dependency strivings except when they were expressed as demands for medical attention. He then, without apparent cognizance of their emotional basis, gratified these needs by resorting to his professional role. A number of patients, for example, who were addicted to drugs, continued to have ready access to them even after the addiction was evident, and in several cases the drugs were furnished by the husbands. Furthermore, of seventeen patients who left the hospital prematurely, that is against the recommendation of their therapists, six were withdrawn by the husband; the other twelve patients did not have any pronounced difficulty in persuading their husbands to condone this action. In many incidences, the husband was unwilling or unable to set limits on his wife's behavior. This passivity, or even cooperation, in his wife's psychopathology suggests that those doctors felt guilty about their own inability to meet the emotional needs of their wives."

Maggie put down the medical journal when the freckled nurse came into the room.

"Would you like something to drink?" the girl asked.

"Yes. A double Scotch—on the rocks."

"The best we can do is Seven-Up—or Coca-Cola."

"Make it a Coke then." As the nurse was leaving the room, Maggie called to her: "This journal belongs in Dr. Rogan's office. Would you see that someone sends it down to him?"

"Of course, Mrs. McCloskey." The girl took the journal and Maggie felt better almost immediately. During the last few moments, the damned thing had seemed like a snake lying there on the table waiting to strike her.

"Nurse," she called, as the girl was at the door.

"Yes, Mrs. McCloskey."

"Will you shut the door, please? I want to be alone with my superego."

ii

Lorrie Dellman's funeral was set for eleven o'clock, in the cemetery back of the old Episcopal church. Only the older families in Weston had lots there; the town had long since been built up around the church and it was no longer fashionable to have a cemetery almost in the center of the city. As a result, new ones had been laid out in the suburbs, complete with perpetual care, fountains, and recorded music played from hidden loudspeakers among the trees.

Della Rogan had gone by the hospital for Grace, who had telephoned that she'd been given a pass to attend the funeral. Elaine McGill came alone. Amy brought Alice Weston with her; living as close together as they did, there didn't seem to be any reason for bringing two cars.

Maggie McCloskey was still in the hospital; Dave Rogan had ordered her not to go to the funeral, knowing that, even though he'd already made considerably more progress toward showing her the path she must follow in the future than he'd expected to make by now, the emotional shock of seeing Lorrie's coffin and knowing that, but for Joe's love and Jeff Long's skill, her body could be inside one just like it, might be too much for her.

As for the others, Lorrie had been their friend and the thought of anyone so alive and vital being shut away beneath the surface of the earth was sad enough to make anybody weep. Besides, all of them felt a little guilty, knowing that under slightly different circumstances any one of them could have been inside the coffin.

Jake Porter had decided on a simple graveside service. Even so, Amy Brennan was surprised by the large number of flowers.

"Uncle Jacob talked to me this morning on the phone," said

317

Alice. "He said flowers came from people all over town. It's surprising how many people knew and liked Lorrie."

"I met one of her college classmates a few years ago at a medical auxiliary meeting," said Amy. "She said Lorrie was the most popular girl in the class—and not just with boys."

"She wasn't always kind to me." Alice wiped her eyes with a tiny handkerchief. "But I loved her."

Mort Dellman was there with Sergeant Jim O'Brien. Amy saw no sign of handcuffs but, from what Pete had told her, Mort was counting on the grand jury to let him off and would have no reason to try to escape. Pete had told her Mort had asked him to make arrangements for a reservation on a plane for South Africa, where he planned to start a new life. Which was probably just as well; they had only tolerated him before because he was married to Lorrie and because of his place in the clinic.

Lorrie's children were with Jake Porter, sitting at one end of two rows of chairs arranged for the family at the graveside under the canopy. Della and Grace stood at the back of the crowd. When Dave and Pete Brennan arrived, Dave made his way across the grass, dodging gravestones, to stand beside Della. He gave her arm an affectionate squeeze and, when she groped for his hand with hers, took it and held it during the rest of the service. Neither spoke, but both knew that her silent reaching out to him had removed in an instant much of the stiffness that had been between them for the past couple of weeks.

The canon of the new cathedral across town was a young and very earnest priest who was causing raised eyebrows among the several Episcopal congregations in the city, particularly the older ones, by spending much of his time with factory workers and their families and Negroes in the slum area called Brooklyn, something no minister in Weston had ever dared to do.

The canon was tall, very young-looking and serious in his vestments. At the stroke of eleven, he stepped up to the head of the coffin and waited for those who had been standing a little outside the immediate area, reluctant to get near the coffin, to move closer.

"It has been requested that I read from the Gospel of St. John, chapter eight," he announced. Opening the Bible, he began to read in a clear voice that carried to the edges of the crowd:

> Jesus went unto the Mount of Olives and early in the morning he came again into the temple and all the people came unto him and he sat down and taught them. And the scribes and Pharisees brought unto him a woman taken in adultery.

The word shattered the placid scene at the graveside like a bombshell. The young canon ignored the gasps from the women and the disapproving frowns of the men as he continued to read:

> And when they had set her in the midst, they said unto him, "Master, this woman was taken in adultery, in the very act. Now Moses and the law commanded us that such should be stoned; but what do you say?"
>
> This they said, tempting him that they might have to accuse him. But Jesus stooped down and with his finger wrote on the ground, as though he heard them not. So when they continued asking him, he lifted up himself and said unto them, "He that is without sin among you, let him first cast a stone at her."
>
> And again he stooped down and wrote on the ground, and they who heard it, being convicted by their own conscience, went out one by one, beginning at the eldest, even unto the last. And Jesus was left alone and the woman standing in the midst.
>
> When Jesus had lifted up himself and saw none but the woman, he said unto her: "Woman, where are those thine accusers? Has no man condemned you?"
>
> She said, "No man, Lord." And Jesus said to her, "Neither do I condemn thee. Go and sin no more."

With no change in his manner to indicate his realization of the effect the passage had caused, the young canon turned the pages of the Bible and began to read the ritual litany for the burial of the dead.

The service was quickly over. Moving along the line of relatives sitting in the chairs beside the grave, the priest came to Mort Dellman and held out his hand to him as he had the others. Dellman hesitated, then shook hands before he moved away with Sergeant Jim O'Brien at his side without attempting to speak to either Jake Porter or the children.

As the crowd began to disperse, the buzz of conversation filled the air. It would be a long time before Weston stopped talking about the effrontery of the young canon in coming right out and mentioning the word "adultery" at the funeral. Things like that just weren't spoken of publicly in an upright moral community, especially during a High-Church Episcopalian service.

"The very idea of him reading that passage," Alice said indignantly as she and Amy were walking toward the car, stepping around the graves in the old cemetery. "Why, it's almost like he was condoning what Lorrie did. And did you see him shake hands with Mort?"

Amy didn't answer. She had seen Pete Brennan with Roy Weston at the edge of the cemetery. And as they moved toward their own cars, she hurried Alice along to intercept them.

"I was just telling Amy it's really sacrilegious, what that priest said," Alice fumed when they caught up with Pete and Roy. "I'll bet the bishop will give him what for, when word of it gets to him."

"He was only reading the words of Jesus," Pete said.

"I don't care. Some things shouldn't be spoken of—and this was one of them."

"Are you throwing stones?" he asked, and Alice stiffened.

"Pete Brennan!" she cried. "I hate you!"

"I'm sorry, Alice," he said. "I guess what the minister said sort of upset most of us. After all, who are we to—?"

"I don't know about you," Alice began angrily.

"Shut up, Alice!" Roy Weston said wearily.

"I won't—"

"Shut up, Alice!" he repeated and Alice lapsed into a hurt silence.

"Uncle Jake told me he had asked the canon to read a special passage." Amy hadn't spoken before during the entire interchange. "Do you suppose that could have been his idea?"

"It must have been." Pete Brennan looked back to where the old man was being ushered to his limousine. "I don't think the canon would have dared do it without a request from the family. As Alice just said, the bishop would certainly give him hell if he had."

"But why would Uncle Jacob do a thing like that?" Alice said.

"I expect because he knows a lot of us have been critical of Lorrie," Amy said, and Pete gave her a startled look.

"Critical because of what she did—or because she was caught?" Roy asked.

"A little of both, I guess." Amy turned to touch Pete's arm, almost apologetically. "Will you be home for dinner, darling?"

"I may have to operate on the Monroe child and I've got a staff conference at the hospital," he told her. "It might be late, but I'll get there as soon as I can."

"I'll let Mary fix dinner and go on home," she said. "We'll pile the dishes in the sink and she can do them in the morning."

He knew what she meant and his pulse quickened as he turned to his own car.

iii

"There's something you hardly ever see nowadays," Grace Hanscombe said as she and Della Rogan were getting into Della's station wagon after the funeral service.

"What's that?"

"An honest preacher—with guts!"

"He only read the words of Jesus himself."

"Jake Sanford's the largest contributor to the church, trying to buy himself a little burn salve, I guess, for the hereafter. From what I hear, he can use it."

"But Jesus forgave the adultress."

"Would you have forgiven Lorrie—if it had been Dave instead of Paul McGill?"

"I don't suppose so."

"And what about Dave—if you were to stray."

"Maybe after a little while; he's more tolerant than I am."

"How do you suppose Elaine felt? She was standing near us."

"She's always been pretty religious, you know," said Della. "I guess that Bible passage would mean something to her."

"If she's got good sense, she won't let this break up her marriage," said Grace. "Sometimes I think I'd love George more, if he would tomcat around a little—at least enough to prove he could still do it. I can't even make him mad any more. When it gets that bad, I guess a marriage is pretty well shot."

"You're talking foolishness, Grace," Della said as she started the car.

"No I'm not. With me it's die with George—or live without him. I don't mind telling you this diabetes episode scared the living hell out of me."

"You're crazy, Grace." Della stopped the station wagon and let another car go ahead. "George isn't Cary Grant, neither is Dave. But he's still a good provider."

"A woman needs more than that. The truth is, I don't think he really loves me any more."

"Why would you say that?"

"Before all this happened I'd been pestering him to let me go back to England—not because I really wanted to go, mind you, but mainly because he didn't want me to. Last night he came to see me in the hospital and suggested that I go to England for a visit."

"Are you going?"

"Sure. But now he's taken all the pleasure out of it, because I won't be making him mad by going."

"How long are you going to stay?"

"I don't know. Maybe for good unless I get to the point where it will feel good to be waked up in the middle of the night by a man patting you on the behind—even if that's all he's going to do."

"I guess Lorrie Dellman getting killed has changed a lot of our lives. I've decided to give up golf tournaments." Della put into words a decision she hadn't known she'd made until that moment.

"I can't believe it."

"Golf's fine when you're playing for the exercise—and the fun of it. But when you've got to stay in training like an athlete, and ride around in one of those damned little carts because you have to save your energy for the strokes, it's time to quit."

"But you're near the top, Della."

"There isn't any top. Tournament play is something like an alcoholic taking the first drink of the day; you can't stop with the first or the second or the third. There's always another tournament ahead that you've got to try and win."

"You almost sound happy about it."

"I guess I am, in a way. Dave wants us to have another child."

"Do you love him enough to go through that again?"

"Yes. I just decided it—out there in the cemetery."

"I saw you holding hands," said Grace. "As for me, I've gotten so used to having George around, I can't tell whether I still love him or not."

"Maybe that's what married love is, being happy to have someone around."

"I didn't say I was *happy* to have him around," said Grace. "I said I was *used* to having him around. Most of the time he irritates the hell out of me."

"Obviously he cares a lot for you or he wouldn't have agreed for you to go to England."

"George is a good doctor, Della; he's always concerned for his patients. He's discovered at last that I'm sick, so he'll do whatever he thinks is best for me. I guess one reason why so many doctors' wives crack up is because the husbands are so busy being concerned for their patients they don't have much time left to be concerned about their wives. I've often heard George say doctors' families are neglected medically."

"He certainly isn't neglecting you. You admitted that yourself."

"Whose side are you on anyway?"

"Both. I'm fond of you and I'm fond of George. I'd hate to see either of you unhappy."

"George won't even know I'm gone—until Saturday night," Grace said with a shrug. "If I do say so myself, I'm pretty good in the hay. I'll give George this much, too. Once he gets out of the starting gate, he can gallop home at a pretty respectable pace."

"Then why are you thinking of leaving him?"

"I guess because the strain of keeping up has finally got to me."

"What does that mean?"

"In England I can grow fat and get a lot of joy out of life—even if I have to take insulin. Here I've got to wear a girdle to keep my fanny from spreading. George is still handsome with that clipped mustache of his and that distinguished little pot, so I have to dress smartly and not look bad compared to the other faculty wives. I drink a lot of liquor I don't particularly care for, because everybody in our group does. Over here I'm fairly smothered in respectability, but basically I guess I'm too much of a slut to enjoy it."

CHAPTER XXI

Paul McGill was out of bed when Dave Rogan came by on the way to the hospital cafeteria for lunch after the funeral. The dermatologist was sitting in a chair by the window, with the distant panorama of the Great Smokies looking like a movie backdrop on the western horizon.

"I saw Elaine at the funeral, Paul," said Dave. "She'll be by to see you after lunch."

"I don't know what I ever did to deserve something as wonderful as she is," said the dermatologist.

"I don't have to ask how it's going with you." Dave stretched out in the one easy chair the room afforded and stuffed his pipe with Rough Cut. "Imagine having your heart opened up day before yesterday and being out of bed already. When I was an intern we used to keep appendix cases down longer than that."

"Dieter says there's no sign of any accumulation of fluid in the pericardium or the pleurae. He thinks I'll be able to go home the first of the week. It's a funny thing," Paul McGill added with a wry smile, "but I can even detect a change in the way people treat me since all this happened."

"What kind of a change?"

"I guess I must have been pretty much of a clod medically—and maybe socially; after all, dermatology isn't the most exciting specialty in the world. You can get to be pretty much of an old maid, doling out ointments and freezing hyperkeratoses all day. But now, it's suddenly like I was a hero or something."

"They say every man has a secret ambition to live to be ninety

325

and be indicted for rape," said Dave. "You've made the leap from what you call an old maid to the role of Don Juan. Naturally, a lot of people whose lives are pretty humdrum envy you. Come to think of it, maybe I do myself."

"It's still a strange thing."

"Not as much as you think. A writer friend of mine has made a fortune out of novels based on real-life heroines who were wicked women—people like Jezebel, Rahab the harlot of Jericho, Cleopatra and the like. He believes the books are popular with women because they want to see how much the hussies of history were able to get away with. And men like them because every man secretly wonders what it would be like to have one of those females around the house."

"I guess there's a lot in what he says."

"Not that Lorrie was basically wicked. Psychiatrically she was more normal than most of us, because she had less inhibitions and gave free rein to the instincts most of us refuse to admit, because we're afraid they might bust open the nice little watertight compartments we squeeze our lives into."

"When I look back on it now, I can see that I've been pretty well boxed in ever since I was a child," Paul admitted.

"How old were you when your father died?"

"Four." The dermatologist gave him a startled look. "But how did you know that? Oh, I remember now. The intern who took the history the day after the operation asked me about my family history."

"I didn't look at it."

"Then how did you know?"

"Your whole symptom pattern fits that of a boy who was reared by his mother in the absence of a father."

"Father didn't really die until ten years ago. When I was about four he walked out of the house and never came back."

"That makes you an even more typical case. I suppose your mother was pretty bitter about the whole thing."

"Once I asked her what Father was like and she wouldn't even speak to me for two days. Just put food on the table before me, and didn't answer when I begged her to tell me what was wrong. After that, I never made the mistake of mentioning his name again."

"Did you ever find out what really happened between them?"

"An uncle—my father's brother—came to see me in college and I asked him about it. It was the old story—another woman. They ran off together but weren't married and after a while she left him. Father tried to come back to Mother but she wouldn't let him. She was pretty stiff-necked about such things."

"Count yourself lucky you didn't turn out to be a homosexual," Dave Rogan said. "The family pattern you describe is pretty common among them. I suppose your mother tried to bring you up as Lord Fauntleroy?"

"She did her best, until I rebelled. When I insisted on playing football at school, she kept hammering at me that I mustn't let myself grow up to be like other men, treating the nice women they married like animals."

"Is that why you waited so late to marry?"

"I suppose so. I didn't marry until after she died and I suppose I might have remained a bachelor, even then, but Elaine came along. She's so sweet and gentle—"

"And physically like your mother too?"

"Why, yes." The dermatologist's eyes opened wide. "Are you saying that had anything to do with my falling in love with Elaine?"

"It almost certainly made you single her out from other women. Men who've been close to their mothers in childhood often marry women who are very much like them."

Paul McGill didn't speak for a long moment and Dave Rogan smoked on without prodding him. One of the most important assets of a successful psychiatrist was patience; the willingness to wait while the patient searched his soul and finally saw the motive for his own acts.

"Elaine is like mother in many ways," Paul said at last. "Could that have anything to do with . . . my trouble?"

327

"It probably has everything to do with it. I suppose Joe Mc-
Closkey has checked you out for physical defects?"

"Joe says there's nothing wrong with me and Jack Hagen gave
Elaine a clean bill of health, too. Surely you don't claim my seed
aren't able to join with hers because of some psychological factor."

"There are investigators who go that far, but not me; I think
the union of sperm and egg is too elemental an affair to have
been left to anything except mathematical probability. Even
there, the odds are weighted so heavily in favor of conception
that it's a miracle it doesn't occur every time."

"Jack did a viability test on my sperm and nothing's wrong
there either," said Paul. "My personal belief is that Elaine has
some kind of hyperacidity in her generative tract that kills them
before they reach the ovum."

"Are they ever really deposited there—inside her generative
tract, I mean?"

Paul McGill flushed. "I get that far—but not much farther."

"What about Elaine?"

"What do you mean?"

"Does she achieve orgasm regularly?"

"I don't know. She's never complained."

"Most women don't until they turn up with something psychosomatic, or a real neurosis. Then we psychiatrists have the devil
of a time working out the real cause of the trouble."

"You mean this sort of thing is common?"

"Most of the married patients I see give a history of disturbed
sexual functions. I'm downright ashamed of you, Paul. The students call you Old Dermatographia because you're always stroking
patients' skins to show their nervous make-up and how it affects
their symptoms. Yet here you have a prima facie case on your own
hands and you don't even recognize it."

"You mean Elaine?"

"She seems somehow to have escaped the Doctor's Wife syndrome so far, in spite of the fact that less than twenty per cent of
women suffering from that trouble report a normal sex life. In
this case, I'm talking about you."

328

Paul flushed with obvious irritation. "Maybe you'd better explain."

"You already know the answer, but you're too stubborn to admit it. Your mother raised you to believe most men mistreat their wives, especially in connection with the sexual function. I don't know whether she told you that in so many words, but she managed to imply it. The act of deserting her was enough mistreatment in her eyes to condemn your father, though I suspect he was justified in leaving her."

"That's a strong statement, Dave. I'm not sure I like it."

"I didn't expect you to. This kind of truth is rarely pleasant."

"What next?"

"You marry Elaine, who's a lively girl and perfectly normal—except that she looks like your mother and reminds you of her. Naturally you love your wife, but when it comes to going to bed with her, your overdeveloped superego keeps getting in the way."

"Why?"

"A lot of things influence that sort of a mechanism. Offhand I'd say the main thing is fear of incest."

"Good God!" The other man's face was a mask of horror.

"There speaks the overzealous conscience. One part of your emotional system has a perfectly normal desire to make love to your wife, Paul, but another part keeps insisting it's too much like making love to your mother. So you get part of the way but can't go the rest—before there's no need and no capability to go any farther."

"But Lorrie?"

"Lorrie was nothing like your mother—or Elaine. In fact, I'd be willing to bet you had wondered more than once what being with her would really be like."

"I wouldn't have admitted it an hour ago," Paul McGill confessed. "But lately that idea had driven me almost nuts."

"I guess all of us had it at one time or another—unless we found out. Most any attractive woman can make a man wonder just that if she wants to. And you can be damn sure they know it,

329

or they wouldn't dress the way they do—to say nothing of advertisements.

"But getting back to your case, Paul. You don't fool the old unconscious mind very long. Down deep inside your mind, you suspected what was holding you back with Elaine, but you needed to be sure and about the only way was to try someone else. You're a pretty moral sort of a guy, like me, though, and you love your wife too much to go philandering. That's why you jumped at the chance to take those samples to Lorrie."

"But—"

"The clinic pharmacy could have delivered them," Dave reminded him. "The truth is you were as ready to be seduced Wednesday afternoon as a Vassar girl on a Yale weekend. But don't tell Elaine that. Let her keep on thinking Lorrie caught you in a moment of weakness."

"You're not going to put any of this on my record, are you?"

"And make you lose the Don Juan reputation?" Dave Rogan grinned. "Just be sure you don't go running after my wife, you lecherous old bastard."

ii

As he was leaving the Intensive Care Unit where he had been talking to Paul McGill, Dave Rogan met Jeff Long in the corridor.

"The brain scan on Jerry Monroe was negative for tumor, Dr. Rogan," said the anesthesiologist. "I just came from the radioisotope lab."

"Thank God for that. Is Dr. Dieter going to do the angiogram?"

"It's set up for three o'clock. Before I start the pentothal I thought the kid ought to rest a bit and get some fluids to wash out the radioactive mercury salt they gave him for the scan."

"I'll try to get up to X-ray for the angiogram, but tell them not to wait for me," said Dave. "How's Janet taking it?"

"She'd made her own diagnosis of brain tumor. Now she's so happy it isn't that she hasn't started worrying about the rest."

"We won't mention the other possibilities until we're sure then," said the psychiatrist. "Statistically, the chances with a congenital arterial condition are a lot better than with a brain tumor anyway." He glanced at his watch. "I've just got time to see Mrs. McCloskey before lunch."

A glance at Maggie McCloskey's chart told Dave the psychiatric journal article had precipitated some of the effect he'd been hoping to obtain. At midmorning she'd had an attack of hysteria and the resident on the Psychiatric ward had given her a sedative. When Dave came into the room, he was carrying the medical journal she'd sent out to the desk under his arm.

"What's the trouble?" he said. "Couldn't you take it?"

"None of your business," Maggie said, sullenly.

"Did you read the article?"

"Yes."

"The nurse told me you asked her to take it out of the room. Why?"

"It was like a snake, waiting there to strike me."

He grinned. "The article—or your conscience?"

"Then she told you about that superego crack?"

"Of course. We keep full records on this ward. I didn't know you were *au courant* with Freudian terminology."

"I went to college, you know—even if I did have to leave in the middle of it."

"Is that why you feel yourself inferior mentally to Joe?"

"Inferior? To that clunk?" Maggie lapsed into incoherent rage, and Dave Rogan took time to light his pipe again.

"Why can't I go home?" she demanded after a while.

"You can—if you really want to."

"Do you mean that?"

"Of course. This isn't a closed ward and you haven't been committed."

"I should hope not."

"But if you're worth salvaging, as I think you are, Maggie, you'll stay here for a while."

"So you can go digging into my unconscious mind and see what dirt you can dig up? Didn't you read the article yourself? I've got an Oedipus conflict; I want to go to bed with my father."

"I didn't know your father. How much is Joe like him?"

Her eyes suddenly filled with tears. "Damn you, Dave Rogan! Do you have to know so much about people? It's . . . it's indecent."

"You've got me wrong, Maggie," he said cheerfully. "I'm a run-of-the-mill psychiatrist whose wife has got the Doctor's Wife disease just like you have."

"Why don't you cure her then? If you know so damn much."

"I don't want to cure her. Golf is a lot easier on her psyche—and on me—than alcoholism or drug addiction would be. Or even lower back pain."

"What about Grace Hanscombe? Is she a patient of yours, too?"

"Not of mine—Dr. Feldman's. You know she has diabetes, don't you?"

"It's only a mild case. She doesn't even take insulin."

"Grace isn't a mild case any more. Her blood sugar shot up all at once yesterday. If she hadn't been testing her urine regularly, she might have missed it and gone into coma."

"You can't put diabetes down to the Doctor's Wife syndrome."

"Grace's diabetes was mild and fully under control; it only went haywire yesterday morning."

"And Mort killed Lorrie the afternoon before. I guess that was the shot heard around this little world of ours, wasn't it?"

"It may turn out to have blown a lot of lives apart," said Dave soberly. "I'm praying it will blow a few together, or at least leave the pieces where we can get at them."

"How's Paul?"

"Fine. Dieter is letting him up."

"And Elaine?"

"She's the picture of health—and happiness, too. Even a psychiatrist doesn't always understand women, Maggie. Can you tell me why Elaine would be proud of Paul, even though he was shot making love to another woman?"

"That's simple," Maggie said with a shrug. "Every wife likes to think her husband is attractive to other women; it builds up her ego to know he chose her over them. Elaine has just had proof that Paul isn't the clod he seems to be, and with Lorrie dead, she doesn't have to worry about his trying to do it again."

"If you can be that analytical," Dave said with a grin, "I don't need to be giving you any psychotherapy."

"Then you really think it's safe for me to go home?"

"No."

"Why?"

"There's a part of that article you apparently didn't read—at the end." He opened the journal he was carrying and leafed through its pages until he found what he was seeking. "Listen to this: 'A number of factors should be considered in the therapeutic approach to this type of patient. First, symptomatic relief of depression and the fulfillment of dependency needs inherent in the hospital situation often enables such patients to return rapidly to a high level of social functioning, without necessarily effecting a change in the underlying psychopathology. The patient and her family may then conclude that she is well and ready to return home. Second, the natural desire to maintain a good relationship with the professional colleague may cause the therapist to acquiesce consciously or unconsciously to the patient's neurotic demands, for instance to requests for intensive investigation of physical symptoms.

" 'Third, the transference feelings of patients with a high index of hysterical fixation may be complicated and difficult to treat. They carry many of their feelings toward their physician-husband into their relationship with the physician-psychiatrist.

" 'Fourth, because of the likelihood that the husband will continue to be absorbed in his professional commitments and can no longer serve as the principal source of gratification for his wife's dependency needs, the patient must be encouraged to establish a separate and personally meaningful role for herself.' "

"Is that what you're trying to do for me?" Maggie asked. "Establish a separate and personally meaningful role?"

"No, Maggie. I want to do exactly what the article says, encour-

333

age you to establish a separate and personally meaningful role for yourself. The trouble is, you haven't been willing to let anybody help you—not even Joe."

"But he—"

"I know you've got that 'born across the tracks' complex where Joe's concerned, but you couldn't be more wrong. You were my secretary, remember? I know your intelligence and your capabilities—if you'd only stop running yourself down."

"Why don't you straighten me out without leaving everything to me?" she flared. "You're the psychiatrist. You're supposed to know what makes me tick."

"I've got a pretty good idea, but I don't think you're so far gone that we have to start digging so deeply into your unconscious."

"Not even after what I tried to do?"

"I'm counting on your having sense enough to realize that's no way to treat the mind God gave you," he said bluntly. "Believe me, talking to you like this is a lot better than having to give you electric shock."

He'd fired the shot deliberately, counting on the fact that she had seen some shock being given, when she'd worked as his secretary, to help him appeal to the intelligence he knew she possessed. And when she suddenly paled a little, he knew the missile had found its mark.

"What is it you want me to do?" she asked.

"There's an A.A. meeting scheduled for Saturday night not far from here. I want you to go to it."

"Alcoholics Anonymous!" Her voice rose sharply on a note of near hysteria. "Are you crazy?"

"It's the only thing that's going to help you, Maggie. Once you try suicide, you've stepped over the line. Nobody can tell when you'll follow the same pattern again—and Joe may not be there next time to bail you out."

The thrust shook her up, as he had intended.

"Do you really want to die?" he demanded, following up the advantage it had given him.

"I want—things back like they were when we all started here," she wailed.

"You can't go back. Nobody can do that. But you can change the future, so it's even better than the past, if you're willing to work and help yourself. The question is, are you ready to admit you've got to have help—or you'll die?"

"You and your damned medical journals," she wailed, and he knew he had won the first skirmish. From here on it was going to be up to her—and to Joe.

CHAPTER XXII

Pete Brennan came into the X-ray room a little after three thirty. Little Jerry Monroe lay on the table on his right side, his head still strapped to the flat surface with adhesive in order to hold it still. Jeff Long was sitting beside the child, his finger on the pulse at the temple. On the tray beside him were the syringe and needle with which he had given a small dose of sodium pentothal intravenously to keep Jerry from moving during the injection and the taking of X-rays.

On another table were the syringe and needle with which Anton Dieter had skillfully sent a probing point deep into the tissues of the small neck, searching for the carotid artery pulsing there. Finding it, he had swiftly injected a solution of sodium diatrizoate that had filled the arteries of the brain for a brief period, allowing them to be visualized with the X-rays.

Now the films were coming from the automatic developer. Six of them had been taken in rapid succession following the injection, with the tube exactly thirty-six inches above to capture the pattern of the brain's arteries as the dye coursed through them. A technician took the finished films from the dryer and placed them against the ground-glass fronts of a battery of view boxes fixed to the wall.

"There you are," said Dr. Sam Penfield, the hospital roentgenologist. "A small aneurysm of the anterior communicating artery— as pretty as you please."

There was no doubting the evidence. The pattern of blood channels at the base of the child's brain was outlined by the opaque dye and the X-ray as clearly as if drawn there in an anatomical diagram, the arteries white against the darker background, where the rays had gone through the soft tissues of the brain without being impeded, photographing themselves upon the sensitive chemicals of the film. Where the dye had filled the vessels, the rays had been held back by the metallic salt that was its main constituent, forming a sharply contrasting pattern of white against the dark background.

Pete Brennan moved close to the bank of viewers, studying each of the films carefully. Anton Dieter had made the injection, but the condition it revealed was now within Pete's own field of neurosurgery, a tiny sac connected to a blood vessel lying at the base of the brain where branches of the carotid artery formed a pattern called the Circle of Willis.

Suddenly he gave an exclamation of surprise and looked closely at the fourth in the series of films, the one showing the aneurysmal sac at its greatest degree of filling by the injected dye.

"Take a look here, Sam," he said to the roentgenologist. "Isn't that a leak of dye through the wall of the aneurysm?"

Penfield came closer with Anton Dieter at his elbow and examined the film a moment. Calling for one of the technicians to bring him a magnifying glass, he studied the part of the film in question once again, then stepped back and handed the magnifier to Pete Brennan.

With the area enlarged several times, it was obvious that some of the dye had indeed leaked out from the sac, proof of a rupture which at any moment might become a massive hemorrhage. Handing the glass to Anton Dieter, Pete went into the other room, where Jeff Long was watching Jerry, who lay on the table sleeping.

"Any sign of convulsive movements, Jeff?" he asked.

"No, sir. What's the trouble, Dr. Brennan?"

"We can see a small aneurysm on the anterior communicating artery, but there's a slight leak into the surrounding tissues. We can detect the shadow of the dye outside the aneurysmal sac."

"That must be where the original hemorrhage occurred. Doesn't leave you much choice, does it?"

"We'll have to go in," Pete agreed. "What sort of shape is he in?"

"Fine, sir. I put him pretty well out with a sodium luminal injection before he left the room so it took very little pentothal for the angiogram—just enough to keep him from squirming at the needle prick."

"I'm going to use a stereotactic approach so it will take several hours to get ready," said Pete. "Will your basal anesthesia hold out that long?"

"I'm sure it will."

"Good; then you might as well take him back to the room now. Dr. Dieter and I will have a talk with his mother."

Anton Dieter was still studying the X-rays when Pete came back into the viewing room. "It sure looks to me like a good case for the injection of iron sludge," said the neurosurgeon. "Do you agree?"

"Perfectly."

"I would appreciate your working with me, Anton, if you have the time."

"For this, I would make the time," said Dieter promptly.

"I'm going to try a stereotactic approach through a burr hole, so we'll need a lot of films," Pete told the roentgenologist. "Do you think there's a chance of overradiation?"

"Not of the skull area," said Penfield. "We'll put a lead shield over the lower half of his body while he's on the operating table, to protect the reproductive organs." More and more, careful X-ray specialists were using such protection for young boys, lest they accidentally be made sterile by X rays while the other parts of the body were being studied.

Janet Monroe had been sitting in the waiting room of the X-ray department; she was in uniform, ready to go on duty. "Your son's doing fine," Pete Brennan told her when a technician brought her into the viewing room. "Jeff Long is taking him back to the room."

"Then it's nothing—" Janet stopped. "Excuse me, please, Dr. Brennan. I guess I'm pretty jittery."

339

"Something would be wrong with you, if you weren't," he assured her. "We've located the trouble. It's just what we thought."

"Not a tumor?" she asked quickly.

"No. There's a small aneurysm of one of the arteries beneath the brain. Come closer and you can see it here." He took a pointer and indicated on an X-ray film the location of the trouble.

"It—it's very distinct, isn't it?"

"That makes our job a lot easier," Pete assured her.

"You'll have to operate, won't you?" Janet was too good a nurse not to know the significance of the aneurysm.

"Yes."

"When?"

"This afternoon."

"But why the hurry?"

"Ordinarily we might be able to wait a few days," Pete explained. "But there's a complication. When Dr. Harrison found blood in Jerry's spinal fluid yesterday, we knew something had been leaking. Obviously, in the light of these X-rays, it was the aneurysm."

"But it stopped."

"Only for a little while. These films show that it's leaking again, which is what we would expect. About half the cases of hemorrhage from an aneurysm inside the skull have another episode of bleeding within six months. Half of these occur within ten days."

He didn't tell her that with those who rebled, the mortality was often as high as 75 per cent, knowing how that information would make him feel, if Michael or Terry was involved.

"A year ago the outlook for your son would have been very grave," he continued. "Fortunately a new procedure was described recently by some West Coast surgeons. The risk with their operation is much less than with the old way of going in and tying off the vessel the aneurysm is connected to."

"A new operation?"

"For us, yes. But those who have used it report excellent results. Dr. Dieter and I have been waiting for a suitable case. Jerry seems to fulfill all the requirements."

"What—what is this new procedure like?" Janet asked.

"It's amazingly simple. A small amount of what is called a sludge containing very fine iron filings is injected into the aneurysm itself and held there by means of a small magnet until a clot can form and obliterate the sac."

"But how can you locate something so small deep inside the brain?"

"That problem was solved a number of years ago by what we now call the stereotactic technique," he explained. "By taking measurements on X-ray films shot from several angles, we can calculate just how deep the aneurysm lies and the exact angles the magnetic probe must take to reach it. Then, using the stereo-tactic frame, we need only make a small opening to insert the magnet and inject the sludge."

He didn't amplify the description of the operation further. There was no point in worrying her with the knowledge that plac-ing the magnetic probe—upon which the whole success of the procedure depended—exactly so it would touch the wall of the aneurysm involved an extremely delicate technique in so small a patient.

"When will you operate?" Janet asked.

"It will take a couple of hours to get the stereotactic setup ready in the O.R." Pete Brennan glanced at his watch and saw that it was already past four o'clock. "If we all have an early dinner, we should get started around six thirty."

ii

Amy had attended a luncheon meeting of the Symphony Guild after leaving the cemetery following Lorrie's funeral. There'd been an executive committee meeting afterward and she hadn't gotten home until after five.

All through the afternoon, she'd been conscious of a nagging feeling of unease whose cause she refused to admit to herself. As she came up the steps to the portico of the majestic house, with its tall fluted columns located on the knoll overlooking the river, she was debating in her mind whether or not to ask Pete about the thing that was troubling her.

"Dr. Brennan just phoned, ma'm." The maid had come from the kitchen when she heard the front door opening. "He said he's got to operate on Mrs. Monroe's child around seven o'clock so he'll be late getting home."

"I'll have dinner alone, then, Ethel." Being the wife of a neuro-surgeon, Amy had long since learned that such operations could frequently run to five and even eight hours. "Dr. Brennan will probably get a sandwich on the way home, if he's very late. Or I can fix him one."

"Yes'm. You want your dinner now?"

"Might as well."

Amy barely touched the food. The feeling of uneasiness she'd had almost all day was still with her, like a lump in her throat she couldn't swallow. When she finished, she went up to the bedroom she shared with Pete and, picking up the telephone, dialed the number she'd been trying to decide to call all afternoon.

"Uncle Jake?" she asked when the old man's voice sounded in her ear. "Are you all right?"

"Sure, Amy. What's the trouble?"

"Pete has an emergency operation, so I thought I'd see whether you needed anything."

"The children are here; they're all I need. You troubled about something, Amy?"

"No. Y-yes."

"What's bothering you, girl?"

"The passage of Scripture the minister read this morning— about the woman taken in adultery. You asked him to read it, didn't you?"

"Yes." The old man chuckled. "He balked a little at first. But he knows I'm the biggest contributor in the diocese, so he finally gave in."

"Why did you do it, Uncle Jake?"

"I thought some people around here needed reminding about

the virtues of forgiveness and tolerance—one person in particular."

"Was . . . am I the one?"

"Yes, Amy."

"Something you said this morning made me think I was."

"If you thought in your heart that it applied to you, then it must have," the old man said.

"But why, Uncle Jake?"

"Like I told you this morning, Amy, I'm very fond of you and that husband of yours. But a woman never was meant to be the boss of any household; that's a man's job. Whenever somebody takes it from him there's bound to be trouble."

"What do you know that I don't know, Uncle Jake?"

"Nothing—but if I had a wife that seemed hell-bent on being a bigger man than me, I'd either tan her behind or leave her. You've got a fine man, Amy; all the man any woman could want. Don't run him away. Good night."

She felt the first throb of pain in her temple as the receiver clicked in her ear and knew the tension which had been building up inside her all day was finally ready to explode into the agony of migraine. Hurrying to her dresser, she opened the drawer and searched beneath the lining paper for her small cache of morphine syrettes. Finding one, she unsheathed the tiny needle, swabbed off the skin of her arm with alcohol, and thrust the point through the skin, pushing it into the tissues beneath where the injection would be absorbed quickly. Squeezing the small tube, she rolled it up carefully until it was empty and the last precious drop of the narcotic solution had been injected.

As it had done two nights ago, the warm sense of relaxation began to spread through her body at once, fanning out from the tiny needle prick in an ever widening circle. She didn't yield immediately to the languor of sleep, however, wanting her body to be fresh and sweet with the perfume Pete liked when he came home. Taking a quick shower, she dried her skin, powdered her body and dabbed the perfume here and there. Then, putting on the nightgown she'd bought before leaving the District Six meeting place—could it only be two days ago?—she stretched out on the bed with a magazine to wait for him.

Her eyes soon began to droop, however. After a while, the magazine dropped from her fingers as she drifted off to sleep.

iii

Roy Weston was about ready to call it a day at five thirty on Friday afternoon, when the telephone rang in the outer office.

"The jailor says Dr. Dellman wants to see you," his secretary called to him through the open door.

"Tell him I've already left for the day."

He saw her speak into the telephone; then she turned to call through the door again: "They say upstairs he's pretty insistent. Claims he's going to demand a habeas corpus or something."

"All right, I'll see him. Tell the turnkey to have him brought to the interview room."

The snotty bastard! Roy thought as he rode up in the special elevator from his office in the courthouse to the jail above. It was bad enough for Mort Dellman to torpedo any chance he might have of running for state attorney general; now he had to go throwing his weight around, just because he knew he had the screws on a lot of people who were close to Roy himself.

The more he thought of Lorrie, vital, warm, fun-loving—and his first love long ago—lying in that coffin under six feet of earth, the more Roy relished the idea of prosecuting Mort Dellman for shooting her—and the devil take the consequences. When the biochemist was ushered into one of the small offices around the central interview room shortly after Roy arrived, the attorney was ready to chew him out. Mort, however, looked cocky and Roy felt his hackles rise even higher at his manner.

"All right," he said shortly. "What is it?"

"I want out of this place."

"You're a prisoner. It's not for you to say when you can come and go."

"It will be—unless you take action to get me out of here."

"What kind of action?"

"You can bring me before the grand jury whenever you want to, Roy—I want it to be now. Your damned jail isn't exactly the Waldorf, you know."

"I'll take it under advisement."

"You'll damned well be advised to get at it now," said the biochemist. "The law says you can't hold me without some sort of a charge—and that means a hearing."

"All right," said Roy. "Tomorrow's Saturday and Monday's Labor Day. I'll arrange for you to be brought before the grand jury on Tuesday."

"No go. I want the hearing tomorrow."

"On Saturday?"

"I don't give a damn whether it's Saturday or not. Either you order the hearing or I'll institute habeas corpus proceedings."

"Since when have you been reading law?"

"I know my rights." Mort Dellman grinned wolfishly. "You ought to know that from the way I foxed you on that confession."

"Suppose I don't buy your request?"

"Like I said, it will be habeas corpus. And you can bet I'll reveal some facts that will make newspaper headlines over the weekend."

Roy was tempted to let Mort Dellman do just what he'd threatened and start talking, on the chance that when he talked in court, the prisoner would admit that he'd gone to the house on Wednesday afternoon planning to shoot Lorrie and the medical student, thus hanging a noose around his neck. But he put the thought away, tempting though it was.

It was true that Roy's own chances of going on with the campaign against Abner Townsend next year for the attorney general post in the state seemed hardly worth anything now. But if Mort accused him in court of prejudice because of that puppy-love affair with Lorrie years ago, the newspapers would blow it up into a *cause célèbre*. Then any small chance he might still have of going to the state capitol in the future would have been destroyed.

"All right, Mort," he said. "I'll call the grand jury together to-morrow."

"What time?"

"Elmer Hill's the foreman, but he's out of town and won't be back until tomorrow afternoon. I'll have the rest of the panel called for seven o'clock tomorrow evening; Elmer ought to be here by then."

"That will have to do, if you can't make it any earlier. Will Paul McGill be able to testify?"

"I wouldn't think so; he was only operated on forty-eight hours ago. Why?"

"I want a deposition from him stating clearly what he was doing at my house that afternoon with my wife. Will you have it taken, or shall I get my lawyer to do it?"

"Who is your lawyer, by the way?"

"I haven't fully decided yet but I can get one in a hurry if I need him."

"I'll take Paul's deposition in the morning," Roy promised. He didn't think the dermatologist would be able to give any testimony that would be damaging to Mort Dellman's case but if there were any such possibility, he could take advantage of it by taking the deposition himself and asking the questions. "Anybody else you want called?"

"No. Once Paul admits what he was doing with Lorrie, that should be all the evidence I need. Just be damned sure you ask him the right questions."

"I'm as interested in justice as you are," Roy said shortly. "If the jury can't meet tomorrow evening for any reason I'll notify you."

"You'd better damn well see that they do meet," Mort Dell-man told him. "See you at the trial, Roy."

Watching the prisoner leave the office, Roy decided he'd much rather see Mort Dellman in hell. But the way things were going, that possibility seemed remote indeed.

iv

The chief nurse of the hospital had found someone to relieve Janet Monroe for the three-to-eleven shift and Janet was sitting beside Jerry's crib on the Pediatrics ward when Jeff Long came down with the stretcher about twenty minutes to six to take him up to the operating suite. The child had been sleeping quietly since he'd been brought back from the X-ray department after the angiograms had been taken.

Jeff gave Janet a keen look, noting the droop of her shoulders beneath the white uniform, the drawn lines about her mouth, and the redness of her eyes from weeping. "Don't take this so hard," he told her. "It could be a lot worse, you know."

"I don't see how."

"There's only been a small leak of blood this second time. It could have been a massive hemorrhage that would have made using the new operation impossible."

She put out her hand to touch his arm with an instinctive, pleading gesture that tore at his heart. "Tell me the truth, Jeff. What chance does Jerry have?"

"Every chance in the world; that's the beauty of the iron sludge technique. Dr. Brennan described it at a staff meeting right after he first saw it used in California. Believe me, the results are miraculous."

"I could see the aneurysm in the X-ray," she said, still doubtful. "But finding something that small inside the skull must be like looking for a needle in a haystack."

"You're wrong, darling." The orderly had lifted Jerry to the stretcher and was waiting for Jeff outside the door. "With the aneurysm demonstrated so well in the films, Dr. Brennan can tell exactly where to place the stereotactic frame. With that to guide him, placing the probe is only a matter of determining two mathematically exact angles. Where they intersect is the path the probe will take."

"I . . . I guess I'm too worried to comprehend," she admitted.

347

"Of course you are. Tomorrow, when it's all over and Jerry is fine, I'll take you up to the O.R. and get out the stereotactic frame so you can see exactly how it's done. Now cheer up and don't start worrying if we're up there a long time. This sort of thing takes a lot of measuring and figuring to get the exact angles. Most of the time Jerry won't even be under anesthesia at all, but I'll be right there with him every minute."

"What have I ever done to deserve somebody like you?" she said impulsively and Jeff Long grinned.

"You're yourself, and you're Jerry's mother. We three are going to have a lot of fun together when this is all over."

v

More than an hour had passed since Jeff Long had given Jerry Monroe a light preliminary anesthesia and passed a tube into his trachea through which the anesthetic had been given during the first stage of the operation. The stereotactic frame, a circular ring of metal, so calibrated that measurements could be read off it in millimeters, had been placed on the small shaven head and locked into place exactly by means of adjustments fixing it to the ear openings, the orbital rims above the eyes and the hard palate inside the mouth. With the frame thus fixed, two basic planes from which to measure and construct angles had been set up: the horizontal one running from the upper eye-socket rims through the ear openings, and the vertical perpendicular to it at a point exactly dividing the between-ears distance and thus at the exact center of the skull.

Using extensions attached to the basic ring of the frame, Pete Brennan had located exactly a point at the back of the skull. There he had made a small incision, barely an inch long, and through it had drilled a small opening into the skull with a burr-shaped trephine. Introduced through this opening, a slender, flexible tube, smaller in diameter than a grain of rice, had been pushed easily through the brain tissue into one of the cavities of the brain—the ventricles, as they were called in medical terminology.

A small amount of a chemical like the one used to visualize the arteries and the aneurysm in the X-ray had then been introduced into the brain cavity through the small tube and, by moving the patient's head, allowed to flow forward into the front portion of the third of the four brain ventricles. It was visible now on the X-rays taken immediately afterward as a blob of white opacity, establishing the location of what was called the anterior commissure, the main point of departure as far as the brain itself was concerned for calculating the distance and the angles necessary to reach the aneurysm that was threatening little Jerry's life.

"That angle should do it," Pete Brennan announced with satisfaction as he looked up from the table at one side of the X-ray room, where he and Anton Dieter had been making calculations and measurements on the films taken of the anterior commissure with the metal stereotactic ring in place. "I take it that we are all in agreement concerning the angles and the distance?"

Dr. Sam Penfield, the radiologist, had also been watching the measurements and calculations being made from the X-ray films. When he nodded agreement, Pete Brennan said, "Shall we get to work, Anton?"

Jeff Long looked up quickly when the surgeons came back into the operating theater, which they had left at the end of the first stage of the surgical procedure in order to study the X-rays. "We've got it all worked out as neat as a pin—I hope," Pete Brennan said in answer to the younger doctor's unspoken question. "Is he all right?"

"Fine," said Jeff. "The basal is holding him nicely."

"I'll make the second incision under local then," said the neurosurgeon. "It's better to have him as near conscious as possible, so we can detect any untoward effects as the probe goes through brain tissue."

Concentrating on the delicate task of making the final angle adjustments and locking in place the metal sleeve through which the magnetic probe would be inserted, Pete Brennan felt all of the troublesome details that had taken so much of his time since he'd reached the marina dock two afternoons before and heard the shocking news of Lorrie Dellman's death, fade into the background. His entire world at the moment had shrunken to only the brightly lit operating room, the table, and the drapings, beneath which Jerry Monroe's little body was completely hidden now except for the shiny metal ring of the stereotactic frame, its several attachments, and a small circle of bare scalp beneath it, painted a brilliant scarlet with the antiseptic used in preparing the operative field.

The years of education and technical training which had prepared him for his profession, and the minutely exact measurements of angles and distances he had just finished making from the preliminary X-ray studies—all of these were as much instruments of use as the metallic bridge he now attached to the circular frame and the calibrations upon the smaller attachment affixed to it, by which the predetermined angle of entry was exactly reproduced.

Using a blunt probe exactly similar to the grooved magnet which would be inserted later, he located on the small patient's scalp the spot where the second burr-opening would be made through the skull to expose the brain beneath. A small wheal of novocaine at that point removed any possibility of causing pain, since both the bone and the brain beneath were quite impervious to it. The small scalp incision was carried down to the bony outer layer of the skull and a burr-shaped trephine quickly made the opening through it. Then, using a sharp-pointed scalpel, Pete nicked the outermost of the meningeal layers covering the brain, allowing the vital tissue of the very heart of the nervous system to be visualized in the depths of the small skull opening.

For the blunt probe he had used to locate the skin and skull incisions, Pete now substituted the magnetic probe, with a slot down its side through which the needle for injecting the iron preparation would be passed, once the instrument was in place and its position verified by X-ray. As Dr. Sam Penfield read off the angle settings for the slender permanent magnet, Pete Brennan once again checked the angulation of the sleeve through which the magnet would be inserted. When the two sets of figures agreed exactly, he began to push the probe gently into the brain tissue.

"Watch him closely, Jeff," Pete told the anesthesiologist. "If there's any change tell me right away."

The warning of encroachment upon some vital center of the brain might come in a dozen ways—a sudden change in the pupil of one of the eyes, a slight convulsive movement, alteration in the vital functions of respiration or pulse.

No change occurred, however, as the probe was pushed ever deeper into the brain tissue. Only a short portion of the metal shaft remained outside the skull, when the surgeon reached the mark he'd nicked on the outer surface of the magnet with a file, indicating that it had penetrated to the exact distance the earlier measurements had predicted mathematically would be necessary to reach the small aneurysm located at the base of the brain itself.

"It's in place, Sam," Pete Brennan told the roentgenologist, and the waiting X-ray technicians quickly took films in two planes, the vertical or anteroposterior—known in hospital jargon as A-P —and the lateral, directly from the side. Developed rapidly, they were returned to the operating room and the view boxes on the wall, where the surgeons studied them with the roentgenologist.

"That small leak we noted in the angiogram is right at the end of the probe." Everyone in the operating room could feel the pride and pleasure in Pete Brennan's voice. "I'd say the probe's against the wall, wouldn't you, Sam?"

"Right on the nose," Dr. Penfield agreed. "You had your sights on it all the time, Pete."

Since the probe had been introduced through a fixed metal sleeve whose angle was locked into place on the stereotactic frame, the task of inserting a slender needle along the groove in its side without disturbing the magnet was simple. Holding the needle— without a syringe attached—between his right thumb and fore-finger and steadying the probe with his left hand, Pete Brennan slid the needle slowly along the groove in the probe. He had previously marked off on the shaft of the needle the length of the magnet, so he could tell when the point, probing deep within the brain, had reached the aneurysm.

When the tiny file mark on the shaft of the needle was opposite the outer end of the probe, indicating that the point was now just touching the wall of the aneurysm, he paused a moment. When he began to push it a little farther, perhaps it was only his imagination that made him feel an increased resistance to the needle point as it pressed against the wall of the aneurysm sac. In any event, he was sure he felt a faint snap or click inside the brain, tangible if not audible, as the aneurysm wall was penetrated.

A deep indrawn sigh went up from the tensely watching spectators when a tiny stream of blood suddenly spurted from the open end of the needle. Pulsing with the heartbeat in an arc of crimson to spatter upon the green draperies, it told them they had hit their target deep inside the brain.

"*Ach Himmel!*" Anton Dieter's explosive grunt of elation punctuated the scene.

"Ditto!" Pete Brennan grinned. "The sludge, please."

The scrub nurse had been waiting with a small amount of the viscous iron mixture in a syringe. She handed it to him now and, shifting the fingers of his left hand to the shank of the needle, he attached the syringe to it carefully, stopping the arching pulse of blood. When he drew back gently on the plunger of the syringe, a drop of red spurted into the syringe, telling him the point was still inside the aneurysm, and he began to inject slowly, forcing the somewhat resistant iron mixture down through the needle and into the aneurysm sac. He continued the injection until the entire amount he had calculated would be necessary to fill the sac by measuring its diameter on the X-ray films of the angiogram Anton Dieter had taken earlier that afternoon was injected. Then steadying both needle and probe, he stood back so the X-ray technicians could snap confirming films.

While the latter were being developed, the tiny skin wound

was closed around the probe with several silk sutures to prevent the entrance of infection over the several days it would be left in place. During that time, if all went well, the powerful magnetic field around the end of the probe would hold the iron particles fixed inside the aneurysm and promote the formation of a tough metallic clot. This in turn would gradually be replaced by fibrous tissue growing in from the aneurysm wall, thus closing it forever.

The final films showed a small blob of sharply outlined metallic particles exactly where the aneurysm had been, the effect for which they had been striving. Pete Brennan felt a surge of satisfaction as he carefully placed a small doughnut of cotton and gauze over the projecting outer end of the probe to keep it from being jarred out of place, then covered that with a voluminous dressing to further protect the vital magnet. When the draperies that had hidden the anesthesiologist were removed, Jeff Long looked up and grinned.

"Not a quiver, Dr. Brennan," he reported. "You were right on target all the way."

From the watchers in the gallery, there came a sudden spatter of applause, audible even through the thick glass of the observation window.

vi

Marisa Feldman had been half-expecting a call from Anton Dieter that evening. When it didn't come by eight o'clock, she decided to take a shower and get into bed to look at television. She was just stepping out of the shower when the telephone rang. Wrapping a towel about herself, she went into the bedroom and picked up the phone.

"Marisa?" She recognized his voice at once and was startled by the sudden feeling of warmth it engendered within her.

"Yes—Anton."

"I tried to call you earlier, around six."

"I was with Mrs. Hanscombe, working out her diet and insulin dosages. She plans to leave for England on Monday."

353

"I went into the operating room a little before seven," he explained. "Dr. Brennan wanted me to work with him on the Monroe child."

"Did the operation go all right?"

"Perfectly. I'll tell you all about it, if you will have a drink with me."

"Now?"

"There's a cocktail lounge in the next block, a nice quiet place."

"But I just stepped out of the shower."

He chuckled. "In that case, I'd better come up there."

"No." She found that she was laughing, a pleasant feeling she didn't remember experiencing for a long time. "I'll dress quickly. Will slacks and a blouse do?"

"With you in them, they'll be sensational. I'll meet you at the front of the Faculty Apartments in fifteen minutes."

Marisa's excitement mounted steadily as she dressed. She was almost like a schoolgirl, she thought, on her first date. When she came down the steps at the front of the Faculty Apartments, wearing silver slacks, a loose white silk blouse, and with her dark hair tied with a silver ribbon, Anton Dieter gave a low whistle of appreciation.

"Would you like to walk awhile?" he asked as he took her arm.

"I'd love it."

The night was warm and the stoops of the houses along the street were alive with people. The older among them were just talking or sitting quietly, enjoying the evening, while here and there in the shadows, the younger could be seen in close embrace.

"You'll love this town when you've had a chance to get accustomed to it," he assured her. "This area around the hospital houses a lot of people who work in the rug mill. Some of their forebears came here from New England, when the mills moved a long time ago."

"Parts of Boston are like this, especially such older neighborhoods as Cambridge," she said. "I love it already."

They soon reached the cocktail lounge he had spoken of. Instead of going in, however, Anton Dieter said, "There's a little park about a block away overlooking the river. Would you just as soon sit there for a while? We can have the nightcap later."

"I'd much rather stay outside."

At the end of the street they came to a small park with benches scattered among the trees. It occupied a slight elevation overlooking the river that wound its course around much of Weston's outskirts before widening out markedly downstream nearer the dam. One of the benches in the shadows at the far end of the park next to the riverbank was vacant and Anton Dieter guided her to it.

"When I first came to Weston I used to walk down here at night and sit by the river, thinking how lucky I was to be here," he said. "Now that you've come, I'm sure I have even more reason to feel lucky."

Things were moving a bit fast for Marisa. To gain time, she asked, "How did you ever happen to come to Weston—after New York?"

"The main attraction was the offer they made of my own research institute in experimental surgery, with no politically appointed board to tell me what I can do and not do. After my years at the Institute of Experimental Medicine in Russia, this sort of setup looked like paradise."

"Has it proved to be?"

"That and more. If I were in private practice, I would have to devote at least a third of my time to the business side of medicine, cultivating good will among other doctors, so they would send me patients—and sending patients to them. Here at Weston, the medical school pays my salary—with help from the Porter Foundation—and finances my experimental laboratory. I hold operative clinics for the students and make teaching ward rounds, all of which I love. But, the major part of my time is spent in experimental studies, without having to worry about whether or not they will ever bring in a cent of income."

"You promised to tell me about the aneurysm operation," she reminded him.

"Are you familiar with the case?"

"Yes. I didn't see the X-rays though."

"They showed a definite aneurysm at the base of the brain. We decided to use that iron sludge technique."

"The one that was described in a news magazine some time ago—I think it was *Newsweek*?"

"Very much like it. Pete Brennan is a very fine neurosurgeon and has added some touches of his own. He knows of my interest in these blood vessel disturbances, so he asked me to scrub with him."

"It must have been exciting."

"The most exciting thing is the possible future applications of this process. Take apoplexy, for example; the one thing a stroke patient dreads more than anything else is a repetition of what happened to him the first time. With this technique, it may eventually be possible to close off the section of vessel that ruptures in a stroke and prevent a second hemorrhage. Besides, if we can prevent the slow leak from a ruptured artery that continues in so many stroke cases, we can prevent extensive brain damage and give the injured parts a chance to heal."

"Listening to you makes internal medicine seem pretty humdrum."

"Don't you believe it," Dieter laughed. "I had an ulcer while I was planning to escape from East Germany. It almost perforated before I could get out of there."

"How did you manage it—the escape."

"The Russians thought they were doing me a favor by making me a surgical fellow at the Institute of Experimental Medicine— and they did. Some of the most advanced vascular work in the world has been done there, but I didn't like the idea of spending my life working with a political commissar looking over my shoulder. So, when they let me attend a medical meeting in Yugoslavia, I sneaked over the Italian border. How about you?"

"They kept me in prison in East Germany for two years." She couldn't keep the pain of the memory out of her voice and, sensitive to her every mood, he said quickly, "Don't speak of it if it causes you pain. I saw some of those prisons and I know what they are like."

"Talking about it always disturbed me before," she admitted. "But strangely enough, it doesn't seem to bother me with you."

"That is the nicest thing you could have said to me, *Liebchen*."

They had been sitting close together on the park bench, drawn by the sense of comradeship that had developed between them. When he felt her suddenly stiffen and draw away, he said quickly, "Forgive me if I am presumptive."

"It's just that my father used to call me *Liebchen*," she explained, and he saw that her eyes were troubled and afraid. "There's something you should know about me, Anton—if we're to be friends."

"I hope we will be more than that. But don't speak of it unless you're sure you want to tell it."

"I do. It wouldn't be fair to you not to."

He listened in silence while she told the story of her stay in prison, the months when she'd spent two nights a week in Colonel Geitz's quarters, so her father wouldn't be tortured with the pain of angina. And particularly the way she had been able to endure it all by shutting away all feeling from the most intimate parts of her body.

"How can you be sure this anesthesia you speak of will persist?" he asked, when she had finished the account.

"There was an instructor at Harvard; I was fond of him."

"He made love to you?"

"You could hardly call it that. I felt nothing—just as it was with Colonel Geitz."

"And you think that means it will always be the same?"

"I'm trying to tell you I'm not really a woman at all, Anton." It was a cry of pain—and desperation. "The woman in me was killed in the prison at Frondheim."

"I refuse to believe that, *Lieb*—"

"Please don't call me that."

"Surely you know how I feel," he said gently. "How I've felt since I first saw you that afternoon in the emergency room."

"But it cannot be." She was close to tears. "Don't you understand? You're fine and decent and honorable. How could I ever love you as you deserve to be loved, when my body would feel nothing?"

When he put his arm about her, she stiffened instinctively against the contact, then leaned wearily against his shoulder, drawing solace from his strength.

"You are wrong about many things, Marisa. First about your lack of response."

"But—"

"I heard it in your voice when I called you tonight. And I can feel it in your body now."

Remembering the warmth that had flooded her when she'd recognized his voice over the phone earlier that evening, Marisa dared to hope he was right. But she was afraid to let herself believe it, lest the old sense of disappointment and frustration seize her again.

"At Frondheim you initiated a conditioned reflex," he explained. "The Institute of Experimental Medicine, where I studied, was once headed by Pavlov, and much of his work was done there. Pavlov first conditioned a dog to produce saliva by ringing a bell and giving it food immediately afterward. Later, he found that saliva would flow when only the bell was rung, even though food was not given."

"I know about those experiments. That really may be the mechanism in my case, but—"

"What you have forgotten is that Pavlov was also able to decondition the same reflexes he created."

"But how can an entire organ system of my body be taught to live again, when it hasn't responded for almost four years?"

"The response began tonight, *Liebchen*—and you didn't have to teach it," he reminded her. "You tell me you taught yourself to shut off all nerve impulses that would normally respond to the touch of a man. Yet I am touching you now."

He turned her face up to him and kissed her gently. In spite of wanting desperately not to resist, Marisa felt her lips close tightly. But when he started to draw away, she suddenly put her arms about his neck and pressed her mouth against his, holding it there until she felt the tension of the muscles relax and her lips soften and yield beneath his, as she responded to his kiss.

"So!" He was a little breathless—as was she—when finally they drew apart; and she could feel his heart beating rapidly against her breast. "We have begun successfully with what the anatomy book calls the *musculus orbicularis oris*. Already, *Liebchen*, the deconditioning has started."

When she found herself laughing as she settled once more into his embrace, Marisa could at last dare to hope her cure had indeed begun.

CHAPTER XXIII

It was after nine o'clock before Pete Brennan finished talking to Janet Monroe about the operation. Figuring that Amy would have had her dinner before Ethel left, he stopped at the Snack Bar for a quick hamburger and a cup of coffee, but it was still not ten when he let himself into the house.

Downstairs was dark, but he could see a spill of light from their bedroom at the top of the stairs and decided that Amy must be reading there, or looking at TV on the bedroom set. Moving quietly, in case she had fallen asleep, he climbed the stairs and came into the bedroom.

The bedlamp was still burning and the magazine Amy had been reading when the narcotic had taken full hold, was lying beside her. She looked young, defenseless and very lovely, lying there in the filmy nightgown that allowed the flesh tints of her skin to show through. Her cheeks were somewhat flushed from the effects of the drug and her breathing was slow and even. Nor did she respond when he touched her bare shoulder gently.

Puzzled by her failure to awaken, he did what any doctor would have done automatically; placing his hand on her forehead, he lifted her left eyelid with his thumb, and what he saw there sent a shock wave of alarm through his senses.

The pupil of Amy's left eye was almost pinpoint in size, nor did it contract with the light as it should normally have done, although he lowered the lid and raised it again twice so the light could strike the eye. The right eye was the same and a sense of horror and apprehension began to grip him as he fumbled for her pulse. It was slow and steady, with a rate of eighty, which was normal, but her respirations, when he counted them with the sweephand of his wrist watch, were only fourteen to the minute.

Almost dreading what he would find, Pete went to the closet and opened the small medicine case he kept there for emergency calls. Only two of the dozen morphine syrettes he usually carried remained and he racked his memory, trying to recall the last time he'd used the case, or had examined it. When he did remember, he closed the case and put it back on the shelf. There'd been twelve of the syrettes in the case when he'd last opened it—of that he was sure. Now there were two.

Amy showed no sign of wakening while he searched the room. Nor did it take him long to find what he was seeking, for in her haste she'd neglected to hide the evidence of what was causing the stupor in which he'd found her. At the bottom of the waste-basket under a pile of tissues, he discovered the small flattened-out syrette tube, with the needle attached. Just how long she'd been taking morphine, he had no way of knowing. Only Amy could tell him that and she was still sleeping under the influence of the powerful opiate.

His steps dragging, Pete left the bedroom and went downstairs to the kitchen. He dialed George Hanscombe's home telephone number and when there was no answer, tried to calm his racing thoughts long enough to figure out where George might be. Other than his work, his home and the club, the internist had no interests Pete could think of. He wouldn't be at work this late at night, for the clinic was always covered by one of the younger staff men as night duty officer. And he wasn't at home—so only the club was left as a likely choice.

"Dr. Hanscombe's in the bar, Dr. Brennan," the attendant who answered the telephone said. "Shall I get him for you?"

"Please."

George came on the phone a few moments later.

"Since when have you hung around the club at night?" Pete asked.

"Grace is leaving for England Monday, Pete. I'm accustoming myself to being alone—by getting soused."

"She'll be coming back."

"I wouldn't count on it and I'm not even sure it's the best thing for her. I guess I've been getting on her nerves; the diabetes almost slipped up on us yesterday."

"I'm sorry, George. With the troubles you've got, I don't feel like saddling you with mine."

"What's wrong?"

"Amy's having one of her migraine attacks. I know you've treated her for it and I was wondering what you were giving her."

"I haven't seen Amy for migraine in quite a while," said the internist. "Thought she'd stopped having the attacks. Did this business about Mort Dellman upset her?"

"Could be."

"I was giving her an injection of ergotamine tartrate to reduce the spasm of the internal carotid artery and Demerol to relieve the pain. I can call the hospital and have the night nurse in the emergency room fix up the injection for you."

"Don't bother," Pete told him. "I've got some quarter-grain morphine syrettes in my case—"

"I wouldn't do that." The other doctor's voice was suddenly crisp.

"Not in just this one instance?"

"Migraines are recurrent affairs, Pete. A strong neurotic element often triggers the attacks, if it doesn't actually cause them. Morphine's bad for it, especially in doctors' wives."

"Why them?"

"There's an article on the troubles doctors' wives have in the *American Journal of Psychiatry*. I wouldn't have seen it myself, if Dave Rogan hadn't called my attention to it."

"I always thought the Doctor's Wife disease was a joke."

"Being a neurosurgeon, you wouldn't see many cases, except maybe the disklike syndromes of lower back and neck pain," said George Hanscombe. "But believe me, it's no joke. A lot of women who develop it wind up eventually with narcotic addiction. And they usually get started with morphine from the husband's medical bag."

Pete stared mutely at the phone, until George Hanscombe's voice in his ear caught his attention again. "You there, Pete?"

"Yes."

"I thought we were disconnected for a moment."

"Thanks, George. I'll give Amy some aspirin and codeine. If that doesn't relieve it, I'll call the emergency room and have them fix a hypo of ergotamine tartrate. We're close to the hospital so I can easily run over and get it."

"If Amy's having that much trouble, I ought to see her again," said the internist. "I hadn't felt she needed to be kept on preventive medication because her attacks were infrequent. It could be that the situation has changed now."

"Is there a preventive medication?"

"A new drug called methysergide maleate seems to work very well in preventing migraine attacks. But it's still closely connected with emotional tension, so maybe Dave Rogan ought to see her, too."

"I'll talk to her about it. Thanks, George."

When he hung up the phone, Pete realized he was still hungry. Opening the icebox, he took out a can of beer, some bread and a package of sliced ham. While he made a sandwich and ate it slowly, he went over again in his mind the implications of what George had said. Any way he added up the facts, they gave a troubling answer.

Amy had apparently not been subject to migraine attacks for quite some time, since she hadn't consulted George Hanscombe. Yet tonight she'd had one that was apparently so severe, she'd filched a morphine syrette from his case and given it to herself. What was more, nine additional syrettes were missing from his bag besides the one he'd found in the wastebasket in the bathroom.

Had she been taking them long? he wondered. Or was tonight the first attack? And if so, had Lorrie's funeral brought it on?

He remembered speaking to Amy at the cemetery but she'd

seemed to be her usual self, so that didn't seem likely. Then he did remember something. The night Lorrie had been killed and he'd come home late, Amy had mentioned that she'd had a migraine attack but had taken something for it and the pain had been relieved.

Her behavior that night certainly hadn't been normal for Amy, but he'd put it down to her being emotionally excited about what had happened that afternoon and to the stiff drink she had said she'd taken. Now he wondered whether she had taken an injection, too, an injection which, combined with alcohol, would have swept away the inhibitions that were a part of her normal make-up.

The more he thought about it, the more certain he became that this must have been the sequence of events that evening. There was one possible way to find out, if he were lucky; finishing the sandwich and the can of beer, he went upstairs to the bedroom.

Amy was still asleep but had turned over on her side, so he could be sure she was not dangerously affected by the drug. A quarter-grain of morphine wasn't really a very large dose for an average-sized individual and, judging by the effect it had had upon her, he was fairly sure she hadn't been taking the drug very long. If she had been, a larger dose would have been required, since the body quickly became accustomed to it.

Looking around the room, he asked himself where she might have secreted the other morphine syrettes and his eye lit upon the dressing table beside the bed. Pulling out the drawers one by one, he looked through them, searching particularly under the lining paper, where anyone hiding something would be most likely to place it.

He found what he was looking for in the third drawer he opened—eight of the morphine syrettes. And he was filled with a great sense of relief, for whether or not Amy planned to continue taking the drug—and her having hidden eight of the syrettes seemed to indicate that she did—he could be reasonably sure now that she had only taken two lately, probably one the night after

Lorrie was shot and another tonight. Which meant, fortunately, that if his assumptions were true, the danger of addiction was not yet very great. And Amy was intelligent enough, he knew, to understand the danger, once he pointed it out to her.

But what had made her take the drug in the first place? he asked himself as he undressed slowly and got into bed—unless she'd heard about him and Helen Straughn. The likely answer seemed to be No, for Amy was not one to avoid facing up to facts, even the truth that her own marriage might be in danger.

Was she troubled by some pain that might have meant a serious illness then? Or something like a fear of cancer so great that she was afraid to seek medical advice?

Lots of women did avoid going to doctors on just that account, he knew, but that answer didn't seem logical as far as Amy was concerned for she was an intelligent and highly sensible woman.

As for a love affair with another man, he didn't even consider it, certain that Amy's stern conscience wouldn't let her engage in the sort of bed-hopping that was so frequent at their level of Weston society.

One by one, he canvassed the possible things that might have disturbed her deeply enough to bring on two severe migraine attacks in four days and lead her to filch morphine from his case in order to get relief. And one by one he discarded them until he came to a final possibility—her ambition.

Amy had survived one major disappointment some five years ago, when he'd chosen a clinical professorship and the lucrative clinic practice over the position of Professor of Surgery. She had actively promoted him for the professorship, but she'd seemed to adjust, after he'd explained that organizing the Faculty Clinic would forbid his taking the full-time teaching job. And when the clinic had proved a bonanza from the start—only partly because their streamlined diagnostic setup, the first really automated clinic in the country, had received a lot of publicity—his position in the university community had quickly risen at least as high as it would have been if he were Professor of Surgery.

It was about then, he remembered now, that Amy had set her

sights on promoting herself into a high position in the state
medical auxiliary. And though after their one major quarrel over
the professorship, she had appeared to sublimate her own desires
to his—at least he had thought so at the time—he wondered now
whether the nagging unfulfilled wish to see him professor could
have been there all the while. And whether it might have had
something to do with her present difficulty.

When he considered that question seriously, however, he didn't
think it was the answer either. For with his decision to go ahead
in medical politics and seek actively the office of president of the
state association, Amy had been assured of a position in the medical hierarchy that was actually considerably higher than would
have been hers if he were simply Professor of Surgery at Weston
University Medical School.

All of which got him nowhere in deciding what had happened
to Amy, and finally, his brain wearied from thinking, he drifted
off to sleep.

ii

When the taxi stopped in front of the house where the Alcoholics Anonymous meeting was to be held that night, Maggie
McCloskey almost told the driver to take her back to the hospital.
It wasn't that there was anything about the house, or the neighborhood, to disturb her. It sat back from the street on the west
side of town looking toward the mountains, the neatly clipped
lawn, the bright-colored drapes at the windows, and the warm
light shining through from the inside giving it a welcoming touch.

What troubled her most about the place—and this whole venture that Dave Rogan had practically strong-armed her into—was
the obvious normalcy of the house, its frank wholesomeness and
the air of neighborly invitation that practically oozed from it.

"You won't be called on to say or do anything; in fact, you
don't even have to give your name, if you don't want to," Dave
had promised. And so she'd come, clutching at straws because she
knew that the next time she came home drunk and took sleeping

pills, she might not be rational enough to regulate the dose and could easily wind up like poor Lorrie, down there in the cold ground of the churchyard.

The thought made her shiver, as if she were already walking over her own grave, but it also made her more and more doubtful of finding anything here that might help her. For this was obviously a normal house, inhabited by normal and probably happy people, judging from the warmth of the drapes and the light, people who had never come near to suicide—or wished for death.

While she was waiting, a man and a woman walked up the driveway from a car that had parked farther down the street. They were welcomed at the door by a rather dark-skinned woman with a coil of dark braids piled upon her head. When the door opened, a gust of human voices engaged in pleasant social conversation had momentarily escaped from the house and Maggie looked once again at the slip of paper Dave had given her, to make sure the address on it and the number on the door were the same.

"You going in, ma'm?" the driver asked and she wondered if he had sensed the sudden fear that had gripped her. Or if he knew what this place was?

But that seemed ridiculous, for it was just like a dozen houses on the same street, except for slight differences in construction.

"Yes." Maggie fumbled in her purse, took out two one-dollar bills and gave them to him. "Keep the change."

"Thanks, Mrs. McCloskey." Maggie knew now why the driver's face had seemed familiar when he had picked her up in front of the hospital. Weston's taxi drivers had taken her home drunk so many times from the club that most of them knew her well by now.

Until that moment, she'd been telling herself she had nothing in common with the people she could see moving about inside the warm bright home. Now she knew she wasn't any better than they—or even than the wino bums who cadged handouts along Main Street downtown. And that knowledge gave her the strength to follow the gravel walk to the front door and push the bell.

"I'm Eve Santo." The woman with the dark braids greeted Maggie at the door. She was comfortably plump and her eyes were warm with welcome. "Come in and meet the bunch. You're Margaret McCloskey, aren't you? I've seen your picture on the society page."

"Not lately. I've been busy—with other things."

"All of us have been through that, too," said Eve Santo. "You're among friends here, Mrs. McCloskey."

"Please call me Maggie." It was impossible not to like the other woman.

"Of course. This is my husband Harry."

Harry Santo was as thin as his wife was plump and Maggie found herself reminded of Jack Spratt who, not eating fat, was as thin as a rail. As a child she'd always felt sorry for the poor man. But now, with cholesterol out of practically everybody's diet and fat long since indicted as a killer, he was revealed as one who had only been following a healthful course.

Eve Santo took her around the two rooms that were filled with people, drinking coffee and eating little sandwiches and cookies. Most of them were completely at ease and Maggie could see no difference between this party and hundreds she had attended on the other side of town—except that there was no bar and no liquor.

Strangely enough, though, they seemed to be having as good a time with each other as people had in the groups of which she had been a part. There was much good-natured raillery but, though Eve Santo introduced her to everyone and she participated briefly in conversation with a few, Maggie soon began to experience a sense of withdrawal, a feeling of standing aloof that made her responses to the friendly conversation of those in the house grow less and less warm, until suddenly she decided she had to leave.

"Can I use your phone to call a taxi, Mrs. Santo?" she asked.

"Of course. Some of those here tonight live near you, though. They'll be happy to drop you by your home a little later."

"I'd rather go now, if you don't mind." She didn't want to admit that she had come from the hospital and was going back there.

"I'll call you a taxi right away." Eve Santo dialed the phone and gave the order, then turned back to Maggie.

"Please don't be depressed," she said. "These first meetings are always difficult; that's why we try to make them social occasions, if we can. But you're still with new people and it disturbs you because you feel they know your troubles and are feeling sorry for you. A.A. doesn't work on that principle, Maggie."

She opened the drawer of a small table in the hall where they were standing and took out a booklet. "Take this with you and read it later. The information it contains will clear up a lot of misunderstanding you may have about us."

Maggie dropped the booklet into her bag, trying to hide the trembling of her fingers.

"Here's your taxi." The lights of a moving car had just appeared in front of the house. "Good night, Maggie. And good luck."

"Good night, Eve. And thanks."

Maggie almost ran down the walkway to the car, not even noticing in her haste that it wasn't a taxi after all—until she recognized a familiar figure holding open the right front door.

"Hello, Maggie," said Joe McCloskey. "Will I do instead of a taxi?"

"Joe!" She went into his arms and he held her for a long moment standing there by the car, while she wept.

"How did you happen to be here?" she asked as he was backing out of the driveway.

"When Dave told me he'd talked you into coming to an A.A. meeting here, I figured this wasn't for you. Dave's like most psychiatrists; he figures he can pull strings and make people behave like puppets, but he wasn't married to you for fifteen years. If he had been, he'd have known you've got too much sense to ever be a real alcoholic. I've been parked across the street ever since before you came. When the taxi you ordered just now stopped down the street looking for the house, I figured you must have called it, so I gave the driver five dollars and sent him on his way."

"Oh Joe! It was awful in there!" She sat close to him, seeking to gain strength from him. "Everybody was so nice."

Joe grinned. "Obviously lower middle class."

"I could just see them feeling sorry for me and that was the worst of all. I need a drink, Joe. Let's go get a drink."

"Sure, darling."

She'd expected him to object. When he didn't, she lay back against the cushion of the seat, closing her eyes and letting the rush of cool air from the car's air-conditioning system soothe her flushed face. Only when the car drew to a stop, did she open them —and was startled by the bright glare of fluorescent lights and neon tubing spelling out in flashing letters:

BURGER HEAVEN

"I said I needed a drink!" She caught the angry note in her voice before it could rise to a screech, and bit back any further words.

"The thick milkshakes they have here are the best you ever tasted," Joe said cheerfully. "I've been having one every night before I went to bed."

"After you'd seen that I got back to the house?" She was suddenly quiet.

"Y-yes."

"Oh Joe!" Her irritation at him, even the craving for a drink, was washed away by a surge of tenderness. "Can't we start over?"

"Sure, darling. That's what this is all about."

Minutes later they were startled by the voice of a carhop girl standing beside the car: "You'd better order something, mister. The boss don't like people sittin' here just neckin'."

iii

Mabel was cleaning up in the Snack Bar, getting ready for the eleven o'clock rush, when Marisa and Anton Dieter came in. They were holding hands and the girl was flushed and happy, like a college girl on a date with her steady.

371

They ordered coffee and drank it almost in silence, obviously still a little stunned by what had happened to them. When they finished, they went out and across the parking lot toward the entrance to the Faculty Apartments, still holding hands.

"I told you they'd make it, Abe," Mabel said triumphantly. "Did you see the look in her eyes?"

"A Jew and an ex-Nazi." The short-order cook shook his head. "It just don't make sense."

"The trouble with you is you don't have any faith," Mabel said loftily. "If you'd been at Mrs. Dellman's funeral this morning like I was, you'd have seen that these people over there"—she nodded toward the hospital across the street—"are just like everybody else. When folks're in love, it don't make no difference who they are—or where they come from."

"But a good-lookin' Jewish gal like that Doctor Feldman. Why does she want to waste herself on a German like Dieter?"

"You ought to read the Bible more," Mabel reproved him. "Don't you know it says that the lion and the lamb shall lay down together?"

"I guess you're right." Abe grinned. "From the way them two were looking at each other, there's sure going to be some layin'—"

"Oh you!" Mabel exclaimed in disgust. "Go fry an egg!"

CHAPTER XXIV

In the living room of Helen Straughn's apartment, across town from University Hospital, she and Pete Brennan were watching the Saturday afternoon football game on the television screen—without seeing it at all. Wearing golden sandals, gold-colored slacks and a white blouse, with her red bronze hair—almost hidden in the operating room by the helmetlike caps the scrub nurses wore—tumbled about her shoulders, Helen was an extraordinarily beautiful woman. None of the look of stern discipline she wore during her working hours was in her eyes as she looked across at Pete, then leaned over to kiss him.

"I'll get you a beer," she said. "Poor darling, you look like you need it."

"This business of buying Mort Dellman's share of the clinic has run me ragged." He raised his voice so he could be heard in the small kitchen where she was opening the beer. "To say nothing of the trouble he caused by shooting Paul McGill."

"That's not really what's troubling you." She brought the tray with the beer on it and put it down before him. "You might as well face the truth; I have already."

"What truth?" He took one of the cans of beer and began to fill a glass, pouring it expertly down the side so it wouldn't foam over.

"Ever since night before last, you've had all the symptoms of a man who's having second thoughts about leaving his wife." She reached over and switched off the TV. "I haven't exactly lived like a nun, you know. By now I can recognize a guilt-stricken husband when I see one."

Pete shook his head in a bewilderment that might have been comic, if it hadn't been so troubled. "Before Mort shot Lorrie, I was certain that I wanted to divorce Amy and marry you."

"And now?"

"I'm not sure it would be best for any of us."

"At least you're honest," she said. "I guess that's what really made me fall for you in the first place."

"What do you mean?"

"You've got something, Pete—integrity I suppose is the best word for it. Anyway it appeals to an orderly sort of person like me."

"It could be that I've got cold feet because I'm afraid what happened to Lorrie could happen to you or to me."

"That never crossed my mind. Your wife has the strait-laced New England conscience her ancestors handed her. She would never go gunning for the woman who broke up her home."

"Don't put it that way."

"If you'd divorced her and married me, what other way could it be put?"

"It's not your fault—or mine—that we fell in love."

"That argument won't hold water either—it never does. I've had other affairs and I don't claim to be anything but what I am, a rather passionate woman who attracts men—and needs them."

"Don't make yourself sound like a Jezebel."

"I'm rather like her, you know. Jezebel was a determined woman —with principles. She thought the worship of Baal and Ashtoreth was best for her husband's people and almost succeeded in convincing them—until she ran up against Elijah."

"Where did you learn all that?"

"The Bible. I'm also religious—which may strike you as sort of odd. The fact of the matter is, your wife and I are alike in some ways; we're both very determined."

"Are you determined to give me up?"

"I thought you settled that just now."

"I said I wasn't sure. Now you seem to be."

"I haven't been certain from the first that it was best for you to divorce Amy and marry me. Now I know it isn't. Until this Dellman business came along, I kidded myself that the community you and I live in by day over at the hospital and the medical school was sophisticated enough for our marriage to work. Of course, people would have done their best to make me feel like a pariah for a little while, but I told myself they'd forget, after I'd proved myself to be the proper wife."

"They still might."

"Unh-unh! Three days ago, a husband caught his wife and another man together in adultery. In a fit of righteous indignation, he killed her and wounded the man, which makes Weston just like any other community, with everybody conforming to what's expected of them. The Bohemian period is over—if it ever really existed. Every husband is going back to his own wife—at least for a while—and the grand jury will set the killer free, because there's an unwritten law that a man has to protect his home."

"You think Weston's going to change that much?"

"The town isn't changing, just going back to what it originally was. One thing's sure, it will never be the same again."

"And you think that's what happened to me—this conformity idea of yours."

"I know what happened to you," she said. "You've fallen out of love with me and back in love with your wife. I can't tell you how it happened or why—only you can do that. But it did happen, so somebody had to lose you. And now that my dream of respectability is over, I'm glad I was the one and not her."

"You're pretty philosophical about all this."

"What do you want me to do?" she said with a shrug. "Go on a crying jag and beg you to marry me?"

"Of course not. But what will you do?"

"What I've done before. You don't own me, Pete Brennan; I've never even let you give me jewelry, remember? We'll break clean, like the honest fighters we are. You go back to Amy and I'll take that Mediterranean cruise I've been wanting to take. You're not going to suggest that we keep on with this affair, are you?"

"No."

"It wouldn't be good for you to come around here anyway." She grinned crookedly. "One day you'd find another man here and that would be a real blow to your ego."

"There's no reason we still can't be friends."

"No reason at all. We're adults. We respect and like each other. But our relationship must end there."

He couldn't help feeling a sense of relief and also guilt, but it seemed best not to mention either.

"You'd better go back to Amy now," Helen Straughn told him. "Don't make the mistake of believing she's as strong as she appears to be—no woman is. That's only a front we put up to keep the men we love from walking over us. My guess is *L'affaire Dellman* has shaken her up as much as it has the rest of us. If she cracks, be sure you're there for her to lean on."

ii

"What I don't understand is why all this secrecy, just to examine a couple of slides," said Lew Saunders, as he took his student-days microscope out of its case in the room he shared with Mike Traynor in the intern quarters of University Hospital and set it on the table. "Or why you're so concerned. You've been hopping around like grease on a hot griddle."

"Just examine the slides." Mike's eyes were feverish and his hands shook as he took a cigarette from a crumpled pack and lit it.

Methodically, Lew Saunders set up the microscope, placed the slide Mike had prepared and stained under the objective, put a drop of cedar oil on it and lowered the oil-immersion lens until it just touched the globule of oil.

"This is a lousy light," he grumbled as he adjusted the goose-neck reading lamp until it was centered on the reflecting mirror beneath the microscope, sending a concentrated beam of light up through the slide and the lens system of the instrument.

With his eyes glued to the twin oculars of the microscope, Saunders began to turn the adjustments: first the gross, until the cells on the slide came into rough focus; then the fine, sharpening the picture until it stood out in the field of the instrument, with the colors and structure of the material sharply defined.

"Jesus Christ!" he exclaimed.

"What is it?" Mike Traynor demanded. "What do you see?"

"The finest preparation of intracellular, biscuit-shaped diplococci you ever saw."

"Oh my God!"

"Whoever you got this smear from has got the hottest dose of—"

"G.C.?"

"No doubt about it. Take a look." When Mike turned away from the microscope, Lew Saunders saw the stricken look on his roommate's face and realization hit him.

"You, Mike! It's yours!"

Mike Traynor nodded; at the moment, he was beyond speech.

"Man, you've really got yourself a dose. I never saw pus cells more crowded with the old Neisseria gonorrhoeae." Suddenly Lew began to laugh.

"It's nothing to laugh about," Mike Traynor said furiously.

"Don't you see?" Saunders went into another fit of laughter. "This is poetic justice, if there ever was such a thing. Mike Traynor, the Casanova of Weston Medical School, has got the clap! Ohh! This is priceless!"

"Shut up," Mike snarled. "Do you want to broadcast it all over the place?"

"Who gave it to you?"

"That bitch from Vassar. The one with the tape recorder."

"It's a hot case all right; three days after exposure is about the shortest time I ever heard of symptoms occurring. Man, when this gets out—"

"You wouldn't do that to me, Lew." Mike Traynor looked as if he were going to faint. "I'd be ruined."

377

"Your supply of women around here would certainly dry up, that's for sure. But when you're admitted to the hospital, it's bound to be on the record. And you know the grapevine."

"I'm not going to be admitted."

"You may not know it, boy, but by this time tomorrow you're going to be sick as hell."

"By this time tomorrow, I'm going to be practically well. Penicillin still cures G.C., doesn't it?"

"Sure—unless that babe was treated before and got herself a penicillin-resistant bug."

"I'll have to chance that. What's the biggest-size ampule made for injecting penicillin?"

"I saw some in the emergency room with five million units."

"If I inject one of them today and one day after tomorrow, I ought to be cured in forty-eight hours."

"Probably. Unless the bug turns out to be resistant."

"Can you get the ampules for me, Lew?"

"I don't know. A thing like this could be pretty sticky, if you have to be admitted later and it comes out that I knew. Besides, if I inject you and next week you start shedding your hide with a drug reaction—"

"Just get me the penicillin and I'll inject it myself. If there's any trouble, I'll swear I diagnosed myself and tried to treat it."

"Well, all right."

"You're a real friend, Lew. I'll get you a girl sometimes."

"Oh no," said the other intern. "You're jinxed." He began to laugh again. "Talk about poetic justice."

"You already said that," Mike Traynor told him. "Get the penicillin."

"I'm going." Lew Saunders reached for his white coat. "But while I'm gone, be thinking about what a hell of a fix you'd be in if Dr. Fleming hadn't discovered the notatum mold that makes penicillin one day about thirty years ago. And thank God for him."

iii

Dave Rogan had been making rounds on the psychiatric wards; whenever he was in the city on the weekends, he always paid a quick visit to his department of the hospital before dinner on Saturday. As he was leaving, he saw Elaine McGill pull into the parking lot, and crossed the street to where she was locking the doors of her station wagon.

"Got a minute, Elaine?" he asked.

"Sure," she said with a smile. "I'm on my way to see Paul."

"He's fine. They moved him from Intensive Care last night to make a room available for Janet Monroe's little boy."

"I hope the child's all right. Paul was talking about the operation last night."

"Pete Brennan did a brilliant job. The only trouble now is keeping the kid still with that magnetic probe in his brain but they've got enough personnel on Intensive Care to look after him."

"That's the second miracle in three days. The first was what Dr. Dieter did for Paul."

"You could call it that. If Pete had been forced to go after that aneurysm the old way, the chances of saving Jerry wouldn't have been much better than fifty per cent. Now, it looks like he's going to come through beautifully." He glanced toward the Snack Bar and saw that it was almost filled. "I'd buy you a cup of coffee, but what I have to say is sort of private."

"We're private enough right here," said Elaine. "I'd invite you to sit in my car but the way things have been around here lately, I'm afraid it might cause talk."

"Maybe we'd better not tempt fate." Dave grinned. "Tell me, do you have a picture of Paul's mother in your house?"

"Of course. You know the kind of retouched enlargements that used to be fashionable thirty years ago."

"Ever look at her? And then at yourself in the mirror?"

"Paul has told me more than once how much I resemble his

mother. At first it made me mad; I guess I even hated her for a while. But I've gotten used to it now."

"I'm going to ask you a pretty intimate question, Elaine. But only because I'm very fond of you and Paul and want to see both of you happy."

"I know that, Dave."

"You say you used to hate Paul's mother sometimes. Was it after you and Paul had made love?"

When she didn't answer right away, he knew he was on the right track.

"How did you know?" she asked finally.

"Paul sent for me the day after the shooting. Something was troubling him."

"Then he *was* potent with Lorrie?"

"Yes."

"I've wondered. But Paul never talks about intimate things and I hesitated to ask."

"He was worried because he was potent with her and isn't very often with you."

"I guess that would be a normal male worry, wouldn't it?" She laughed, but not very convincingly.

"It wasn't himself Paul was worried about, Elaine. I think he realized for the first time the part a woman who really enjoys sex can play in it."

"And how a man can fail his partner?" Remembering what had happened earlier that fateful Wednesday afternoon, Elaine looked away lest Dave notice the warmth that the memory of it brought to her cheeks.

"The important thing," he said, "is what are you going to do about it?"

"Me? How can I keep Paul from remembering his mother?"

"By not being like her."

Elaine caught her breath. "Are you saying I should be like Lorrie?"

"Only where Paul is concerned. If you try, I think you can give a pretty good imitation of her." He grinned. "Maybe I'm older than I thought, or I would know already. But isn't there a pretty interesting pair of knees under that too-long dress Paul makes you wear?"

Her eyes twinkled. "It's a little public here, but if you really want to find out, I can always get back into the car."

"I'll take your word for it; after all, Della's been away a lot lately. But if you have an entirely new—and a lot smarter—wardrobe when Paul comes home, I don't think he'll mind paying the bill."

"I'll be a hussy." Elaine's eyes were shining. "But if Paul doesn't deliver, warn Della she's going to have competition. Don't forget Pygmalion and Galatea."

iv

The weather had been worsening to the south toward Atlanta since morning, and Elmer Hill, foreman of the Weston County Grand Jury, was delayed in his flight home. It was after seven Saturday evening before the jury was finally assembled in the courthouse and the hearing on Mort Dellman could begin.

When the prisoner was brought into the locked room where the jury was sitting, Roy was surprised to see that he was accompanied only by the bailiff, who had brought him downstairs from the jail.

"It was my understanding that the accused had engaged counsel," he said to the foreman.

"I plan to be my own counsel," Mort Dellman interposed blandly. "Since I have done nothing that any normal man wouldn't do to defend the sanctity of his home and his marriage, I don't need anyone to twist the law in my behalf."

It was a clever move, the sort of thing Roy should have expected, particularly after Mort's slick ploy with the confession on the afternoon of the killing. But Roy wasn't at all sure he had a case anyway, so he hesitated only a moment before turning to the court reporter, who was taking down the proceedings word by word on a shorthand machine.

"Let the record show the prisoner was warned of his constitutional right not to give testimony and to be represented by counsel," he directed.

"I waive both rights and throw myself upon the mercy of the gentlemen of the grand jury," Mort Dellman added.

"That should be sufficient, shouldn't it, Mr. Weston?" the foreman asked.

"Yes—so long as it is a matter of record that the prisoner was warned of his rights and that he is not required to testify."

"Are you ready to proceed with the hearing then, Mr. Weston?"

"Yes, sir. I shall read first a deposition given under oath this morning by Dr. Paul McGill, a patient in the University Hospital, who is unable physically to attend the hearing and testify himself."

"Any objection?" the foreman asked Mort Dellman.

"None whatever, sir."

"Proceed then, Mr. Weston."

The reading proceeded briskly.

Q.—Your name?

A.—Paul McGill.

Q.—Occupation?

A.—Physician. I am a specialist in dermatology—diseases of the skin.

Q.—Where do you reside?

A.—At 2625 Sherwood Ravine Road.

Q.—Where were you about 4:30 P.M. on the afternoon of July 1?

A.—At 5051 Sherwood Ravine Road.

Q.—What were you doing at the time?

A.—I was engaged in sexual intercourse.

Roy had tried to get Paul to avoid the word, knowing the effect it would have on the jury in Mort Dellman's favor. But Paul had insisted, for the same reason.

"I'll be damned," one of the jurors said in an awed voice. "He's a regular studhorse, ain't he?"

Roy ignored the interruption and continued with the reading:

Q.—With whom were you having intercourse?

A.—With Lor—Mrs. Mortimer Dellman.

Q.—What happened then?

A.—I'm not sure.

Q.—Did you see Dr. Dellman come into the room?

A.—No. Suddenly I heard a shot and at the same moment I . . . I blacked out.

Q.—When did you next regain consciousness?

A.—Around midnight, I guess it was.

Q.—Where?

A.—In the Special Intensive Care Unit at University Hospital.

Q.—And you knew nothing of what happened in between?

A.—Nothing.

Q.—Did you see Dr. Dellman at any time that afternoon?

A.—No.

Q.—Did you know who shot you?

A.—No. When I first became conscious at the hospital I didn't know what had actually happened. In fact my first thought was that I must have had a heart attack.

Q.—One other question, Dr. McGill? How long had you been engaged in sexual intercourse with Mrs. Dellman when you heard the sound and blacked out?

A.—Maybe five minutes.

"Didn't even get to finish," said the juror who had spoken before. "What a shame."

"This is the end of Dr. McGill's deposition." Roy Weston ignored the interruption.

"Call your first witness, please, Mr. Weston," said the foreman.

"Bailiff, call Dr. Sylvester Short, Medical Examiner for Weston County."

Dr. Short, a portly man of some sixty years, who was also Professor of Pathology at the medical school, gave the usual background information for the record concerning his training and qualifications.

"Dr. Short," Roy said. "Did you on September 1, examine the body of Mrs. Loretta Porter Dellman, deceased?"

"I did."

"Would you tell us your findings, please?"

"Death came from a wound in the left side of the heart, damaging both the cardiac muscle and the left coronary artery."

"The coronary artery? Would you explain, please?"

"The coronary arteries are two in number and supply blood to each side of the heart muscle. The bullet destroyed at least a half inch of the left coronary artery, thus depriving a large portion of the heart of vitally needed blood. The effect was the same as massive coronary thrombosis."

"And that was?"

"Instant death."

"Did you find the bullet that caused this extensive damage?"

"No, sir. The bullet passed entirely through the body of the deceased. The wound of entry was in the back of the chest on the left side. The wound of exit was in the front of the left chest."

"And death was instantaneous?"

"No question about it."

"No more questions."

There were none from the jury and Dr. Short was allowed to leave.

"Call Sergeant Jim O'Brien," Roy directed.

Sergeant O'Brien settled into the witness chair, nodded to several members of the jury, and was sworn. He was obviously an experienced witness.

"Sergeant, were you called on September 1, to the home of Dr. Mortimer Dellman at 5051 Sherwood Ravine Road at about four thirty in the afternoon?"

"I was."

"By whom?"

"By Dr. Dellman. He called the police station and reported that he had killed a man who was with his wife."

"Did he identify the man at the time, Sergeant?"

"No sir."

"Did he say he had killed his wife?"

"No sir."

"What did you find when you reached the house?"

"Mrs. Dellman was dead, shot through the chest. Dr. Mc-Gill was seriously wounded. I didn't think he would live to get to the hospital."

"Where was Dr. Dellman?"

"In the adjoining room. He gave us the weapon when we came in."

"We, Sergeant?"

"Lt. Vosges was with me."

"What kind of a weapon was it?"

"A twenty-two-caliber target pistol."

"How many shots had been fired?"

"One."

Taking a small box from his pocket and opening it to show a bullet lying on a piece of cotton, Roy held it close enough for the sergeant to examine it. "This one?"

"Yes sir. I scratched an identifying mark on it."

"Are you sure the bullet came from the pistol Dr. Dellman handed you?"

"Yes. I fired another bullet from the weapon later and had them compared ballistically by the FBI. Dr. Dellman's pistol unquestionably fired the shot that killed Mrs. Dellman and wounded Dr. McGill."

There were no more questions and the sergeant was dismissed.

"Call Dr. Anton Dieter, please," Roy Weston directed.

Dieter came in, was sworn and gave the usual background information.

"Dr. Dieter," said Roy. "Did you, on September 1, operate upon Dr. Paul McGill?"

"I did."

"And what did you find?"

"A bullet, twenty-two caliber, steel-jacketed, located inside the right ventricle of the heart."

"Did you remove the bullet?"

"I did."

"Can you tell us its approximate course."

"The bullet entered Dr. McGill's chest about a half inch to the right of the sternum—"

"The breastbone?"

"Yes. It penetrated the chest wall and also the wall of the right ventricle, one of the four chambers of the heart, landing inside the ventricle."

Roy Weston took the small box from his pocket, opened it and once again showed the jury and the witness the bullet lying on a piece of cotton at the bottom of the box.

"Is this the bullet you removed, Doctor?"

"Is it the one I turned over to Sergeant O'Brien at his request following the operation, Mr. Weston?"

"It is the same bullet."

"Then it is the one I removed."

"I have no more questions of the witness," Roy Weston told the foreman of the jury.

"You may step down, Dr. Diet—"

"One minute." It was the rather garrulous juror. "Did you say the bullet entered the front of Dr. McGill's chest?"

"I did."

"Wasn't he something?" the man said, with obvious admiration. "Not only takes a man's wife but makes her do the work." When a titter of amusement passed like a wave over the faces of the jurors, he added, "Lazy bastard, ain't he?"

"We will present no more evidence at this time," Roy Weston announced. "It seems proved beyond question that the prisoner killed his wife and wounded Dr. McGill. I ask therefore that he be bound over to Circuit Court on a charge of manslaughter."

"Just a moment!" It was Mort Dellman. "Don't I have the right to testify?"

"In my opinion, your testimony is neither necessary nor advisable at this time, Dr. Dellman," Roy Weston said coldly. He didn't know exactly what Mort was up to, but he preferred to have as little of the details of the sordid affair brought out as possible, even in the relative secrecy of the jury room.

"I think the jury is entitled to know the facts before they consider whether or not to bring an indictment against me," Mort Dellman insisted. "Both my life and my professional reputation are at stake here."

"It is my duty to warn you, both for yourself and for the record," Roy said formally, "that since you have been apprised of your rights and have chosen to be without counsel, any statement you make can be introduced in evidence as part of your trial, if an indictment is returned."

"The truth never hurt anyone," Mort Dellman said in a tone of pious righteousness.

"You may make a statement, Doctor, if you believe it will assist us in arriving at a decision in your case," said the jury foreman.

"I do believe that, sir," Mort Dellman assured him.

"Proceed then. But please remember that you may stop at any time and refuse to answer any questions put to you without in any way prejudicing yourself."

"I understand." Mort Dellman turned to face the entire jury. "On the afternoon of September 1 of this year, gentlemen, I came home earlier than usual. It had been brought to my attention previously that a Buick Wildcat automobile had been seen parked in front of my house on several afternoons, but a number of people I know own such a car, so I merely thought some woman friend might be visiting my wife. She grew up in this community and had a large number of friends.

"When I entered the house, I found no one downstairs—our children are all away at a summer camp and the maid was off on Wednesdays. I climbed the stairs and approached the bedroom my wife and I share, but when I was about six feet from the door, I heard voices inside the room. The room was somewhat dark but the door was partly open. When I heard a man's laugh, I guess I sort of lost control of myself. There is a small study on that floor where I keep a pistol since a rash of burglaries occurred in our neighborhood lately."

He paused and, pouring a glass of water for himself from a pitcher on a small table nearby, drank it down before continuing.

"As I have said, I was laboring under a very strong emotion. I think any of you would feel the same if you heard a man's laugh and your wife's voice from a darkened bedroom in your home at four thirty in the afternoon. I remember throwing open the door of the bedroom and seeing my wife in the arms of another man. As to what happened then I can't be sure. I remember raising the gun but I don't remember firing it. When I regained control of my senses, I found that my wife was dead and her lover was unconscious. I called the police at once and you know the rest of the story."

The foreman looked at the rest of the jury. "Any questions?" he asked.

Watching them, Roy Weston saw that the man who had spoken several times before was frowning. "How good a shot are you, Doctor?" he asked.

"I qualified with a pistol as an army officer in Korea. And I also shoot sometimes in local contests at the pistol range."

"How far away were you when you fired?"

"As I said, I'm not sure exactly what happened. I may even have taken several steps into the room; the venetian blinds were drawn and it was rather dark."

"Any further questions?" the foreman asked and the juror shook his head.

"Any questions from you, Mr. Weston?"

"No," said Roy. "I have no more witnesses to bring in at this time either."

"The bailiff will take Dr. Dellman into custody," said the foreman of the grand jury. "I would appreciate your waiting outside the jury room until we reach a decision, Mr. Weston, in case we need to call you back to explain any points of the law."

"Of course." Roy followed the court reporter outside and offered her a cigarette. She was a pert young woman, an experienced reporter and, he knew, very sharp.

"What do you think the verdict will be, Mr. Weston?" she asked, as she accepted a light.

"An indictment for manslaughter—what else?"

"They're going to turn him loose."

"Why do you say that?"

"Only one guy on the jury saw that this whole thing smells to high heaven."

"What do you mean?" Roy asked warily.

"Loretta Dellman was no saint; that's common knowledge. But Dr. Dellman also makes a play for anything wearing skirts whenever he can. My roommate's a secretary at the Faculty Clinic and gives me all the dirt."

"Like what?"

"Mrs. Dellman was playing cozy with a curly-tailed wolf of a medical student. I had a few dates with him, until I found out I'd have to learn judo. My guess is that Dellman couldn't stand the idea of knowing the students were talking about him being cuckolded by one of them, and went there that afternoon to get the guy. But Dr. McGill was there instead and got the bullet intended for somebody else."

"Do you have any proof of this?"

"All I know is what I read off the stenotype." The girl grinned. "These high-society shenanigans are not for the likes of me."

The door to the jury room opened and the foreman looked out.

"Please come in, Mr. Weston—also the reporter," he said. "We have reached a decision."

Inside, the reporter took her place at the stenographic machine and the foreman put on his glasses before taking up a piece of paper on which something had been written with a ball-point pen.

"We, the Grand Jury of Weston County," he read, "sitting on

the fourth day of September, find that Mrs. Loretta Dellman came to her death by the accidental discharge of a weapon in the hands of Dr. Mortimer Dellman, her husband. We therefore find no cause to bind Dr. Dellman over for trial and he is hereby ordered released from custody."

CHAPTER XXV

Dave and Della Rogan were sitting on the sofa in the cypress-paneled family room watching TV, when the broadcast was interrupted by a local news bulletin that the grand jury had freed Mort Dellman with a verdict of accidental death.

"How could they figure that?" Della asked.

"Mort undoubtedly claimed the unwritten law, as far as shooting Paul was concerned, and the jury must have figured that Lorrie got in the way of the bullet. It's a screwy sort of a verdict, but I guess it's the best for all concerned. Now everything can go back to normal again."

"Except that Mort's a hundred thousand dollars richer."

"He's more than that. The rumor is that Jake Porter gave him two hundred thousand not to claim custody of the children and let the old man adopt them."

"So Mort came out better than anybody else?"

"I guess you could say that, though getting Joe and Maggie back together means a lot to me—and more to them. They're going on a world cruise the first of October; Maggie told me when I saw her this afternoon. The one I really feel sorry for is George Hanscombe."

"Why? If he'd ask Grace to stay here, I think she would."

"Maybe. But George is a good enough doctor to know that wouldn't be best for Grace, after the diabetes almost got away from them a few days ago. He's letting her go to England because he loves her enough to see that it's best for her."

"She can always come back."

"George is gambling on that but my guess is she won't. Grace never consulted me and I probably couldn't have helped her if she had. There are too many points of frustration between her and George and they're both too old by twenty-five or thirty years to really make any basic changes in their approach to life and each other. Grace can adjust; after all, she'll have enough to live on comfortably and she'll be in England where she has relatives. But George's life has been arranged in pretty watertight compartments for so long, it's going to be hard on him."

"Do you think Pete and that nurse will go on?"

"That nurse, as you call her, happens to be an extremely capable and fine woman, hon. Like George, Helen probably loves Pete enough to give him up. I've always figured that in the end, Pete would go back to Amy anyway, once he realizes how brittle Amy's defenses really are."

"And us? What about us, Dave?"

He moved his arm to draw her more closely to him. "I'm pretty sure Mort's bullet missed us." He yawned. "It's about bedtime. What say we go to church in the morning, then drive down along the lake for dinner? The kids will be back Tuesday and things will be pretty lively around here—for a while."

At the foot of the stairs, Della turned back to where he was checking the latch on the front door.

"I stopped taking the pill a couple of days ago, Dave," she said casually.

"Hmm." He grinned and the look in his eyes set her heart beating a little faster. "What day would this be in your cycle, by the way?"

"The thirteenth or fourteenth. I haven't paid much attention to it for quite a while."

"We may be too late this month, but it's still worth a try. Next month we ought to hit that old ovulation date right on the head. You go on up; I'll fix us a drink and bring it with me."

It was going to be fun painting the crib that had been stored up in the attic more than ten years now, he thought as he mixed bourbon with ginger ale. Almost as much fun as having a little fellow toddling around the house again.

ii

It was nearly eleven o'clock before Roy Weston finished preparing and signing the documents connected with Mort Dellman's release from jail, following the decision of the grand jury. Mort had insisted on their being prepared tonight. And though Roy knew what was in Mort's mind—the possibility that one of the county judges might become disturbed over the rather summary action of the grand jury in freeing him and order his re-arrest—Roy was anxious to get the whole thing off his mind, too, so he'd stayed at the courthouse to prepare them.

By encouraging the jury to sweep the whole affair under the rug, so to speak, Roy had the satisfaction of knowing he had saved many of his friends—and himself—from the scandal of epic proportions that could have resulted if Mort had been brought to trial. But he also knew he had removed any possibility of running for the job of attorney general of the state in the forthcoming election, since Abner Townsend would certainly seize upon Mort Dellman's release as a major campaign issue if he did.

It didn't really matter any more, Roy tried to tell himself, but without much success. Weary and discouraged, he took a bottle from the lower drawer of his desk and poured a glass half full, drinking it down without even noticing the sting of liquor upon his throat. In the parking lot outside, he got into his Cadillac, but when he reached the street, didn't turn toward his home. Instead, he headed westward toward the new apartment complex the Biesons were building on a hillside around a small lake.

The apartment he sought was on the third floor, but the window was dark. Ordinarily, she never went to bed until after midnight, he knew. But on the chance that she might have decided to go earlier tonight, since she wasn't expecting him, he took the elevator up and rang the bell. When no one answered after a few moments, he went back to his car and headed toward home.

The clouds had been lowering all afternoon and now it had begun to rain. Usually, when he was out late Roy called Alice before starting home; even though they slept in different rooms and she was often asleep when he got home, she didn't like for him to come into the house at night without her knowing it. But tonight, he was too depressed and tired to stop on the way and, putting the car in the garage when he reached the house, let himself in with his own key.

A small light burned downstairs, since Alice sometimes had to go down in the middle of the night for the green medicine, if her colon started acting up. Stepping out of his loafers so as not to disturb her on the landing upstairs, Roy stopped at the downstairs bar off the family room for another quick drink, then climbed the stairway in his sock feet.

The entire upper floor was dark but he didn't turn on the light in the hall. He'd come home so many times late at night that he knew the way to his own room by instinct now. As he was passing the door to Alice's room, he heard what sounded like voices and, thinking that perhaps she had forgotten to turn off the small television set in her room, he moved to the door. Before he could open it, the sounds came again and, startled by their nature, he put his ear to the wooden panel.

In much the way a stethoscope magnified the hidden sounds of breathing and the heartbeat inside the body, the wooden panel of the door and his eardrums magnified the sound within the room. He heard Alice's gurgling laugh and then the throaty tones of another woman's voice, a voice that sounded familiar, but which he could not place at the moment.

Shocked by the implication of what he was hearing, Roy considered for a moment going on to his own room and leaving Alice and whoever was in there with her alone. But the whiskey he'd drunk before leaving the office and downstairs just now was beginning to heat up his brain and with it another, headier excitement started to rise. Turning the knob of the door carefully so as not to warn those inside, he pushed it open with his right hand and reached inside quickly, flipping the light switch with his left.

As the room was flooded with light, a shriek of surprise came from Alice. She rolled over, scrambling desperately for a sheet to cover her naked body, but the other woman made no move to cover herself. Instead she raised herself on her elbows and looked up at Roy with a mocking light in her eyes.

"Don't stare, Roy," said Corinne Marchant. "You've seen us both naked before."

As Roy gaped at her and at Alice, now sitting up in bed, with the sheet drawn up under her chin, watching both him and Corinne warily, the Frenchwoman added: "You've got what we French call a ménage à trois, darling, so why not make the best of it? I can assure you that you'll find it interesting."

Roy stared at them while the liquor rose in his brain and the pounding of his pulse accelereated steadily. The contrast between the two women was remarkable: Alice all soft, pink and very feminine, with her rather full breasts and rounded hips; Corinne, slim and tanned, like the athlete she was. The more he looked and the more his pulse pounded in his ears, the more he could see that Corinne's suggestion made sense. What decided him, however, was the sudden avid look in Alice's eyes and the way she let the sheet fall and shoved it away from her body with a casual movement.

Beginning to loosen his tie and unbutton his shirt, Roy started to laugh, and, after a startled moment, the two women joined him.

"Two for the price of one!" he chuckled. "By God, Corinne, I think you're right."

iii

It was shortly after midnight when Mort Dellman reached Weston County Airport. A single attendant was at the counter of the only airline serving the city with night flights.

"Is the 1 A.M. flight to Atlanta on time?" he asked.

"We're socked in, sir."

"What d'ya mean, socked in?"

"The flight's been canceled out of here on account of bad weather."

"When's the next one?"

"Nine o'clock tomorrow morning."

"Nine o'clock?"

"We can't be too sure of that one either, sir. The weatherman says this front is going to hang around for a while. As long as it does, there won't be any planes landing here."

Nine o'clock! He couldn't chance it!

The morning papers were already off the press. He'd picked one up outside when he'd come into the airport, and the first thing everyone would see in the morning would be the bold headlines:

GRAND JURY FREES DOCTOR

Roy Weston had been a fool not to prosecute him, Mort knew, but the state attorney general was far too astute a politician to overlook the chance to torpedo Roy's chances of running for the post. An hour after Abner Townsend saw the morning papers, he would be dragging a judge in the capital from his Sunday paper, asking for another warrant. Which meant that Mort Dellman had to be out of Weston and across the state line—preferably out of the country, too—before that could happen.

His escape plan was foolproof and he could have made it, too, if the rain hadn't socked in the flight to Atlanta. The reservation he'd had Pete Brennan make for South Africa had been only a feint. His real destination was Brazil, where there was no extradition treaty with the United States. With a hundred thousand for his share of the Faculty Clinic and another two hundred from old man Porter in the kitty—plus what he had been stashing away through the years in Switzerland and the lever the accidental death verdict of the grand jury would give him when he had a lawyer claim the benefits for the accident policy he'd taken out on Lorrie a year ago, he could have lived high in Brazil, while he decided what to do next—until this damned weather had upset his plans.

There was only one answer—a rental car. Even then he'd never make it to Atlanta before nine o'clock, which meant the people he rented the car from would certainly recognize him and the police would know almost immediately where he had gone. He'd have to take that chance though, and try to sneak across the state line by taking a back road.

The car rental booth was across the foyer of the airport and he was striding toward it when his eye was caught by a sign over an empty booth:

CHARTER FLYING SERVICE

And underneath it the promise:

WE FLY YOU ANYWHERE AT ANY TIME.
IF BOOTH IS UNATTENDED, DIAL 389–7677

Stepping into a telephone booth, Mort dropped a dime into the slot and dialed the number. It rang several times before a sleepy feminine voice answered.

"Charter Flying Service?" he asked.

"Just a minute, please."

"This is Charter," a man's voice said.

"I want you to fly me to Atlanta."

"The weather's too bad, sir. Nothing's coming into Weston Airport tonight."

"That doesn't mean nothing can leave it," Mort Dellman said. "How does a thousand dollars sound to you for flying me to Atlanta. Or fifteen hundred to New Orleans?"

"It's still pretty risky."

"I'm paying you well."

"Who is this?"

"My name's Richards. I'm at the airport now and I'm ready to go whenever you are."

"Why do you have to get to Atlanta in such a hurry, Mr. Richards?"

"A member of my family is dying in Dallas. It's important that I get there as quickly as possible."

"You said fifteen hundred to New Orleans, didn't you?"

"Yes. If you hurry."

"I'll be at the airport in twenty minutes. You'll know I'm there when you see the lights go on in my hangar. It's close to the airport building."

"I'll come over to the hangar when they go on."

It was a little over fifteen minutes before the lights went on. Picking up his bag, Mort crossed over to the hangar in the rain. A man was busy working on a light plane, filling the wing tanks with gasoline.

"I'm Mr. Richards," Mort called to him. "How soon can we take off?"

"Right away, sir—as soon as I finish filling the tanks and file a flight plan with the tower." He looked more closely at Mort. "You say your name's Richards?"

"That's right. You want me to pay you in advance?"

The man hesitated only momentarily. "Yes."

Mort counted out the money and put it into the pilot's hands when he finished filling the tank.

"This is a helluva night for flying, Mr. Richards," the man said. "But I can't afford to turn down fifteen hundred bucks."

And I can't afford not to get out of the country, Mort Dellman thought as he swung his bags up into the plane. From New Orleans, he was pretty sure he could get a plane for Mexico City before Abner Townsend could stop him. And once there, it would be a simple matter to go on to Brazil.

iv

After leaving Helen Straughn's apartment Saturday afternoon, Pete Brennan had driven home and taken Amy to dinner at the club. It hadn't been a very festive occasion, however. Amy seemed depressed and several times he thought she was going to tell him something, but each time she'd turned the conversation along another line. Around nine o'clock, they returned home and, after the ten o'clock news broadcast announced the action of the grand jury in freeing Mort Dellman, they went to bed.

It was just before dawn when Pete awakened. A glance at the other side of the king-sized double bed told him it was empty. The door to Amy's bathroom was closed but a line of light showed beneath it, telling him where she was. While he was debating knocking upon it, the sound of retching made the decision for him.

When he opened the door, Amy was standing in front of the washbasin, her head held tightly between her hands and a look of agony on her face. When he took her in his arms, she clung to him like a child. Reaching for a washcloth, he moistened it beneath the tap and gently wiped her face and her mouth with a cool cloth.

"Migraine?" he asked.

"Woke up with it," she gasped. "Nauseated."

He drew a bath towel from the rack and threw it over his shoulder, in case she had another fit of vomiting. Guiding her back to the bed, he helped her lie down. Then, placing the folded-up towel beside her where she could reach it, he moistened the washcloth again and put it on her forehead.

"Lie as quietly as you can," he told her. "I'll call the emergency room for a hypodermic."

Using the extension in the next room, Pete rang the hospital and got the night emergency-room nurse immediately. "I need a hypodermic of ergotamine tartrate and Demerol, Miss Tabor," he told her. "Mrs. Brennan's having a severe migraine attack. I'll run over and get it."

"We're not busy, Doctor," said the nurse. "The night orderly can bring it over to you in my car."

"That'll be fine. I'll meet him at the front door."

"He should be there in ten minutes."

When he came back into the bedroom, Pete saw at once that

Amy had moved while he was away. The dresser drawer where she had hidden the morphine was not quite completely closed, though he remembered closing it tightly after he'd found and removed the drug. She was lying upon the bed again, however, with the washcloth pulled down over her eyes.

"The night orderly is bringing over the injection George Hanscombe always gives you, dear," he said. "Do you need anything else?"

"Some ginger ale over ice might help my stomach."

"I'll get it while I'm waiting for the hypo," he said, although he was pretty sure the request was only a device to get him out of the room. By the time he'd found the ginger ale and poured it into a glass filled with ice in the kitchen, the grizzled night orderly was at the door, with the sterile syringe and needle wrapped in a sterile towel.

When he came back upstairs, Pete saw at once that Amy had been up again—as he had expected. This time the door to his closet was not quite shut and he was sure she had been looking there for the medicine case, which he had removed after finding the syrettes and put in the glove compartment of his car.

"This will straighten you out in no time," he told her as he made the injection with the plastic disposal syringe most hospitals used to prevent the possibility of carrying the deadly virus of serum hepatitis from one patient to another.

"Hold me, Pete." It was a whisper of entreaty and, slipping into bed on his side, he took her in his arms. Her body was tense at first but as the medicine began to take effect, he felt the tension gradually lessen.

"Head feel better?" he asked after a while.

"The pain's almost gone now."

"You might feel better if you drank some of the ginger ale. I'll get it for you."

"No. Don't leave me. I'll get it." She turned over and, taking the glass from the bedside table, drank it through a straw he'd put into it in the kitchen. Turning back, she nestled against him once more, and after a little while moved even closer. When her

400

lips sought his, he kissed her and found her mouth soft and labile beneath his own. Her arm tightened about his neck and when his hand touched the warm skin of her back, where her nightgown was rolled up, she shivered a little and pressed herself against him.

He made love to her gently then, filled with a great tenderness he'd never remembered experiencing before. Amy had always seemed so self-sufficient she'd never aroused that sort of a feeling within him. When it was over and she was close against him, warm and relaxed, he said, "Is there anything you want to tell me, dear?"

She'd been lying with her eyes closed, utterly relaxed from the drug and from the love-making. Now she opened them and looked up at him, as he propped himself up on his elbow so he could look down upon her face. There was no tension now and no apprehension in her eyes.

"It all seems sort of foolish," she said.

"What does?"

"Worrying about what I had to tell you."

He grinned. "Maybe if more husbands and wives prepared for serious discussions as we just did, there wouldn't be any need for the discussions after all."

"There's need for this one. You found the little tubes?"

"The syrettes? Yes. I still don't understand why you used them."

"It was Wednesday night, after Lorrie was shot. I got a severe migraine on the way home from the District Six meeting, even before I heard the news on the radio. The presidency was cinched. I had enough votes to win but—"

"Was? Had? Isn't the present tense appropriate?"

"Not any more. When I saw myself in the mirror while you were downstairs just now, scrabbling around hunting for that morphine because I couldn't face what I had to do, I realized I'm no better than Maggie McCloskey, or any other alcoholic or addict. Being president of the auxiliary before you became head of the state medical association didn't seem important to me any more."

"Was that what brought on the attack when you were on the way home?"

"I'm sure it must have been. I'd been under a lot of tension over there but what really worried me was my selfishness in wanting to get ahead of you."

"You're wrong."

"How?"

"What really troubled you was the fear that you might hurt me. But you couldn't be afraid of that, unless you love me even more than being auxiliary president."

"I know that now, but for a while I was in danger of letting it become too important. Driving home from the meeting, I began to realize that, and something inside me triggered the attack. I was on my way to George Hanscombe's office to get an injection when the radio broadcast told me about the shooting. After that I was so concerned that you might have been hurt—"

"Didn't you call the hospital?"

"Yes. But the Cardiac Alert was on."

"The clinic operator could have told you it was Paul."

"By that time I was too upset to think clearly. When I left the hospital after we talked to Dave Rogan, the clinic was closed and by the time I got home the pain was so bad I was almost blind. I was undressing up here, when I happened to see that little case of yours. I don't know what made me do it, Pete. I guess I was upset about so many things—worrying about losing you because of my ambition, worrying about your being shot, disturbed about Lorrie and troubled for Elaine and Paul—that it all sort of piled up on me. When I saw the little tube, it seemed to offer a way to relieve the pain."

"As I remember that night, it did a lot more than that."

"If I didn't feel so wonderful now, I'd feel ashamed of the way I acted then."

"But you're not?"

"No."

"You don't need to—not ever again. A husband and wife who

really love each other shouldn't be ashamed of anything that expresses their love and makes them happy."

"From now on I'm going to spend my time trying to be what you want me to be, not what I thought I wanted to be," she promised. "I'll start by calling up the delegates today and releasing them."

"I don't want you to do that."

"Why?"

"You're a person, Amy, an individual in your own right—with a lot of drive. When a woman like you marries, she almost always uses that drive to make her husband over into whatever she decides she wants him to be. Five years or so ago, you were hell-bent for me to be Professor of Surgery. When you failed, your ego felt slapped down and resented it, so you went on the auxiliary kick to get ahead of me."

"I don't want to get ahead of you any more."

"You don't now—because you've just been made love to. You're enjoying what the sexologists call postcoital lassitude."

"Hurrah for postcoital lass—whatever it is."

"I couldn't agree more. A few hours from now, you'll be Amy Weston Brennan again, with all your energy intact. And believe me, I'd rather have that energy directed toward making you president of the national medical auxiliary than making me over. I happen to be a stubborn Irishman who's perfectly satisfied with the way he is."

"I'm satisfied with the way you are, too." She took his face between her hands and pulled his head down to kiss him. "Right now, I want to be made love to again."

"Not unless you've got an ampule of testosterone propionate hidden somewhere that I can give myself with that syringe," he told her with a grin. "I'm almost forty-five years old, you shameless wench, so what you have in mind is physically impossible for another couple of hours at least. Let's go to sleep."

CHAPTER XXVI

Alice was already at the breakfast table when Roy came down shortly before eight Sunday morning. Sitting across from him while the maid served them, she was as demure and composed as if nothing that had happened last night had actually transpired.

Women! he thought. I'll never understand them.

But why try when they were far more interesting and exciting if you took them as they were. He had been taking Alice for granted all these years. And looking at her now, with every hair intact, the epitome of the successful professional man's wife in the upper social level, you would never think she could—

"The paper says the grand jury turned Mort Dellman loose." Alice looked up from the headlines, which were all she read— except the funnies.

"I guess I was too busy after I came home last night to mention it."

"I've been wondering why he shot Lorrie. But I guess it must have been because Uncle Jacob changed his will."

"What?" Roy looked up from his section of the paper, startled by what he thought he'd heard—and couldn't believe.

"Uncle Jacob changed his will several weeks ago—put everything in trust for the children, with the bank as trustee."

"How do you know this?"

"Uncle Jacob told Amy about it day before yesterday, when she went to see whether he needed any help about the funeral. Amy told me yesterday at the funeral but I was so upset about Lorrie being bur— I guess I just forgot it."

"The conniving bastard!" Roy exploded. "I knew something about that statement of Mort's before the jury didn't jibe with Paul McGill's deposition, but I couldn't figure out what it was. Mort said the room was dark but Paul didn't, so Mort actually knew who he was shooting all the time. This was a chance to get back at Lorrie over the medical student and clean up on his own account with the hundred thousand he'd get for his share in the clinic, plus the two hundred thousand he planned to stick Uncle Jake for letting the children stay here, and the insurance. I've got him."

"But the jury set Mort free."

"I can always reopen the case with new evidence and I'm going to do it, no matter what the consequences. This establishes a clear case of premeditated murder." He reached for the telephone book, and finding the number he wanted, dialed it rapidly.

"Jim," he said when Sergeant O'Brien answered his phone, "I want you to haul Mort Dellman in wherever you can find him. I've got new evidence and I'll get the warrants—"

"You're too late."

"You mean he's already skipped town?"

"He skipped all right. The eight o'clock news is just coming on. Turn on your radio and you'll get the details."

Roy reached over to the sidetable and switched on the small radio they used sometimes for listening to the early morning news. When the first words of the broadcast struck his ears, he hung up the telephone and sat listening closely:

> The identity of two men killed in the crash of a private plane just north of Birmingham early this morning has now been definitely established. One was Percy Damon, owner of Weston's Charter Flying Service and pilot of the plane. The other was Dr. Mortimer Dellman, freed only last night by the Weston County Grand Jury in the killing of his wife, the socially prominent former debutante, Loretta Porter, daughter of Jacob Porter, a leading industrialist.

According to the tower at Weston County Airport, the plane took off in very bad flying weather shortly after midnight, the pilot having filed a flight plan showing New Orleans as its destination. Police authorities who found the plane several hours ago reported that Dr. Dellman was carrying a large amount of money on his person.

"So that's that." Roy reached over and shut off the radio when the announcer turned to national news. "Abner Townsend won't be able to make anything out of the case now."

He looked across the table and grinned at Alice. "You look mighty pretty this morning, sweet. I think you're going to enjoy being the wife of the next state attorney general."

ii

Sunday mornings, Mabel always went to early Mass, then came by the Snack Bar for breakfast. The terms of her employment allowed her one free meal a day, in addition to the one she ate while on duty in the evening—usually on the run.

"Everybody at church was talking about Dr. Dellman getting off and then being killed in a plane," she said to Geraldine, the morning-shift cook, as they were enjoying coffee and cigarettes together in the almost deserted restaurant.

"In here, too." Geraldine was inclined to be phlegmatic.

"It's funny." Mabel looked across the almost deserted street to the emergency entrance of the hospital. "To look over there now, you'd hardly believe all hell could break loose before you could say boo—like it did last Wednesday afternoon."

"That was something," Geraldine agreed.

"I guess Dr. Dellman getting killed sort of wraps the whole thing up. From what I've been hearing across this counter the past few days, a lot of people have had their lives changed since last Wednesday. It was pretty exciting while it lasted, though."

"Yeah," said Geraldine. "I guess it was."

407

"It's sorta like the passage the priest read from the Bible this morning. I think I still remember it:

> A *generation goes, a generation comes, yet the earth stands firm forever. The sun rises, the sun sets; and then to its place it speeds and there it rises* . . .

"That reminds me," Mabel sighed. "Monday morning you'd better tell the assistant manager to take that other waffle iron and have it fixed. The upper-class medical students will be coming back to school next week. They sure do like our waffles."